SAINT JOHN OF THE FIVE BOROUGHS

Saint John of the Five Boroughs

EDWARD FALCO UNBRIDLED BOOKS

This is a work of fiction. The names, characters, places and incidents are either the product of the author's imagination or are used fictitiously, and any resemblance to actual persons living or dead, business establishments, events, or locales is entirely coincidental.

Unbridled Books
Denver, Colorado

Library of Congress Cataloging-in-Publication Data

Falco, Edward.
Saint John of the five boroughs / Edward Falco.
p.   cm.
ISBN 978-1-932961-88-1
I. Title.
PS3556.A367S35 2009
813'.54—dc22
2009012626
1   3   5   7   9   10   8   6   4   2

Book Design by SH · CV

First Printing

For Susan and Will

Blasted

PEOPLE were checking her out from the balconies. Avery knew it, she could feel it, and so she was conscious of how low her slacks rested on her hips, how much of her stomach showed, how her breasts pushed up by her bra rode just slightly higher than the straight neckline of her tank top. Part of her squirmed, part of her preened. An old Rolling Stones song charged down from a second-story balcony a dozen feet in front of her, the driving rhythm doing its magic, dance welling up through her legs and backbone to her shoulders like someone flipped a switch and for an instant she was wildly happy, and that was a pleasure for the moment it lasted before she started wondering about the actual party where she was headed and about whether or not this night she might really hook up with some guy just because she liked his looks or the way he was built or whatever. Because she didn't want to go back to ice cream and an old movie with Melanie. Because the summer at home that had just passed was all ice cream and old movies, only with mother, with Kate.

Mel bumped shoulders with Avery and said, "Look. That's Billy and Chack."

Avery saw Chack first. He was an Indian guy with big eyes and short, scruffy hair. He had on a short-sleeved madras shirt and khaki slacks, which was like a uniform with him. Sometimes Mel called him Professor Madras. He was a grad student in chemistry or something like that. He and Billy were one of those sets of guys who seemed to exist in a kind of magnetic relationship so that wherever one was, the other was circling nearby. She was still looking for Billy when she heard him scream out Melanie's name and then hers as he emerged out of the crowd and climbed over the balcony railing. He was barefoot and wearing pants that only reached midcalf and a bright red shirt that looked like it was probably a woman's blouse given the fat collar and the lack of top buttons, a small, skinny guy with long hair slicked back and dripping water on the shoulders of the shirt-blouse. When he let go of the railing to wave them up, Chack grabbed him around the waist and yanked him back to safety. Then someone turned up the volume on some Salt-N-Pepa cut, and heads nodded and bodies bobbed in a ripple of motion.

Melanie said, "What's up with that boy?"

"Let's go see." Avery started toward the balcony and then stopped to say maybe they shouldn't, since Dee was expecting them at Vince's party.

Melanie said, "Screw her. She's been a bitch all night."

Avery thought it over for a second and then continued across the lawn. At the crowded doorway, she wanted to turn around, repulsed by the prospect of trying to wedge her way through the dense crush

4

of bodies inside, but Melanie grabbed her by the arm and yanked her into the swarm. "I need another drink," she said. "I'm losing my buzz."

"Buzz?" Avery shouted. Melanie had her wrist in a death grip as she pulled her through pounding music and sweaty bodies. "You're out of it, girl! You left *buzz* behind hours ago!"

Melanie yelled something Avery couldn't make out, and then a body stumbled in front of her. Melanie's grip broke, the crowd closed around her, and Avery found herself toe to toe with a guy so big she had to look up to see his face, which was amazingly square and flat. "Yo, Missy," he said. "Looking good!"

Avery was about to slide around him when someone knocked into her from behind and pushed her flat against his unmoving body, which was so rock-hard and solid that it startled her. Banging into him was like running into a boulder. "Jesus," she said, the words spilling out without thought, "what are you, like a weight lifter or something?"

The guy's face lit up. "You don't know who I am?"

"I'm supposed to know who you are?" Avery stepped back to get a better look and saw a guy who did in fact look a good bit like a boulder. He was tall and wide, with a neck the size of an average guy's thigh. "Let me guess," she said. "Football player."

He offered her his hand. "Zachary Snow," he said. "I'm pretty famous, but I guess you don't follow football, huh?"

Avery said, "Do we have a football team?"

Zachary's face went slack with confusion before Avery smirked, cluing him in that she was making a joke, and he laughed a weird, high-pitched, tittering laugh. "You're funny," he said.

"I'm only funny when I'm drinking," she said. "Otherwise I'm pretty dull."

"Well, shit …" Zach pulled a silver flask out of his back pocket, took a swig, and offered it to her. "Can't be talking to no dull girls."

Avery managed one big gulp of bourbon, which she recognized from its familiar sweet burn, before she coughed and handed back the flask. "That's good," she said. "Smooth."

"Booker's," Zach said. "Fifty dollars a fifth."

Avery stalled a moment, offered Zach a coy smile. She was getting that fluttery feeling she got when she didn't know for sure what she was doing but was pretty sure she was about to do it. "So are you one of those football players everybody's trying to get with because they're, like, on the cover of *Sports Illustrated* and stuff?"

"Nah, not like that," Zach said. "But, you know, maybe. If I have a good season. This'll be my first year starting."

"Starting what?" Avery asked. She had to smirk again to let him know she was joking.

"You're pretty funny," he said.

"So, like, Zach …" She reached up and touched the biceps on his right arm, which was significantly bigger than the width of her outstretched hand, thumb to pinkie. "How much can you lift?"

"I can bench four hundred," he said. "I got a shot at the Iron Man title. You into lifting?"

She smiled her cutest, girliest smile. "Do I look like I'm into lifting?"

Zach said, "You look good." He pulled the flask from his back pocket and handed it to Avery.

Avery took another big swallow, shook it off, and looked over Zach one more time as she handed the flask back to him. "So, Zach," she said, "you want to come out to the balcony with me and meet my friends?" She offered him her hand.

Zach said, "Aight," and flashed a bright, happy smile.

Avery gestured toward the balcony and then followed Zach as he bulled through the crowd. She was getting dangerously close to being *too* drunk, though she wasn't there yet. Sound buzzed and swooped over her, color flashed and flared. Breasts were in fashion again, which was a good thing for her, since she had 'em, but rough on girls like Mel, who didn't have much at all. She briefly pondered this—the current fashion of displaying breasts—as she was pulled through the party, past one girl after another wearing a variety of revealing tops.

On the balcony, Mel was leaning against the railing next to Chack. She held a gigantic plastic cup of beer frozen an inch or so from her lips as she watched Avery approach hand in hand with Zachary. Billy appeared to be passed out. Chack was holding him up with an arm around his chest. The boy looked like a rag doll, his head and arms dangling loosely, his legs bent under him.

"Is he okay?" Avery had to shout to be heard over the music. She touched Billy's hair, which was dripping wet. The clothes he had on—close up, clearly a woman's blouse and slacks—were damp. "What," she shouted, "did he fall in a pool or something?"

"You got it," Chack said, "only dove. Lydia's got his clothes in the drier."

Mel said, "Lydia?"

"S'er place." Chack touched his fingertips to his forehead, as if he were about to read someone's mind. "Hey, dude," he said, "do you know who you are? You're Zach Snow."

"See?" Zachary put his arm around Avery. "I told you I was pretty famous."

Mel brought the beer down from her lips without taking a drink. "D'you guys just meet?"

Someone turned up the volume on the music until the glass in the balcony doors rattled. Avery hissed in Mel's ear, "He's huge!"

"No kidding," Mel said, looking up at Zach.

Chack said, "You're starting linebacker this year, right?"

"Dude," Zach said, nodding.

"Sweet." Chack returned the nod.

Avery said, "Chack, Zach," and the boys shook hands. She leaned over Mel and kissed her loudly on the forehead. "This is my room-mate, Melanie."

"Hey," Melanie said.

Zach said, "Pleased to meet you," and winked at her. He looked down at Billy. "You sure he's okay? I had a buddy almost died last year from alcohol poisoning." He pulled his flask from his back pocket and offered it to Chack.

Chack waved off the flask and looked down worriedly at Billy. "You think he might have alcohol poisoning?" He gave Billy a shake and the boy's body flopped around like it was boneless. "Alcohol poisoning," he repeated, as if the idea were new to him and perhaps worth considering.

Zach said, "Dawg, don't they get alcohol poisoning where you're from?"

SAINT JOHN OF THE FIVE BOROUGHS

"I'm from Connecticut," Chack said, staring down at Billy. "Shit . . ." He got to his feet and yanked Billy up with him. "Hey! Billy!" he shouted into Billy's ear while shaking him.

Mel said, "How much has he had to drink?"

"Incalculable," Chack said. "We both been drinking since this morning."

Avery said, "Since this morning?"

"Well, so, you don't have alcohol poisoning," Zachary said to Chack. "He probably don't either."

"He's twice Billy's size," Avery said.

"Point," Zach said.

"Nah . . ." Chack seemed to have come to a decision. "Dude's just passed out." He looked up at Zachary. "Hey, man," he said, "be a prince and help me get him down to my car."

Mel said, "You're driving?"

Chack pointed out into the darkness off the balcony. "I'm just over there. I cut across the grass, don't even go on the road."

"Cool." Zach grabbed Billy's feet. "Lead the way." To Avery, he said, "Don't go noplace. Be right back."

"I'm not going anywhere," Avery said. She sat down next to Mel and watched as Zachary and Chack carried Billy through the opened screen door and into the seemingly still growing crowd of partygoers. Zachary yelled, "Casualties! Coming through!" and when no one budged, they hurled themselves into the mass of bodies, two huge guys carrying Billy's scrawny ass through the sweaty hordes.

When they were out of sight, Melanie said, "Av! You're not!"

"I think so," Av said. "I think I am."

"A-ver-y!"

"What?" Avery said. "It'll be fun."

"Fun? Jesus. He's a monster."

Avery grinned.

Melanie looked off into the scores of bodies packed onto the balcony. For a long moment she watched the crowd, and then she looked back and said, "Are you really?"

"Pretty sure," Avery said. "'Less something happens."

"Like what?"

"How would I know?"

"You drunk?"

Avery nodded. "You?"

"Yeah," Melanie said. "We shouldn't drink any more, though."

"Why not?"

"We want to know what we're doing, don't we?"

"We?"

"What do you think of that guy?" Melanie gestured toward the apartment, where the balcony railing met the wall. "The one sitting on the railing smoking a cigarette."

Avery checked out the guy Melanie was talking about. "In the T-shirt?"

"Smoking a cigarette."

The guy was older than the rest of the crowd, maybe late twenties, maybe even early thirties, dressed in black chinos and a white T. He wasn't especially big, five ten, five eleven, maybe, but his chest had a sculpted look, as if he might be a bodybuilder, a tight set of abs clearly defined through the T, the muscles of his biceps and forearms sleek. Avery studied him a moment longer.

Melanie said, "You don't think he's hot?" She sounded shocked.

Avery squinted, making a show of checking the guy out. He was peering off into the distance as if lost in thought, as if he might as well have been sitting on some lonely mountaintop as on a balcony railing in the midst of a noisy party. His hair was cut close to his scalp in a military-style buzz cut, the dark hairline curving down deep into his forehead so that it looked like it wanted badly to grow back wild and thick. He held his cigarette pinched between the thumb and forefinger of his right hand, which was dangling loosely at his side. His left arm lay crossed over his lap. Something about him, she decided, looked brutal. It wasn't just the compact, muscular body and the practically shaved head, it was something in the way he held himself. "I think he looks creepy," she said, turning back to Melanie. "What about him?"

"Creepy? You think so? Don't you think he's good-looking?"

Avery shrugged. "Yeah," she said, "he's good-looking. So?"

"I caught him checking me out before."

"Really?" Avery watched him another moment. He still hadn't moved. A line of ash dropped from his cigarette. "Don't you think he's way too old?"

"For what?"

"For you. He looks like he could be in his thirties."

Melanie made a face that suggested Avery might be out of her mind. "I'm not thinking about making a life with the guy. Why, you have long-term plans for Zach?"

"All I'm saying is . . . I don't know. Whatever." Avery searched the crowd, looking for other possibilities, and then leaned closer to Mel. "You really want to pick up some random guy? You sure?"

Mel turned a sober gaze on Avery. "Are you sure?"

"Pretty," Avery said. "But Zach kind of picked me up, which is a little different."

"Oh, bullshit," Mel said. "He picked you up like this guy is about to pick me up." She stood and brushed herself off. "Come with me," she said. "For backup."

Avery said, "I don't know about this guy. Really."

"Well, let's go find out." Melanie ran her fingers through her hair and then shook it out briskly. "We'll just go over and talk to him." She hesitated a moment, as if having slight misgivings, and then said, "He is handsome, don't you think?"

"Yeah," Avery said, "if you're into the silent, brooding type."

"I'm into it," Mel said. "For tonight, anyway." She started into the crowd and then looked back to make sure Avery was following.

Avery laughed, more a giggle than a laugh, which reminded her that she was still drunk. "Okay," she said. "Whatever."

Mel mouthed, "Don't embarrass me," and pushed forward.

LINDSEY sat up in bed with a hot cup of peppermint tea and a Land's End catalog that pictured a beautiful twenty-something model walking barefoot on a pristine beach of white sand beyond turquoise water, wearing a subtle pink top and SwimMini™ skirt and trailing a matching beach towel, her eyes downcast as if shy about being photographed. She flipped the catalog to the foot of the bed, where it landed on top of several other magazines and catalogs, and pulled a Victoria's Secret out of the night-table drawer. Here barely dressed women were all looking directly at her. She tossed the Victoria's Secret on top of the Land's End, poured a shot of Bacardi into her cup, and stirred it in with the tea bag, bouncing the porous sack of herbs around on its string as if were a dancing puppet. The house was quiet except for occasional TV sounds coming from the basement, where Hank was watching a football game. Keith, her seven-year-old, was asleep at the end of the hall. This was ten o'clock on a Saturday night, and when she thought about that and about not yet being thirty years old, a little hot flash of fury ripped through her, which she calmed with a swig of rum straight from the bottle.

Lately Lindsey's sense of humor was failing her. She considered herself someone who took the world in stride and with humor, but lately— Her younger brother, Ronnie, was in Iraq, and that weighed on her because she loved the little shit, but she was simultaneously furious at him. He had gone to Iraq because his friends were going. That was what he'd told her. *What kind of reason is that? You're going to Iraq because Willy and Jake Jr. are going?* She talked at him and talked at him about the stupidity of it, and he was just, *Well, Willy and Jake Jr. are going, and we all went over to the recruiter's together, and they said*—Willy and Jake Jr. and Ronnie, who were all still little boys in her mind, kids screaming on the Slip'N Slide, boys off fishing on Claytor Lake together every chance they got. Now the three of them were in Iraq and every time an IED killed some boy on the news or in the paper—which felt like it was every god-damned fifteen minutes—her heart went to ice and her blood stopped till she heard or read the names and they weren't her boys. This war was killing her sense of humor. Mostly she put it out of her mind as best she could, but it weighed on her and that was part of it.

Then there was her father, who was in the early stages of Alzheimer's. He was fifty-five when he married her mother, who was thirty-eight at the time, her second marriage, his third. Now her mother was dead some nine years, from breast cancer, and he was pushing eighty-five and in assisted care, which, luckily, he had the resources to cover, but, still, to see him going downhill so fast, a man who had once doted on her and now sometimes had trouble remembering her name. Still, still, still. She was alive and young and she had her health and her family, her baby boy, Keith, and . . . That brought her around to Hank. She sipped her tea.

It wasn't even September yet and already he was down in the rec room watching some college football team play some other college football team somewhere out West. And he'd been looking forward to this event all week, yet. This, for Hank, was a big Saturday night: alone in the basement of his house watching television while his twenty-nine-year-old wife, who was pretty damn good-looking, lay in bed reading catalogs. How Hank could care so much about which bunch of boys scored more points than which other bunch of boys while boys he actually knew and loved were in real danger at first baffled her and lately was getting to downright piss her off. When she was inclined to think badly of Hank, which was not a rare thing anymore, she saw him as a moron, a gape-mouthed, mindless slug stuck to his La-Z-Boy, an idiot who had traded real life for a series of games, for *watching* a series of games.

Still. When she wasn't inclined to think badly of him, which was most of the time, she loved him. Just, things were getting away from her. She started to pour more rum into her teacup, thought better of it, and took another swig straight from the bottle. Eventually this would put her to sleep. For the moment, though, she was stuck on the thought that this was a Saturday night, and she was still young, and there was something very wrong with feeling so alone in a house where her husband was in the basement and her sleeping son down the hall. When she felt, suddenly, as if she might break into tears, she got out of bed and walked through her dimly lit house to the patio.

It was hot out. She was wearing white linen pajamas and carrying the bottle of rum, and within moments after she pulled open the glass patio door and walked out into the heat, a patina of sweat coated her forehead. Hank had mowed the lawn late in the evening, and the smell of cut grass was still in the air. She sat on the wood swing, pushed it once for momentum, and then pulled her feet up under her. She loved this swing and she loved her yard. Their house backed up against undeveloped land, Roanoke Mountain looming in the nearby distance, and on summer nights like this one, the dividing line between their neatly mowed lawn and untended land was marked by swarms of fireflies. She held the Bacardi bottle to her nose, inhaled the rich aroma of rum. She took a sip and placed the bottle on the concrete patio under the swing. Across the yard, the fireflies were doing their magic, scores of them slow-blinking that bright dark yellow light.

The summer she was twelve and Ronnie was seven, the family spent two weeks on Smith Mountain Lake, a close-to-home vacation. Days were spent on a pontoon boat fishing and swimming, nights in the big, fancy house with a backyard on the lake. At twilight she'd chase lightning bugs with Ronnie. They'd put them in a Mason jar, punch holes in the lid, stick some grass in the jar. "How many'd you catch?" "How many'd you?" Dozens each, till it was time to let them go and they'd set up a folding chair out on the dark lawn and Lindsey'd settle in to watch and Ronnie'd place the two jars side by side, pop the lids off quick, then run back and jump into Lindsey's lap, and sometimes, as often as not, he'd fall asleep while she held him cuddled against her watching fireflies float up into the darkness, spilling up out of the unseen Mason jars, drifting away into the night. It was almost as if, Lindsey now grown and married with children and Ronnie half a world away doing whatever a soldier does in the morning in Iraq— It was almost as if, swinging gently in her yard on a hot summer night with her son asleep and her husband in the house— It was almost as if she were that twelve-year-old girl again, she could feel the past that vividly, so sharp it was like it wasn't past, and that might be Ronnie in the house sleeping peacefully, and Mom and Dad in the basement watching TV. Then, when a couple of things happened at almost the same time, when Lindsey missed her mother and father so powerfully it was as if Mom had just died and Dad had overnight grown old, and she could almost feel her little brother's warm body wrapped in her girlish arms, the physical senses of that memory, the heat of Ronnie's sleeping body, the weight of it, his little-boy's sweet, sweaty smell, when that came back to her tangibly for the briefest of seconds and then disappeared, leaving her bereft—when those two things happened so quickly, one instantly after the other, then she cried. Her face scrunched up like a child's and warm tears seeped out of the corners of her eyes. Once it was gone, the moment passed, she felt a little better.

A swell of dizziness hit her when she sat up so that she had to lean back and close her eyes and wait it out. She was sweating more than she should be, more from the rum than the heat. She took off her pajama top and wiped her face with it before tossing it onto the lawn because she wanted to see the white splotch against the deep green of grass in moonlight, a token of abandon, as if some wildness had just gone on here in the backyard of this quaint, two-story colonial in quiet Salem, Virginia. Then she took off the bottoms, tossed them next to the top, and laughed. Wasn't anyone to see within a half mile in any direction, so why not? She looked up and saw a sea of stars scattered across a dark sky.

Someone cried out in the house and she was alarmed for a

moment until she realized it was Hank and that he was shouting in reaction to something that had just happened in his game, a score no doubt. She spread her arms and spun around on the patio and then held the pose. She was a middle-sized woman, middle-sized everything: middle-sized height, five six, middle-sized weight, 135, middle-sized breasts, 34C, middle-sized looks, not beautiful but certainly nice-looking, certainly attractive; middle-sized ass . . . well, that she had to work at. She had to diet and exercise to keep her ass under control, otherwise it would mushroom into a monster ass, like her mom's when Ronnie was twelve and used to sing in Lindsey's ear, *Mom's-got-a-monster-butt*, whenever he wanted to make her laugh. But for now it was a middle-sized ass, and all that middle-sizedness made her perfect for spinning, which was something else she used to do with Ronnie when she was a girl, the spin-until-you-fall-down-and-then-try-to-walk-a-straight-line game. She grinned at the memory of the game and then spun like she did when she used to play ballerina, an all-alone girl game. She spun around and let the momentum of her spinning carry her out to the grass and the yard, all the way across the lawn to the line of trees and wild grass and scrub, where she stood a while with her eyes closed as if blindly offering her middle-sized dizzy undressed self to the huge untended firefly night, and when the night refused to ravish her and the dizziness subsided, she went back into the house and down to the basement.

Hank at first didn't notice that she was naked. His eyes were fixed on the TV and as she passed in front of him he ducked his head, not wanting to miss a second of the action. "It's fourth and goal," he said. "We're on the two-yard line," and then, as if her nakedness had indeed registered with him on some deeper level, he turned his head slowly toward her, seemingly wary about confirming that he'd just seen what he thought he'd seen. He looked at her worriedly for a moment before the play went off and his head snapped back to the TV.

Lindsey looked down at her pale body against the black leather couch. The air conditioning had raised goose bumps on her arms and legs. Her nipples had popped up. She grabbed the lightweight red throw from behind Hank, where he had placed it to support his bad back when he wasn't leaning, as he was now, so far forward that it looked like he might leap into the action. She draped it over her and propped her legs up on the coffee table. She always felt a little like an intruder in this room, which seemed to belong in some deeply gendered way to the boys. She and Hank had fought for a week after a delivery truck showed up on a Saturday morning and two workers hauled out a monstrous sixty-inch rear-projection TV. It took Lindsey the longest time to understand that the tank-sized package was a television set. They had to take the back door off its hinges to get the damned thing into the rec room, where it loomed over the furniture like a billboard. Once the TV was installed, with its array of speakers and amplifiers, Hank camped out in the room for a month. Keith, following his daddy, brought his favorite toys down, so now the carpeting was strewn with so many Lincoln Log cabin pieces and Lego parts and Tinker Toy crap and Erector Set contraptions he and Hank built together, she thought of the room as a cave where the boys played, with a huge electronic portal into every hockey arena, football stadium, and basketball court in the universe.

Hank cursed and turned off the television, which said good-bye with a four-note melody of electronic beeps. "They can't get two damn yards," he said and then leaned back into the couch. Lindsey felt as though she could actually see the various molecules and particles of his essential self recomposing as they transitioned back into the real world, where they suddenly found themselves sitting on a black leather couch in a dimly lit basement alongside a naked woman draped in a red throw. How strange that must be. Gone, the screaming crowd. Gone, the intense game. Here, dark, quiet room with a woman draped in red.

"Why," Hank said, the annoyance in his voice obvious if restrained, "are you naked?"

"You're upset?" she said. "I come to you naked late at night with Keith asleep—and that's a problem?"

Hank locked his fingers behind his neck and looked at the opposite wall. "Lindsey," he said, as if he had something significant to say and was prefacing it with her name to signal its importance.

"Yes?"

He sighed and closed his eyes. To Lindsey he looked, for a moment, almost beatific. His blond hair, bleached by the sun, was curly and thick as a boy's, though he was coming up on his forty-first birthday. His face, big and squarish, was largely uninteresting except for those striking pale blue eyes, which every woman who ever saw him noticed first thing.

Lindsey moved closer to Hank and laid her head on his shoulder. His gut may have grown out over his belt buckle, but his arms and shoulders were still thickly muscled. She put her hand on his thigh and stroked gently upward.

Hank shoved her hand aside.

"What?" She pulled away from him. "What the hell is that?"

"You've been drinking," he said. "I smelled it as soon as you came in the room."

"So? I can't drink now?" She kicked his calf with her ankle. "Could you look at me?" she said. He was staring straight ahead. "If you're going to criticize me, could you at least look at me?"

"At what point—" he said, and he pulled his feet up under him as he shifted his position, turning his body toward Lindsey, "at what point does your drinking become a problem?"

"Beats me." She clutched the throw at her neck. "Why would my drinking be a problem? Do I sound drunk to you?"

"No," he said. He folded his arms over his chest, as he always did when he was getting ready to settle into an argument. "You never sound drunk, not at all. But you are. You are drunk. We both know, regardless of how you sound, that you're drunk right now. Aren't you, Lindsey?"

"I don't know," she said. She shrugged and offered Hank a little smile. "Define drunk."

Hank was a smart guy whose job was mostly about lifting heavy things and arranging them. His father had started a landscaping and construction business half a century ago, and now everyone in their huge family, including Hank, was part of it. Lindsey watched with intense interest as his eyes narrowed and his lips opened. She was often impressed at the sheer bulk of him, the six foot–plus frame, the thick chest and broad shoulders and wide, muscular thighs. There was something purely animal and thoughtless in her attraction to all that mass of body, and when he screwed himself up and concentrated it was almost as if he were doing something against nature, like *the beast speaks* or something. Though they had met in college, at VCU. Though she had always known he was smart. "When you're drunk," he said finally, "it's like you're not really here. I'll talk to you and you'll talk back to me, but on some level—which I can always sense—you're gone. It's like having a conversation with someone who's not here. Not really."

"I'm here," she said. "What could that possibly mean, *like I'm not really here?* You ask me a question, I respond. I'm engaged. Perhaps," she said, "this is more about you than me. Have you considered that possibility? Maybe you just don't think it's appropriate for women to drink because the women in your family are all churchgoing teetotalers. Maybe you just want me to be more like your mother," she said. "Could that be it?"

The color in Hank's broad face, tanned almost to a shade of brown, deepened. His breathing turned shallower and more labored. "You're not here," he repeated, "and the person who turns up in your place is sarcastic and dismissive, and sometimes, like now, she's mean."

"What was mean about that? Just because I suggested you might sometimes act like you want me to be your mother as much as your wife?"

Hank looked away from her to the opposite side of the room. His eyes fell on a half-finished Erector Set cement truck. He turned back toward Lindsey and stood up in the same motion. "When you're drunk," he said, "like this, like you are now, I feel like you despise me." When a second or two passed without any response, he left the room.

Lindsey considered calling after him but instead only listened to his heavy footsteps on the stairs and along the hall to their bedroom. She knew he was angry and she knew she should be concerned—but she wasn't. If he wanted to run away, fine. Had he stayed, she might have gotten around to explaining that a woman doesn't like to be left alone on a Saturday night while her husband watches a football game. But he hadn't, so the hell with him. Let him be all hurt. *Like she's not really here.* Well, who would want to be, with him plastered to the television set watching some idiot game like it mattered? Meanwhile she had to worry that Ronnie was going to get himself killed being where there was no reason in the world he should be. *Like she's not really here.* Because it sure as hell felt like she was here. It felt like she was right smack-dab here in the middle of Salem, Virginia, U.S.A.

Still. It would have been nicer had he comforted her and held her in his arms. Which was what she really needed.

She pushed herself up off the couch and draped the throw over one shoulder like a toga. She heard Hank's footsteps again as he crossed the bedroom floor to the bathroom, where he would brush his teeth and take his Prilosec before curling up on his side of the bed the way he did, like a little boy, folding his hands between his knees, which struck her alternately as cute and ridiculous for such a big guy.

Lindsey clicked off the lamp by the La-Z-Boy after a bug flew into its halogen bulb and the acrid smell of its bit of existence burning up began to saturate the room. She waited in the stinking dark while she listened to Hank push the medicine cabinet closed a little too hard and swing open the bathroom door with a little too much force before crossing the hall with long, angry strides, closing the bedroom door behind him, and getting under the covers, the metal bed frame creaking under his weight. Through the rec room's single porthole window, only an inch or so above ground level, a tributary of moonlight trickled down the wall and along the carpet. For several minutes Lindsey waited in silence, hoping that Hank, given some time to get over being angry, might come back and they might pick up the argument where it had left off and then eventually get around to the part where he comforted her and the good stuff started up. Part of her expected it. It was like Hank to get angry and walk away, but it was also like him to come back when he calmed down and was ready once again to talk. Part of her thought, *Not tonight, not likely.* For months now she had ignored the looks, the expressions of dismay, as he let her know he was not happy about how much she was drinking. *At what point does your drinking become a problem?* How about maybe drinking isn't the problem? How about maybe the problem's something else and drinking at least takes the damn edge off? That might be a place to start talking. That might actually do some good, Hank, trying to talk about that. Because what is the problem, really? Ronnie. Dad. You. Me. Lindsey. Is Lindsey the problem?

Who was Lindsey in this dark, in this little trickle of light? Who would Lindsey be when the lights went out at last altogether in her father's mind? Who did Lindsey become once she was no longer any living man's daughter? Who would she be without her brother?

Lindsey said aloud, to the dark, "Why shouldn't I drink?" She locked the back door and then went through the house turning off lights on the way to the patio, where she considered taking one last drink and then thought better of it and left the Bacardi in the moonlight under the wood swing. She turned off the last of the lights and felt her way along the hall to her bedroom door and then hesitated. She almost knocked. The idea amused her sufficiently that she held it in serious consideration long enough to actually make a fist and lift her arm before dropping the notion when it suddenly no longer seemed like a funny thing to do. She touched her forehead silently to the door and leaned into it with her eyes closed, the darkness slowly revolving around her as if she were the nucleus of some really really slow-spinning atom. A delicious tiredness descended on her. She might crumble at the door and sleep in the hall, a dog snuggling up as close as possible to its master. No. No. Nor would she crawl into bed beside him, where they might sleep back to back like a couple of stones. Or put her arm around him—because she didn't want to put her arm around Hank.

The knot at her neck came loose and the red throw dropped to the floor, and at the same moment she heard a small cry from Keith's room, a nighttime sound, nothing unusual, but it pulled Lindsey out of her drowsy, drink-stunned world and she opened the bedroom door and walked through the room without so much as a glance at Hank. She found a cotton nightgown in her dresser and went back down the hall to Keith's room, where he was sleeping, just like his daddy, with his hands pressed together between his legs. He had kicked his blanket off and his tiny moonlit body was dark and wiry, a shadow on the white sheets—except for the brightly colored Super-man briefs that covered his little butt. Lindsey reached across Keith for the blanket and pulled it over both of them as she lay down beside him. She wrapped her arms around him and held him tightly to her breast and he didn't so much as stir. Outside, where Keith played all day, it was still summer and hot, and the dank musty odor of things growing wild seemed to have seeped into his blood so that she could smell it now in his hair, in his sweat. She laid her head down on his bright yellow pillow cover, the top of his head pressed into her neck, her chin touching his forehead, their bodies fitted together like puz-zle pieces. For a while she watched the trees through his window. A breeze had come up and leaves were fluttering like birds' wings, like a forest of birds, going where? All the small dark birds flying in the moonlight nowhere.

A watery rumbling in Avery's belly woke her, and when she sat up in bed the headache she had been dully aware of in her restless sleep expanded suddenly, as if unseen hands had yanked a too-small hat down over the back of her head. She gritted her teeth against the pain and lay back down, keeping as still as possible while she waited for the throbbing to stop. She had been dreaming about a lake . . . and a boat . . . a dark lake, a small boat. Her father was on the shore. She was in the boat. It was night and the lake was still, a dark glassy surface, and the boat was floating away, but . . . a strand of her hair connected her to the shore. Her father was holding the other end of the strand, and she was leaning toward him . . . then the hair snapped and she watched it dent the water's surface in a long straight line to the shore where her father was a shadow that grew smaller as the boat kept drifting away.

When the throbbing finally let up and Avery opened her eyes again, the memory of the dream settled over her like a heavy blanket.

Her father had died the summer after her high school graduation, suddenly, of a cerebral aneurism, in his sleep. She dreamed of him regularly, and often the dreams were comforting. He'd hug her, or give her a kiss on the forehead the way he used to. But sometimes the dreams were like this one, and she'd wake up feeling heavy and slow, as if the air around her were so dense she could barely move.

Zach rolled over and put his hand on Avery's knee, and she looked down at him as if she were annoyed at discovering someone else in her bed. He asked if she was okay in a voice that sounded impossibly gentle given the hulking mass of body out of which it issued. She told him to go back to sleep, which he did instantly, closing his eyes and snuggling his forehead against her thigh. She was fully awake then, lying in bed next to a football player she had met only a few hours earlier—and as the events of the night came rolling back through her sober memory, she groaned and checked the alarm on her night table. It was a little after three in the morning. She had been in school all of one full week, this her senior year. Her room was dark, but there was enough light from her various electronic devices to see the mess of clothes scattered over the floor and the disorderly array of cosmetics covering the top of her dresser. In the pulsing white light of her sleeping iBook, the rose-colored walls lightened and darkened as if breathing peacefully. On the wall opposite her bed, the muted greens in a poster-sized photograph of the Folly Beach pier echoed the steady green light of her recharging cell phone. She had bought the framed picture for ten dollars at a yard sale in Salem, where an elderly man had held it up and pitched the value of the frame—but she had bought it for the picture, which captured the elaborate crisscross of mossy pilings beneath the pier as they narrowed in diminishing perspective to a flash of bright light where the pier ended and frothy ocean waves surged. That flash of white light in the distance looked to Avery like a cathedral door, like an opening into another, utterly different world.

In this world, her head was still aching. Gingerly she slid out of bed and into the first things she found at her feet, which were a frayed pair of denim cutoffs and an ancient band T. She paused a moment at her bedroom door when she thought she heard a sound coming from Melanie's room. She pressed her ear to the wall beside her dresser and listened, and when she didn't hear anything more, she went quietly along the hall to the bathroom, where she washed down three aspirin in a palmful of water and then chewed four Tums on her way back to her bed. The living room was a disaster. The couch was overturned where Zach had tripped over it, and there was a stain on the carpeting where the wine bottle he had just opened had spilled as he'd fallen on his face. Drunk as he was, he wasn't drunk enough not to be embarrassed. He kept promising to clean it in the morning or to pay the damage deposit until Avery finally shut him up by taking him by the hand and pulling him into her bedroom. What she remembered most vividly, though, was the way Grant, Melanie's shaved-headed pickup for the night, had calmly watched Zach from where he leaned back soberly into the window frame, and then the way his eyes met hers just as she was closing the bedroom door.

While she was gone, Zach had stretched out like a skydiver, his spread-eagled arms and legs reaching to the four corners of the mattress. His body was freakish, and Avery observed him for a long moment with fascination. From head to toe, he was everywhere twice as thick as most other guys. His calves had the girth of telephone poles, and they widened proportionally to massive thighs, a back broad as a coffee table, an impossibly thick neck, and an almost square head with fleecy dark hair. It seemed impossible that she had actually just had sex with this guy. It looked like the weight of him alone would crush her.

She went to the window and looked out over a narrow strip of moonlit lawn that ended at a line of tall trees, beyond which was the highway, and while she was at the window, a doe wandered halfway through the tree line, looked about for a few seconds, and then bounded away through the trees and out onto the quiet highway. Avery went back to her bed, sat on the edge of the mattress, and shook Zach's arm. "Zach," she said, and he opened his eyes instantly.

"Hey—" He blinked a few times and looked as though he were working to pull himself back fully into consciousness. "What? Are you okay?" He propped his head up on his elbow and then, as if to announce he was now awake, smiled sweetly.

"Sure," Avery said. "I'm fine. But, look, you have to go."

"Really," he said. "You want me to leave?"

"It's just, you know—" She made a face, as if she expected him to understand, naturally, why it was obvious he should leave.

"What?" he said. "Was I snoring?"

"Loud," she said. "Really, I'm sorry. I'm not used to it."

"Oh . . ." He grimaced. "I do that." He thought about it for another second and then added, "I could try to stop."

Avery brushed a long strand of hair back off his forehead. "You've been sweet," she said. "You're not at all like you seemed at the party."

"I'm not?" he said. "How did I seem? At the party."

"Yo! Missy!" Avery mocked his voice.

Zach laughed. "That's just—" he said. "I'm not like that. I've got to drink to put on that whole thing."

"Why?" Avery folded her hands in her lap and looked at him like a schoolteacher working with a student. "Why do you have to put on that whole thing?"

"Otherwise I never meet anyone," he said. "The guys make fun of me. They're all like—" He looked away for a moment, up over Avery's head. "They make fun of me is all." He laughed, as if amused at himself. "I realized, you know, I've got to act a certain way or else they make my life miserable."

"You have to step in front of girls and go, *Yo! Missy!*" She did his voice again, which made him laugh again.

"Exactly." He leaned close and kissed Avery's thigh through the shreds of denim fringe. "You sure I have to go?"

"I need to get some sleep," she said, "and I'm not used to anybody else in my bed."

"That's good," he said. "That's encouraging."

"Really? Why?"

Zach watched Avery as if he were trying to say something to her with his eyes and a slight, mischievous, smile. Then he spun around and out of bed and stood naked in front of her.

"You're full of yourself, aren't you?" she said.

"Me?" He sounded as if he had no idea what she was talking about, even though the grin on his face said he did. "Why?"

"'Why?' Are you modeling for me?"

"Oh." Zach looked down at himself. "You think I could be a model?"

Avery said, "I think you should get dressed." While Zach was getting into his clothes, she cocked her head at what she thought was the sound of the refrigerator door opening.

Zach apparently didn't hear anything. He said, "Want to see me out?"

"Sure." She slid off the bed and gave him a hug. "You're sweet," she said again and led him out into the living room, where she was startled by the reflection in the sliding glass doors to the balcony. She saw herself a step in front of Zach as he loomed hugely behind her, her head reaching up only to his shoulders, her body dwarfed by his bulk. With her braless, in fringed jeans and snug T, and Zach in tight denims and short sleeves that threatened to rip at his biceps, they looked like a couple of characters out of the *Dukes of Hazzard*. In the background of the reflection, Grant stood at the refrigerator with a bowl of ice cream in one hand and a spoon in the other. He nodded at Zach and Avery before he lifted the spoon to his mouth. The couch had been turned upright, and a wet towel lay over the wine stain on the carpet. "Shit," Zach said, looking down at the towel. "I forgot about the wine."

Grant nodded toward the towel and said, "I thought that might help." Then he shrugged as if he actually had no idea whether or not it would do any good.

Avery liked the sound of his voice. She asked another question mostly just to hear him speak again. "You know something about cleaning up spilled wine?"

Grant smiled enigmatically and then took a seat on the couch, turned on the television, and started flipping through channels.

Avery gave Zach a look, and he hesitated at the door, as if to ask if she were wary of Grant. She leaned against him and stood on her toes to kiss him on the cheek. "Good night, Zach," she said.

"Can I call you tomorrow?"

"I made plans with my family for tomorrow. Call me during the week."

Zach nodded, the disappointment on his face obvious. Before he left, he glanced over to Grant on the couch, where he had settled in before a black-and-white movie.

Once Zach was gone, Avery locked the door and leaned back against it. The movie on the television was *Casablanca*. She had seen it ten times, at least. It was coming up on the scene where the Nazis are in the club and Rick has the band play *"La Marseillaise."* "I love this scene," she said and sat on the other end of the couch.

Grant's eyes were fixed on the television as he held the bowl of ice cream in his lap. Avery was tempted to ask how old he was. She also wondered why he was out here and not with Melanie. He was, she decided again, handsome—in an interesting way. His lips were pink and shapely and full—the kind of lips women hope for when they get collagen injections—but the top of his nose was flat and wide, the broad lines merging with thick eyebrows that looked like a pair of wings over intense dark eyes. His ears were smallish and pressed back almost flat against his head. The overall effect, emphasized by the military haircut, was brutal, warrior-like, at least at first glance, though the lips undercut the harshness and suggested other possibilities.

"I think," she said, referring to the *"Marseillaise"* scene, which had just ended, "it's, like, the hopelessness of the gesture, standing up to the Nazis, that's so moving." She surprised herself with her sudden talkativeness. She seemed, out of nowhere, full of questions and observations.

Grant muted the sound on the television and then settled back on the couch facing her. "It's the defiance," he said.

Avery said, "I think it's stirring." When Grant didn't keep up the conversation, she added, "Don't you think?"

Grant watched her long enough to make Avery uncomfortable. Finally he said, "I think there's something special about you."

Before the words were fully out of his mouth, Avery half laughed, half snorted—a dismissive response that happened without thought, mostly out of surprise. "Did you tell Melanie that tonight, that there was something special about her?"

"No," he said. "Did you tell Zach he was special?"

Avery considered getting up and going back to her room. Instead she said, "I'm just trying to be friendly."

"Really?" Grant turned back to the television and clicked on the sound. In a moment, he seemed absorbed again in the movie.

"Dude," she said, "you're majorly fucked up."

Grant didn't look at her but laughed quietly. *"Dude,"* he said, under his breath. *"Majorly,"* he added.

Avery got up slowly, hoping the right rebuke would come to her, and when it didn't she had to settle for a contemptuous snort that came off as theatrical even to her. She went back to her room, closed the door quietly behind her, and sat on the edge of her bed in the dark. Part of her wanted to slip under the covers and go to sleep. Part of her wanted to go back out to the living room and tell Grant to get the hell out of her apartment. *Dude. Majorly.* Jesus, what was she, fifteen all of a sudden? She heard him again, mocking her under his breath, contemptuous—and she had to swallow and her fists clenched into little rocks. The room approached and retreated in the throbbing light from her iBook, rose walls appearing and fading. The dresser top cluttered with makeup and jewelry, the Folly Beach pier, a framed Picasso print, a framed Dali: here and gone, here and gone. She should just march into the living room and ask him who the hell he thought he was, hitting on her after just having slept with her girlfriend, knowing she had just slept with Zach. What kind of freak was that? How was she supposed to react?

Unless he wasn't hitting on her . . . though of course he was. *I think there's something special about you.* What else was that?

In her quiet bedroom, Avery paid attention to the palpitating of her heart, the quick shallow breathing, the tingling of her scalp that signaled the approach of a panic attack. She hadn't had one in almost a year. She had stopped taking her Zoloft at the end of the spring semester. But here it was, coming on, and now she was almost as furious as she was scared. Scared of the fear approaching, the way it cramped her heart and overwhelmed her so that she couldn't breathe, but furious at the same time. Why should something like this bother her, why now? Though it wasn't just this, it was the dream too, the dream of her father and the lake, and the weight that had settled over her afterward, the heaviness of being alone, unmoored.

She got up and turned on a light. With the back of her hand she swiped away the sweat on her forehead. On her desk, a thick art book, *Sister Wendy's 1000 Masterpieces*, was propped up against her computer. She flipped through the pages until she came upon a quote from Gerhard Richter, *Art is the highest form of hope*, beneath a painting that looked like a blurred photograph of a young woman holding a hand over her mouth, looking either terrified or bored, all her edges jittery, as if she might be coming apart. She continued turning pages until she came to an oil titled *Monk by the Sea*, which was what she had been looking for—though not that specific painting, just something calming, peaceful, beautiful, which was a technique she had learned back when the panic attacks were frequent and bad: immersing herself in the right kind of image, forcing herself into it, pushed her out of herself. And it helped, this particular painting a gorgeous play of blues: light blue sky, inky blue water, icy blue land, and a lone figure in the midst of the vast blue expanse, but somehow not overwhelmed, solitary, not lonely. She imagined that she was the figure in the painting, which was not hard, and after a while her heart stopped palpitating and her breathing returned to normal. She bookmarked the page and turned off the light and then knelt in front of her window.

I think there's something special about you. She had reacted viscerally—as if he had called her a whore, as if she would get out of bed with one guy and into bed with another. Though, now, kneeling at the window, looking out at nothing, she considered the possibility that it was all in her head, that he might have meant nothing like that at all; that she was, on a not very deep level, ashamed of herself for going to bed with a guy who meant nothing to her, who, if anything, amused her. She wondered if her reaction to Grant's words weren't more about her own unhappiness with herself and the uneasiness of her mood than anything he had actually said. *I think there's something special about you.*

She went from the window to her bed, where she stripped out of her clothes and pulled the sheet to her neck. She lay on her back, her head propped up on two pillows. From the kitchen, she heard the refrigerator open and close, then the clank of a dish in the sink, and then, Jesus, she tightened up at the prospect of listening to him go back to Melanie's room. She could feel it in her shoulders and her neck, the clenching against the unpleasantness of it, listening to him as he opened and closed the door and got back into bed with Melanie—and when he didn't, she was relieved. She got up and looked herself over in the full-length mirror beside her dresser.

There she was, staring back at herself, the whole of her reflected in the mirror—and it was as if she could see only her thighs. She grasped the extra handful of flesh in her fist and then quickly let go, a little angry gesture without thought. She laid one hand flat over her stomach, over the pouch of belly that she never saw on one model in the whole world of television and magazines and movies, but most of her friends and most of the girls at the pool and the gym had at least a little belly, a little looseness or jelly there—and the older women, Jesus, clearly there came a point when all of them gave up the battle. But her thighs—they weren't that bad, not really. Her legs were fine. Her breasts were nice. Lots of guys thought she was pretty. She might have to diet a bit. Just a little. She thought she sort of looked like Uma Thurman in *Pulp Fiction*. A little anyway. She had the dark hair and the straight bangs, and the way her hair fell on the sides, lustrous and straight, to her chin, framed her face in three neat sides of a rectangle, which was the Uma Thurman/*Pulp Fiction* part. She had pretty eyes, a little bigger and rounder than most. Her eyes were dark and with the dark hair, she liked that too. She decided not to turn around and check out her ass, and then she did anyway. And there it was. Her ass. It was okay. She pulled on the same shorts and T-shirt, so he wouldn't think she had changed for him, straightened out her hair, and then went out to the living room.

Grant was on his back, apparently doing leg lifts. He lay stretched out parallel to the television set, his hands clasped around the back of his neck, heels six inches off the floor. The way he was holding his feet up with legs out straight tensed the muscles of his stomach, the broad chest and magazine-ad abs clearly defined under the cotton of his T. With great effort, Avery could hold that position—legs out straight, heels six inches off the ground—for about two seconds. Grant seemed to hardly notice it. He had turned his eyes to Avery as soon as she had entered the room, and he watched her now as she took a seat on the couch, folding her legs under her.

"All I meant," he said, "is that there's something about you that's intense. It's like an aura around you."

Avery gave him her most skeptical look, one she hoped would encourage him to drop the subject.

"So," he said and then fell quiet and stared at her unabashedly, his eyes roaming over her face and then meeting her eyes and staring into them with a disorienting objectivity, as if he were examining them, as if he were a physician looking for signs or symptoms. "So tell me," he said finally. "I'm a good listener. I feel like we could connect."

"Tell you what?" Avery looked at him as if he were a little crazy. "What do you mean, *connect*? What does that—"

With a small shake of his head, Grant dismissed her questions. "You're the one I noticed at the party," he said. "It was you I was staring at, not Melanie."

"You were staring at me?" Avery heard herself raising her voice and was immediately frustrated. "Why would you be staring at me?"

"Why wouldn't I be staring at you?"

Avery laughed. She could hardly believe . . . "Why are you coming on to me like this?" she said, her voice suddenly quieter. "You just got out of bed with my girlfriend."

"What makes you think I'm coming on to you?"

"Are you serious? *Why wouldn't I be staring at you?*" She mimicked his suggestive tone.

The refrigerator clicked on loudly and rumbled for a second before settling into its white-noise hum. "All I'm saying," Grant said, "there was something happening with you, something special about you. Even through the drinking, it was there. I could see it."

"What was there?" Avery shrugged as if she had no idea what he was talking about. "I don't have a clue."

"Yes, you do," he said, and then he appeared to suddenly turn off, as if a switch had been thrown in some internal circuitry. His face turned hard and impassive, and he went back to looking at the ceiling.

Avery watched him. His feet were still floating effortlessly six inches off the floor. His eyes were fixed on a spot directly above him, though he obviously wasn't seeing a thing. He was so inside himself it was as if he had disappeared. "Can we try again?" she said. "I'm Avery. I'm a student here, in the Art Department. What about you? I don't know a thing about you. You could be . . . anybody."

He said, "I'm here spending a couple of weeks with a friend." He turned to look at her. "He used to be a street performer. Now he's a professor. It's like— The guy wears a jacket to class." He seemed amazed at the unlikeliness of it. "It's— *Man. Who are you?*"

"What do you mean, *street performer?*"

"The thing that got him famous—" Grant let his feet drop. He turned on his side and propped his head on one hand.

"How long could you have done that?" Avery asked. "Keep your legs lifted like that."

"Forever," he said, uninterested, and then went back to the subject of his friend. "One of the things that got him famous, anyway. He stabbed himself in front of the Met. A Sunday afternoon in spring. Beautiful weather. French Impressionists show. Tourists? Coming out your ears."

"He literally stabbed himself?"

"Once in the chest, once in the stomach. Screaming some shit or other about art."

"And he *teaches* here?"

Grant nodded.

"So. But. That was it? He stabbed himself? That makes him an artist?"

Grant looked away, as if momentarily annoyed. "He's a performance artist," he said. "He's in the Theater Department." When he looked back at her, he said, "Do you want to go for a ride?"

"Now?" Avery leaned forward, partly taken aback and partly, to her own surprise, excited. "It's four in the morning."

"We could watch the sunrise. There's a lake not that far from here." He sounded as though he were merely putting a proposal on the table, as if he were curious whether she would take him up on his offer.

"So, what?" Avery said. "You're a professor too? You were teaching here?"

"Just visiting," he said. "Are we going?"

Avery looked over her shoulder at Melanie's closed bedroom door. As if Melanie sensed her attention, a small sleep sound issued from the room, a soft groan and a rustling of sheets. Avery waited, and when the sound was followed only by silence, she turned back to Grant. "You know," she whispered, "if Melanie finds out that I went for a ride with you at four in the morning . . ."

"I'll have ruined your reputation," Grant said.

"I'll have to find another place to live is what I was thinking." Avery got up, about to go back to her room to change. "I have no idea why I'm doing this." She hoped her expression conveyed at least a little of her genuine amazement.

Grant said, "Wear something warm and put on a jacket. I ride a bike."

Avery said, mostly to herself, "Should have figured . . ."

Once she closed the door to her room, Avery turned off the lights, as if she needed the help of darkness to think. In the softest of whispers, but aloud, she said, "What are you doing, Avery?" and she pulled off her T-shirt and sent it sailing over the bed. No answer came immediately to mind, but a small voice out of some corner of herself urged her to change her mind, to go back out into the living room and tell him she was just too tired, or, even better, to just go to bed and leave him waiting; and as that quiet voice spoke to her, she got out of the rest of her clothes and then turned on the lights and rummaged through her dresser. While she was putting on her jeans and finding a clean blouse and then searching through the closet for her best buttery black leather jacket, she continued to entertain the possibility of not doing it, of not taking a four A.M. motorcycle ride with a guy who'd just gotten out of bed with her best friend after she'd just gotten out of bed with another guy. It was too crazy. She couldn't do it; and then, a few minutes, later, she was dressed and out on the streets of State College with Grant, heading for town.

His motorcycle was parked in a lot behind the Days Inn. A sleek machine that looked as much like a missile as a bike, its compact black body soaked up light, a kind of shadow tilted cockily to one side. Grant had her wait while he went up to his room and returned with a pair of black helmets with black Plexiglas face masks, and a moment later they were riding into the night, slowly at first through town, then flying over lonely state routes faster by far than she had ever experienced before, trees and road rushing by in a dark blur, her arms wrapped around Grant's waist, her head pressed into his back to block the wind. When what seemed to be a half hour or more had passed and they were still speeding over unfamiliar roads, farther and farther from civilization, she felt the first creeping traces of uneasiness working their way through her, and, later, as the ride went on and on, part of her turned unambiguously frightened—though another part of her, perhaps the bigger part, was thrilled. The dark flew by all around as she held tightly to Grant, her arms around his waist, her body against his. She leaned into the turns with him, hurtling over the road only a few feet off the ground, nothing to protect her but him, his solid body piloting a sleek shadow through shadows.

When they came to a stop, eventually, on the wooded shore of Raystown Lake, it was still dark, but morning and sunrise couldn't be far away. She climbed off the bike and pulled off her helmet, and then they both moved toward a fallen tree at the edge of the water. The lake was glassy and quiet, dark and unmoving as a sheet of black plastic. She sat on the log and looked at the opposite shore, where trees crowded a hillside and descended to water. The early-morning air was crisp against her skin, and it smelled of pine and something else she couldn't name, something rank that seemed to rise up from the water's edge. The earth at her feet was covered with an inch-deep layer of moss that extended halfway to the lake like a blanket, and on a whim she pulled off her boots and socks and pressed her toes into the cool moist ground. She heard the crack of a breaking branch, and then Grant stepped over the log and sat beside her holding a small tree limb in his hands like a fishing pole—and at the sight of the fishing pole/tree limb, her dream came back to her and her head snapped back to the lake as if she might see herself floating away from the shore in a small boat, a strand of her hair stretching across the water.

Grant said, "Did you hear something?"

She shook her head, dismissing him, and continued staring out over the water, where again she saw the lake from her dream—the strand of hair her father was holding connecting her to him and to the shore, and then the strand snapping and then her drifting away. While she stared out over the black water of the lake, the dream's images shifted into a flurry of memory and feeling, and a breeze slid over the water and through the underbrush along the shore. It was like something coming at her, this breeze she could see in the ripples on the lake and the fluttering of leaves and then feel against her skin and it seemed to carry with it a moment when she was a child and her father was holding her in his arms and pointing up at the moon and telling her he loved her, that he'd always love her, under that fat white moon, the same fat white moon floating now somewhere out of sight.

Beside her Grant sat quietly in a tongue of moonlight watching her. After a while, after a long silence, she told him about her father and about the dream, how strange it made her feel to wake up from a dream about a lake and then find herself sitting on the shore of just such a lake only a few hours later.

Grant said, "What do you believe?"

Avery slid away from him. "What do you mean?"

"I'm asking what you believe. Spiritually."

"Spiritually," she said, working to grasp the question. She looked into the woods, as if the answer might be waiting for her there. She tried to think about the question seriously, but nothing came to her. She said, "My family is Episcopalian," though she knew that was no answer. "I don't know. We never really talked much about that stuff growing up. We never went to services or any of that either, so . . . I guess I don't know what I believe." She folded her hands in her lap and looked at Grant. "Why?" she said. "What do you believe? Spiritually?"

"I don't know either," he said, "but I can't believe it's a coincidence you'd dream about a lake exactly like this lake and then find yourself here."

"Then what?" she asked. "If it's not a coincidence?"

Grant bent over and undid his laces, and he seemed to be thinking in the process. "Then it's a mystery," he said, and he kicked off his shoes.

"What are you doing?" Avery leaned back and stretched.

Grant undid the buckle and zipper of his chinos and pulled them off. Beneath them he was wearing a pair of white briefs. "I have an urge to get in the water."

"You're shy," she said.

He looked down at his briefs. "More modest than some bathing suits."

"I suppose." Her thoughts flashed back to Zach a few hours earlier, showing himself off in front of her.

Grant went down to the water and stepped in, gingerly at first. "Huh," he said, "the water's warmer than the air." He walked in all the way up to his waist and looked toward the wooded tree line across the lake. "It's beautiful out here." He took off his shirt, threw it to the shore, and dove into the water.

Avery thought *he* was beautiful. Unlike Zach's freakishly huge body, Grant's was sleek and compact and beautifully muscled. Michelangelo's *David* came to mind, the gracefulness of the musculature, Grant's skin looking as hard and flawless as the statue's marble. While she watched, he surfaced, took a deep breath, arched his body, and dove again, this time going deeper, she could tell by the breath he took and the way he dove. She went to the edge of the water, her bare toes sinking down into mossy silt. The surface had closed over Grant's dive, and the lake looked unchanged, peaceful and dark. If she hadn't seen him disappear, there'd be no way to know anyone was in the water. When he came up again, he was only a few feet away from her. He exploded out of the lake, shaking off water, and the spray caught her in the face and chest. She jumped back, startled, and then laughed.

Grant took a moment to catch his breath. "It's like being in a deprivation chamber down there," he said. "You can't see or hear anything and the water's so warm—"

Avery picked up his shirt, which was caught on a bush beside her. She wiped her face with it. "You got me wet."

"What I was thinking, down there," he said, "is that it feels like you and I are supposed to be here. I mean," he said, "the way I felt when I saw you. Your dream. Some things, they feel—" He looked at the sky and placed one hand flat over his heart, as if he were about to pledge something. "They feel as if somehow they had already happened." He looked back to Avery, his hand sliding down to his belly.

"Is that what you were thinking," Avery said, "that we were destined to meet?" She had a slight, wry smile on her face, and she meant to sound at least a little dismissive, but she wasn't sure it had come out that way.

"There are people who believe," he said, "that we're all spirits, and that the ones you connect with in this life, the ones you love or have deep friendships with, they're from previous lives. You're meeting them again, and it's like seeing someone you've missed for a very long time."

Avery was acutely aware of the distance between her and Grant. It was strange. She could tell he was trying to say something meaningful, but it was as if he needed the barrier of the water between them to do it. She wasn't entirely sure what he was talking about, but the gist of it was that he felt a special connection to her—and she realized that was what he had meant all along. That was what he had meant when he'd said there was something special about her. She was flattered, but also wary.

Grant watched her, waiting for some response. Finally he said, "What are you thinking?"

Avery stripped out of her clothes down to her bra and panties and waded into the water. When she reached Grant, he took her hand in his and then stepped closer and put his arms around her. She let him hold her for a moment without returning the embrace, as if she were thinking about something else. Then he took her head in his hands and kissed her, and again she let him. When his hands slid down the small of her back to grasp her and pull her into him, she didn't resist. She felt him stiff and warm pressing against the bare skin of her stomach. "Hey," she whispered, meaning to turn down the heat of the moment, but no other words came, and when he lifted her up and carried her back to the shore, she laughed, partly like a child laughing at being lifted and carried and partly in amazement at the power in his arms and chest and thighs. She recognized both excitement and fear at the strength in him as he carried her out of the water and onto the shore, where he pushed her back against a tree, the rough bark scraping the soft skin between her shoulders. She tried to speak, meaning to ask him with humor just what he thought he was doing, but he kissed her again, hard, and she kissed him back in a daze of sensation and movement and heat—and then, in an instant, his foot hit the inside of her ankle and pushed her leg aside as his hand simultaneously reached between her legs, and then he was inside her with a single movement that made her gasp, partly in shock at the ease of the entry and partly out of simple surprise and unreadiness.

She said his name aloud, sure the urgency in her voice would make him stop, and when he didn't, she said it again, louder, a command—but instead of stopping, he brought his right hand up around her neck, his thumb and forefinger digging into either side of her jaw, and pressed her head back against the tree as he pushed harder and deeper. His hand around her neck terrified her, and her body went slack with surrender. There was, then, the briefest of moments that felt like a hinge, an instant in which things might swing one way or another: in one direction, screams, scratching and fighting; in the other, abandon, immersion in movement and feeling. Even though the moment was so fleeting it barely happened, she recognized it with an out-of-body clarity, that hinge moment, a point of turn. She made her choice by grabbing his ears as if she might rip them off and locking her calves around his thighs as she pushed back against his push with equal power. His hand came away from her neck and he was thrown backward as he spun around, holding her in the air a moment before kneeling and laying her down in the bed of moss, cool and wet against her skin. Under him, on her back, she grasped his ears tightly, her fingernails digging into them while he continued pushing as if he were desperate to reach up into her belly. When she yanked his head up to see his face, she found a turbulent mix of pain and pleasure there. Inside her she felt the familiar build of heat and sensation, and she willed herself into it until, finally, it released and washed over her, accompanied by a long guttural note, half growl, half moan.

On top of her, inside her, Grant kept at it until he was done. When he got up and walked away, Avery closed her eyes, turned on her side, and curled up into herself. Outside the blind circle she identified as her body, she could hear Grant getting dressed, the sound of clothes sliding over limbs, the rattle of a belt buckle.

After sex, she usually wanted more of a man, she wanted to be held while he was still inside her, but now she was content with the feel of moss under her cheek and the low, rustling half whistle of wind through leaves. She didn't want to think. All she wanted was to lie there quietly with the sound of wind and the odd, dreamy sensation of movement that she knew was an illusion but felt real, a sensation of sliding and sinking as if everything outside her were drifting away and she was falling backward into a dark space. In her mind's eye, she saw herself lying on the ground while Grant stood over her, watching her. In her mind, she saw him scowling, and when she opened her eyes, there he was, just as she had imagined, standing close by and looking down at her—only he wasn't scowling. She couldn't name the expression on his face except that at first it seemed impassive, merely observing—and then in the instant after she opened her eyes, it changed to a smirk, and he turned his back to her and walked off along the path toward his bike, leaving her where she lay, a white body curled up on a bed of dark green moss. She didn't get up until she heard the roar of the motorcycle engine behind her, and only then because she thought it was possible that he might simply drive off and leave her there—but when she came up off the trail, he was waiting for her astride his bike, his helmet pulled down over his head, his face hidden behind the black mask. She pulled on her own helmet and pulled down the mask, and they drove off without a word, her arms again wrapped around him, the bike again speeding over dark roads.

KATE was barely conscious of the rosary's polished black onyx stones sliding between her fingertips as she waited apart from dozens of other churchgoers clustered in bright sunlight outside St. Andrews. Behind the elaborate Gothic facade of the church, in the stone and marble vestibule, Corinne was flirting outrageously with Dave Price, who was several years too young for her and had been separated from his wife, Lucille, for about five minutes. When Corinne had volunteered to drive to church, Kate had explained that Hank was stopping by and that she needed to get back in time to straighten out her house. Corinne had said, "Sure, no problem," and now Kate was nonetheless waiting at the curb, her hand buried in a leather pocketbook strapped to her shoulder, running her fingers along the polished stones of her rosary. Still, the sun felt good on her arms and shoulders. She tilted her head toward a perfectly blue, cloudless sky and tried to relax, though her fingers kept working the linked black stones, following the circular path down to the medal of the Virgin Mary, down to the cross.

A month after Tim had died suddenly, thanks to an aneurysm that had probably been waiting to kill him since birth, Corinne's husband, Stan, had died suddenly from a heart attack that was almost certainly connected to his liberal use of cocaine. Kate and Corinne, church acquaintances, had become friends, even though they couldn't have been much more different as people. Kate was thin, always had been, a few pounds over skinny, with a fair complexion and auburn hair she kept cut in a bob, and she had a cheerleader's cute if unremarkable face. Corinne was wide in the hips, big-boned and fleshy, a few pounds short of being fat, with long, curly hair that cascaded over her shoulders. She had a round, strikingly pretty face. Kate typically wore loose-fitting dark slacks and a light-colored blouse. Corinne was given to flowing dresses in a variety of floral patterns. Kate was small-breasted; Corinne's breasts were ample. Kate worked in an office for a modest salary. Corinne made jewelry, which she sold at art fairs around the country, though she didn't have to work thanks to a substantial inheritance. What the two women shared, however—each waking one morning to find her husband's lifeless body alongside her in bed—made up for their differences. When Corinne was in town, they met regularly for lunch or coffee, went to movies together on weekends, and were walk-in-without-knocking guests at each other's houses. At the moment, the friendship was strained. Corinne was getting to be expert at annoying Kate, currently, for example, by flirting with Dave Price, who should be thinking about his marriage, not Corinne.

A blond-haired boy in a red shirt ambled boldly up to Kate and then stared. She let go of the rosary, squatted to his level, and said hi. The boy smiled shyly before turning and running back into a cluster of women. Kate straightened up to find Corinne approaching her, shoulders bobbing from side to side in a little dance of pleasure once they made eye contact. When she was close, she leaned into Kate and whispered, "Guess who's stopping by Dave's tomorrow night with a bottle of wine?" With exaggerated suggestiveness, she added, "To comfort him."

Kate laughed and tried to look amused. "You're too much," she said, and then put a hand on Corinne's arm, directing her toward the parking lot. "Come on. I have to get my house cleaned up. I've got guests coming."

"What?" Corinne said. She linked her arm with Kate's. "You disapprove?"

Kate hadn't meant to sound disapproving. Ordinarily she would have denied it, but now she found herself walking alongside Corinne in silence.

"Oh, come on, Katie." Corinne bumped shoulders with her playfully. "Dave needs a good roll in the hay, and so do I."

Kate said, "I'm not saying anything."

Corinne said, "I know you're not," meaning her silence was saying it all. "You think because he's only separated a couple of months—"

"Has it been that long?" Kate waited at the passenger door of Corinne's car. She drove a vintage Thunderbird convertible.

"Don't get bitchy. You know I hate bitchy women." Corinne went around the car to open the door and glared exaggeratedly at Kate over the roof.

Kate laughed because she knew that was what Corinne wanted.

Once in the car, she said, "I guess I do think it's fast with Dave. He and Lucille haven't been split up more than a month. If you get involved with him now, you know what people will say."

"Okay, first," Corinne said, one hand on the ignition key, leaning forward, her head resting on the steering wheel as if she were tired, "they may only have been split up a little while, but that marriage was winding down for years. I know for a fact they were in counseling at least two years. And next, I don't give a flying fuck what people say—except maybe you." She leaned back and started the car. "You want to take the top down?"

"Too hot," Kate said. "Plus the wind'll make a mess of my hair."

"And can't have that when Hank's coming over." Corinne started the car and pulled slowly out of the parking space.

"What's that mean?"

This time it was Corinne who was quiet. She negotiated the lot and nosed out into the Roanoke traffic.

Kate said, "Oh, please, Corinne. He's my brother-in-law. My *married* brother-in-law," she added. "My married brother-in-law with a seven-year-old son."

Corinne's eyes were fastened on the car in front of them, an aging green minivan with a couple of toddlers throwing things at each other in the rear seats. She brushed a hand over her breast, smoothing the fabric of her dress. "Look," she said, "Katie . . ."

"Yes?"

Corrine was watching the car in front of her, but she seemed to be someplace else, someplace far away. "Sometimes," she said and stopped abruptly, as if she needed another second to think.

"Honey," she said, "it's like, with you— I don't know what you're thinking."

Kate said, "What are you talking about, Corinne?"

Suddenly Corrine's face was red and she was angry. She said, "How do you see yourself, Kate? Do you plan on living the rest of your life— I mean, is Avery and your job— Is that all you want?"

Kate laughed. "Okay, look," she said, "go ahead and sleep with Dave. I'm sorry I questioned you. Really."

"I'm serious." Corinne tossed her hair back, as if shaking off Kate's attempt at humor. "What's your plan, honey? *My* plan is— Truth, Dave's lonely and he'd love to get me in bed. So why not? It's not like either one of us is a kid. I'm *not* lonely, but I like sexual intimacy."

"Really?" Kate said. "Oh, yes, you've mentioned that."

"Well, I do." Corinne gave Kate one of her bemused looks. "I love the whole thing, especially the cuddling and talk. I love that and I don't want to live without it. *And,*" she said, raising her voice as if the next point were both important and not easy to say, "And there's still a part of me that hopes every time that I might find a real partner. I know I'm never going to have again what I had before, but I want a partner. I'm losing hope rapidly, I admit."

"I understand—" Kate started to sympathize with Corinne, which was pretty much what she always did. Their friendship had started out with her offering Corinne sympathy and support, and it had never changed.

Corinne said, "What do you understand?" She looked at Kate long enough for Kate to point to the windshield, reminding her that she was driving a car.

"I understand about wanting a partner," Kate said, "but you've got to consider . . ." She hesitated a second and looked out the side window at the sidewalk streaming by, at rows of weathered and beaten-up houses. "It's only been a few weeks," she went on, "and what if he gets back together with Lucille? Then you'll be this thing between them. You might even be the thing that pushes them to break up when they otherwise might have gotten back together."

"And this is my responsibility?" Corinne said. "I'm responsible not just for what Dave does but for how what he does might affect his relationship with Lucille? Are you serious?"

"Oh, Corinne . . ."

"Oh, Corinne what?"

"Look," Kate said, surprised by the snap of anger in her voice, "you're being glib."

"I am?"

"Yes." Kate folded her hands in her lap and sat up straight, as if good posture and a ladylike demeanor might be useful in an argument. "I suppose ultimately we're all responsible for our own behavior and for the consequences, but please— That's not an excuse to do anything you want. It's not."

Corinne pulled the car to the side of the road and cut the engine. She looked as if she might be trying to keep herself from exploding.

Kate put her hand on Corinne's knee. "Corinne," she said, "I don't mean to be judgmental. Honestly."

They were parked in front of a row of tawdry-looking shops, one of which was a bookstore of some kind, with piles of old paperbacks

54

stacked high behind a storefront window, the bright colors on the spines faded by sunlight. Two girls walked past and glanced into the car, then looked at each other as if to say, *What's that about?*

Corinne said, "If I waited around in this town for the right man—" She looked hard at Kate, as if she were holding herself back from what she had intended to say.

Kate said, "Go ahead. If you waited around, what?"

"I'd have to live the kind of life you've been living for the past four years, which, I have to tell you, Kate, looks emptier and lonelier and just plain sadder than I could bear. I'd rather drown myself, I swear. I'm sorry, but Jesus—"

"You think it's that bad?" Kate looked away and laughed quietly to herself.

"It's not?" Corinne said. "I'm your only friend, and I'm away half the year. The only thing you ever talk about with any real interest is Avery. Avery this, Avery that. Plus you're only forty-five, and you haven't had sex in years."

"I hardly miss it," Kate said.

"Bullshit."

"Not everyone has the same—"

"Bullshit."

Kate said evenly, "You don't know as much about me as you think you do."

"I'll tell you what I do know," Corinne said. Then she stopped again, her lips pressed together.

"Oh, for heaven's sake. Just say it, please. What do you think you know?"

Angrily, as if she needed the anger to get it out, Corinne said, "I know you're in love with your brother-in-law. When I've seen you two together alone, it's as obvious as daylight."

Kate said, "You're just wrong about that, Corinne." When Corinne was quiet, she added, "The thing I have with Hank is about Tim. It's not about us. It's not like what you're thinking."

"You're lying." Corinne shook her head, as if to say she were disappointed that they couldn't talk about this. "I'll tell you what else," she said softly, "as long as we've gone this far: if he left that bitch of a wife of his, and if you both had the nerve to face all the shit you'd have to face to do it, you two could be happy together."

Kate pointed to the ignition. "Please take me home," she said. "You're out of your mind. This is my brother-in-law you're talking about."

"Sure," Corinne said, and started the car. "Whatever."

For the remainder of the ride, Corinne kept her eyes on the road. Kate watched houses pass by for a while before closing her eyes and laying her head back against the headrest. When they finally arrived at her house, a tire scraping against the curb as Corinne pulled over, Kate took her time draping her handbag over her shoulder. "Corinne," she said, "you're all wrong about this, and I just hope to God it's not something you're repeating to others."

"The thing with Dave Price," Corinne said, "I'm not letting that pass because of what people might say. You make your choices. I'll make mine."

Kate looked up the driveway at her house, at the sea-blue aluminum siding that Tim and Hank had put up together, sweating through one of the hottest days of that summer. She wanted to say something more to Corinne, to make her promise she wouldn't go around talking about her and Hank, but she couldn't find the words, and she was angry enough that she could feel her heart bumping against her chest and a tight anxious knot in her throat. Finally she just got out of the car without even looking back at Corinne.

Near the house, she stopped to pull some weeds from a flower box at the foot of the three steps to the front door. The neighborhood was quiet, as usual, and when she looked up, there wasn't a soul to be seen anywhere on the street or a sound to be heard other than the occasional chirping of crickets or the intermittent call of a bird.

Tim's funeral had been a grim, miserable, weekday-morning affair, and the memory of it, even now, four years later, with his wife and son in the car as he drove to the cemetery—even now there were moments so vivid that Hank's eyes might well up with one thought and his cheeks might burn with another. He had been a pallbearer, with all his brothers, and he had fainted carrying the casket down the church steps on the way to a black hearse. He still had a scar where he'd gashed his head on the stone steps. He'd been told that he fell over suddenly, smacked his head hard on the edge of a step, and rolled all the way to the street with half his family scurrying after him.

But he didn't remember any of that. What he remembered was the heavy weight of the casket, the way the hardwood carrying pole felt in the tight grip of his hand, the way, at the top of the church steps, his knees got watery and the corners of his vision went green and red and fluttery as he looked down at the black hearse and the long line of cars and the milling crowd of family dressed in black— and the realization that Timmy was dead and they were about to put him in the ground came over him along with something like shock, as if he'd just been told. That moment when a fully formed sentence emerged, *Timmy is dead*—that moment he remembered. He had been at his mother's house, in the kitchen having a cup of coffee with her, when the phone rang and she answered, and his father, sensitive as always, gave her the news over the phone. She leaned back against the wall and slid down it and landed with her legs at a right angle to her body, the phone clutched to her chest, her face half dazed, half anguished. That instant on the church steps was like that, like he had just been given the news bluntly, and it brought him down.

Keith bolted out the rear door once they arrived. They were supposed to park in the lot and walk to the grave, but Sherwood Memorial was a quiet country cemetery in the shadow of the Blue Ridge, and no one minded that he left his car on the side of the road while he spent a few minutes standing at the foot of his brother's grave. He knew half the people who worked there anyway. Sometimes he felt like he knew half the people in Salem, period.

"Does Kate ever come out here?" Lindsey asked. She took his hand as they walked across the grass toward the tombstone. Keith took her other hand.

"She says she doesn't." He was about to explain that Kate didn't come to the grave because it made her think of Tim's actual body buried a few feet under the ground, what it would look like decomposing. She had come out a few times and always wound up trying to imagine what would be left of him at that point. What the hands that used to stroke her face would look like. What would remain of the lips she had so often kissed. "She feels like she can talk to him just as well at home," he said, and with his eyes told Lindsey he couldn't explain fully with Keith there.

At the grave, Hank folded his hands together and lowered his eyes. Alongside him, Keith and Lindsey did the same. The site was marked by a marble stone engraved with his brother's name and dates: Timothy Mason Walker, 1955–2002. In the sunlight, the gravestone glistened. With its rolling green lawns divided by lines of neatly kept graves, surrounded by a network of paths and gently curving blacktop roads, mountains in the background, the cemetery was a restful place, and Hank supposed that was mostly why he came, for the few minutes of serenity in a tranquil setting. In the beginning he would close his eyes and say a few words to Timmy, and he still did occasionally. Mostly now he just closed his eyes and was quiet for a minute or so.

Lindsey told Keith to wait for them in the car, and the boy walked away without a question. He put his hands in the pockets of his shorts, bobbed his shoulders, kicked playfully at something in the grass, and then took off, zigzagging around graves as if avoiding gunfire. "I'm sorry about last night," she said. She looked up at Hank with an expression composed and sincere, as if she had carefully thought through what she meant to say. "I know I've been drinking too much," she said, and then stopped, her composure suddenly weakening as her face went slack. A moment later she was silently crying, her eyes closed, the tears spilling out, her head turned away.

Hank put his arms around her to comfort her. He intended to say that if she felt her drinking was a problem she couldn't handle on her own, they could try to get her some help, they could work on the problem together, but when he put his arms around her, she was rigid and ungiving. He let her loose and took a step back.

"We should just go," she said, sounding for all the world like she was angry at him. She wiped the tears from her face with a tissue and, without giving him another look, started for the car.

He took a couple of quick steps after her, meaning to make her stop and explain herself; but when he remembered where he was, in public, at the cemetery, with Keith nearby, he stopped and turned back to face his brother's grave. To anyone looking he would have seemed like an ordinary guy in a moment of contemplation. He waited there a long time, several minutes, until the heat and frustration boiled away and he was able to go back calmly to the car.

Three summers ago, the first summer after his brother had died, she had tried to kiss him on a sweltering evening under a black sky, out in the yard, with constant cicada night music in the weeds, in the fields. He was back from a long weekend fishing trip on the Jackson, and she'd missed him. In some ways it wasn't a complicated thing, and in other ways she was still trying to figure it out three years later. He was standing in the grass with his hands clasped behind his neck looking out at empty fields. She had just put Keith to bed after the three of them had spent a half hour rocking on the wood swing, Hank with his arm around the child's shoulder, she with a hand on his knee. She couldn't remember what they had talked about, but it was an easy back-and-forth, probably about nothing at all. She could still feel it, she and Keith and Hank on that swing in the backyard on a beautiful summer night. Then she put Keith to bed and came back out to find Hank standing at the edge of the patio light. She came around him and put one hand on his chest and the other around his neck as she closed her eyes and tilted her head up, lifting her lips to his. He was supposed to wrap his arms around her back and pull her tightly to him and kiss her hard because he loved her, because he had missed her, and what she was starting there, by the way she touched him, by the way she offered herself to him, was supposed to end in the bedroom—but when she opened her eyes she saw him looking back at her as if she were a mystery to him. He lowered his head to hers and gave her a peck on the lips, followed by a friendly smile. That was all that happened. She let him loose and then she went in to bed and was asleep before he came in, whenever he came in and joined her.

The next day, nothing was said. The next day or ever, and yet her mind often wandered back to that moment. It was like a door had been slammed shut in her face. She could feel the back of his neck ungiving under her fingers, his closed mouth glancing against her lips, the hard little peck and the dismissive smile. The memory now brought tears to her eyes, and then Hank, in the present moment, in the car on the way to Kate's with Keith quiet in the backseat, leaned over and whispered, "Can we please keep it together. Please," as if they both somehow knew what they were talking about, when neither one of them, she'd guess, if someone put a gun to their heads, neither one of them could have found the words to say exactly what it was.

WHAT did people see when they saw her? Cute girl, jeans and a T—a mom in a few years driving her kids to soccer. But that was not Avery. Whomever she was, that was not it. Sometimes she thought that was what the tattoos and the piercings were about, all her girlfriends: a way to say, *This is really more like who I am.* Nipple ring: *I like that I know I don't look like it, but I do.* Nose ring: *I'm different than what you would otherwise have thought. There's something strange and savage inside me.* Indian tribal armband, Cecilia Brown. Snake coiled around the base of her spine, Leslie Weinstein. Sorority girls. Tiger clawing up her arm, scorpion on the back of her neck. Alice Wen, Ashley Caputo, intramural soccer team. Avery said, "Oh my God!" loudly when she saw Gabrielle's tattoo. Gabrielle: quiet demure shy girl with an angry edge. Avery knew her from art history, a few other art courses; they were sort of friends. In the shower, after gym, Gabrielle pulled away her towel and there, below her hip bone, low, toward the inner thigh, a trompe l'oeil rip in her skin out of which black spiders poured. "Don't ask," she said, and rubbed at the spiders with her fingertips as if she might erase them that easily. "I was not in a healthy place," she added and turned on the water and stepped under the shower with her head turned up to the cascading stream. That was all that was said. Avery didn't ask. She knew "healthy place" meant healthy emotional place, and she had wondered ever since what might have happened, what might have been going on in Gabrielle's life to make her choose that tattoo.

As she thought about Gabrielle, Avery buried her head under pillows to block out noise. Melanie was up, doing something in the kitchen. It sounded like Dee might be in there with her, and someone else. People kept knocking at the front door. She pushed her head into the mattress, struggled to hold on to the dullness of sleep, where her thoughts could bounce off the one thing she didn't want to think about yet. Instead she thought about Gabrielle's tattoo. She wondered what might have happened to Gabrielle. Avery had gone through her own terrible years from middle school, roughly, through sophomore year, when things had changed a little for the better. She remembered those two years, junior and senior year in high school, as a respite, a little halcyon period between the fury of her early teens— when she had talked to almost no one and lived with Nine Inch Nails and Marilyn Manson blaring through earbuds—and the blow of her father's death. She saw her childhood as ending somewhere around age ten, when she could still remember her father putting her to bed at night, tucking her in, reading her a book until she was sleepy and then she would give him a hug, and tell him she would always love him, always, and he'd tell her the same, a little ritual between them. Sometime after that the anger came on and she wouldn't let either of her parents into her room. They let her put a bolt on the door and she lived alone in that room behind that bolted door.

Something about Grant brought her back to those years, to thinking about those years, as if somehow he stirred up the same intense feelings, or as if those feelings had never gone away, really, she had only mostly successfully tamped them down, and then Grant had dug them up again.

She didn't really understand what had happened. She hadn't been able yet to think it through. She was furious with him but not done with him yet, the feelings, whatever it was about him, still there. Whatever it was. As if whatever he was, she might fall into it, and something about that pulled at her like gravity. It seemed to Avery sometimes—she knew this, she had thought about this—that there wasn't one thing about her life that was hers. Sometimes she thought she hated her friends and was only with them because, what else? Sometimes she thought she would give anything if she didn't feel she had to be what Kate needed her to be, for Kate, not for her, not for Avery. She didn't want any of it sometimes, and lately it was most of the time, and something about Grant was like all that dark music when she was a teenager. She felt pulled to him, even after what he'd done, even after that.

She liked it. She came. Was that who she was? That moment, that hinge, when she might have tried to stop him, when she might have fought, what was that about, the way she threw herself into him instead? She might as well have screamed like an animal, she might as well have clawed and bitten. And Grant— He wanted to rip her open. She could still feel him in her belly, the way he pulled her apart. Was that who she was? Even now in the warmth of her bed, her head buried under a pillow, the thought of it made her heartbeat quicken. She had clung to him on the back of his bike while the night softened to day, and by the time he let her off it was light and she walked away from him, his face hidden behind a black shield.

At the sound of someone knocking on her door, Avery yanked another pillow over her head and burrowed into the sheets, pulling her knees up to her belly as if she might knot up into a tiny ball and disappear. "Hey," Melanie said, her voice inside the room. "Bitch," she said, and she sat on the bed. "Are you getting up today or what? It's like eleven o'clock."

Avery turned over and peered out from between the pillows. Melanie had on baggy gym shorts and a blue T-shirt with *Nittany Lions* scrolled in white letters over her heart. The girl smelled like perfumed soap and shampoo, her hair damp, her skin pink and shower-fresh.

Melanie said, "Zach's called twice already this morning. What did you do, throw him out?"

"Sort of," Avery said. "Not really." She pulled herself upright, her back against the headboard, and rubbed the sleep out of her eyes.

"Sort of?" Melanie said. "You sort of threw Zach Snow out of your bed?" She pulled up the shuttered blinds and let a flood of sunlight into the room.

Avery covered her face with her arms.

Melanie sat on the edge of the bed. "Did you throw him out like he was a pig or something? What happened?"

Avery gave up and took her hands away from her face. "I didn't throw him out. You said that. I didn't say I threw him out."

"So! What? What happened?"

"Nothing happened." Avery slid down under the covers again and settled her head on the pillow. "I just didn't feel like waking up with him in the morning."

"I get up first," Melanie said. "I'm like, no way I'm letting a guy see me first thing in the morning. Plus," she added, "morning breath."

Avery said, "You get up and brush your teeth and wash your face before the guy's even awake?"

"I fix my makeup too," she said, and added, "Oh, like you've never done that!"

Avery said, "Jesus, Melanie, I'm—" She was starting to say that she was still half asleep and hadn't even gotten out of bed and wasn't ready for this conversation. She thought she might ask Melanie sweetly if she could manage to go away—but she stopped when she realized she was glad Melanie was there chattering at her.

Melanie said, "Yes?" and then added, apparently startled by a sudden thought, "He didn't want you to do something that was, like—"

Avery said, "Oh, just stop, please." There was a loud knock at the door and Melanie bounced up and ran to answer it, as if she were expecting someone special. Avery slid down in the bed and pulled the covers over her head, giving herself a moment in the warmth and darkness before Melanie came back into the room with Dee.

Dee yelled, "You're so bad!" and jumped on Avery, smothering her with a hug before rolling over and sitting up beside her. She straightened herself out and said, as if she'd just remembered she was mad, "You bitches ditched me! I'm like, *Where are my girls?*" She looked back and forth from Avery to Melanie. "Where'd you go?"

"We got sidetracked," Melanie said.

Avery said, "Wound up at a different party."

"Bitches," Dee said to both of them, and then, as if done with the anger, she said to Avery, "Is that where you met Zach? It's like, already I must have had like five phone calls and they're all, *Avery and Zach, Avery and Zach.* He told Leslie he's in love with you."

Avery said, "Who's Leslie?"

Dee said, "Friend. So? Did you sleep with him? Because he's telling people you did."

"He's telling people I slept with him?"

"You didn't?"

Melanie laughed and said, "Right, she didn't sleep with him."

"Of course I slept with him, it's just—"

"Avery!" Dee said. "Zach Snow!"

Avery said, "Why? Is he like—"

"He's gorgeous!" Dee said. "Not to mention he'll get drafted and be megarich like a week after he graduates."

Melanie said, "Avery doesn't think that way."

Dee said, "I think that way."

Melanie said to Avery, "I think they're both gorgeous, don't you? Zach and Grant?"

Dee said, "Who?"

Melanie said to Avery, "Wasn't he unbelievably intense? Oh my God!"

"Who's Grant?" Dee shouted.

Avery said, "Melanie's date last night."

Dee said, "You both— What was this, like orgy night?"

Melanie said, "Please." To Avery she said, "He's thirty-three! Can you believe it?"

"He told you his age?" Avery sat up and crossed her arms over her chest.

"Why *wouldn't* he tell me his age? I'm into older men—"

"Oh, *puh*-lease," Dee said, "like you're all about older men. Who was this guy?" she asked Avery.

Avery said, "I thought he was a little creepy, actually."

Dee said, "Is he good-looking?"

"I think he's gorgeous," Melanie said. To Avery she said, "He's got like a perfect body, don't you think?"

Avery said, "When did he tell you his age?"

"Son of a bitch," Dee said.

Avery said to Melanie, "You asked him in bed how old he was?"

"I don't think it was in bed. We got *busy* in bed."

"Oh, fuck you," Dee said with a wiggle of her shoulders, meaning Melanie was all proud of herself. "So was he good?"

"At first—" Melanie started. Then she stopped and smiled, as if luxuriating in the memory. "At first he was all, I don't know, like in some other place or something." She seemed to think a moment, looking for the right way to explain him. She had Dee and Avery's attention. "I think he's like really deep," she said, "because I'm— There was nothing happening at first, you know? I'm like in bed with him, *Hello? I'm over here?*"

Dee said, "What was he doing? Gazing at the ceiling?"

"Really," Melanie said.

"So what happened?" Avery asked.

"So I got *busy*," Melanie said, doing a tough-girl parody, making Dee laugh. "I did some of the *nasty* things get a boy's *attention*."

Dee said, "That's so fucked up."

Melanie kept going, on a roll. "Used my feminine *wiles!* Did some *nasty* stuff."

Avery said, "Oh, shut up, please."

Dee said to Avery, "Bitch is full of herself. I think she's love-struck."

"Well, where is he, then?" Avery said to Melanie. "Where'd the boy go?"

"He leave in the morning?" Dee asked. "'D' you go out for breakfast?"

"Uh-uh," Avery said. "He was out in the living room watching television when Zach left, and I'm pretty sure I heard him leave a little after."

"Watching television?" Dee said, looking accusingly at Melanie.

Melanie said, unfazed, "He couldn't sleep."

Avery said, "Really."

Melanie took a neatly folded slip of paper out of the pocket of her shorts and read it aloud, *"Can't sleep. See you tomorrow. You were wonderful."* She lingered long over each syllable of *wonderful,* drawing an "Oooh," from Dee.

There was another knock at the door, followed by a shout. Avery said, "I'll get it," and jumped out of bed.

When she opened the door, she found Chack and Billy. Chack, as always, in khaki slacks and a madras shirt, Billy in loose-fitting greenish polyester pants and an orange T-shirt that read "Kill Me" in clashing red letters. Billy's face looked like he might be serious about the message on the T.

Avery said, "Chack, you know, I got to tell you, nobody in this whole fucking country wears madras except Indian guys. What the fuck is that about? Where do you even find that shit?" When Chack's expression went from cheerful to dumbfounded, she said, "Forget it. I'm having my period. Party's in my room," and she left them standing in the doorway as she headed for the bathroom, her head fuzzy and her back and shoulders a little stiff and tingly.

In the relative quiet of the bathroom, behind the locked door, she pulled down her pajama bottoms and panties, sat down heavily on the john, and then ripped a clump of toilet paper off the spool and slammed it between her legs. While she peed with the toilet paper clutched angrily in her fist, she stared at the opposite wall with enough intensity to burn a hole through it, but there wasn't a thought in her head. She sat slightly crouched, her back hunched over a little, her hand between her legs, her eyes on the wall, hovering above the familiar watery melody as if suspended in time. She ached a good bit down there. She felt raw. When she was done, she washed her hands and then hesitated in front of the medicine-cabinet mirror. She straightened out her hair, massaged her eyes hard and deep, and then stood there with her hands over her face in the shifting patterns of dark. She wanted to slap Melanie, and not for the sappy *you were wonnnnderfulllll* but for the gleam in her eyes when she said it, like she was all in love with Grant after one night.

You were wonderful. What was that about? With Melanie, he's *you were wonderful.* With Avery, he's an animal. What was that? Really? Avery looked at herself in the mirror and saw that she was glaring and that her face was red. She grabbed a clean washcloth off the shelf above the john and gave herself a cat bath. She had slept in an old short-sleeved blouse over an equally old pair of pajama bottoms, and she straightened the blouse as she stepped out into the hallway.

She heard a loud outburst of laughter, and when she got to her room, she found Billy standing on her dresser, barefoot. She said, "What's this?" and Chack said, "He's illustrating his diving technique."

Melanie said, "Crazy bastard dove into the apartment pool." She was stretched out on the bed next to Dee.

Billy jumped down from the dresser. "I was slightly drunk," he said to Avery. "Were you at the party?"

Billy was cute—a little dopey but basically sweet. Avery sat beside Melanie. She said, "What are you going to do when you run out of stunts, Billy?"

Billy touched his heart, as if he were about to pledge allegiance. "Who? Me? What?"

"To call attention to yourself," Avery said.

Billy said, "What do you mean?" He lifted himself onto her dresser.

Avery said, "Please don't sit on my dresser."

Billy slid off the dresser and then leaned back against it.

Dee said, as if suddenly developing interest in the conversation, "She means when you run out of crazy stunts, what are you going to do so that people notice you?"

The room got quiet for a moment while Billy shifted from foot to foot, looking a little confused. Chack, who was sitting on the floor by the window, looked up at Billy with what appeared to be interest, as if he were genuinely curious about how his friend would respond.

When the silence got awkward, Melanie said to Avery, "What are you, like on bitch pills this morning?"

Avery said, "I'm just asking."

Dee said to Melanie, "Who wears a T-shirt that says 'Kill Me'?"

Chack jumped up and shouted, "My man does!" He picked up Billy and tossed him onto the bed, on top of Melanie and Dee, causing shouting and laughter as Billy scrambled to the floor.

"Okay, okay, okay," Avery said. "Everybody out. Really. Let me get dressed." She went to the door and held it open. "I'll be out in a few minutes."

Dee said, "I have to go anyway," and kissed Avery on the cheek as she left the room. "I'll call you later," she said. "I want more details."

Billy and Chack filed out after Dee. Melanie waited a second. On her way out of the room, when the others were out of hearing range, she whispered to Avery, "Dee's so jealous I swear she's turning fucking green."

Avery closed and locked her door, fell into the bed, and curled up under the covers, where she lay in silence for several minutes. From the living room, she heard Chack and Billy chatting with Melanie for a while before they left together, laughing back and forth out in the hall, talking loudly about something that had happened at the party. When the apartment was blessedly quiet for a few minutes, she felt herself getting sleepy again. She burrowed down under the covers, pulled her knees to her chin, and drifted toward sleep nestled in an inarticulate funk.

KATE and Lindsey were talking politely in the kitchen, seated across
from each other at a round oak table with claw feet, and Hank was
in the living room on the sofa, sipping a cup of coffee as he watched
Keith sprawled across a throw rug over a jigsaw puzzle, a semicircle
of scattered pieces spread above a partial rectangle, blue-black at the
top edges, black and yellow at the bottom. Keith lay on his belly as he
worked on the puzzle. He had sorted the pieces into piles of similar
colors, and his legs kicked lazily at the air, as if he were slowly jog-
ging somewhere. He examined a pair of emerald-green shapes and
then looked at the cover of the puzzle box propped against the coffee
table. Hank said, "What's it going to be, bud?" and the boy quickly
showed him the box cover picturing a black highway cutting through
a sage-covered desert. "Sweet," Hank said, and Keith tossed the cover
down on the rug and went back to work.

What would Tim think, what would he say, if he could see this
scene, if he knew the way things were? He'd be pleased to see Keith

doing a jigsaw puzzle in his living room. He loved the boy. There was a connection because Tim never got the son he wanted and because he and Hank were so close. He'd like to see Kate and Lindsey talking over coffee on a Sunday morning. That much he'd like anyway: Keith working on a puzzle, the women talking in the kitchen, his little brother relaxing with a cup of coffee on the couch.

Hank was a teenager the first time he met Kate, and that thought troubled him a little. Tim started dating her when she was still in high school, her senior year, and she was five years older than Hank, so, yes, about thirteen. He remembered Timmy's first car, a chartreuse Fiat Spider that was a family joke—and it *was* a piece of crap, broken down every other week, parts impossible to find. But Tim loved it and so Hank did too, because when he was nine and Tim was twenty, Tim could do no wrong.

"Hank," Lindsey called from the kitchen, "are you hearing this?"

Hank roused himself from the couch, lurching forward as if he had been caught sleeping. He spilled a little coffee on his pants. "Look at this!" he said, holding the cup out in front of him.

Lindsey said, "Did you get any on the couch?"

Kate went to the sink for a dishrag. "It's not a problem." She wetted the towel and tossed it to Hank.

Hank said, "Couch survived," and dabbed at his pants with the dishrag. Keith watched, mildly interested for a moment before returning to his puzzle. "Hearing what?" Hank said and went about emptying his coffee cup and refilling it from what was left in the decanter.

Lindsey said, "Corinne De Haven is going after Dave Price."

"Really? What's Lucille think of that?"

Kate said, "They're split up."

Hank took a seat between Kate and his wife. He held a black mug wrapped in his hands, as if he were trying to absorb its warmth. His wife was not yet thirty and Kate was forty-five, but as far as he could see, they might have been sisters, only a few years between them, Kate with just the slight hint of wrinkles around her eyes radiating out into her temples to give away her age. They talked with the same energy, were interested in the same things, had the same womanly air about them—that proficiency at the domestic that Hank associated with women, or at least women in his small circle, in his piece of the world, Salem, Virginia, the outer edge of the South. He had a momentary urge to take hold of both their hands, as if they were a religious family about to say grace, only he wanted to bow his head and ask God for forgiveness and maybe just a small piece of illumination, since at that instant he had a profound sense of not knowing who he was or what he thought he was doing.

Lindsey said, "Hello? Anybody home?"

"I don't know," Hank said. "What am I supposed to say?"

"Just grunt," she said and rolled her eyes.

Kate put her hand on Hank's forearm. "Corinne's going to Dave's tomorrow night with a bottle of wine. You *know* where that's going to lead, and he's only split with Lucille not even a month."

"So," he ventured, "you think Corinne's being a bitch? She should give him more time?"

Lindsey said, "Duh."

Kate said, "Don't you think so?"

75

"I guess," Hank said. "But, hell, they're both grown-ups."

"Oh, please," Lindsey said. To Kate she added, "Typical male point of view."

Kate said to Hank, "I think Corinne should respect the place he's in right now, which has to be confused and emotionally vulnerable."

Hank gave Kate a look. "Men are not children," he said, and he lifted his cup to his lips. "They know what they're doing." He sipped his coffee and made a show of savoring it.

Lindsey said, "Since when are men not children?"

Kate laughed, and Lindsey looked as though she were about to say something else when the tinny opening notes of Beethoven's Fifth issued from someplace in the back of the house, interrupting her.

"It's Grandpa," Keith said without looking away from his puzzle.

Lindsey said, "I left my pocketbook in the bathroom." She had her cell phone programmed with different rings for her principal callers. Her father was Beethoven's Fifth. Hank was the theme song from *Gilligan's Island*. As she got up from the table, she looked at her wristwatch. "I've got a couple of hours before I'm supposed to be over there."

Hank said, "He likely got the time confused."

"Probably hit the wrong speed dial," she said, mostly to herself, and then disappeared down the hallway between the kitchen and living room.

Once Lindsey was out of the room, Kate got up from the table and went to the sink with her saucer and cup in hand, then stood quietly looking out the kitchen window. With his back to Kate, Hank watched her nonetheless, her reflection mirrored in the protective glass of a framed photograph hanging on the kitchen wall. The picture was a dramatic early-morning image of mist rising off a stream that cut through a lush pine forest. The atmosphere of the picture was serene and primeval, as if the photographer had found the last place on earth untouched by time or civilization. For a long moment, the house was silent. Lindsey had exchanged a few sentences with someone obviously not her father and then gone quiet, though Hank could hear her footsteps as she paced the hall. In the living room, Keith was entirely lost in his puzzle, and at the kitchen window, Kate appeared to be lost in thought.

Hank and Lindsey were seniors at VCU when he proposed to her. He was thirty-two and Lindsey had just turned twenty-one. Lindsey had gone to college straight from high school, while he had spent ten years after high school working in the family business. During that time he had learned enough about landscaping construction to be convinced that he would never find the work fully satisfying, so he had gone to VCU to pursue a new career and get some distance from Salem and his family, which had roots in Salem going back three generations. Once at VCU, he fell in love with the first girl he met from Salem, married her upon graduation, got her pregnant on their honeymoon, and found himself back where he'd started, only now with a family. Sometimes all this amazed him.

When Lindsey appeared in the kitchen doorway, she was clutching the cell phone to her heart. "Ronnie's being airlifted somewhere," she said. "He's been wounded. Jake Jr. called Friendship looking—"

"Goddamn it," Hank said, and he surprised himself by how loudly he said it. "Do they know how bad?" He turned to Lindsey and leaned forward but didn't get up. "Who were you talking to? Your father?"

Kate was at Lindsey's side immediately, touching her arm, looking ready to embrace her. "I'm so sorry," she said. "My God."

Lindsey said, "Somebody called from Friendship. One of the nurses took the information. She had Dad's phone."

"Does your father know?" Kate asked.

"They didn't tell him. They wanted to tell me first, and then—" Lindsey's thoughts seemed to shift suddenly, and she stopped speaking.

"Honey," Hank said. He went to Lindsey and touched her shoulder. "Did they say how badly he was wounded?"

"Just that he was being airlifted and he'd undergo surgery—and then they're supposed to call again after . . ."

"Surgery," Hank said, the worry clear in his voice. "Was there any mention of where he was airlifted?"

"Yes," she said. "It didn't register, though. I need to call back." She started pressing buttons on her cell phone. "For God's sake," she said, "what are we supposed to do, just sit around and wait for someone to call? That's crazy."

"Lindsey," Kate said, "sit down, honey. Let me make you some tea."

As if she hadn't heard, Lindsey walked to the front door with the cell phone to her ear. When she stepped outside, Hank tried to follow, but she held him at arm's length. "I want to be alone," she said. "Let me try to figure out—" When someone answered the call, she started asking questions and walked out into the front yard. Hank watched her from the steps as she paced the lawn. A minute later, she disappeared around the corner, walking away from him as if she didn't want him even looking at her. He went back inside. The kitchen was empty and Keith was sitting up beside his puzzle with his hands folded in his lap. He watched Hank carefully, with wide eyes, in silence.

Hank said, "Buddy, it'll be all right."

Keith opened his hand and looked a little surprised to find that he was clutching a puzzle piece. "Did Uncle Ronnie get shot in Iraq?" he asked, his voice so soft and quiet that Hank had to lean forward to catch all the words. "Will he die?" he added.

"No, no," Hank said, and he knelt beside the boy. "I mean, yes, Uncle Ronnie was wounded in the war—but we don't even know if it was a bad wound yet. It could just be something that's not really serious at all, that, you know, he'll recover from and be good as new."

"Do you think that's it?" the boy said, and Hank heard in his voice more of a plea than a question.

"Yes," Hank said. "That's what I think. We won't know anything for sure for a while yet—but I think Uncle Ronnie's going to be fine."

"Are you sure?" Keith asked.

Hank squeezed the boy's shoulder. "You keep working on that puzzle," he said, "stay out of everybody's hair for a little bit. That'll be a big help."

"Okay," Keith said, and he stretched out again on the floor, as if grateful for permission to go back to his puzzle.

Hank said, "Where'd Aunt Kate go?"

"Down the basement. She said she'd be right back up."

Hank found Kate standing in front the washing machine, her arms resting atop it as she looked out a narrow window only inches above the ground. When he came up behind her, he saw that she was watching Lindsey in the backyard, where a breeze was ruffling her sundress and she was holding it down with one arm while pressing the cell phone to her ear with her free hand. She looked besieged as she turned in small circles, taking a few steps one way and then the next to best position herself against the wind. On the horizon, a bank of clouds turned the sky that deep slate blue that announces an oncoming storm. Hank said, "It's going to pour in a few minutes." He put his arm around Kate's waist and leaned into her.

She reached back and rubbed his thigh. "You should go be with her," she said.

"She doesn't want me with her."

Hank kissed the back of Kate's head, and she turned and held him close, wrapping her arms around his waist. "It's terrible," she said. "She's so close to Ronnie."

Hank nodded, agreeing. "We don't know if he's hurt badly yet," he said, "but—"

"What?"

Hank pushed back from her a little. "Being airlifted isn't good," he said. "There's a U.S. hospital in Balad where he'd go if the wounds weren't bad."

"Where's Balad?"

"Iraq someplace."

"Where would they airlift him?"

"Landstuhl, probably. Germany. That's where they flew those reporters, the ones that got blown up on air."

Kate shook her head as if she didn't know what he was talking about but didn't want the explanation either. "How come I feel guilty?" she said, and then her eyes were suddenly full of tears.

Hank rubbed her back and neck to comfort her and she rested her head on his shoulder. In the yard, Lindsey was talking heatedly into the phone. She was angry at something or someone, and her head bobbed a little with the force of her words. In her anger, she had forgotten about her dress, which was blowing up into her face, exposing a white slip with a gauzy patterned fringe that was pushed up over her knees. He thought that she was beautiful still, her hair, so thick and dark down to her shoulders, whipped around her head now by the wind.

Kate whispered, "She's as much a mother to that boy as a sister."

Hank said, "I hate this. It's all—"

"I know," she said, and she kissed him on the lips, tenderly, before turning to look again out the window.

AVERY slept until late afternoon and awoke to rain and gusty wind tapping at her window. She listened a while to the music of the weather in an otherwise quiet apartment. By the quality of the silence, she could tell that Melanie was out somewhere and the door was locked and she was blessedly alone on a rainy Sunday afternoon. She stared a while at the picture of the Folly Beach pier on the wall above her dresser, the muted green pilings walking out into the ocean and that wave, tossed-up foam caught before it could fall back to the water, something spiritual and alluring in the quality of the light. She wished she had snapped that picture and not simply found it.

With the quilt still wrapped around her, she slid to the floor and pulled a box of her prints from under the bed. These were prints intended for her senior portfolio, her graduation project: a series of self-portraits, nude and in costume. In her heart, Avery believed that even her best work sucked. The costumes shouted *Cindy Sherman* and the nudes shouted *So what?* She looked at the top image for a moment, a picture of her dressed as the cliché of a sexy nurse, the white uniform, white shoes, tight dress unbuttoned deep into cleavage. She kind of thought it was interesting because of the furious look on her face—but she could barely stand to look at the picture, and she put the top on the box and slid it back under the mattress. From a crate beside the bed, she pulled out an oversized gift book titled *Goddess* and opened it to *Demeter Mourning for Persephone*, a full-page reproduction facing the first page of a chapter titled "The Suffering of the Goddess." With the book in hand, she slid along the floor to the window, where the light was better.

In the painting, Demeter was portrayed as a woman weeping roses. Actually, the roses seemed to be falling from her hair as she knelt on craggy rocks in flowing sunlit robes and pulled at her golden hair, braided in cornrows, festooned with roses. Avery couldn't remember much of Demeter's story. Pluto, god of the underworld, carried her daughter, Persephone, down to Hades. When Persephone was in Hades, it was winter and the crops died; when she returned to earth, it was summer and the crops flourished. There was a pomegranate somewhere in the story. Avery put the book aside, and in the subdued light from the window, she practiced Demeter's pose. She grieved. She pulled at her hair and moaned, and she was surprised by how genuine the acted-out grief felt, how a feeling of release and relief rushed over her and her eyes welled up with tears, which she brushed away and then laughed at herself, half frightened and half amused at the power of the feelings brought on by acting.

From behind the sliding doors of her closet, she retrieved her camera and tripod and set them up in the corner of the room, looking along the outer wall toward the window so that she wouldn't be shooting into the light. She framed the shot before setting the timer and retaking her pose at the window. After the camera blinked and fired, she checked the shot in the monitor. With her dark hair and crumpled bedclothes, she didn't look much like Demeter, nor did she look particularly grief-stricken. She set up the camera again and then quickly stripped off her clothes, and when she knelt again at the window, she moaned aloud and tore at her hair and banged her head against the ledge. This time when she checked the image in the monitor, she found it much more interesting. The camera had caught her just at the moment when her head touched the window, and there was an interesting sense of motion. It looked less posed than the first shot, which wasn't good, since the idea in the rest of her portfolio was to emphasize the artificiality of a pose rather than try to hide it. Still, she liked the second shot better. Her nakedness was stark in the window light and her grief looked real, as if she had genuinely caught herself in a tragic moment. She was also sure that it was a picture no one else would think particularly interesting. She shut off the camera and, finding herself naked in a quiet apartment, decided to take a bath.

Once she was comfortably settled in steamy water, she folded her arms behind her head and concentrated on relaxing, allowing the sharp caress of hot water to go about its soothing work. She found herself thinking about Kate. At the funeral they had waited hand in hand at the grave as the casket had gone into the ground, and neither had cried, but Avery had felt that if Kate let go of her hand she would die, she would fall on the spot, unable to bear it; that night, alone together in the kitchen, Kate had told her the same thing.

It was late, neither could sleep. A sliver of moon high in the kitchen window and they were both quiet at the counter drinking tea, looking out the window at nothing. Kate said, "This morning, at the burial, I thought I would die right there if you let go of my hand." Avery dropped her head to the counter and cried. She never told Kate why. She didn't tell her she had felt precisely the same thing. She didn't know why she never told her mother. She wanted to keep it, to save it for another time. Kate came up behind her and massaged her shoulders, and then they said something, they talked. Kate would have tried to comfort her. She would have given her advice. Avery would have allowed it then, that night. That was what Kate did. That was how Kate loved her, by giving her advice, by looking out for her, by wanting to help.

Avery sank back in the hot bath. She cupped a handful of water in her palms and brought it to her face, letting it spill soothingly over her cheeks and down her neck as she rubbed her eyes gently, in small circles, moving outward to her temples. In the quiet, she heard again the steady, incessant tapping of rain against the windows. She moved down in the bathwater until she was submerged to her chin, and then, on an impulse, she slid all the way under, the way she used to when she was a little girl, when she would hold her breath and stay under long as she could.

But she wasn't a little girl anymore. The thought came to her clearly—she was grown-up—and with that thought a sense of loss shivered through her, and not just the loss that had loomed so huge in her life the past four years, since the death of her father, but something that included that and was more. It was also the loss of herself, or a sense of disconnection from herself. For a moment underwater she was no one because she was attached to no one, as if she were suddenly cut loose from herself, a consciousness floating without an identity. She popped up out of the water breathing raggedly, her heart palpitating. She took a deep breath and exhaled slowly. She thought of her mother. She thought of her family, all her aunts and uncles and cousins. It calmed her some to place herself, to think of where she belonged, of the people to whom she mattered. Though they seemed far away, all of them.

There had been a time in the terrible first year after her father's death when she had felt so lost, it was almost as if she had forgotten everything she might have once known about herself, about who she was and where she came from and what she knew and believed. Grant had asked what she believed as if asking what she ate for breakfast. The question had startled her. When she was little, she had believed there was a God who lived in heaven, which was where the good people went when they died, which was why it was important to be a good person. As she grew up, all that just faded away to be replaced with . . . nothing much. She needed to read a lot more. She had no idea, really, what she believed. She was a hodgepodge of notions, and sometimes she thought she'd gotten most of them from growing up watching television shows, that her beliefs were formed more from *Frasier* and *ER* than religion and philosophy.

She believed in art. She liked making it. She liked looking at it. Some art had an awful, gripping power over her. In high school, in art class, her teacher had brought in a painting called *Cave, Narcissus, and Orange Tree*. She couldn't, at the moment, remember the art teacher's name, nor the artist's, nor could she recall a single fellow student in the class—but she remembered the title of the painting and she remembered sitting quietly in a red-backed desk chair looking at a sky-blue, half-human, half-animal creature bent to its reflection in water, encircled by a black shell-like dragon-ridged cave above which a tattered black bird with frayed feathers struggled to fly. She didn't know then and she didn't know now what the painting meant, but it spoke to her powerfully. She could almost hear Grant's voice as he posed the question, so casual, so nothing. *What do you believe?*

Avery's stomach rumbled, the sound of it loud in the quiet bathroom, and she said, aloud, "I believe I'm hungry," and pulled herself up out of the bathwater. Thinking about the Deli and a macho chimichanga, she grabbed a towel off the rack and went about getting ready for the walk into town.

Salem High School floated by in the periphery of Lindsey's vision, a blur of dark blond brick, greenery, white roof, and the round island-bench out front where she used to stand in the morning among crowds of teens waiting for the school doors to be unlocked. She drove slowly. She was on her way to see her father, and she didn't know yet what she would tell him—or if she should tell him anything. She felt weepy and heavy, as if she could curl herself up in a ball, sink down into the earth, and cry. She pulled the car to the side of the road, rested her head on the steering wheel, and wept quietly, sobbing a little between small, ragged breaths. Ronnie could be on an operating table and in the hands of strangers, or he could be unconscious recovering somewhere, or he could even, God help her, be dead. He could be legless, armless, brain damaged . . . "Or he could be fine," she said. "Stop it." And she did. She needed to be composed when she saw her father. Hank had offered to come with her, but he so rarely came she thought it might throw her father off and make things harder, and she needed him, anyway, to stay with Keith—but Keith could have stayed with Kate, that would have been easy enough, and her father, it probably really would have made things easier, so . . . Why wasn't he here? Because she didn't want him. And what the hell did that mean?

Their families were so different, hers and Hank's. He was part of a clan, all those brothers, sisters, aunts, uncles, cousins, nieces, nephews, friends—they numbered in the hundreds. With Lindsey, it was just the four of them: Lindsey and Ronnie, Mom and Dad. Both of her father's parents were gone by the time he married her mother. He had one brother, who lived someplace in South America and whom he hadn't seen in more than forty years. Her mother was originally from Iowa, an only child, and her parents were gone before she was thirty. A job teaching art history at Roanoke College brought her to Salem, and she taught there eight years before she met Lindsey's father and first got pregnant and then got married and retired from teaching to raise her children. They were an island, the four of them, odd and isolated and happy together. By the time Lindsey was a teenager, her father was in his seventies and her mother was in her fifties. People often mistook them for her grandparents. Hank had met Lindsey's mother only a few times. She died in the fall of '97, and Lindsey married Hank in the summer of '98. She wondered, even at the time, if his big family weren't part of the attraction: all those people bonded by blood and history. Marrying Hank was like gaining citizenship in a friendly country, like moving from an island to the mainland.

Lindsey sat back in the driver's seat. She needed to be composed when she saw her father. She had to tell him about Ronnie, but it would do no one any good if he got too upset and agitated. She felt angry then, if only for a moment, about the reversal of roles between her and her father. He had always been the one looking out for her: the smart, steady, solid center of all their lives, hers, her mother's, and Ronnie's—and now, now she had become the parent at twenty-nine. Now she was the one who gave advice. She was the one who listened patiently while her father repeated the week's worries and concerns for the hundredth time, as if they hadn't discussed and settled the same issues over and over again.

She started the car and pulled out onto the road. This was the way things were, and there was nothing to do about it but get on with it. Ronnie was wounded. He'd been airlifted to a hospital. That was all she knew. For now. She was working on getting more information. She'd tell her father that gently but firmly. And then she'd have to tell it to him again, endlessly, as the slippery words squirmed in and out of his consciousness. He'd probably say *far out* at some point. He'd recently taken to saying it in response to just about everything, which was one more cruel, cosmic irony, since no one hated '60s slang more than her father. She was surprised the gods hadn't stuck *groovy* in his head, one of his least favorite all-purpose '60s slang expressions. Ronnie used to say *groovy* whenever he wanted to annoy their father, and later it became a joke between them, between Ronnie and Lindsey. *Groovy*, he'd say whenever he saw something interesting, and they'd both laugh. This was when she came back to Salem and married

Hank, after Richmond and VCU—when she came back and found that Ronnie had grown into a gawky, awkward teenager who compensated for his lack of cool with a wicked sense of humor. Lindsey used to take Ronnie and Avery, Kate's girl, who was around Ronnie's age, out to Roanoke. They were good company, and the three of them had fun together, Ronnie cracking jokes a mile a minute, managing even to pierce poor Avery's stunning case of teenaged angst and surliness. Avery picked up on the joke, and the three of them wore it out, commenting on everything from art to fashion. Everything was *groovy*, followed by laughter. They had fun, Lindsey and the kids, back then, not even ten years ago, when she was the married grown-up at all of twenty-one or so, introducing the kids to culture in metropolitan Roanoke. Another lifetime.

At Friendship, she pulled into her regular spot outside her father's apartment. The literature referred to the grounds of the Friendship Retirement Community as a campus, and the place did have that feel, with its neatly mowed lawns and carefully attended shrubbery. She jogged from the parking lot through the light rain and used her own key to enter the apartment. "Dad!" she called once the door was open a crack, and then again, "Dad!" as she entered the apartment. "It's Lindsey!" she yelled, and then waited a moment. The living room was dark, neat and orderly as usual, which was to be expected given housekeeping came in daily—and her father had always been neat to the point, at times, of fastidiousness. Most of the surface of the living room table was covered with an unfolded map, its parallel creases dividing a field of light blue into which a peninsula of land descended, crisscrossed with a spidery web of red highway lines. "Dad!" she called again, but more softly, as she entered the room and saw that it was a map of Greece covering the table, with Crete in an inset. A red wildflower guidebook held down one side of the map, and a yellow *National Geographic* held down the other. As she leaned over the map to look at it more carefully, her father ambled through the bedroom door.

"Arthur," she said, addressing him as her mother had whenever he'd done something surprising, "why do you have a map of Greece open on your living room table?"

"I was in the bathroom," he said. "That's why it took me so long." He kissed her on the cheek and Lindsey returned the gesture with a hug.

"The map?" she said, nodding toward it.

He leaned across the table and looked over the map. He seemed hesitant about explaining. His once wiry build had diminished to an unattractive thinness that made him look frailer than he actually was. But he *had* grown frail, and it surprised Lindsey every time she noticed it. Everything about him was thinning, from his hair to his body to his mind. His face, in the dull light of a cloudy day through the living room windows, looked pinched and sallow. The crown of his head was speckled with liver spots, and there was a raw indentation above his right ear where the doctors had removed a cancerous mole.

"Are you planning a trip?" Lindsey said. "You weren't going without me, were you?"

Art placed his palms on the map, flattening it out, and nodded toward the inset. "I hitchhiked around Crete, right after the war." He shrugged as if bemused. "Just, memories," he said and then laughed, but not without a touch of bitterness. "This—" he said, and he pushed the map half off the table, "This I suddenly remember like it happened yesterday—but *yesterday* is a fog."

Lindsey shifted a chair and sat down. "Tell me about Crete," she said, and she folded her hands under her chin, adopting the posture of a interested listener.

"Long time ago," Art said, and he pulled the map back onto the table and went about refolding it.

"That's what you always say." Lindsey tugged the map away from him. "You know," she said and then hesitated, wary about following through, afraid of upsetting him. "You know," she repeated gently, "it's just that eventually, Dad, you're going to forget all this"— she pointed to the map—"all your history. I know, really, next to nothing about your life before you met Mom. I mean, I know you fought in World War II, in Europe, and you were wounded—"

"Three times," Art said. He took the map back from her.

"Three times? See? I had no idea. Where were you wounded? How badly? Why haven't you ever told us any of this? I mean, I used to wonder if you weren't an ax murderer or something before you met Mom, your life was such a mystery."

Art smiled at that, and for an instant that old, wonderful light came back into his eyes. He ran his fingers through the few strands of thin gray hair remaining atop his head. "An ax murderer," he repeated, and then said, "no, nothing as dramatic as that."

Lindsey knew her father had been married twice before he'd met her mother, but she knew nothing about the women or the marriages. She knew there were no children, her mother had told her that. According to her mother, Art thought he was incapable of fathering children until he got her pregnant with Lindsey, an event about which they were both ecstatic—even though they weren't married. Vivian, her mother, had been married for a little over a year in her twenties, and not having gotten pregnant during the marriage, she had her own doubts. When she told Art that she was pregnant, they both cried for the joy of it. Lindsey had these kinds of scraps of knowledge about her parents' lives before they married, but next to no details. She wondered if now, in his old age, on the verge of losing all his memories, he might finally be willing to share them.

Art finished refolding the map and then pulled out a chair and collapsed into it. He seemed tired, as if the work of folding up the map had exhausted him. "Have you heard anything from Ronnie?" he asked. "I feel like it's been a long time since we've heard from him. Have I forgotten? Did we hear from him, and I've forgotten it?"

Lindsey didn't answer right away, and for several seconds the two of them sat in the quiet, dim light of a rainy afternoon, watching each other in silence. She ran her fingertips over the warm wood surface of the living room table. "Actually," she said, "it's uncanny you should bring it up because, actually—" She closed her eyes and hesitated, annoyed with herself for being so nervous. She was afraid she would burst into tears once she tried to talk about Ronnie being wounded, which she knew would only make the situation more difficult since her father was at his worst, his most confused and unmoored, when he was stressed or anxious.

"What is it?" Art leaned across the table to lay a hand over Lindsey's wrist, stopping the nervous, repetitive movement of her fingertips on the table. "Is something wrong?"

"No." Lindsey couldn't keep the tears out of her eye. She took her father's hand. "Listen," she said, "Ronnie's been wounded, but it's not bad." As soon as the words were out of her mouth, she wished she could yank them back out of the air.

"When did you find this out? Why didn't you tell me?" Art pulled his hand out of hers. "Lindsey," he said, "I'm not senile yet. How badly was he wounded?"

"Actually," Lindsey said, and suddenly she was once again the child. She felt as if her father had caught her in a lie and now she feared the punishment. "Actually," she repeated, "I really don't know anything about the nature of the wound, Dad. I'm hoping it's not bad. All I know for sure is that he's been wounded and he's in surgery."

"In surgery . . ." Art repeated, as if the concept were a little too much to grasp all at once. "In surgery," he said, and then he began to shake, first his arms and then his whole body, and at that sight—the sight of her father's frail body shaking—Lindsey laid her head in her arms and cried, the tears and sobs issuing out in great, body-wracking waves. And then, a moment later, her father was standing beside her and rubbing her back. "It's all right, honey," he said, one hand on her shoulder, the other running up and down the length of her spine. "It's okay," he said.

"Jesus . . ." She grasped his hand on her shoulder and held on to it tightly. "I'm sorry, Dad," she said. "I'm falling apart. Jesus." When she looked up, she saw her father looking out the living room window as if he could see all the way to Iraq. "Ronnie'll be okay, Dad," she said. "I just feel it. I just know somehow."

Art patted Lindsey's head and ran his hand over her hair, his eyes fixed on the distance beyond the window. "In Italy," he said, "it was so cold, honey." He wrapped his arms around himself as if he could feel the cold he was remembering. "I never knew cold before that. And wet, to the bone."

"When was this?" Lindsey asked. She got up and helped Art into her seat. "What are you talking about, Dad?" She was still sobbing a little, and she worked to control it as she pulled another chair next to him and sat down.

"In Italy," he said, "where I was wounded. We were there all winter, in the mountains, and that's were I was . . ." His voice trailed off.

Lindsey said, "Ronnie's in a hospital, Dad. I'm sure he's getting the best of care."

Art said, "Why am I talking about me?" and then he looked away again, off into the distance over Lindsey's shoulder. He seemed to be seeing something far away, and tears filled his eyes before he shook his head, as if shaking off a vision. He got up abruptly. "Some things," he said, "it will be God's greatest blessing to finally forget," and he walked into the bedroom as if with a purpose.

"Good job," Lindsey whispered to herself. She thought her father must have gone to the bathroom, so she waited silently, her head empty for a few moments. She noticed a lemon smell and was perplexed until she pegged it as the polish housekeeping used for the table. She went to the window and looked outside at rain beading on the roofs of a line of cars in the parking lots, all the same subdued colors: silvers, greens, reds, blues. When, after a while, she didn't hear any noises from the bathroom, she grew concerned and went into the bedroom to find her father sitting in the black recliner next to the window, holding a nicely framed picture of her mother in his hands. "She was so beautiful," he said, and he turned the picture toward Lindsey.

Lindsey nodded. It was a picture of her mother at seventeen, wearing a knee-length white dress, her hands clasped gracefully in front of her. She was stunning in the photograph, her skin resonant with youth, and she was smiling at the camera as if the person taking the picture had just said something that deeply amused her. "That's her graduation picture," she said. "When did you have it framed?"

"One of the girls did it for me," he said and propped up the picture on the end table beside the chair. "I was looking at it one day, and . . ."

"Yes?" she sat on the edge of the bed, her knees almost touching her father's knees.

"What was I telling you?"

"About the picture. You were telling me about someone having it framed for you."

"That's right," he said and looked over at the picture again. "She was so beautiful then. I never knew a woman more beautiful than Vivian at that age."

"But," Lindsey said, "you know . . . you didn't actually know her at that age, right?"

"Sure, I did," he said. "When she was seventeen? Sure, I knew her then."

"No." Lindsey gestured toward the picture. "That's Vivian, Dad. That's my mother."

"I know who this is," he said angrily—though more frustrated, really, than angry. "I knew her in high school," he said, only the slightest note of uncertainty in his voice, the words posed as a statement with the tremulous note of a question just under the surface. "I took her to the prom, and then after that—"

Lindsey said, "Are you thinking of your first wife, Dad? That's Vivian in the picture. You didn't meet her until you were in your fifties."

Art shook his head, disgusted with himself. "Of course," he said, "of course. I'm thinking of my first wife. Oh, Lord," he said. "No, I'm not even. I'm thinking of a high school sweetheart. For heaven's sake," he said. "I know I didn't know Vivian in high school. For God's sake . . ."

Lindsey said, "It's okay," and she knelt at his feet and put her head in his lap. "You're upset," she said. "You're upset about Ronnie." At the mention of Ronnie, Art's body stiffened, and when Lindsey looked up, she saw that he was frightened.

"What's going on with Ronnie?" he said tentatively. "I know something just happened. It's— What is it? What happened?"

"He was wounded," Lindsey said. She patted his leg. "He's fighting in Iraq, and he was wounded."

"Is he hurt badly?" he asked.

"We think he's going to be okay."

"All right," Art said. "Okay." And he looked out the window again.

Lindsey could see the confusion in her father's eyes. He had lost track of what was going on. Ronnie and Iraq and all his family, all his history fogged up somehow. "You have to relax," she said. "You'll feel better when you relax a bit."

Art nodded, acknowledging that he had heard her. His eyes were drowning.

Lindsey pulled herself up, sat on the arm of the recliner, and put her arm around her father. Together they looked out the window at rain falling on a long expanse of green pastures, in silence.

When Hank got to his sister Liz's, Keith bolted from the car to join his cousins. His sister Tammy was already there with her three boys—her Subaru was parked at the curb, and he could hear the boys shouting through the open front door—and his brother Steve was just pulling into the driveway with his crew, the wife and kids piling out of his van as soon as it came to a rest, the three girls sprinting for the front door. Hank watched from his car while Steve walked toward him and his sister-in-law went about unbuckling their youngest, who was screaming and flailing his arms and legs, hysterical to be set free. It was raining lightly, a misty drizzle under a gray sky, but there were darker clouds approaching and it looked like it might rain hard on and off the rest of the day. Steve was two years older than Hank, but he'd put on weight steadily since he'd gotten married in his twenties, and he already looked solidly middle-aged, all the youth gone out of him, as he labored across the front lawn, hauling his meaty thighs and arms as if each step took effort. Hank powered down the passenger window. He didn't feel like getting out of the car just yet. Word had obviously already gotten around about Ronnie: there was no other reason for Steve and Tammy to be at Liz's.

"Hey, buddy," Steve said. He crouched by the door and crossed his arms on the edge of the open window. "You doing okay? You holding up all right? Son of a bitch," he said. "This whole goddamned war. How's Lindsey?"

"She hasn't said much." Hank pulled keys from the ignition. "Mostly she just looks scared shitless," he said. "I'm dropping off Keith and going to meet her over at Friendship."

"At her dad's? Is he— Does he know what's going on?"

Hank said, "I haven't been there yet, Steve." He gestured for Steve to back away from the window so he could close it, and by the time he unbuckled himself and got out of the car, Steve was waiting for him, wrapping him in a big embrace.

Hank patted Steve on the back and waited to be let loose.

"Goddamn shame," Steve said.

When he looked toward the house, Hank saw both his sisters crossing the lawn toward him, followed by a horde of kids. Liz stopped halfway to the car and shooed all the kids back into the house. "It's raining!" she shouted. "Y'all get back in the house—and don't track dirt on my rug!" She was a big woman, both his sisters were— not fat but big-boned and tall. Liz stepped in front of the car and pulled Hank into her arms just as Steve let him loose. "How's my baby brother?" she said, and when she took a step back, he saw that her eyes were full of tears. "It's terrible," she said. "I've been so afraid for those boys, all three of them. They're all like family, the way they did everything together."

Tammy said, "They were joined at the hip, those three." She squeezed Hank's shoulder and kissed him on the cheek. "It's godawful," she said. "My heart goes out to Lindsey—and to you, honey."

Hank said, "Lindsey'll be all right," a little annoyance in his voice at all the fuss. He swiped a hand over his head, wiping away the rain.

"Could be nothing much at all. Could just be pulling some shrapnel out of the boy, something like that."

Tammy took a step back from him, and Steve started to say something before he stopped abruptly and turned his eyes down.

"What?" Hank said. "What's this?"

Liz put her hands on her hips, as if she were suddenly a little angry. She was still in her church clothes, a pale blue dress with a white-and-yellow floral pattern, and her face looked ruddier than usual in contrast. "You said she went to tell her father about Ronnie."

"Being wounded and needing surgery," Hank said.

"Oh, honey . . ." Liz's face turned deeply solemn. "We've heard from Barbie."

"Who's Barbie?" Hank asked. "Lindsey—" He paused and then asked calmly, "What's going on?"

Liz said, "Barbie is Jake Jr.'s mom," and then she faltered, seemingly at a loss how to continue.

Steve leaned against the car and finally looked up to meet Hank's eyes. There were trickles of rain spilling out of his hair, but he didn't seem to notice. "Jake Jr. called home with the news about Ronnie," he said. "It's bad."

"How bad? Is the boy dead? Is that what—"

Tammy said, "He's lost both his legs, Hank. He's mangled all over. They're trying to save what's left of him." Liz was leaning against the car next to Steve, and Tammy joined them, her shoulder against her sister's shoulder, the wet hood of the car soaking the back of her blue dress. "It was one of those IEDs. The boy, Jake Jr., he says better we pray . . ." She covered her face.

"That he die?" Hank said. "Better we pray that he die?"

Steve nodded. "But he don't know," he said. "That boy was never the brightest bulb."

"Lindsey . . ." Hank said. "Lindsey . . ." Then the words seemed to drain out of him and silence descended on the moment, leaving only the background sound of drizzling rain. Hank stared blankly at the solemn faces of his sisters. He joined them in leaning against the car, squeezing between them, and each sister took one of his hands in her hand. He couldn't imagine how he would deliver this news to Lindsey. "God," he said, and then his head seemed to empty of thought and he stared blankly at the street.

"We're getting soaked," Tammy said, and she squeezed Hank's hand, meaning it was time to go inside.

When Hank looked around him, he saw that there were faces in every window of Liz's house looking out at them: kids in the doorway watching in silence, friends and neighbors and family in the living room, many more people in the house than he had imagined. Then he turned to the surrounding houses and saw people in the doorways and windows, one older man standing out in his driveway holding his chin in one hand looking as if he were struggling to keep his composure. Hank let his sisters lead him into the house.

"We'll get you a little something to eat," Liz said.

Tammy said, "We'll give you some food to take with you to Lindsey and her father."

"Okay," Hank said. The rain started to pick up some. "But I can only stay a minute."

"Just have a bite to eat," Liz said.

Tammy said, "Probably a good idea to give Lindsey a little time alone with her father, too."

Hank said, "That's true. I mean—" And then he had no idea what he meant. It was as if all thought emptied out of his head for a second, and he simply followed along between his sisters.

The slick blue hood of Avery's raincoat dipped down over her forehead, protecting her from the weather and offering her a degree of anonymity by shadowing her face. The hood worked like a cowl, the way the thick strips Velcroed under her chin and the sides covered her face and the top dipped down. When she lowered her head, it was as if she disappeared. Something about that she liked: walking along streets in the rain, there and not there, seen and not seen. Ahead of her, rain poured off a line of blue umbrellas over the Deli's outdoor seating. She took her time, ambling along the sidewalk, in no hurry, though she was hungry. Her friends would all think her weird for going to the Deli alone. It was a girl thing, like girls somehow were never supposed to want to do anything alone, which was such bullshit. *You went by yourself?* How many times had she heard that in her life? *You went by yourself?*

Inside the Deli, she pulled the hood back, shook off the rain— and saw Melanie and Dee leaning across their table while talking, their lips practically meeting, apparently not wanting anyone else to hear what they were saying. The Deli was bustling, as usual, packed mostly with students, an array of youthful bodies and faces and styles of dress, though khaki and denim dominated. Avery noticed one of her art professors sitting across the room with his back to her. He was an older guy with long gray hair, and he was sitting across the table from another professor, a woman in her forties, maybe fifties, not in the Art Department, but Avery had seen her before on campus. Dee, as if she sensed Avery's entrance, looked up and grinned at her. She nudged Melanie, who turned around, smiled hugely, showing long white teeth, and waved her over to their table. Avery sat next to Dee and folded her hands demurely in her lap. "So what were you girls whispering?" she said, and she leaned toward Melanie as if she wanted in on the conspiracy.

"You're all wet." Dee swiped at Avery's jeans and then looked at her fingers as if rainwater were a disgusting foreign substance. "Don't you own an umbrella?"

Melanie said, "Why didn't you drive?"

Dee said, "You meeting someone?"

Avery said, "I had a craving for a macho chimichanga."

"Yuck," Dee said.

Mel said, "What? They're good."

Dee rolled her eyes.

Avery said, "What are you guys getting?"

"Chicken salad," Dee said, "if it ever gets here."

Mel said, "Burger. So? D'you talk to Zach yet?"

Avery made a face, as if she had mixed feelings about Zach. "I turned off my phone," she said. "I've got, like, five missed calls."

"Oh, please." Dee dropped her face into her hands and leaned on the table.

Avery said, "What's that about?"

"She thinks Zach's a catch."

"Not really," Dee said, exaggeratedly perking up. She tossed her hair back. "Big handsome guy, football star, word is, going to be rich. He's not much," she said. "Why don't you toss him back?"

"He's *sweet*," Avery said, announcing that as her only real interest in him, "and he's funny and guileless in a way that's charming."

Mel said, "What-less?"

"Guileless," Dee said.

Avery said, "Like he's not deceitful."

"Grant is *so* not sweet," Melanie said. "That's what's so hot about him."

At the mention of Grant, the table went silent for a moment before the waitress hustled over with their food. A thin older woman with frizzy gray hair tied back in a ponytail, she looked at Avery with annoyance and then asked if she could take her order. Avery asked for the chimichanga and the waitress scuttled away. Mel bit into the hamburger and Dee said, "Ex-hippie," gesturing with her head toward the departing waitress.

"Not particularly friendly," Mel said with her mouth full.

Avery glanced around the room while the girls went at their meals amid the modulating rumble of voices and the tinny background hum of indistinguishable music coming from someplace overhead. Her art professor had been joined by two more faculty members from the Art Department. The four of them were drinking beers and chatting amiably with each other, not looking much like artists, looking in fact like every other middle-class comfortable well-adjusted body in the place.

"Grant," Melanie said, holding her half-eaten burger between the plate and her mouth, "has this birthmark on his thigh? It looks like a dog, I swear: little head with like dog teeth, little body, and like four long legs."

"It's not a tattoo?" Dee said, as if she found something about the birthmark distasteful.

"Birthmark," Mel said. "Got to use your imagination a little, but the teeth are like right there." She bit into her burger and a funnel of a yellowish-red grease spilled onto her plate.

Avery said, "Do you think you'll see him again?"

Mel, chewing on her mouthful of burger, snatched a cell phone out of her lap and plopped it on the table beside her plate.

Dee, without looking at either of them, said, "She's been waiting for a call all day, God help us."

Melanie swallowed hurriedly and said, "If he doesn't call, I swear to God I'm going to die." She leaned toward Avery. "I am, like, so hot for this guy. I don't know what's got into me, I swear."

Dee said, "I know what got into you."

Melanie said, "Oh, shut up," and grinned and took another bite of her burger.

Avery reached for Mel's Coke and looked at her. Mel nodded and Avery took a sip and slid the glass back to her. "What do you like about him?" she asked. "Why are you so into him?"

"Oh, my God," Mel said, leaning over her plate. "He's. So. Hot."

"You've said." Avery straightened herself in her chair. She looked annoyed. "But what? What do you like about him?"

Dee said, "He's got a big dick."

"Shut up!" Mel said, dropping the remaining bite of burger onto her plate.

"Really," Avery said. She folded her hands in her lap again and waited for an answer.

"I don't know," Mel said, and she looked suddenly aglow with the pleasure of getting to think about the question. "He's just like, I don't know— There's something *manly* about him, you know? Like he is definitely not a boy."

"So," Avery said, "he's not a boy? That's it?"

"There's something magic about it," Mel said. "How can you explain that? He just, he makes me tingly."

"Fluttery," Dee said, correcting her. Deadpan, she added, "He makes you all fluttery just thinking about him." She forked a single small bite of chicken from her salad and brought it, almost reluctantly, to her mouth.

"That too," Mel said. "Tingly and fluttery." She snatched up the last bit of her hamburger and popped it into her mouth. "Plus he's utterly gorgeous," she mumbled.

Avery picked up the salt shaker and fidgeted with it. *"He's hot,"* she said. *"He's gorgeous.* You're devolving into a twelve-year-old, Mel."

Dee said, "Amen."

"You're both just jealous." Mel slid her plate away from her. She looked smug and amused.

Dee said, "What's Avery got to be jealous about?"

"Yeah," Mel said, "what are you jealous about?"

"I'm not jealous. I'm just curious." She returned the salt shaker to the center of the table. "I want to know what makes you so into him."

Melanie gazed off into space as if she were working to come up with a good answer. Before she could say anything, the waitress returned, delivered Avery's chimichanga, asked if anyone wanted anything else, and then hurried away after dropping the checks on the table. Across the room, a group of young men burst into loud raucous laughter. One of them, a skinny boy in a blue Penn State T-shirt, shouted, "Dawg! Dawg! No way!" and the boy opposite him shouted back, "Way! Man! I swear!" leading to another round of shouting and laughter. For a minute, everyone in the restaurant was watching them, and then everyone went back to their own affairs and there were a few seconds of quiet in which Avery made out the tune coming through the overhead speakers as an orchestral version of the Beatles' "I Want to Hold Your Hand."

"Okay," Mel said, and she looked suddenly a little embarrassed. "You've got to promise you won't laugh at me if I tell you this."

"Go ahead," Dee said.

"You especially!" She pointed at Dee.

"Yeah, yeah, yeah," Dee said. "I promise." She slid her plate into Mel's, finished with her salad.

Avery took a bite of her chimichanga and stared at Mel, announcing she was listening.

"Okay," Mel said. "I know this will sound a little sappy-girly . . ." She was smiling slightly but turning red too, as if truly reluctant to say what she wanted to say.

"Oh, my God," Dee said, annoyed. "What?"

"Just," Mel said, and then sighed and spit it out, "he told me he thought I was special."

"That's it?" Dee said. "He told you you were special? That's the big deal?"

"It's the way he said it." Mel turned to Avery as if looking for confirmation. "You know what I mean? I felt like he was really see-ing into me."

Dee said mockingly, "Seeing the *special* you."

Melanie said, "You promised, Dee."

"Okay, okay," Dee said. "No. You're right. It's nice. I see what you're saying." She pushed a stray lock of hair out of her eyes and smiled genuinely at Melanie.

Avery looked past both girls to the window beyond them with its view of the street. She could feel her body getting hot, as if someone had turned up a thermostat and heat were rising through her legs and chest to her cheeks. Outside, the rain was coming down hard, streaking the window and splashing off puddles on the blacktop. A girl in a red raincoat sprinted past, clutching the flaps of her jacket tightly with one hand and pulling the hood down to her nose with the other. A moment later, she came through the front door of the Deli, shaking herself like a wet dog.

"You know her?" Mel asked.

"Who?"

"*Who?*" Dee said. "The girl you're staring at."

Avery wasn't aware of staring at anyone. All the sound in the Deli, the voices, the music, the rising and falling chatter—it all co-alesced into a background hum as her breathing got so shallow that she felt a little like she was suffocating. The word *special* kept bouncing around in her head, and in her mind's eye she saw Grant at the lake standing in the moonlit water, his skin bright against the dark surface of the lake. She saw him carrying her in his arms, and then she saw herself lying on the ground, curled up into herself as he stood over her.

"Earth to Avery," Mel said. "What up, girl?"

When Avery turned her attention to the table, she saw that both her friends were looking at her with concern. "What?" she said, and then, before either could answer, she said, "Okay, look. I just think—" She realized she was raising her voice when the people at the next table turned to look at her. "I just think," she said to Mel evenly, "that you need to be wary about this guy."

"Grant?"

"Yes, Grant."

"Why?" Dee said. "Did something happen between you two?"

"What?" Mel said. "Something happened between you and Grant?"

"Oh, shit," Avery said, and she melted a little as she saw the worry in Mel's face. "Look. I'm just— He said the same thing to me, Mel. I mean, he wasn't out of bed with you ten minutes—"

"When? When did he say that? He said you were special?"

"Oh, my God," Dee said in a harsh whisper, leaning over the table, her eyes bright. "Get out of here. Really?"

"Now, wait a second," Mel said, raising her voice. "What exactly did he say to you?"

Avery said, "Look, Mel. I'm sorry—"

"Don't be sorry, just what did he say?"

Dee said, "Hey, Mel—"

"I want to know." She leaned closer to Avery. "You're waiting till now to tell me this? I mean, you're acting just a little bit like a cunt, don't you think?"

"Calm down," Dee said.

"Fuck you." Mel took her napkin from her lap and tossed it onto the table. "I don't even believe it," she said. "Tell me what he said."

"He told me he thought I was special—"

"You already said that." Mel's face was twisted up in a look somewhere between contempt and a snarl. "He told you he thought you were special. When? What were you even doing hanging out with him, Av? What? While I was sleeping in the other room?"

"Exactly." Avery folded her arms over her chest. "He chatted me up with you sleeping in the other room, and then he asked me to take a ride to Raystown Lake with him on his bike, which I did, at like four in the morning. Don't ask me why. I honestly don't know. And then, at the lake, I didn't intend it—it's so fucking complicated, I swear—but at the lake we had sex. What am I supposed to do now, just let you go on thinking he's some kind of romantic hero?" When she finished speaking, both girls were looking at her in silence. "I'm sorry," she said.

"You're sorry?" Mel looked at Dee and then back to Avery. "Let me be sure I have this straight. You fucked Zach at like two in the morning, and then Grant at like four in the morning—" She looked at her bare wrist as if checking a watch. "Shouldn't you be fucking somebody else about now?"

"Stop it."

"Stop what?"

"I didn't mean to—" Avery's eyes were suddenly moist, which made her furious, and she covered them briefly with both hands, as if she didn't want to see anything for a second or two.

Mel said, "What didn't you mean to?"

"I didn't mean for anything to happen."

"At the lake? You didn't mean to have sex with him at the lake?"

"I didn't—"

"Will you give me a fucking break?" Mel said. She was shouting now. "You went to the lake with him at four in the fucking morning after you must have just gotten out of bed with Zach? You're a fucking slut," she said. "I can't believe it."

On either side of the table, two men appeared, one in a jacket, the other in an apron. They stood in matching postures: hands on their hips, feet spread slightly, as if bracing themselves for a tackle. The man in the jacket said, "I'm going to have to ask you girls to leave. This is a family restaurant. You ought to be ashamed of yourselves."

Dee looked at him as if he were a bug and said, "Fuck you."

Mel said, "We're going. " She fished her check out of the pile and slid one to Dee.

The men waited as Mel walked off to pay her check at the counter, forgetting her jacket on the back of the chair as well as her cell phone and a purse. Dee gathered up Mel's stuff and her own. Before she left, she said to Avery, calmly, "Girl's got a point. That's pretty fucking unbelievable," and then she joined Melanie at the counter. Avery looked at the men and then down at her plate. An orchestral version of another Beatles tune was playing, and she realized that she could hear it clearly because no one else in the restaurant was talking. "I'll leave in a second," she said, and the men seemed to think about it briefly before they both walked away. Avery glanced over the room and saw her art professor looking at her, and when their eyes met, the professor turned away, and then a moment after that, people started talking again, and the rumble of voices returned and blotted out the music. Avery waited until Mel and Dee were gone before she put on her jacket and went to the counter. The cashier was a guy she knew from around town, and usually he'd be friendly and they'd exchange a few words. She made a point of meeting his eyes and smiling ruefully at him, but he acted as though she were a stranger as he rang her up and then dropped her change on the counter.

Outside, it was still pouring. Avery hesitated near the entrance to the Deli as she gazed up at the sky and let rain splash off her face. She had neglected to put her hood up, and her hair was instantly soaked. Water spilled down her forehead and into her eyes. It felt good. Instead of putting up her hood, she took off the jacket. She felt like getting wet. She felt like getting soaked. She walked aimlessly along the street, knowing she didn't want to go back to her apartment and not knowing where else to go.

In a photograph propped on the sitting room table, Hank looked like a gawky teen. He was dressed awkwardly in an ill-fitting black tuxedo, with a frilly blue vest that must have—given the look on his face—embarrassed him even then. Tim was standing beside him, his arm around Hank's shoulder. Hank was fourteen in the picture, Tim twenty-five. It was from their marriage, and Kate had to remind herself that she was only nineteen at the time, the same stubborn five years then that separated them now, when Hank was forty and she was forty-five and the five years seemed like nothing at all. Kate picked up the photograph and held it in her hand, not to see it better so much as to touch it, as if touching it could bring her back for an instant to the instant captured. She was sitting in a polished mahogany chair, an antique probably: Tim had found it at a yard sale, ugly, painted glaring white, and he had stripped it, sanded and stained it, and turned it into a beautiful piece of furniture. She was in her mahogany chair, in her sitting room, facing the backyard window and her garden, where a heavy rain was drenching the already soaked grass. The sound of the rain was soothing. It lulled her. The Hank in the photograph was still a boy, but even back then he had those blue, blue eyes. She used to call him her little brother, and that memory *did* disturb her, thinking of it, recalling then how she wanted to be to him what Tim was, a kind of parent.

Things change. Things always change, she knew that, but before she hadn't really understood. At forty she was a wife and mother, seemingly still in the middle of her life, and still at forty her husband was dead and her daughter was gone, away at college, and she felt old. It still shocked her, the suddenness of it. After Tim's funeral there were days when she could hardly breathe. For months she struggled through every day feeling like she was drowning, and there was only Avery to cling to. Poor Avery. Kate held on to her for dear life; she couldn't help herself. She hovered, she was suffocating, and she knew at every moment what she was doing and that she shouldn't be doing it and she couldn't help herself nonetheless. When Avery finally left for college, it was a relief for both of them.

Kate ran her thumb over the picture of fourteen-year-old Hank, as if she were touching the boy himself. It was a kind of kiss before she slid the picture back to its place on the table. The rain had let up a little bit, but the sky was still thick and dull with dark clouds, and in the distance were even darker clouds. She felt terrible for Lindsey, and she feared for Ronnie, whom she still thought of as a teenager— but her sympathy and concern for Lindsey were complicated by

Hank. She wanted to help, she wanted to offer support, but she didn't want to be a hypocrite, which was how she always felt around Lindsey. If she was honest with herself, anyway, her real concern wasn't for Lindsey at all, but for Hank. She couldn't help it. Her thoughts were all about Hank: how he was feeling now, how he would deal with Lindsey's grief and anger, if Lindsey would take it out on him, making her troubles somehow his fault, as she usually did.

When it started with Hank, the first time, there were no words spoken. Hank and Tim used to watch football together—football and everything else. Lindsey never could stand sports, though she occasionally made a feeble effort to pretend she was interested. Sometimes Tim would go over to Hank's, but mostly it was Hank and Tim in the den watching one game or another, and Kate would make snacks for them and bring them beers, and eventually she got into the games and watched with them, cheering along with them. After Tim was gone, Hank would still come over occasionally to watch the games, and after the games they'd talk, about Tim, about Avery, about Lindsey, about Keith, about their families, about everything, really, sometimes until late into the night, over a couple of glasses of wine or a few beers, and then one night Hank sat next to her on the couch, where she was stretched out, half asleep because the game had been boring. She smiled at him, a little confused, wondering why he had crossed the room to come and sit on the edge of the couch, at her hip, but once he put his hand on her shoulder, she knew. He didn't say anything. He was wearing jeans and a white cord sweater, and the sleeves of the sweater were pushed up on his forearms, which were muscled in a way she felt in her belly, in her thighs. She knew better than to say anything at that moment because she knew there was nothing to say that would make it right, and she wanted it anyway. She touched his face, sliding her hand along his cheek and up to the back of his head before she clutched his hair and pulled him down to her.

Neither of them spoke. When it was over and they were together on the couch, a thin sky-blue throw draped over them, her head on his chest, her body draped over his, Hank tried to speak, the choked, awkward beginning of a sentence struggling on his tongue, but she touched his lips, quieting him. She knew from the start that there would be no comfort in words. If you couldn't be honest, you might as well not speak at all. The moment Hank had touched her shoulder, she had agreed to lie. She knew that one lie would engender a thousand more lies, to Lindsey, to Keith, to Avery, to the family, to everyone. She knew for certain that no one could ever know without bringing disaster to Hank and to herself. The family would never forgive either of them, and Hank's family was his life, whether he knew it or not, whether he accepted it or not. His every thought, his every breath, his every act had its roots in his family. So what happened between them would have to always be a secret. She was clear on all that from the beginning. She knew the right thing to do, and she didn't care. She should have gently removed his hand from her shoulder, slid off the couch, and pretended nothing had happened. But she never even considered it. Not for a second. She would never have done it herself, she had never seriously considered doing it herself, but once he touched her that way, words and reason, right and wrong—it all disappeared like nothing at all and she pulled him down to her and accepted whatever might follow.

Kate's cell phone, upstairs on the kitchen table, began issuing what were supposed to be clapping noises but actually sounded more like little firecrackers going off. It was Corinne's ringtone. The morning's argument had largely gone out of Kate's head, and she found herself anxious to talk to Corinne about Lindsey and Ronnie. By the time she got to the kitchen, the phone had gone quiet—but Corinne was standing on the other side of the window in the kitchen door, slipping her own cell phone back into her purse.

Kate let her in and said, "Wouldn't the doorbell have been simpler?" She gave Corinne a hug and pointed her to the kitchen table. "Want a cup of coffee?"

"Love one," Corinne said, following her to the counter and coffee maker. "I just heard about Ronnie," she said. "I had to come over. I'm so sorry, Kate."

Kate turned around and the women embraced again, the bulk of Corinne swallowing up Kate. When Kate tried to let go, Corinne tightened her grip, pulling her into the musky perfume splashed on her neck and chest. Kate patted Corinne's back. "It's terrible," she said.

Corinne said, "I can't imagine." She let Kate loose, stepped back. "To lose a loved one," she said, "in—forgive me—in an idiotic blunder of a war like this one. My God."

"He's not dead." Kate's hands went to her belly, as if she were protecting herself. "He's wounded. They don't have any facts yet," she said. "It might not even be bad."

"Oh, honey," Corinne said, and she touched Kate's arm, massaging it a little. "That's not what I'm hearing."

"What are you hearing? How could—"

"The boys have called and talked to their families."

"The boys? Willie and Jake Jr.?"

"They've both called."

"But he's not dead, is he?"

Corinne nodded. "That's what I heard," she said. "I'm so sorry, Kate."

"Wait a second." Kate's knees felt like they might buckle. She pulled out a kitchen chair and sat down. "Wait a second," she repeated. Her eyes were full of tears, and she brushed them away.

"Jesus Christ," Corinne said. She pulled a clump of tissues out of the pocket of her dress and blotted the tears running down her cheeks. "Oh, my God," she said. "I'm sorry, Kate. I was sure you knew."

"But wait a second . . ." Kate heard the pleading tone in her voice and tried to shake it off. "Wait a second," she repeated. "Wouldn't Lindsey have heard first? How is that possible? How could others know before the immediate family?"

Corinne said, "The boys are probably breaking rules, honey. You know—"

"Or there are rumors going around. I mean, that could possibly be what's happening here, don't you think?"

"I suppose." Corinne took a seat next to Kate. "I suppose it's possible."

"You're humoring me," Kate said. "Don't do that."

"I'm not." Corinne looked away for a long moment, at the photograph of a forest stream hanging on the wall, the kitchen counter and the coffee maker reflected in its glass, along with rain falling on the front lawn and a part of the driveway. "It is possible," she added softly, "that there are rumors going around. You're right."

"But you think it's true," Kate said.

Corinne didn't answer. She looked up at the photograph again and then out to the driveway, where an old station wagon had just pulled in. "Damn," she said. "It's Evelyn and Gilda." Kate watched the car in the driveway as the door opened and two elderly women from their church group got out carefully. Corinne touched Kate's wrist. "Do you want me to tell them you're in bed? Go ahead," she said. "I'll say you're not feeling well or something."

Kate shook her head, but she got up anyway and started for the back of the house. "Just entertain them for a moment." She pointed to the bathroom. "Just give me—"

Corinne waved her away. "Go, go. I'll make some coffee."

In the bathroom, with the door locked, Kate sat on the john. She didn't believe that Ronnie was dead. It didn't feel possible, and part of her was somehow certain that it was all a rumor. The part of her that wasn't certain, though, felt shaky and unmoored. Ronnie and Avery had spent a lot of time together when they were teenagers. They both adored Lindsey, who was fresh out of VCU in those days and posturing as a young artist. She carried a sketch pad at all times and was always making drawings of the kids. She took them to the art museum in Roanoke, and she took them on several weekend trips to D.C. It was Lindsey's influence that made Avery start taking art courses in high school. Kate had been jealous, a little, not a big deal—but she remembered feeling like Lindsey was stealing Avery from her. And Ronnie . . . he was just . . . sweet. Avery was probably the only girl in the world he felt comfortable around. He was such an awkward and shy kid, the kind of local boy who had a hard time looking anyone other than family and friends in the eye. But he was easy and jokey around his big sister, and that transferred to Avery. He couldn't be dead. He was too young. It would be like thinking of Avery as—Kate couldn't even let herself think it. Avery was her beautiful girl: smart and complicated, talented and often angry at the world, long before Tim died. Somehow accepting the possibility that Ronnie had died made Avery's death seem possible—and she couldn't allow that thought.

From the kitchen, she heard Corinne talking quietly with Evelyn and Gilda. She couldn't make out what they were saying. The rain picked up again: it beat against the narrow bathroom window. Kate got up and turned on the lights, and the room seemed impossibly bright for a moment, light bouncing off the floor's blue tiles and echoing off the white porcelain tub and sink. She closed her eyes and then splashed water on her cheeks and pressed a thick cotton towel against her face. "Okay," she said, aloud but softly, and then she said it again, "Okay," and she took the towel away from her face and gave herself another minute to fix her makeup before she went out to talk with her guests.

Zach's meatball sub, still fully wrapped in its wax-paper shroud, lay in front of him on the booth table, bracketed by a big bag of chips and a giant yellow cup of Coke. When Dee had called and said she needed to talk to him, he'd told her to meet him at Subway, where he'd planned on going for a snack anyway, and now he had met her and she had told him about Avery and Grant, and he was staring at his sub as if it were a mysterious object that had somehow suddenly appeared in front of him. Across the table, Dee leaned toward Zach, hair falling to her shoulders, bright strands of it shining blond against the deep blue of a boatneck top that revealed more and more cleavage the more she leaned toward him, a look of deep empathy and concern in her eyes. On the other side of the room, a girl walked away from the jukebox followed by the opening twang of a country song.

Zach said, "That's just hard to believe."

"I know," Dee said. She pushed a loose strand of hair away from her eyes. "I've known the girl for, like, years—and I was just, oh my God."

"Both of us?" He looked at Dee as if he doubted her. "She slept with both of us last night?"

"I wouldn't be telling you," Dee said, her voice thick with the deep regret she felt at having to pass this news along to him, "but it was like the whole Deli. I didn't even get back to my apartment"—she clapped her hand over her breast as if pledging allegiance—"and Chack's on the cell, like, *Is what I just heard true?*"

Zach began slowly to unwrap his sub. He looked as if he were still searching for some way to discredit the story. "How did Chack know so fast?"

"Billy's got a friend who was working the counter." Dee toyed with her Coke and then leaned down and took the fat plastic straw gently between her lips but didn't take a sip. She seemed to be thinking something over. When Zach looked up at her after the silence grew awkward, she held the straw another long moment before letting it loose and saying firmly, "I just didn't think it was right. I mean, I only met you this morning, but— You're sweet. You've got this guilelessness about you—"

"What?"

"Niceness," she said. "I mean, what she did? That's just wrong. I don't want anything to do with her anymore, and Melanie's the same. We're both, like, we don't want anybody thinking we'd do anything like that. You know, just because we're her friends. *Were* her friends, anyway. You know what I mean?"

Zach leaned back in his seat and laid his hands flat on the table. He looked as though he were finally accepting the truth of what he'd been told. "Shit," he said. "Damn it."

"I know," Dee said, and she reached across the table to touch his arm. "We're all, like, damn— Chack and Billy too. Nobody wants anything to do with her anymore. I mean, come on, that's disgusting."

Zach pushed his sub aside. "Lost my appetite."

"I'm so sorry," Dee said. "Look . . ." She took a sip of her Coke as if giving herself a second to rethink what she had started to say. "Look," she said again, more firmly, "why don't you let me take you to dinner tonight? We'll go to the Tavern." When Zach didn't answer right away, she added, "I feel guilty about what happened. We all do."

"Why would you feel guilty?"

"Because, you know, you come into our circle of friends and then this happens? That's, like, so wrong. We're not like that. That was just— Who knew? We can't believe it either."

Zach toyed with his drink. "You don't have to take me out."

"I want to," Dee said, and she smiled, showing off brilliant white teeth. "I swear," she added, "I didn't sleep with anybody last night."

Zach laughed. "All right," he said. He pulled his sub back in front of him, looked at it a moment, and then took a bite. With his mouth full, he said, "Might as well eat."

"Good," Dee said, and then leaned over her Coke and sipped it slowly while Zach ate.

Hank found the door to Art's apartment ajar, a section of the *Roanoke Times* wedged between the lock and the door frame. It was pouring again, rain coming down thick and loud, splashing off the roof, thudding into the ground, spilling out of gutters in little streams. He hesitated at Art's doorstep, under the wide black circle of a big umbrella that Liz had insisted he take with him when he left her house. The propped-open door was an invitation to enter without knocking, and he guessed Art was sleeping and Lindsey didn't want him disturbed. She used to do that when Keith took naps as a baby, wedge open the front door. Visitors knew not to ring the bell or knock. Hank had complained about it once, worried that any stranger might walk in on her and the baby. Lindsey had laughed and said, "In Salem?"

Hank opened the door and found Lindsey sitting at the head of the dining room table watching him. He turned his back to her, collapsed the umbrella, propped it up against the stoop railing, and then closed the door quietly, muting the noise of the rain. The first thing he had noticed was that she had a bottle of Woodford Reserve open in front of her and a tumbler of ice and bourbon in her hands. A flash of anger shot through him at the sight of her drinking so early in the day, but he dismissed it before he turned to face her again. She looked beat, as if she hadn't slept for days. Her hair was messed up, two thick clumps sticking out above her ears, where she must have been massaging her temples repeatedly, running her fingers along the sides of her head, pushing her hair back and up. Her unkempt hair along with an expression, mostly in the set of her eyes, that was a mix of anger and exhaustion gave her a dangerous, slightly crazed look. She was wearing one of her father's robes, a matted terrycloth garment that was probably older than Lindsey. At her neck, where the robe opened in a V, a bright yellow flower against the green background of her summer dress looked like some happier self peeking out into the gloom.

Hank sat alongside her at the table, met her eyes, and waited. She stared back in silence, as if furious with him about something. He asked, as gently as he could manage, "Is Art sleeping?"

She nodded, and he saw that she wasn't angry with him. The response was so indifferent, a reporter might have asked the question.

"I take it you told him about Ronnie," he said. "How did he handle it?"

Lindsey didn't respond. She continued watching him, the hardness still in her eyes but shifting from fury toward sadness. Hank looked out the window at the rain, gathering up his resolve, intending to tell her what he had learned from his sisters, but when he looked back, she said, "Ronnie's dead."

Then it was Hank's turn to be silent. Questions came to mind, but no words came to his lips.

"He's gone," she said. She wasn't whispering, but her voice was soft and low. "Jake Jr. knew somebody," she continued, "who knew somebody else at the hospital. They got word back to him a little while ago, and he just got through to me." She nodded toward her cell phone where it lay on the table beside the bottle of bourbon. "He waited to call me until he knew for certain." She paused a moment as if replaying the conversation in her mind. "He was sweet," she said. "He couldn't stop crying once he started. He said he knew—" She stopped, and the slightest part of a smile suggested itself on her lips. "He said he knew I'd rather hear it from him. He said he wasn't supposed to—but he feared for the lives of the soldiers who'd show up to tell me." She paused again. "I feel like I'm the one who's dead," she said, and her voice was so emotionless she might have been talking about the weather. "I feel like I've been killed."

At first Hank didn't even know he was crying, the tears welling stealthily in his eyes before dropping onto his shirt, but then he was sobbing, his head on the table, buried in his arms. Lindsey's hand, gentle on the back of his head, touching his hair, made him cry even harder.

Avery sat on a bench in front of the Days Inn, soaked to the skin. When she'd left the Deli, there had been no intention on her part—conscious, at least—to see Grant. She had just . . . started walking. Then she was on Pugh Street, by the Days Inn, and she walked over to the parking lot and saw Grant's motorcycle. She thought about kicking it over. She thought about keying it—maybe scratching her name in the enamel. Instead she went around to the front of the hotel, stood a moment in front of the sliding glass doors, and then took a seat on a nearby bench when she realized that she didn't know what room he was in, and she didn't even know his last name. With the back of her hand, she tried to dry her eyes and her forehead, but it was useless. Her hands were wet, her eyes were wet, her forehead, her hair— She felt as though she had just taken a shower fully clothed. She bent over and whipped her hair back and forth like a dog shaking off a bath.

At the height of the scene in the Deli, when the whole place had gone quiet and everyone was watching them, an odd, tingly sense of anticipation had come over her. It was very strange. It felt like a kind of debut, a coming out, as if some chrysalis she had been encased in was cracking open and she was emerging to an audience. She couldn't find the words to pin it down, and she played over the sensation again and again walking through the rain, getting drenched, getting washed away. She felt that too in the rain, like some part of her was washing away. First there was the emergence in the Deli—the emergence of the Avery who sleeps with Zach, a guy she doesn't know and cares nothing for, and then a few hours later has confused, angry sex with Grant, a guy she at least finds attractive in the way danger's attractive. The unveiling of that Avery. Zach— Her friends had no problem with Zach, their Avery picking up some hulking boy with whom she never in a million years would have any real connection, that was fine because their Avery could do something like that and apparently it was okay. On some level of herself, some deep, deep level, she knew this to be the truth: that the person others saw in her, both friends and family, that Avery was not her, was not Avery. Their Avery was some other person composed of all the things both she and they thought she was supposed to be, and for a very long time now it had been getting harder and harder to live with the Avery she wasn't—and maybe that was what was washing away, that composite, unreal Avery she had been stuck with for so long. The new Avery who emerged . . . she might be every bit as dangerous as Grant, and that might have been the connection she'd felt all along. The new Avery was not a bright shiny thing, polite speaker, good companion, nurturer, caregiver. It seemed possible that the new Avery was not nice at all. Wasn't that what she'd seen in the eyes of the audience watching her emerge, that recognition, that this was not a nice girl, this Avery?

Why should she be? Did she feel nice? Did she feel loving? No. No, she didn't.

So maybe it wasn't an accident that she'd wound up at Grant's hotel—though it was not a conscious plan. Maybe she wanted to see Grant again for no other reason than that she didn't want to see anyone else. Going back to her apartment, seeing Melanie and Dee—it seemed impossible. She despised both of them. No, she didn't despise them, she was just sick of them. They didn't matter. They were vacuous, flitting things all about the shape of their asses and what they draped over themselves and who saw them and thought what about them and what boy they might fuck for fun and which one they might fuck for keeps. They made her ill, all of them, and the part of her that was supposed to be like them, let it wash away, let it runnel along the street and waterfall to the sewer. Whatever was emerging might not be nice—but it had to be better than what had been, if only because she just couldn't do it anymore, and she'd rather it rain hard and wash it all away.

The Days Inn's sliding glass doors opened with a low, pneumatic rumble, and an instant later a bulky man in a navy Penn State jacket stepped out under the canopy and looked at her with a mix of wariness and annoyance. At first he didn't speak. He seemed to be waiting for Avery to go first, to explain why she was sitting on a bench soaking wet in front of the Days Inn. Avery ignored him. She stared straight ahead at the street and crossed one leg over the other, as if she were relaxing while, perhaps, waiting for someone.

"Excuse me," he said. "Can I help you?"

Avery said, "No," and smiled at him. She'd have bet money that he was an ex-football player, that all that bulky fat was muscle a decade ago. She guessed he was in his thirties.

"Well, is there a problem?" He came a couple of steps closer, to the edge of the bench. "I'm the manager here."

Avery said, "No. Thank you. I'm okay."

"I'm sorry," he said. "But you're drenched and just sitting here. It looks to me like there's a problem."

Avery asked his name, and he told her it was Howie. "Well, Howie," she said, "I'm fine. There's no problem."

"Well, then, young lady," he said, "I'll have to ask you to please sit someplace else." Howie paused a second and then added, as if dredging up a touch of humanity, "If there's something wrong, perhaps I can help. If you've been drinking, we have a shuttle—"

"I haven't been drinking," Avery said, cutting him off. "Jesus. It's Sunday afternoon."

"This is a college town," he said. "Nothing surprises me anymore."

Avery said, "I'm having an argument with a boyfriend. Does that give me the privilege of sitting on your bench a few more minutes?"

"Is he a guest here?"

"Drives a motorcycle? Pretty much shaved head? He asked me to come here. I'm supposed to call up to his room." When the manager only crossed his arms over his chest, she added, as if annoyed, "Grant's been here a couple of weeks now. I'd think you'd know your guests a little better."

Howie's face turned a little red. "I'm sorry to disappoint you," he said, "but Mr. Danko checked out yesterday."

"Sorry to disappoint *you*," Avery said, "but he's still here."

"Really?" For a moment, Howie looked like he wanted to pick up Avery by the neck and strangle her, but that quickly disappeared. "Well," he said again, "we should straighten this out. Why don't you step inside with me? We can check at the desk."

Avery said, "Whatever," and followed Howie into the hotel, her jacket slung over her arm and dripping water.

At the desk, Howie typed a few commands into a computer, and the look on his face made it clear that Grant was still at the hotel. He cleared his throat. "He's staying an extra day."

"The rain," Avery said. "Not a good day for a motorcycle."

Howie jotted down a number, handed it to Avery, pointed to a wall phone, and then disappeared quickly into a back room as if he had pressing work to do.

Avery looked at the slip of paper. The number of the room was written above the phone number. She glanced from the wall phone to the elevator and then to a nearby exit sign over a fire door. She checked the door and, finding the stairwell, climbed to the second floor, where she followed a nondescript hallway, narrow and dimly lit, like every other chain hotel hallway in the country. Grant's was the last room, beside a window that overlooked the parking lot. She knocked and then leaned against the wall, her hands folded in front of her.

Grant opened the door wearing a white cotton undershirt and

faded blue jeans. He was barefoot. His eyes brightened with amusement at the sight of Avery dripping water onto the hall rug. "Surprise," he said. "What are you doing here?" When Avery didn't answer, he stepped aside and held the door open for her.

Avery walked past Grant without a word and sat on the heating unit at the far end of the room, in front of the wall-length window. The curtains were open and she had a view of rain falling on the apartment complex across Pugh Street. She tossed her jacket onto the windowsill. The room looked un-lived-in: bed neatly made, no clothes scattered around, no suitcase, nothing on the desk. The bedspread wasn't even rumpled. "Where's your stuff?" she said. She pulled off her sneakers, Nikes with bright red tongues, and tossed them toward the bed.

Grant leaned against the bathroom door, the length of the room between them. "You're all wet," he said. "What happened?"

Avery peeled off her running socks and dropped them on the rug, where they landed with a wet thud. "I can't believe," she said, "that you told Melanie you thought she was *special*, and you left her a note telling her how *wonderful* she was."

"So?" Grant said. "What's that to you?"

"Really? What's that to me?"

"Yes," Grant said. "What is it to you whatever I said or did with Melanie?"

Avery said, "You're unbelievable," and looked out the window, where a gust of wind was blowing through trees along the sidewalk.

Grant sat at the foot of the bed. "Are you telling me," he said, "that you've been out walking in the rain because you're upset over what I said to Melanie?"

Avery said, "Not at all." She peeled off her jeans and panties and tossed them on top of her jacket on the windowsill. She was still for a moment, framed by the window behind her, wearing only her soaked, summery shirt with its wet red fabric stuck to her skin, her hair plastered to her head. "I'm telling you that I think you're the kind of shallow liar who spews whatever bullshit comes to mind." She met his eyes and tried to stare him down. "What?" she said when he didn't flinch. She took off her blouse and bra and stood there in the window a moment. "Is every girl you meet *special* and *wonderful?*" She yanked the bedspread back and slid under the blanket, pulling it up to her neck and snuggling into the bed. "Aren't you even a little embarrassed?" she asked. "I'd be." She settled her head on the pillow. "If someone called me out on being so insincere. Or are you so glib and phony that it doesn't bother you?"

Grant said, "So what are you doing here?" He went to the bathroom and came back with a towel, which he tossed onto the pillow beside her. "Dry your hair. The pillow's getting soaked."

Avery ignored the towel. She had gotten chilled in the hotel's air conditioning, and she was starting to warm up deliciously under the covers. Grant, standing at the foot of the bed, seemed completely comfortable with himself. His arms hung loosely at his sides, bent slightly at the elbow. His untucked white T-shirt fell over the waist of his washed-out blue jeans, and she could see the outline of his stomach through the crisp cotton.

Grant climbed onto the bed and knelt beside her. He took the towel from the pillow and began to dry her hair. "What did you say to Zach last night?" he asked. "Were you mean to him? Were you cruel?"

"A little," Avery said. "I sure as hell didn't tell him he was special."

"Why not? You were making love to him and you couldn't be nice to him?"

"It was what it was," Avery said. "He knew that. It was nothing special, and I wouldn't have been a hypocrite and told him that it was."

Grant finished drying her hair and laid the towel over her shoulder. "Do your hair up," he said, "so that you don't get the pillow any wetter than it is." He stretched out alongside her, his head propped up on his hand.

Avery tied her hair up in the towel. "That better?" She pulled the blanket around her again, tightly, to her chin. Between the towel and the blanket, only the circle of her face was exposed as she peered up at Grant, who was watching her with what looked like interest, nothing more. A long time passed like that: Grant watching her and Avery watching Grant, trying to read him but finding nothing she recognized, except, perhaps, that slight smugness that had made her angry the night before, that air he gave off of someone slumming, hanging out with people who were less fully evolved. Throughout the whole of that long stretch of staring, if Grant was at any time even slightly uncomfortable, he didn't show it. It was Avery who finally broke the silence. "Who am I to you?" she asked. "Truthfully?"

Grant gave himself a second to think about the question, and Avery noticed again the way the womanly sensuousness of his mouth seemed in conflict with a face that was cold and compact, with a military air that came not just from the jarhead haircut but from the way his ears looked pinned back and way the top of his nose was so flat it looked like someone might have pressed a ruler over it in the womb. "You're young, a college girl," he said. "You're a student with whom I had sex last night."

"A student," Avery repeated. "I don't have a particular identity to you. I'm just *a student*."

"I hardly know you," he said, shrugging a little as if offering the mildest of apologies. "How would it be possible for you to have much of a particular identity to me? I mean, are you hoping I'll bullshit you? Or do you actually, like you said, want me to be truthful?"

"Truthful," Avery shot back. She knew her face was turning red, and that made her even angrier. "So," she said, "just so I'm sure I've got this accurately: telling me you thought I was special was, you're saying, the same thing with me as it was with Melanie. With both of us, it was just something you said because you wanted to get with us."

"It works," Grant said. "Women— People— We want to think there's something about us—"

"Please don't lecture me, all right?" Avery yanked the towel off her head and used it to dry her hair some more. "Jesus Christ, you're fucking arrogant. Do you know that about yourself?"

"It's not the first time I've heard it."

"I'll bet." Avery threw the towel across the room and turned over onto her back so that she was looking up at the ceiling. She pulled the blankets up to her chin again. "And all that shit about destiny," she said, laughing at herself a little, at the naïveté of actually having taken him seriously for a second, "that was of course all bullshit too. More crap meant to make me feel special so I'd want you."

"Do you believe in destiny?"

"No."

"Neither do I."

Avery said, "Great," though she had no idea what she meant by it. She was quiet, and the room filled up with the sound of rain.

She considered telling him that the sex hadn't really been entirely consensual, that she hadn't offered and he hadn't asked, and she hadn't really been entirely willing—but there was no way to say that now without it sounding childishly defensive. *Well, I didn't really want to have sex with you anyway. You forced me.* That it was partly true and that there was no way to say it made her furious. "You're, like, some kind of monster," she said finally. "You really just wanted to fuck both of us."

"Not really," Grant said. He sat up beside her so that they were looking at each other again. "I wanted you, but you were with Zach, so I settled for Melanie. Then, when you came out and started talking to me, I went for it."

"You wanted me? Why?"

"Because you're prettier than Melanie."

"Unbelievable." She laughed. "Not because I'm *special*, or you felt something for me—just, you thought I was the prettier of the two college girls."

For the first time, Grant seemed annoyed. "You want to believe I looked at you and felt my heart throb?" He paused as if giving her a chance to respond. "Sorry," he said. "I saw you. I thought you were attractive. I wanted to have sex with you. That's what happened."

"And now," Avery said, "and now my whole life here is screwed. Does that mean anything to you?"

"Why?" Grant said. He crossed his arms over his chest. "Why would what happened between us—"

"Because I told Melanie," Avery said, and then she repeated the story of the scene in the Deli. When Grant didn't respond, she added, "It was a disaster: Melanie screaming about how I slept with you and

Zach in the same night, the whole damn diner watching, including a table with a bunch of my art professors."

Grant said, "You're an art student?"

"I already told you that," Avery said.

Grant thought about it for a while. Then he said, "Look, you attracted some attention." He stretched, locking his fingers behind his neck. "Why should that be a problem? You're an artist. You're not supposed to play by the rules. That's what art's about: stripping away the mask, showing what's under it."

Avery turned her eyes to the mattress. If she didn't look away from Grant, she was going to spit in his face. His patient, lecturing tone felt like an ice pick to the brain. She had a wild desire to dig her fingernails into his cheeks and try to peel his face away. She thought about telling him what a condescending son of a bitch he was, and that if he didn't stop talking to her as if she were a hysterical woman who needed calming, she might have to kill him. Instead she said, "Take me with you." She looked up at him. "Take me with you when you go."

"To Brooklyn?" he said. "You want to come to Brooklyn with me?"

"Just for a while," she said. "I can't go back to my apartment. I can't stand being here." As soon as she said the words, which seemed to have come out of nowhere, she felt a spill of energy, liquid and electric at the same time, as if it were washing through her body and sparking simultaneously. It felt like what she imagined it might feel like to shoot up some drug.

Grant was watching her with interest again. "Do you have money?" he asked.

"Credit cards," she said, "and a bank account I can cash out before we leave in the morning."

"How much in your bank account?"

"A little over three thousand. From working this summer."

Grant said, "You couldn't take much with you. I've only got the bike. I already shipped my stuff."

"That's not a problem," Avery said. "All I need from my apartment is some clothes."

"I thought you were disgusted with me?" Grant pulled back the covers and slid down beside her. "What happened to me being insincere and a liar?"

Avery smiled coyly.

"And a phony," he said. "I think that was also an issue." He rested his hand on her hip and kissed her on the forehead. "And now you're running off with me. You forgive pretty easily. No?"

Avery said, "Who said anything about forgiveness?" and ran a finger down the center of Grant's chest. Before she could think of anything else to say, he kissed her—and then the talking was over.

Saint John

HER arms around his waist holding and the bike solid and powerful under, Grant was moving, doing 85, white needle like a finger wagging over white numbers, 86, 87, 90. He backed off the throttle, leaned into the right lane. The city was still a couple hundred miles in the future. For now, a summery wind rushing over him and a girl on the back of his bike, her arms wrapped around his waist. She was a trip of a little girl, eyes like bullets, anger sparking off her skin like flares. Zoo was going to freak. He'd be, *You're out of your mind.* Maybe. She packed next to nothing. Stopped by the bank, picked up money. Stopped by the apartment, filled a duffel bag, which was now wedged between her body and his. Maybe. Not likely she'd last long in Brooklyn, a few days, a week. Then back to school. Meanwhile, Zoo would have to live with it. She might even straighten the place out a bit. Grant touched her hand, gave her a reassuring squeeze, and she laid her helmeted head between his shoulder blades in response.

Jeshua at Penn State, teaching. How much more improbable

could a thing be and still happen? They should have seen them, Grant and Jeshua, all through the '90s. Those classrooms full of the brightly decorated, the lovely robed, they should have seen Jeshua puking in his sewer of a bathroom, Grant passed out somewhere. They'd both be long dead if not for Zoo. Who knew what it was they thought then, flaming rebellion against what? Such corny bullshit they were so possessed by, as if pain and squalor were transcendent—an ugly innocence to live through. Though. There were moments. Feeling the city inside him, the mass of it reduced to an essence lodged in his heart, feeling that, that for a moment he contained it all, all the people, all the buildings, the water and stone, heat and death and noise of it all like a texture against his skin. They were in Brooklyn, the NYU crew, Mei Mei and Terry, Heriberto and Zoo, Grant and Jeshua. Jesh was playing some firetrap in Williamsburg and they all went to see him and then down to the river after, where they could sit on rocks and look out at the line of bridges linking Manhattan to the rest of the world. It was cold and they were drinking whiskey out of brown paper bags, huddled together by the water's edge, pressing up against each other for heat, laughing, Mei Mei with her endless stories going a mile a minute, all of them full of dreamy ambition, the city light reflecting off the river. It was because he was different and had been different for years at that point, this was some time after the killing and so he was separate from them and still a part of them, laughing with them, passing bottles around like communion, but it was because of the separation, because of the distance that he could step outside the moment and for a heartbeat contain it all, them, the city, everything. That moment on the rocks in the city with his friends when he was twenty-something was as alive to him now, at thirty-seven, roaring over a highway through Pennsylvania with a girl on the back of his bike, as it was then, half drunk and a kid, surrounded by and separate from his friends.

Another hundred miles, roughly, and they'd be near Leigh's. He toyed with the idea of stopping in. She'd be there alone, her husband at work, both her kids out and on their own. She had just turned fifty-one a few days ago, and he might stop in at a drugstore for a card, something tacky, and bring it along, just stopping in to say happy birthday, and meanwhile introduce Avery as his girlfriend. *Avery, this is my sister Leigh.* Maybe he'd emphasize *sister*, just for the cruelty of it. *Leigh, this is my girlfriend, Avery.* His first memories of Leigh were tender, his beautiful sister, fourteen years his elder. She was the only sibling he'd lived with, and she was out of the house before he turned five. But he had memories. Leigh playing with him on the living room floor, tossing him around, spinning him in circles hand in hand and then letting go gently and both of them flying into the couch cushions. His other siblings, Claire and Christopher, were sixteen and eighteen years older than Grant, and he had almost no sense of them as family. He knew them as adults he'd seen now and then at family affairs. Claire was a high school art teacher in upstate New York, Utica, married with three kids. Christopher, the oldest, sold office supplies, a career inherited from their father, though Chris worked for Staples and lived in Los Angeles, whereas their father had owned his own business, a stationary store on Greenwich Avenue in TriBeCa. Claire and Christopher, names and faces, distant as little-seen aunts and uncles. But Leigh . . . Leigh was slim and athletic, pale skin and dark eyes. A mop of auburn hair that framed her face, fell to her shoulders. Her beauty was in her spirit and her spirit was in her eyes. She was gentle. She was a playful moment. And when she moved out, she left him with their father.

Grant was the ring bearer, eight years old at her wedding, and that was the first time he suspected, though he could never have given it a name—but he felt it, the vibration of it, the unspoken word of it. At the church, he marched solemnly along the aisle, accompanied by organ music, carrying a pair of rings in the center of a satiny white pillow, and when he reached the altar and Leigh in her white gown, her hair resplendent cascading to her shoulders, her eyes welled with tears at the sight of him, and there was something in her look, something like longing or sadness, that he felt acutely, as if a message were being spoken to him in a language he couldn't understand. Later, at the reception, she took him by the hand and led him out of the hall to a quiet place by a circular pool. She held his hand while they sat on the stonework at the edge of the water. Grant had no memory of what they talked about, but he remembered vividly the talking and the pool and the way she held his hand, and, again, that sense of something that he didn't understand under the words being spoken, and he remembered that his mother came out searching for Leigh, looking hurried and frazzled, and when she saw them she stopped and her expression changed from anxious to sad, and she turned and walked away.

Behind him, Avery leaned back and shifted her weight as she rearranged the duffel bag between them. The day had turned glorious, a serene blue sky almost cloudless, and lush green Pennsylvania countryside, the bike sailing easily through a warm rush of air. He might stop at Leigh's. One day he would ask her the question he had always wanted to ask her, and it wouldn't be the one she expected.

How, he wanted to know, *could you have left me with him?* He was a tyrant. Some of it could be explained away: the frustration, because the business was always precarious; the anger, because he spent most of his life as a slave to the business; the physical violence, because his generation had been raised to believe children needed beating now and then. Beyond the frustrated anger and the beatings, though, there was something more, a meanness, a twistedness. Not child abuse, not holding a kid's hand over a fire, not breaking bones—but an ugliness, a need to dominate that had driven all the children out of the house and away from home as soon as possible. Christopher, across the country to L.A.; Claire, six hours away upstate. Leigh was the closest, and she was a two-hour drive. Not that any of them ever visited. Maybe once a year, and Christopher never. Christopher and Claire, names attached to faces, nothing more. She knew. That was the only unforgivable thing. He grew up like an only child under the thumb of a tyrant, and she knew it would be exactly what it was.

He might stop in. He still owed her more than thirty thousand, and he might stop by and not mention it just so she knew for sure she'd never see a penny. When he was accepted to NYU out of high school and wanted to study literature, his father wouldn't help. He claimed it was Grant, his politics, his thinking—he said, *I won't subsidize your kind of thinking*—but it was the money. He wouldn't have subsidized any kind of thinking. He didn't want children who thought at all. They were an affront to him. Any independent thinking was an affront to him. So Grant worked and Leigh came through with the rest and that pretty much sealed his suspicions. He thought at the funeral that something might be said, but nothing was. His father dead of a heart attack, Grant twenty and a junior at NYU.

Grant thought maybe at the funeral he'd turn a corner with Leigh, but no, didn't happen.

At the funeral, he met Billy. *Who is that?* Man standing in the chapel dressed immaculately, youthful, handsome, something magnetic about him, a celebrity entering the room. Black suit with soft gray shirt, matching tie, wingtip shoes that looked new. Salt-and-pepper hair, all gray at the temples. He was short, five eight at the most, built thick and solid. He gave off an impression of rootedness, as if someone running into him full speed would bounce off. Grant's mother, sitting beside him in the first row of seats, in front of an open coffin, *That's your father's only brother.* Grant's father didn't have a brother. He had two younger sisters, who were at that moment approaching the man in the black suit and embracing him. Both sisters were sobbing. Grant said, *Dad had a brother*, a flat but amazed assertion and a question. *He wouldn't allow any mention of him. He was dead to your father and he insisted that he be dead to the rest of us.* Grant asked why and his mother didn't answer. She said, *His name is Billy. He's your uncle.* Billy approached the casket amid a murmur of voices. He knelt beside the body and clasped his hands in prayer, just as a dozen others had before him. Grant's mother said, *Where are your sisters?* They weren't in the chapel, they had stepped out for a moment. She twisted in her seat, looking for them. The man in the black suit—Billy, Billy Danko, Uncle Billy—seemed to be collapsing. His head dropped lower and lower until his forehead was resting on the edge of the casket and then his hands gripped the frame as if to hold himself up as his body convulsed with choked sobs and his sisters went to him, one on either side, their arms around him. Laura, Grant's mother, said gently, *He loved your father.*

Kurt Danko, Billy's only brother, Grant's father—even in his casket, the toughness, the hardness in his eyes. A brawny man with wide shoulders, long muscular arms, a powerful chest. Grant had once seen him knock a man's teeth out. Grant was a boy sitting on the stoop outside his house, a summer night in Brooklyn, in Williamsburg where he grew up, only a few miles from where he lived now. He was sitting at the top of the stoop and his father and mother were a few steps lower. A sweltering night. Everyone out of their apartments sitting on stoops or on chairs in the small fenced-in concrete slabs that served as front yards. The wood and stone maze of Brooklyn alive with voices, some kids still running the streets, shouting and squealing. A man coming down the sidewalk looked up at Grant's parents. He was a big guy, tall, bigger than Kurt. He had slicked-back hair and he was wearing a black T-shirt untucked over white jeans. He smiled up at the stoop, and Grant noticed the smile with some surprise since he didn't know the man and people didn't generally smile at his parents—but it was a friendly smile, nothing more. Then, as he neared the stoop, he winked at Grant's mother and made a kissing sound with his lips that he hardly had a chance to finish before Kurt was off the stoop and on him, his left hand around the man's neck as he pinned him against a car and punched him mercilessly in the face until he slumped down to the street on all fours, spitting out blood as he tried to crawl away. Past that image of a man crawling spitting blood, Grant didn't remember much. Neighbors came and led the man away. His parents went back into the house. His father's hand was bleeding. There was a bloody tooth on the gray slate of the curb.

Kurt. Grant could not think of one single moment of tenderness between them. Even now, after he'd been dead all these years, Grant dreamed about him at times and woke up surprised he was not alive, not sitting at the head of the dinner table, all that twisted intelligence and anger bubbling in his eyes.

Billy came to the interment. Grant was with Terry then, and they both thought they'd get married eventually and settle down in the city to pursue careers together. They were both writers. Grant was twenty, Terry nineteen. She was tall and interesting-looking, not beautiful but sexy. She held his hand through the service while the family wept and the casket descended. It was misting, an almost-rain, clouds a dense gray-blue ceiling low over the heads of the family. At the end of the ceremony, Billy came up behind Grant and asked politely for a moment of his time. Grant had heard the story by that time, how Kurt had raised Billy—their father useless, their mother indifferent—how Billy had gotten into the streets, running numbers, then dealing, then marrying into one of the families, and Kurt had told him that if he went that route he'd have nothing to do with him, he wouldn't be a brother to someone like that. And when Billy did go that route, Kurt kept his word. Grant excused himself from Terry and walked away from the mourners with Billy, deeper into the cemetery along a blacktop path. Billy told him stories about Kurt, how Kurt had looked after him growing up, how sorry he was about all that had come between them—and he gave Grant a card with his phone number. He told him if he ever needed money, if he ever needed work, if he ever needed anything. Grant listened. He told Billy he was doing fine, that he was a student at NYU, that his sister Leigh was helping with tuition and expenses, that he was a writer and an artist, and that he planned to pursue writing as a career. Billy listened. He said, *You're not like your father.* Grant said, *I'm not much like your brother, no.* Billy smiled at that and pointed to Grant's jacket pocket, where Grant had put his card. *Call me,* he said. *I'm family to you.* They shook hands and walked back to the cars together.

Jeshua was with Mei Mei then, and Heriberto was with Zoo, and after the interment, they drove back into the city together. Over the next several years they would all break up with each other and then go on as friends. It was like something they needed to get past, the sex, and then their friendships deepened, or maybe solidified, as they went on to other people. Now, in their midthirties, they were all still single. They had come to be a family of singles, bringing other people into that central relationship for short periods of time but always bonded essentially with each other. They were ambitious, all of them. They were full of the city. Jeshua was the first and only one to leave Manhattan, abandoning them for a professorship at Penn State. When he came back to the city, he stayed with Terry, who had a good career writing for television. She had a place in TriBeCa. Most nights some combination of them ate dinner there, usually delivered and eaten on trays in front of the TV set, which was on to fill the time when conversation flagged or to provide topics for the endless chatter. They had known each other so long and so intimately that they had developed their own language, with its own codes and signals. Others, joining them, were amazed by how fully they were excluded from the conversation.

Avery squeezed Grant to get his attention and shouted that she had to pee. Grant nodded toward an approaching exit. He slowed, signaled, leaned into the turn. At the gas pump, Avery propped her helmet on the back of the bike before heading off in search of a bathroom. When he was done filling the tank, Grant drove around to the back of the station, peed behind a Dumpster, and then rode out to the exit and waited astride the bike. The day was beautiful, but all the sunlight and crisp, fresh air in the world couldn't make a pair of run-down service stations separated by a torn-up road attractive, and Grant found himself staring first at the blue sky and then at the red streak of a cardinal as it dashed from a fence post to a small square of grass, where it hopped about for a moment before rocketing up into the branches of a lone tree at roadside. When his thoughts flashed to his apartment, which he had left a mess and which would be stifling and stuffy from having been closed up for weeks, he snatched his cell phone from his shirt pocket, took a picture of the seedy gas station across the road, trucks blazing past on the interstate behind it, added a short voice message—"Zoo, I kidnapped a coed and will be home with her in a few hours. Could you open my windows an inch, maybe get rid of anything that smells bad, like two-week-old unwashed dishes? I'll owe you. Thanks"—then hit *send* and watched an icon dance and spin until the message was transmitted. Next he sent a text message to Heriberto: "Your place tonight for dinner w/schoolgirl," and by the time the message was transmitted and the phone snapped closed and returned to his shirt pocket, Avery was standing beside the bike, getting ready to put on her helmet.

"That bathroom was disgusting," she said. "Are the men's bathrooms that bad?"

Grant said, "Listen, I'm thinking of stopping at my sister's for a few minutes if you don't mind. I hardly ever see her, and she lives, like, two minutes off the exit."

Avery tucked the helmet under her arm. "You want me to meet your family already?" she said. "I don't know that the relationship is that serious, do you?"

Grant started the engine. "Get on," he shouted. "It'll just be for a few minutes, and you can wait on the bike if you want."

Once Avery was settled with her arms around him, Grant gunned the engine and shot out onto the road. In his shirt pocket, the phone vibrated and he figured Zoo or Heriberto had zapped a reply back. He waited until he had merged into the traffic on 80 before he dug out the phone and found a text message from Zoo. Two words: *No problem*. He put the phone back in his pocket, knowing for certain that Zoo was already in his apartment airing the place out and straightening up the mess. Between Jesh and Heriberto and Grant (and also Mei Mei, and sometimes Terry), Zoo had made himself a full-time job looking after his friends. Though everyone was better these days now that they were getting older. Mei Mei's once yearly suicide attempts were history since she had found the right combination of medications, and that had been a decade ago. These days her life looked glamorous. The kind of conceptual art she practiced, which had seemed so radical in her twenties, had long been institutionalized, and now her installations were everywhere, mostly in New York, but all over the country, all over the world. With the influx of money and with precisely targeted prescription drugs, she had stopped needing Zoo to look after her, to let her spend the night sleeping in his bed or just holding her and letting her talk. Jesh, a man who had once stabbed himself outside the Met, a man who at times had been addicted to every legal and illegal intoxicant available in Manhattan, Jesh was now a professor at Penn State. Terry was comfortable. She'd started out big, writing for television, a TV hit of the time, and had being doing well ever since. Heriberto owned a restaurant in midtown and was about to buy a second one in the East Village. Heriberto had always been the most stable mind in the crew, but he had his share of dramas, which Zoo helped him through. And Grant . . .

Grant's life as a writer, his life pursuing any kind of conventional success as a writer—all that had come to an abrupt end after the hijacking. He had been doing well. He published pieces in the *Village Voice*, mostly reviews, and he published his first stories in small-press mags. He felt like he was on his way. An agent contacted him after a story came out, but she wanted a novel and he didn't have a novel, so he let that ride—but it looked like it was there, a career as a writer waiting for him, and he was in no hurry. He was living his life, with a cubbyhole on Barrow Street close enough to Terry's that he'd spend daylight hours in her two-bedroom apartment and go home at night to his closet. He was writing. He was sleeping with beautiful girls. He made money with part-time work and by driving for Uncle Billy, piloting big rigs up from various places in the South into the city.

The day before the night of the hijacking, he'd been with Kellen, an uptown girl, waif-thin, bright red hair, eerie green-gold eyes. They spent the day in bed drinking coffee and smoking and going at it again and again, and in between the sex and the talk, the boy he remembered stretched out on that bed in his Barrow Street place— He could see him. He had a shaggy head of hair that curled over his ears and down his forehead to his eyes. His body was boyish, a little wiry, almost frail. He was almost *pretty* except for his nose with that odd flat line that traveled up from the tip and widened out into the space between his eyebrows. He was a different person then. Sometimes in the moments after coming, he'd pray. In how everything fell away at that moment he sensed a swelling of forces into which he dissolved, in union with them, through her. He would pray, a quick simple prayer, *Thank you God for everything. Thank you for this moment. Thank you for Kellen. Thank you for my life.* He was different then. He could spend an hour in bed with Kellen asleep in his arms, her head on his chest; he could pass that hour listening to the music of street traffic and voices murmuring in passing snatches of conversation. He could lie there quietly and listen with an intense pleasure that he now thought of as innocence. He was a boy. He didn't love Kellen, but he loved being with Kellen. That was a long time ago. Years and years. Now he didn't pray anymore.

Billy paid him three hundred for a typical run, sometimes double that, according to his whims. He'd give Grant a hug and squeeze his shoulders and then pull a roll of bills out of his pocket and peel off a few hundreds. The day of the hijacking, Albert called at five, which was the usual. Albert, a skinny guy in his forties, arranged the runs. He was always nervous and especially careful, and Billy liked him for that. Billy said, "Albert never screws up. Right, Albert?" Albert nodded, and Billy winked at Grant, and the wink said something like *He's an idiot, but we're letting him run the show, so do what he says.* Grant never knew when the calls were coming, but they always came around five o'clock, so he made sure he was near a phone, and that day he was still in bed with Kellen when the phone rang and he knew he was going on a run.

He was twenty-four, a few years out of college, living in an apartment furnished with books and a bed and a hot plate, and he never used the hot plate. By five-thirty he was on the L, clattering through the dark, jammed in a car full of twenty-somethings who couldn't afford to live in Manhattan and could barely afford Brooklyn, where he was heading with them, on his way to the Liberty Avenue station and Uncle Billy's, an old storefront turned into a club. By seven he was on the road. He was liked at the club, and Billy would shout at the sight of him every time—*Hey, it's the kid*, or *Look at this, the poet*. He was *the kid*, or *the poet*, or sometimes *Shakespeare*, because he had a college degree, because they knew he was a writer, and most of the guys at the club seemed to like him for it, but mostly they liked him because he was young and Billy's nephew. By seven-thirty Albert was asleep and Grant was piloting the big rig down I-95 toward Raleigh or Winston-Salem, where they'd pull into a warehouse and load the trailer with could-be-anything but usually cigarettes and then turn around and take it back to a warehouse in Redhook, where they'd unload it and be done with the sun coming up, and if they were lucky beat the morning traffic. But that night a car was stopped in the middle of the road a mile and a half from the warehouse, a couple of miles yet to the interstate, a dark middle-of-nowhere road. It was hot and the windows were open and the night smell from the woods came in through the open windows and filled the cab. Albert woke up as he was slowing down and shouted, *Don't stop, don't stop*, but it was too late.

Men appeared out of the darkness and leapt onto the running boards. Two men. Both with guns. Two more men with guns got out of the stopped car. Albert said, *Son of a bitch*, and his door opened. He said, *Just do what they say*, and then a kid not much older than Grant was sitting beside Albert, pointing a gun at his heart and grinning. A much older guy on the driver's-side running board touched the barrel of his gun to Grant's head and said, *Pull it over*— When he pointed with his gun to where he wanted the truck pulled over, he fell off the running board. The kid beside Albert broke up laughing, like he'd just seen the funniest thing in the world. His laugh was a high-pitched giggle that shook his whole body, and when he laughed Albert knocked the gun out of his hand and hit him in the throat with his elbow so that the laughter turned to gagging in an instant. The gun landed on the seat beside Grant and he picked it up just as the older guy leaped onto the running board again screaming curses, and Grant found himself holding a gun as a gunman appeared furious in the window, and he shot him in the forehead, the barrel of the gun actually hitting the guy's head as he pulled the trigger. The body disappeared into the dark. Albert tossed the boy out the door. Grant hit the gas and slammed into the stopped car as the two gunmen scurried toward the woods. The car slid for twenty feet and then went over on its side and down into a ditch, and the truck hurtled on along the pitted macadam road. Albert said, *Son of a bitch, kid*, then *Slow down, slow down*, and Grant eased off the gas pedal and concentrated on the road, on piloting the big rig toward the interstate.

Grant had gone over the sequence of events endlessly. He figured it had all happened in well under a minute. From the time he saw the car stopped in the road till the time it turned on its side and tumbled into a ditch, a handful of seconds. After that, Albert spent the next hour on the phone, and then the rest of the ride passed in silence. In Redhook, Uncle Billy was waiting for him. He gave him a ride back to his apartment and an envelope with five thousand dollars in new hundreds, and he told him to take a vacation somewhere for three to four weeks. He recommended the Bahamas. Grant went to Italy, where one of Terry's friends had a place on Lake Maggiore. He stayed away for three weeks, and when he returned it was as if nothing had happened. He was assured there would be no repercussions, and there weren't—except that he didn't sleep through the night anymore, except that he had regular dreams in which he was murdering someone, except that he felt estranged from his friends and from himself, except that he couldn't concentrate long enough to write two sentences in a row.

Because he needed the money, he went back to working for his uncle. He told himself again and again that what had happened was self-defense. It was. He was holding a gun when a guy with a gun appeared screaming at the driver's window and he reacted. There was no thought involved. It was self-defense. He was holding a gun, the gunman appeared, someone was going to shoot someone. For a while, he only unloaded trucks at Redhook, and the guys at the club were quiet around him. But he needed more money, so he went back to driving. He started working with Albert again. Billy started shouting, *Hey, Shakespeare* when he showed up at the club. Eventually the night of the hijacking faded from his dreams—but nothing was ever the same.

He stopped writing. He spent more time with Jesh, which meant he spent more time high. He started performing, first with Jeshua, then alone. First he called himself a performance poet, then a performance artist. He developed a persona, Saint John of the Five Boroughs, and performed in a cassock with a priest's white collar. He cut himself with a crucifix while he riffed on God's grace and mercy. His performance was a mix of comedy and outrage. *God is good*, he'd chant while drawing blood with the crucifix or whipping himself with the rosary. His performance included film clips of holy men scourging themselves with chains. He wore a hair shirt and writhed while he ranted. Jesh helped him sketch out the rants, and at first he memorized but after a while he was able to riff on his own, and there were times when he was hot when the words would spill out effortlessly as he talked about God and His viciousness. He developed a following. He was reviewed in the *Voice* and the *Times*. He performed at the Whitney and at MOMA. He did everything but make enough money to pay his rent. For that, he had to work for Uncle Billy.

Behind him on the bike, Avery kissed his neck. He reached back and patted her thigh.

Now Jeshua was a professor at Penn State. Mei Mei was the one-in-a-million artist who actually grew wealthy from her work. Heriberto was opening his second restaurant. Terry was doing fine—though she was currently between shows and boyfriends. Zoo never made much money, but he came from money, so it didn't matter. He was a working actor in New York. There was still hope for Zoo, hope that something bigger might happen. For Grant, such hope had quieted. He hadn't performed anywhere in more than a year. In part because the whole performance scene had faded, and in part because he had lost interest without Jeshua around. In Jeshua's class, where he had represented himself as a performance artist, he'd felt like a fraud. He didn't know what he was anymore beyond a truck driver and an errand boy for mobsters, beyond getting high and moving from girlfriend to girlfriend.

On the road, the exit for Leigh's rushed toward him. He backed off the throttle for a heartbeat and then hit it harder and sped past, flying toward the city.

Revelations

MARCOS handed the last carton of Stoli to Grant and then leaned back against the trailer wall as Grant slid the vodka down the ramp to D'shaun, who loaded it into a bright yellow Hummer and slammed the door closed. He looked back to Grant and Marcos and said, "How many cartons was that?" Then he muttered something else and disappeared through a scuffed metal door into another room.

Grant sat on the lip of the trailer, dangling his feet, and Marcos sat beside him, on the other side of the loading ramp. Though the garage still held the night's chill, they were sweaty from unloading the truck. Sunlight from outside seeped under the closed garage doors. "Where the hell are we?" Grant said, and Marcos laughed. For the last month, ever since Grant had gotten back from State College, they had been moving around between a dozen warehouses and garages. They were someplace uptown now, in Harlem. Marcos said, "I don't even know how to get home from here. I got to ask D'shaun for directions."

"Shit," Grant said, meaning nothing at all. He lay back, rested his head on his arms, and looked around him at the ribbed interior of the empty trailer. A bright red dolly lay on its side next to a pair of lightweight work gloves with the word *Proflex* in yellow letters like a tattoo across the knuckles. The trailer was a belly or a throat, gorged and disgorged. He stuffed stuff in and hauled it out: liquor, clothes, power tools, every conceivable item of electronics. Half the stores in New York had to be stocked with stuff he'd loaded and unloaded.

Marcos fidgeted like a kid, rocking himself from side to side on his haunches. He was short and solid, muscular across the chest and arms. "Bro," he said, "you got the time?"

Grant found his cell phone in the pocket of his jeans. "Eight-oh-five."

Marcos looked pained. "Damn, bro!" He flung his hands up as if in despair. "Traffic everywhere now."

"Get breakfast somewhere," Grant said. "Kill an hour."

"Still be bad in an hour. 'Sides, Em'd kill me."

"Shit," Grant said. Emily was Marcos's daughter. Her girlfriend had left her, and Marcos was helping out by watching her twin three-year-old daughters from the marriage that the girlfriend—the one who had walked out—had broken up. Marcos was in his forties but looked younger. His ex-wife, Em's mother, had divorced him while he was in Fishkill a dozen years back.

"What's your uncle about," Marcos said, "moving around all over the fuckin' place?"

D'shaun came back through the metal door carrying three bottle of Sam Adams. D'shaun was a kid, still in his early twenties, chubby and big, six two, maybe six three. He had his hair done up in cornrows that dangled down to his shoulders.

Grant nodded toward the beer and said, "I was thinking more in the line of coffee, D'shaun."

"Fuck that." D'shaun slapped two of the beers down on the truck and took a long drink from the third.

Marcos asked D'shaun, "What's up with all this moving around? It's making me nervous, bro."

D'shaun said, "I look like I know what the fuck's up with anything? Ask the man," he said, pointing his bottle at Grant.

"Man don't know shit."

Grant said, "You guys want me to ask my uncle for you?" He held his beer between his legs. "I'll tell him D'shaun and Marcos want to know why we we're in a new spot every other trip."

Marcos laughed. "Maybe you better not, bro."

D'shaun said to Marcos, "You afraid of gettin' jacked again?"

"More worried about the law," Marcos said and folded his arms over his chest.

"You worried about the law," D'shaun said, "or you worried 'bout what Em do to you you got busted?"

Marcos said, "Fuck that, bro."

Grant said, "Where the hell's Albert?" and the three of them looked toward the front of the garage, as if Grant's asking about Albert might make him suddenly appear.

When the garage door didn't open and Albert didn't walk in with their money, D'shaun said, "How's your new girl? I got to get me some of that college pussy."

"She's fine," Grant said. "She likes the city."

"She like the lowlife," D'shaun said, patting his chest as if offering himself as an example. "Girls like that shit." His voice seemed amplified by the bare walls and high ceiling. The outside buzz of street traffic dulled by the thick metal garage doors and the closed side door with its blacked-out window.

"College girls, bro," Marcos said. "I heard that." He slid off the truck and raked his fingers though his hair as if suddenly worried about how he looked.

Grant said, "Thanks for the vote of confidence."

Marcos made a face. "What the fuck's that about, vote of confidence?"

D'shaun said to Marcos, "The man sayin' he ain't a lowlife like us, bro."

Grant said, "Get the fuck out of here," and all three of them laughed, but it was as if each of them were laughing at something different.

When the side door rattled, D'shaun said, "There's the man with the money," and a moment later, Albert walked in. He was nattily dressed in a dark gray suit with a light gray shirt open at the collar. He looked like he might be on his way to a dinner meeting.

"Mr. DeLaura!" D'shaun yelled.

Albert approached them with a look of discomfort, as if he weren't especially happy about having to be there—which was how Albert almost always looked.

Marcos looked from Albert to Grant, as if to ask Grant what was up these days with Albert's dress. For as long as any of them had known him, he'd worn neat dress slacks and an overstarched dress shirt and every once in a while a jacket. In the past six months he had started wearing suits—good, expensive, tasteful suits. It was as if he had hijacked a fashion coordinator. Anyone who asked him about the sudden change in apparel got silence in reply.

Albert pulled a folded wad of bills out of his jacket pocket. "Everything went smoothly?"

"No problems," Grant said.

Albert peeled off three hundreds for each of them and then placed the still fat wad of bills in his jacket.

D'shaun said, "Whose Hummer is that? Nice ride."

Albert looked at him as if he were an idiot. "We got another load on Friday," he said. "I take it everyone's available?" When they all indicated that they were available, Albert gestured toward the truck and said, "I see you found the beer." He pulled a ten out of his pocket and handed it to D'shaun. "Put that in the fridge where you took the beer from."

D'shaun took the bill tentatively. He looked like he was torn between apologizing and getting pissed off. Before he could say anything, Albert walked away. When he was out the door, D'shaun whispered to Grant, "What the fuck's that about, man? Guy makes an issue out of drinkin' a couple of beers?"

Marcos laughed and said, "He don't like you, D'shaun."

Grant said, "Albert doesn't like anybody," and then he hurried to grab his denim jacket out of the cab of the truck. "See you guys Friday." He followed Albert out the side door.

On the street, bright sunlight blinded Grant for a moment. He pulled a pair of wraparound sunglasses out of his jacket pocket and slipped them on. Half a block in front of him, Albert was just turning the corner onto Lenox Avenue. Grant called out to him and sprinted along the sidewalk as a pair of yellow cabs flew by with their horns blaring. At the sound of his name, Albert spun around. When he saw it was Grant approaching him, his face went solemn for an instant before it returned to its standard look of semidisappointment.

"Albert," Grant said, "you got a minute? I didn't want to talk with the other guys around."

Albert took a cell phone out of his jacket pocket and showed it to Grant. They were standing in the middle of the sidewalk, with people passing them on both sides. "See this?"

"Your cell."

"Yes," Albert said. "You want my attention and you're far enough away to have to yell? Use the phone."

"Jesus, Albert, I was just—" He gestured toward the corner.

"What can I do for you?"

Grant said, "All right. Sorry." Then added, "Look, I'd like a meeting with my uncle."

"A meeting? You got a business proposal?"

"Yeah. Sort of. Maybe," Grant said. "I'd like to talk to my uncle is all."

"Grant." Albert put his hand on Grant's back and directed him down the street. Albert, in his early fifties, had thinning gray hair that he combed straight back. He was slim and wiry with a narrow face and sharply etched features: a longish nose that seemed to come to a point, thin bluish lips, and eyes accented by half-moon-shaped fleshy bags. Somehow, miraculously, the features came together in a face that wasn't half bad-looking. In the twelve or so years since he used to make the trips south with Grant, he had come a long way in Billy's organization until now he was closer to Billy than anyone else, at least anyone else that Grant knew, and his success seemed to affect both his looks and his manner. "Grant," he said, "the word *meeting* has certain implications. I tell your uncle that you want a meeting with him, he'll think you have a business proposition. Do you see what I'm saying? Do you have a business proposition?"

"I do," Grant said, "but it's something I need to talk to him about first."

Albert shook his head sorrowfully, as if Grant had once again disappointed him. They walked the next half block in silence until they neared Albert's car, a gleaming, black Lexus. For the past several years, Albert had shown up with a new Lexus every September. You could still see the glue from the sales sticker on the back window. "Get in with me," Albert said. He pointed his electronic key at the car and unlocked the doors.

"Nice," Grant said, nodding at the car. He walked around the hood to the passenger door. "But I thought Uncle Billy said you were getting an Escalade this year."

"I was thinking about it." He bent to the door and slid into the car. Inside, with Grant in the passenger seat beside him, he finished his thought. "But everybody's got an Escalade. Your Uncle Billy's got the same one three years. He's in love with the thing."

When Albert was quiet for a moment, Grant said, "Nice interior," wanting to put off the real conversation for a bit. "What's that," he said, "wood steering wheel?"

"Wood and leather trim." Albert gestured around him. "Whole interior," he said.

Grant pointed to the GPS screen in the center of the dashboard. "You use that much?"

"Sometimes." Albert's tone said he was done with the bullshit. "Look," he said, "your uncle doesn't want any business meetings with you. You should know that." He paused and added, "Come on, Grant. What are you thinking? This is a job your uncle got for you; that's all this is."

Grant inhaled the new-car smell and looked out though tinted windows at a bent-over, disheveled drunk stumbling along the side-walk. When the silence started to get awkward, he said, "It's occurred to me recently, Albert— It's occurred to me that I need to make some changes." He turned and saw that Albert was watching him intently. "I always thought I was working for my uncle while I . . . what? I thought I was going to be a writer, but that's— I haven't written a word worth shit since—" He looked away from Albert, out at the street.

"What?" Albert said. "Since what?"

"Since a long time," Grant said.

"What about that performance stuff?" Albert said. "You broke your uncle's heart with that crap."

"What are you talking about?" Grant folded his hands in his lap and backed away from Albert as if he had suddenly become conta-gious.

"I'm talking about that Saint John bullshit. You think there's something about you we don't know? Any jack-off works for us, we know all about him. You? His nephew? You think we didn't send people to see those shows?"

"What the fuck would Uncle Billy—"

"Don't be a jerk, Grant, please." Albert took hold of the steering wheel as if he had to grip something to keep himself from smacking Grant in the face. "You're mocking our religion? You weren't Billy's nephew— Billy wasn't who he was— Still," he said, "it's dis-gusting."

Grant opened his hands, indicating his amazement at this turn in the conversation. "I had no idea. This matters to you?"

"Why do you think it wouldn't matter?"

Grant straightened himself out in his seat and, inexplicably, since the car was parked and Albert had made no move to start the engine, pulled the seatbelt down and clicked it in place. "This is blowing me away," he said. "This matters? Really? This is like, what? Religious convictions are pertinent to your line of work?"

"What is it you think?" Albert said. "You think we're animals? Because of what we do for a living? Because of our *line of work?*"

Grant had no idea how he had gotten into this conversation. Part of him wanted to change the subject and get back to arranging a meeting with his uncle, but another part of him was weirdly pissed off, weird in that he didn't know where the anger was coming from. It felt like something more than annoyance with Albert. When he first started working for his uncle, Albert wasn't all that much higher on the ladder than he was, and they used to drive down south together regularly. Albert had moved beyond that a decade ago, and he hardly seemed like the same person anymore—but back then, when they used to ride together, Grant had to struggle to get a word out of him. All those hours in the cab of a truck together—hauling stolen merchandise and untaxed cigarettes across state lines—and not word one about God and religion. Now all of a sudden it matters to him, Saint John of the Five Boroughs. As if, what? Grant was supposed to explain performance art? He wanted to say, *Where would you like me to start?* He wanted to say, *What the fuck do you know about anything?* Instead he said, "This is crazy, Albert. I'm sorry if I caused my uncle any trouble. That Saint John of the Five Boroughs stuff, I haven't done anything like that in a long time. I want this meeting with my uncle because I'm looking to change direction, and I've got some ideas I want to discuss with him."

Albert straightened out his jacket. He looked at Grant as if he were both curious and interested in him.

"But as long as we're on the topic," Grant said, and he could hardly believe he was saying it, even as he heard the words coming out, "how do you reconcile being religious—believing in God and caring about the church and all—with being a thief and a murderer?"

"What makes you think I'm a murderer?" Albert said without hesitating.

Grant didn't answer. He had heard things about Albert, everyone had. On Lenox Avenue, a hooker wearing red short shorts and a bright green bikini top rode by on an ancient Schwinn bicycle, the kind with the old-style high handle bars. He laughed and said, "Look at this. It's Christmas."

Albert put his seatbelt on and gripped the steering wheel as if lining himself up with the road. "I think you'd find," he said, "that most people who do my kind of work are pretty religious." He started the engine, hit the turn signal, and pulled out carefully onto the street. "But that's not something," he added, "that a guy like you can understand."

"I guess not," Grant said. "Where we going?"

"You said you want to see your uncle?"

"He's not going to make me go to church, is he?"

"Doubt it," Albert said, and then went about silently piloting the car toward Brooklyn.

ON her way to work at Heriberto's, Avery left Grant's apartment at ten A.M. in the late-September sunlight and started along Bedford Avenue, past McCarren Park and the automotive school, where kids milled around looking surly and dangerous. She had made this walk along Bedford fifty times already, more, from Grant's apartment on Lorimer past the park along Bedford to the L on 7th, where she took the subway into Manhattan. Or didn't, in the first couple of weeks before she started working. Then she might have walked around Williamsburg looking at people and places.

When she first arrived in Brooklyn, it was early evening, hot, late August, and she was sore from the long ride on the back of Grant's bike. She leaped off the motorcycle, swinging her leg over the seat a bit too energetically so that she wound up doing a kind of spinning dance move on one leg. She looked around to find only an old man sitting on his stoop who might have seen her. He seemed to be gazing at nothing, holding a plastic cup in two hands: work clothes, heavy shoes, a white short-sleeved shirt. She smiled at him as Grant wedged the bike next to the sidewalk between two cars, and Zoo opened the front door of their building and stepped out front, though she didn't know at the time that he was Zoo, only a tall handsome Asian guy in sandals, black loose-fitting slacks, and a white cashmere pullover with a V-neck over a black T. He was handsome to the point where it edged over into beauty, with long black hair parted slightly off center spilling down over his ears. His face was broad and rectangular, with thick eyebrows dramatic over dark eyes.

That night, her first night in the city, she had met most of Grant's friends, beginning with Zoo—whose name, she discovered, was actually Jun Xu. His parents had been born in Hong Kong. He had one older sister, immensely successful, something in computers. Zoo had set out some cheese and crackers with slices of apple on a dark blue plate and poured them each a glass of a good zinfandel. He seemed more familiar with Grant's kitchen than Grant did. Avery liked Zoo—and Zoo liked her. She could tell. As soon as he had walked out the door and seen her on the street, his eyes had fallen over her appraisingly and he'd smiled, as if he needed only a few seconds to read her.

Zoo looked at his wristwatch and said, "We don't have a lot of time. Heriberto's holding a table for us."

Avery said, "Can I take a quick shower before we go?"

Grant said, "That has everything to do with what *quick* means to you."

Zoo said to Grant, "Oh, stop it," and in the way he said it, Avery saw that he might be gay. There was nothing obvious or overt in his tone, but there was the hint of a gay manner, an inflection, and she was both sorry and pleased. Sorry that he wasn't available and pleased for the same reason. She excused herself from the table, hauled her duffel bag into the bathroom, sat down on the john to begin getting undressed, and was stunned for a moment by where she was and what she was doing.

She had left school. She almost wanted to say it out loud. *I left college.* There was a part of her that felt like a child or a little girl who had run away and was having an adventure—and there was another part of her that was busy calculating possibilities and consequences. On the road to New York from State College, her mother had called, catching her alone at a rest stop. Through tears she told Avery that Ronnie had been killed in Iraq. The news hit Avery at first like a blow, like someone had sneaked up on her and slapped her in the face. Then she heard herself lying, saying she couldn't come home right away because she had a big assignment due. At the time, she couldn't think of anything else to say. She wasn't about to explain that she was on the back of a motorcycle heading for Brooklyn with a guy she had met the night before.

On the other side of the bathroom wall, Grant and Zoo were talking about a play called *Inflictions of Cruelty*. She could hear them perfectly clearly, as if a curtain rather than a wall separated her from the kitchen. Then Zoo started talking about his upcoming role in a new play that Grant apparently knew all about by the way they were talking, glancing off names and sliding over details. Zoo said something about his agent, and then Grant said something about someone named Terry's agent. She would have kept listening intently if Grant hadn't said, raising his voice only slightly, "Avery? Are you all right in there?"

"Fine," she answered and pulled back the shower curtain just to make some noise.

When she came out of the bathroom, her hair still damp from the shower, Grant and Zoo had moved into the living room and were playing chess with a clock, each making moves incredibly quickly and then slapping a button atop the clock. Their concentration on the game was so intense that she doubted they were even aware of her as she watched them from the kitchen, unsure what to do next. Grant's bedroom was between the kitchen and living room, so even the most casual of visitors would most likely walk back and forth through the bedroom a few times. The bed was covered with a lightweight quilt, and there were a couple of pillows stacked up at one side, under a reading lamp atop an adjacent dresser. One wall of the bedroom was taken up with closets and the others held bookcases and music equipment and several small pieces of art, all dark, abstract, and somber.

She sat on the bed, crossed her legs, and waited for the game to end. Zoo was perched on a black leather sofa against the wall as he leaned over the chess set atop a glass coffee table cluttered with books and magazines. Grant was across from him on a desk chair with rollers that looked like it belonged with the old wood drafting-table-turned-desk next to the front entrance. Immersed in the game, they seemed almost boyish, Grant with his nearly shaved head, all that remained of his hair a dark sheen of growth, and Zoo with hair falling to his shoulders. When, suddenly, Grant flung himself back in his chair so that he rolled all the way to the front door and bounced off it with a curse, Avery guessed that the game had ended. Zoo looked at her and said softly, as if sharing a secret, "He never beats me."

Grant said darkly, "I can never fucking beat him," and then laughed. "Are you ready?"

A few minutes later, Avery was in the back of Zoo's shiny blue Mini Cooper driving along Lorimer past the park and onto the Williamsburg Bridge.

If either Grant or Zoo noticed the New York skyline glittering in the near distance, they weren't showing it as they chatted rapidly about mutual friends, who was doing what and where and with whom. Avery, however, noticed the skyline. A sparkling shimmer of light from the long array of buildings streamed over the river. The density of it, all that mass and light in one place, seemed . . . dazzling. She could pick out the Empire State Building and what she thought was the Chrysler building, because of the odd shape of the dome—but except for those two, they were just buildings, a dozen towering over the bulk of the rest of them. From behind her she heard the clattering sound of an approaching train, and she turned to see a line of subway cars rocket into view, the silvery exterior covered with bright graffiti, the interior visible through rows of windows, people sailing past in bright yellow light holding newspapers, reading books, plugged into iPods, grasping poles, slumped in seats and looking out the window at what must have looked to them like a blur of cars against the background of water and city lights. The loud noise of the train rumbled through the car, and she found herself a little giddy with the welter of sensations, the sound and light and movement.

Once they were off the bridge and in the city, they hit a line of stopped traffic. Zoo suggested packing in Heriberto's and just going to Terry's and getting takeout. He flipped open his phone, and Grant said to Avery, "Terry's in TriBeCa, which'll be easier to get to from here than midtown, where Heriberto's place is."

Avery said, "Who's Terry?"

Grant said, "Mutual friend. You'll like her."

Twenty minutes later, Avery was crossing Greenwich Street. Zoo had parked in an underground lot, and they had walked up a long, echoey ramp and out onto a wide concrete sidewalk with park benches scattered here and there. A half-dozen black limos were parked around what looked like a restaurant on a close-by corner. A line of yellow taxicabs flew along the street. On the other side of Greenwich, having bolted to avoid the taxis, Avery asked about the limos. Grant said, "That's De Niro's place."

Avery said, "The actor?"

Grant took Avery's arm and directed her along the sidewalk.

Zoo said, "De Niro's father was a painter. His work's on the walls in there."

Grant said to Zoo, "Avery studied art. She's a photographer."

"Really," Zoo said, and then they were standing in front of the bar, looking through a plate-glass window into a shabby lobby, and Avery's thoughts buzzed around Grant calling her a photographer. She replayed the sound of him speaking the words and decided she liked it. *Avery studied art. She's a photographer.* Grant rang a bell, and a second later a metallic voice said, "Yes?"

Grant said, "It's us, Terry," and the voice said, "Heriberto and Mei Mei are here. Come on up," and Zoo pulled a key chain out of a carry bag he had slung over his shoulder. The lobby was dusty, with an old copy of the *New York Times* yellowing under an array of mailboxes on the far wall. After unlocking a second glass door, Zoo hit the button for an elevator. The elevator's doors were battered, as if someone had gone at them with a baseball bat. Avery said, "Is this thing safe?"

Grant said, "Be thankful it's working."

Zoo said, "Is it working?" and then they were all quiet, listening until they heard a loud clunk as the elevator car lurched into motion somewhere above them.

Avery said, "That wasn't a comforting sound."

When the elevator finally arrived and the doors squealed open, Avery stepped into it with some trepidation. It looked like a service elevator, with dirt and some chalky material, like the inside of dry-wall, dusting the floor. "You sure this thing's safe?" she said.

Grant said, "Not at all."

Zoo said, "It's fine," and the elevator started up with a lurch and then settled into a slow, jittery climb, shimmying every now and then as if some mechanism desperately needing aligning.

Zoo had used a key to operate the elevator and then slipped it back into the carry bag. On the fourth floor, the elevator doors opened into a spacious living room–kitchen area. A frisky yellow Lab, who had been waiting excitedly, leaped onto Grant and licked his face before jumping onto Zoo. Zoo said, "Down!" simultaneously with the other occupants of the living room: two women sitting on an olive-green leather button sofa, one of them with her legs folded under her, and a bulky, balding, well-dressed man in a crumpled linen jacket across the room at a counter near a stainless-steel refrigerator. The Lab sniffed Avery tentatively, then turned and bounded onto the sofa.

Grant said, "This is Avery." He put his arm around her shoulder and gestured toward the woman sitting with her legs folded under her. "Avery, Terry," he said. Then he nodded toward the Asian woman, "And this is Mei Mei," and pointed to the guy in the linen jacket, "and that's Heriberto." They each said hello in turn and then went back to what they had been doing: Terry chatting with Mei Mei and Heriberto slicing a wedge of cheese and dropping pieces onto a plate with mixed nuts and red grapes.

"Sit." Grant pointed to a loveseat situated at an angle to the sofa. "Do you want a snack?"

Avery indicated that she didn't, sat awkwardly rigid for a few moments, and then relaxed when she realized that no one cared that she was there. At first she was insulted. Terry and Mei Mei went on talking, Zoo turned on the television to CNN and flopped back on a lounge chair intently watching Anderson Cooper, and Grant disappeared up a long flight of stairs. She sat stiffly on the sofa, her face a little red.

Heriberto called out to Zoo, asking if he'd canceled his reservation. When Zoo said he hadn't, Heriberto rolled his eyes, sighed, and pulled a cell phone out of his jacket pocket to make the call. When he was done, he brought the snack plate in and placed it on the coffee table in front of Avery. He touched her knee, said, "Hi, sweetheart," and then turned to Zoo. "So?" he said. "How's our boy?" gesturing to the flight of stairs where Grant had disappeared.

Zoo said, his eyes still on Anderson Cooper, "Looking to change his life."

"Really?" Heriberto turned to Avery. "First Jeshua, now Grant?"

Before Avery could say anything, Terry said, "What about Jesh?"

Heriberto said, "Grant's following in Jeshua's footsteps."

Mei Mei said, "There's a surprise."

Terry said to Avery, "*What's* happening with Grant?"

Then everyone was looking at Avery. She made a gesture of bewilderment and said, drawing laughter, "I hardly know him,"

A moment later, Grant descended the staircase and joined the conversation, which was moving back and forth between Terry's pitch for a new show (she apparently wrote for television) and Mei Mei's installation at the Tate Modern (Avery, when she realized that Mei Mei was Mei Mei Tropp, an artist whose work she had studied in several classes, gasped and then pretended to be clearing her throat). No one seemed particularly interested in Grant. There wasn't even much talk about what he had been doing for the past two weeks in State College.

Eventually the food came, and the conversation continued unabated through the delivery of the meals and the distribution of drinks and Styrofoam boxes and eating utensils. Avery was a little awed at how easily the conversation flowed and how frequently it was interrupted by laughter. Mostly Avery was audience to the chatter, but she didn't mind. Sitting almost directly across from her, Mei Mei occasionally met Avery's eyes in a way that suggested she was sizing her up. Mei Mei was not an especially attractive woman, her face was flat and broad with thin lips, but there was something sexy about her. At one point, when Avery smiled in response to her gaze, Mei Mei smiled in return, revealing teeth so perfectly white and aligned that they had to be the result of expensive dentistry. The smile, though, seemed genuine.

Relatively early in the evening, Terry excused herself, explaining that she had a meeting in the morning and wanted to get a good night's sleep. Grant stood and said he'd be going too. He glanced at Avery as if inviting her to join him, and a few minutes later, after she'd said good-bye and thanked Terry for *her hospitality* in a way that seemed to slightly embarrass everyone, including Avery, she found herself out on the street with Grant. He put his hand on her back and directed her down Greenwich toward North Moore and a subway entrance on a little island between two streets. They descended the steps, Grant showed her how to use her credit card to buy a subway pass, and then they were waiting, just the two of them, for the train that would take them to 14th Street, where they would traverse a long tunnel on their way to pick up the L, which would let them off on Bedford.

It was a trip Avery would make many times over the next several weeks, but that night it was all new, and she took in everything: the echoey quiet of the Franklin Street station; the bustle, even late on a Monday night, of the 14th Street stop; the otherworldly feel of the tiled pedestrian tunnel with its graffiti and posters advertising movies and shows; and the people walking toward them from the opposite direction, the way no one made eye contact, the way footfalls echoed; and then, near the center of the tunnel, a middle-aged man who started playing something lovely and haunting on a silvery flute, a hat at his feet with a few bills in it.

Through most of the trip, Grant was quiet. He seemed changed by the city, no longer the arrogant observer she had met in State College, the distant, slightly bemused outsider. On the crowded subway car, he held on to a pole beside her and looked out a black window as if he saw something worrisome there. When she was about to ask him what was wrong, her own thoughts took a sudden turn, back to home and Kate and Ronnie. She'd have to deal with all that—but already those thoughts, those concerns, felt far away, as if the life she had been living twenty-four hours ago was somehow the distant past.

Her first night in Manhattan and she had spent the evening with Mei Mei Tropp. Until a few hours earlier, Avery had had dreams of being a photographer, of being an artist, but then Grant had called her a photographer and Mei Mei had smiled at her—and suddenly, rather than being a far-fetched possibility, a gauzy dream, it seemed possible. Already she was thinking about how to get her portfolio and her camera gear to Brooklyn. She was thinking of how she might get her photographs in front of Mei Mei, wondering how to get Mei Mei to take an interest.

Out of the train station, on Bedford, the night was warm and summery, and a breeze swirled dirt and a few bits of trash along the sidewalk. A dozen people, all young or youngish, were waiting at the corner bus stop, peering down the avenue for an approaching bus. An older man, burly and disheveled, brushed past her muttering to himself, the smell of liquor wafting around him in a cloud. Grant asked if she wanted to take the bus or make the ten-minute walk. His tone made it clear he preferred walking, which was fine with her. She slipped her arm through his, pressed close to him, and they walked along Bedford arm in arm, silently. At the park, a baseball diamond glittered under bright stadium lights as a young man approached home plate with a bat slung over his shoulder. In the field and on the bases, the ballplayers, men and women, wore sneakers and shorts and various Ts, all young and athletic and vivid in bright colors: red shorts on second base, green on third, a white ribbed wife-beater on the pitcher.

Avery said, "It's like a street festival out here."

Grant looked around at the crowds of people enjoying the warm weather, kicking balls, throwing Frisbees, or stretched out on picnic blankets. "It's like this all spring and summer," he said. "Stuff goes on all night," he added and then fell back into silence.

At his apartment, Grant unlocked a pair of outside doors that opened onto a corridor with a flight of wooden stairs, peeling wallpaper, and ancient carpeting. The sharp, unpleasant odor in the hallway came, probably, mostly from the carpet. Past one more locked door, inside Grant's apartment, the odor disappeared and was replaced with a minty smell that she hadn't noticed earlier in the evening. She sniffed the air. "What's that?" Grant turned slowly, puzzled, then grinned and pointed at an air freshener plugged into a wall outlet under one of the front windows. "Zoo," he said. "Must have gotten stuffy in here while I was gone." He pulled the freshener out of the socket and placed it on the coffee table next to the chess set. "Make yourself comfortable." He walked through the bedroom and kitchen and into the bathroom.

Avery took off her shoes and lay back on his bed, her head propped up on a stack of pillows. From the bathroom, she heard the loud splash of Grant peeing, followed by the flush of the toilet and silence. His apartment, she noticed, was remarkably quiet. She had to be still to hear the faint murmur of voices from the park. If there were people living above him, she thought, they didn't make any noise—and then she remembered that Zoo had the apartment above him. She turned off the dresser lamp, casting the room in the softer light from the living room and kitchen. In the back of her mind, a flock of questions fluttered noisily, but it was as if they were safely caged and she didn't have to pay attention to them right at that moment. There was the big question of her mother and the rest of her family and what they were all doing and what they might do once they understood she had left college. She knew Kate. She knew that her mother would think Grant had somehow kidnapped her and stolen her away. Then there was Ronnie. What to do about that? She should at least call Aunt Lindsey, at least that. Her share of the rent at college, she'd have to deal with that too. Tuition and fees, could she get those refunded? That would be a significant amount. Her stuff. How to get it from there to here. And where was *here?* Grant hadn't invited her to live with him, only to stay a while. How long before *a while* became too long? Somewhere in her mind all those questions waited that night, her first night in the city.

When Grant came out of the bathroom and joined her on his bed, she said, "I can't believe Mei Mei Tropp's your friend. Why didn't you didn't tell me?"

"Why should I have told you?" He ran his fingers through her hair. "Does it make a difference?" he asked. "Do you like me better?"

"Absolutely," she said and kissed him on the neck.

Grant smiled in a way that suggested a combination of annoyance and amusement. "You have to watch out for Mei Mei," he said. "She can be voracious."

"Voracious? How?"

"She devours people."

"I don't get it," Avery said. "I need more information."

"What about Terry?" Grant asked. "You think she's attractive?"

"Sure. Definitely attractive."

Grant smiled again, and in the same way.

"But what about Mei Mei?" she pressed. "What do you mean *She devours people?*"

"Why are you so interested in Mei Mei?"

"Why?" Avery didn't know whether or not to take the question seriously. Who wouldn't be interested? "Well," she said, "she is kind of world renowned."

"Do you know her work?" Grant asked.

"What do you mean?"

"I mean," Grant said, "are you familiar with anything she's done? Is there any of her work that you especially like? Or is it just the being famous that counts?"

Avery stretched out alongside Grant and propped her head up on her hand. "We studied her work in my art classes and in art history."

"No kidding," Grant said. "I recommend you don't tell her. She's seriously hung up about getting old."

"She's not old," Avery said.

"That," Grant said, "she'd like to hear."

"But you're not thirty-three, are you?" she said. "You told Mel you were thirty-three."

"I lied."

"I know. How old are you?"

"Why?" Grant turned on his side to face her. "Does it make a difference?"

"Not unless you're sixty or something, with a picture in your attic."

"No picture in the attic," Grant said. He fell onto his back again and looked across the room at a small, gloomy watercolor of what might possibly be weeds but was mostly just a moody abstract. "Terry and I used to be a couple," he said. "Long time ago, right after college."

"Really?" Avery snuggled closer to him. "What's she like in bed?"

Grant smiled and was quiet. He looked like he was thinking about something while at the same time he was obviously ignoring her question. "Thing is," he said, "sorry, but I think Mei Mei's a fraud."

"Seriously? How could she have gotten so famous if she were a fraud?"

At that Grant laughed out loud. "Mei Mei can't draw," he said. "Not to save her life. She's supposed to be an artist, yet she can't even—" He stopped abruptly, as if stopping himself from pursuing a line of thought he found too frustrating.

"What?" Avery said. "What can't she even?"

"She has interesting ideas. Slightly. Interesting. But other people do all the work," he said, his voice suddenly incredulous. "She has no particular skills, even at the rudiments, and yet—she's *world renowned*."

Avery thought to ask him, playfully, if he were jealous, and then thought better of it. Instead she asked, "When did you break up with Terry? You seem like good friends."

"Long time ago," he said. He wrestled a couple of pillows into shape under his head. "Terry's crazy competitive. She loved me, but she couldn't help being jealous of my successes and pleased by my failures. Everything, underneath it all, everything with Terry is a competition. And if she doesn't think she's got the best of it—" He made a sour face.

Avery traced a finger along the dark edge of Grant's hairline, running her fingertip along his temple and across his forehead. Grant closed his eyes, as if relaxing, and she found herself surprised and moved by the obvious pleasure he was taking in her touch. In his face, she saw relief mixed with pain, as if her touch were soothing him and he very much needed soothing. She wondered if Grant knew how much what he was feeling showed in his face. Probably he did, which might be why he usually looked so stony-faced. She unbuttoned his shirt slowly, watching his closed eyes while she worked the buttons. Everything about him seemed suddenly more complicated than she had previously gathered—and she had summed him up from the beginning as complicated. Still, watching him like that, with his eyes closed, apparently letting his defenses down just the slightest bit, she felt as if she could see the tension he carried rippling through his skin, in his face and shoulders and chest, every muscle tight, every nerve ending waiting at attention.

She pulled his shirt open and slipped her hand beneath his undershirt to feel his stomach and chest. With his eyes still closed, he pulled her down to him, and then, for the first time, they began making love like human beings, touching and kissing and comforting. At one point, after taking off his clothes, Grant got up and walked away from her naked, and she was struck again by his body, the hard lines of muscle running up his calves and through his buttocks and his back—and she thought if she could capture that in a photograph it would be something worthwhile, that physical beauty. When he turned off the lights in the kitchen and living room and got back into bed with her, he took a box of condoms from one of the bookshelves beside the bed. Avery laughed and said, "It's a little late for that, don't you think?" He said, "If we're going to be—" She stopped him and explained that she was already taking birth control pills, basically for her complexion, which made him laugh, and then they started again, but in the dark, so that everything was about feeling and touch and sensation. Then the outside door to the building opened and then the inner door, and someone was in the hallway. Grant heard it too. He stopped and they were both quiet in the dark, listening. Grant said, "Probably Zoo." Avery said, "Don't stop," and then they started up again and kept at it until it was over amid the familiar music of creaking bedsprings and labored breathing. Whoever was in the hallway must have climbed the stairs quietly, not wanting to disturb, because Avery didn't hear another sound in the building until much later, when Grant lay asleep beside her in the dark: she heard footsteps as Zoo crossed the room above her, and then the flushing of a toilet, and then silence.

That was her first night in the city. She lay in bed with Grant warm alongside her, mulling over what had been an incredibly long day, beginning in State College and ending in a quiet bedroom in Williamsburg. She was looking forward to the morning, to exploring the neighborhood. She decided to get a newspaper and check out the jobs section. She felt inexplicably good, even with the prospect of calling Kate in the morning looming. It would feel good to tell the truth. She would do her best to convince Kate that she was all right. Kate was going to freak, but all Avery could do was make it as easy on her as possible. She'd try, but beyond trying it was out of her hands. This was a choice she was making, coming to New York. It felt right. Leaving State College felt right. Kate would just have to understand.

Now, on Bedford Avenue, midmorning, on her way to work at Heriberto's, almost a full month after arriving in New York, Avery heard
her cell phone ring in her purse as she walked briskly along the slate
sidewalk. She recognized the ring as her mother's and reluctantly
disconnected the call. She had been disconnecting her mother's calls
for the past week, both because Kate always seemed to call at the
wrong time and because she was tired of explaining herself again and
again, especially since Kate didn't really seem to hear her. No matter
how many times Avery explained what she was doing and why and
her hopes for this time in the city, Kate came back to the same set of
concerns: *How could she leave college in her final year; how could she
move in with a guy she barely knew; wouldn't it be better to wait until she
graduated and then move to the city?* When Avery told Kate about Mei
Mei, who was introducing her to the art world, and Heriberto, who
had given her a good job, and Zoo, who was always looking out for
her, Kate would listen and then go right back to the same arguments:
*How could she leave college in her final year; how could she move in with
a guy she barely knew; wouldn't it be better to wait until she graduated
and then move to the city?* Again and again, endlessly: same arguments, a thousand variations. Avery put Kate and the disconnected
phone call out of her mind and continued along Bedford, past the
coffee shops and bodegas, behind a middle-aged couple talking rapidly in Polish. In front of them, a tall black guy was with an even
taller white girl—she guessed their heights at six two and six four or
five—and they were shouting and laughing and pushing each other
in the midst of an animated conversation so full of slang that their

talk was almost as impossible to comprehend as the Polish couple's. After growing up in a place as homogeneous as Salem, this was fascinating to her—all the languages, all the dialects, the varieties of clothes and styles and manners. She liked being among these people. She walked briskly and purposefully, feeling pleasure and something like a sense of accomplishment—as if she had, by dint of her own will and character, achieved something.

TRAFFIC out of Manhattan was brutal, and it didn't get a lot better in Brooklyn. Somewhere along Atlantic Avenue, stuck behind a produce truck, with Albert unperturbed at the wheel, Grant closed his eyes for a minute. When he opened them, they were parked on Liberty Avenue in front of a clothing store, and Albert's hand was on Grant's shoulder, gently shaking him. Sunlight glared off the black hood of the car. For a moment, Grant could have been a kid again, the boy who used to drive to work with his father on Saturday mornings. His mother, a slim, nervous woman, would come into his room, sit on the edge of his bed, and shake his shoulder gently to wake him. *It's Saturday morning, honey. You're going in to work with your father.* His father was always *your father. Your father* wants you to look nice. *Your father* wants you to help him with the magazines. He saw her sitting on the edge of his bed on a winter morning. They lived in Williamsburg, on Powers Street, in a two-family house, maybe a mile from his place now on Lorimer. Before they moved out to Long Island when he was thirteen, to Babylon, where he was miserable. But then, he was miserable in Brooklyn too, as a kid. Wherever his father was, he was miserable: his father's anger settled over his life like a black mist. The bruises on his mother, not all the time, maybe three, four times that he could remember growing up, but he did remember. Mom at the sink one night, holding a washcloth full of ice cubes over her eye. It was late and dark and something had awakened him. His mother was standing at the sink in moonlight from the backyard window. She was looking out the window into the yard. She looked peaceful, and the house was still, only the sound of an occasional car somewhere on the million streets around them.

She lived in a home now in Bay Shore that Chris and the girls took care of. He hadn't seen her in months. When he had first discovered that his mother wasn't his mother— There were still ways in which it just wouldn't click. That was his mother in memory sitting on his bed in the morning, waking him to go to work with his father, though he knew the right words were *grandmother* and *grandfather*, *grandmother* sitting on the bed, *grandfather* at work in the stationary store, but he never thought that way, never. His mother woke him on a Saturday morning. He went to work with his father. His father sat him down in the back room amid piles of *New Yorker*s and *Esquire*s and *Modern Living*s and a hundred other titles he couldn't remember, and his father showed him how to cut the cords binding them and stack them in neat piles before bringing them out into the store to arrange them on the display stands. His father did that, and *grandfather* was only a word the truth required, or a version of the truth, the biological truth, because *father* was the real truth. His father smashed their car into a neighbor's car in front of their house because the neighbor had parked in his spot, the spot in front of his building that he claimed belonged to him, and he told the neighbor not to park there and then stopped one night, it was snowing, Mom and Dad were in the front seat, Grant was in the back, stopped for a minute and cursed and then hit the gas pedal and sent their car flying into the neighbor's car and Grant flying into the windshield and the neighbors pouring out onto the street. Grant could still see in his mind's eye the neighbor coming out of her apartment wielding a fork like a weapon, a fork held over her head while she screamed at his father. Grant sat in the front seat and watched snow falling over his flailing neighbors, a woman wielding a fork, his father throwing punches knocking one man down and then another and another man jumping onto his back while his mother clawed at the man's shirt trying to pull him off his father, her husband, Kurt Danko screaming curses at them all. It was snowing and snowflakes floated down gently over the whole scene, in Brooklyn, Grant, a boy safe in the front seat of his father's car, his lip cut and bleeding.

Albert said, "You awake, kid?"

Grant took a deep breath. "Long night," he said. "Sorry."

Albert showed Grant his cell phone, meaning he had talked to Billy. "Your uncle's only got a few minutes for you. Like I said, he's not too happy about it."

"About meeting me?" Grant looked out the window at an armless mannequin in a clothing-store window. Albert hadn't made a move to open the car door yet, signaling that Grant could still change his mind. "Look," Grant said, "I need to talk to my uncle. Sorry."

Albert made a face that said, *It's your business,* then pushed open the car door and stepped out onto the busy street.

On the sidewalk, in the shadow of a storefront awning, a breeze whisked a few leaves into the air. With lines of cars and trucks roaring along Liberty, Grant put on his denim jacket and followed Albert down the street to a small restaurant with plate-glass windows. Billy was in a back room, sitting alone at a table, holding a menu. As usual, he was dressed immaculately. Unlike Albert, who had on a gray shirt with no tie and looked almost hip in comparison, Billy wore a dark blue suit over a white shirt with a tasteful pale blue tie. His hair had gone white, but he still had a full head of it, parted neatly on the right and thick and carefully combed across his forehead, tasteful, everything about Billy tasteful.

"Grant," Billy said as they approached the table. He sounded pleased to see him, which was his usual tone. Then he added, "Albert tells me you want a meeting with me," and the way he said *meeting* suggested a degree of amusement at the notion.

Grant took a seat at the table across from his uncle. "I'll only be a minute," he said. "I appreciate your seeing me."

Billy looked at Albert and then to the counter in the next room. There were people in the booths, a couple of middle-aged women chatting and giggling like teenagers and a guy who looked to be in his forties, sitting across from two children who remained silent at their places, hands folded on the table in front of them. Billy said, "Where the hell's Carmine?"

Albert looked at the counter, as if expecting to find Carmine there. "He's probably in the kitchen," he said, finding the counter abandoned. "Should I go see?"

Billy said, "Yeah, why don't you do that?" When Albert was gone, he said, "So what is this you want to talk to me about?"

Grant folded his hands on the table. "I'd like to work for you," he said.

Billy was silent a moment, looking Grant over. He said, "You do work for me."

Grant closed his eyes as if thinking deeply. When he opened them, he said, "I'm thirty-seven, Uncle Billy. Since I went away for a couple of weeks last month— I'm seeing my life from a different perspective."

"And what's that?"

"That it's nothing much, my life."

"Oh." Billy leaned back in his chair. "Tell you the truth," he said, "I'd given up on you." He was silent then, and his eyes seemed to harden into a glare as he watched Grant. "It just occurs to you now, suddenly, that you're not doing anything with your life?"

"It's not like it just occurred to me." Grant leaned over the table. He had an urge to touch his uncle's arm, to do something to soften the look in his eye. "It's more like," he said, "I'm tired of the bullshit." He shook his head, expressing his own dismay with himself. "I'm letting go of this idea that I'm going to wake up one day and find myself some kind of world-renowned artist." As soon as he spoke the words *world-renowned*, he cringed a little, inwardly, remembering where they had come from. "That's bullshit," he said. "I guess I always thought because some of my friends—"

"You mean the TV writer?" Billy said. "And how come she can't help you? How come she's never gotten you work writing for a show, or whatever?"

Grant opened his hands as if he were holding a ball and offering it to his uncle. "Because I'm not a writer," he said. "She knows it. Everybody knows it. I'm the last one to let it go."

Billy appeared confused for a moment, as if he had more questions. Then he seemed to shrug off his concern. "All right," he said. "Whatever. I mean, you've got a degree from NYU, which I'm told is a pretty good school. And I read one of your stories, which, I'm not a literary critic, but *I* liked it. Still, you're right, it's been, what? Ten, twelve years?"

"Something like that," Grant said. "More."

"So you didn't follow through," Billy said, as if accepting and summarizing Grant's arguments, "and now you're giving up. Still, what's this got to do with me?"

Grant bristled, feeling, surprisingly, a sting at being told he was giving up. "What it's got to do with you, Uncle Billy," he said politely, "is that I'm tired of living on five or six hundred a week."

"A grand on good weeks," Billy said. "Tax free. You're not grateful for that?"

"It's not that I'm not grateful," Grant said, his voice still reasonable, "it's just that I'd like to do better. I'd like to do a lot better."

"Really?" Billy said. "And how's that, Grant? How are you going to do a lot better than that?"

Grant wrestled against the frustration he felt rising in his throat, lodging in a knot just under his Adam's apple. "What's Albert do for you?" he asked. "Between the Jay Kos suits and the Lexus, he obviously does well."

Billy looked like he didn't know whether to be amused or

shocked. "You're thinking," he said, "that you could do the kind of work for me that Albert does? Is that what this is?"

"Yes," Grant said. "That's what this is."

"But you don't know what Albert does for me, right? About that, you're clueless."

"Not exactly."

"What do you mean, not exactly?"

"I'm mean I'm not an innocent," Grant said, some of his frustration seeping out. "I mean I know who you are, and I know the kind of business you're in."

"No, you don't," Billy shot back. "I'm sure you think you do—"

Grant said, "Can we please stop playing games here, Uncle Billy? You know what I'm asking. I want to work for you. I want a chance at making the kind of money that Albert makes."

"Playing games," Billy repeated. He looked down at the table, as if taking a second to gather himself. He coughed and then said mildly, "I know what you're asking, Grant. It's you who don't know. You have no idea what you're asking."

Grant said, "So the answer is no."

"Of course the anwer's no," Billy said. "What do you think? This line of work is, what? You put in an application and you get hired? The answer's no because (a) you couldn't do the work, (b) you don't have a clue, (c) my brother's ghost would rise up out of his grave and strangle me in my sleep, I ever tried to bring you into this line of work—which would have had to happen, were it ever going to happen, many years ago. You don't just—" Billy's face had turned red. He stopped and gathered himself again. "Look—" he said. Then he was quiet, apparently thinking something through. "Look," he repeated, "I can get you a union job. You work, you can pull down six figures a year. But you've got to really work, not two, three nights a week, like you've been doing. And then you are what you are. All that work you put into NYU, they'll laugh at you for that. Someone might even try to kick your ass because of it. But you'll be making good money. If that interests you, I'll do it because of my brother, but after that, Grant—" He paused again and met Grant's eyes. "After that," he said, "I don't want to know anything else, you understand? Funerals and weddings, that's about it. Is that clear?"

Grant didn't answer right away. Inside him, a wild urge to reach across the table and strangle his uncle had his heart pounding. He didn't want to speak until he felt sure his voice wouldn't tremble.

Billy folded his hands on the table and gazed steadily at Grant. "You want my advice, though," he said, "as your uncle: do something with that degree you earned. You got sidetracked with that Saint John shit? You got screwed up on drugs for a few years? Which don't think I don't know about. You been wasting your time fucking anything that moves in the city? You think you're the only one winds up throwing away his life? So, what, now the light dawns? Okay. Settle down. You want to write? Put your nose to the grindstone and do it. Go back to school. Get in one of those writing programs. You want help with something like that, I'll help you with it. For my brother's sake. Or take the union job and settle for the money. Whatever you want, Grant. But make a decision." Billy slapped the menu down on the table. "What the hell's going on with Carmine and Albert?"

As if on cue, Albert appeared behind the counter with a guy

who was as stocky and unkempt as Albert was thin and neat. At their appearance, both booths emptied out and approached the cash register.

Grant said, "I'm not interested in a union job. Thank you."

Billy said, "You want to go back to school? You want some help with that?"

"No," Grant said, "that's over with." He hesitated for a second, his eyes fixed on his uncle's.

Billy said, "What? You have something you want to say?"

Grant said, "I was never able to write again after I killed that guy. After I killed that guy, working for you, Uncle Billy."

Billy's face went grim and tight. "I don't know what you're talking about," he said. "I don't know anything about any killing. The only work you've ever done for me is driving and unloading trucks."

"I thought I could put it behind me," Grant said, "but I never did."

Billy looked across the room and barked out Albert's name. To Grant, he said, "I think you must be losing your mind."

Grant said, "I'm not losing my mind. I haven't done anything worthwhile since that night."

Billy leaned forward on the table. "That," he said, "is one of the biggest crocks of bullshit that I've ever heard."

Grant ignored him. "So I figured," he said, "if I can't be what I once had the potential to be, I might as well get rich being what you made me."

Billy said, "This is pathetic." He looked in Albert's direction, but it was as if Albert were invisible to him. Mostly to himself, he said, "You're blaming me . . ." When he looked back at Grant, he said, "Try this as an alternative theory. You threw your youth away partying and you threw whatever talent you ever had away with it, and now that you're life's a total fucking dead end, you're looking for the next easy way out." He raised his eyebrows and leaned closer to Grant, wide-eyed. "How's that for a theory?" he said. "Does that feel about right, Grant?"

Again Grant felt a nearly overwhelming urge to wrap his hands around his uncle's neck and strangle him.

Billy said, "You thinking of doing something, Grant?" He leaned back in his chair, unbuttoned his jacket, and waited. When Grant didn't respond, he said, "Get the fuck out of here," and he waved Albert to the table. To Albert he said, "I'd appreciate it if you would give my nephew a ride home." To Grant he said, "Go wait outside. Albert will be right with you."

Grant left the table without a word, his heart banging in his chest. On the street, he leaned against the storefront wall, sunlight beating down on him like a spotlight. He put on his sunglasses and concentrated on his heartbeat, willing it to slow down. What was he thinking? He didn't have a penny in the bank. He'd have to borrow just to make the rent. The thought of going back into the restaurant and trying to apologize pushed at him for a moment, and his body stiffened in resistance. What he wanted to do was go back in, grab a napkin holder off the counter, and beat Billy's head into ketchup with it.

When Albert came out and found Grant looking up into the sun, he slid his hands into his pants pockets and stood beside him silently, waiting.

Grant said, "I can't believe that just happened."

Albert said, "Neither can your uncle." He touched Grant's arm as he started for the car.

Grant said, "What happens now?"

Albert laughed. "What do you think?" he said. "I'm going to dump you in the river?" He pointed to his Lexus.

Inside the car, Grant said, "What I mean is, am I out of work now? Did I just get myself fired?"

Albert appeared to be sympathetic. "Listen, Grant," he said. "First, that thing you talked about with your uncle— I know you're not wearing a wire, but I've got to check you."

Grant threw up his hands as if he were being held at gunpoint. "Is that what he thought?"

Albert said, "No. He doesn't. But when somebody, anybody, asks for a meeting out of the blue and then steers the conversation around to something like you did—" With that he leaned across the seat and unbuttoned Grant's shirt down to his belly. When he undid his belt buckle and pulled open the top of his pants, Grant said, "Uh, Albert?" and Albert said, "Don't be a comedian." When he finished unbuttoning and unzipping him, Albert frisked him from his shoulders to his ankles. "All right," he said when he was done. "Straighten yourself up." He started the car and pulled out into traffic.

Grant said, buttoning his shirt, "I can't believe he'd think that."

"It was unlikely," Albert said, "but your uncle didn't get to where he is without being suspicious."

Grant found the controls and angled his seat back. He stretched out. "I'm not going to be getting work anytime soon, am I?"

Albert shook his head. "Not likely," he said.

Grant angled the seat back farther as he tried to stretch out his legs.

Albert said, "You comfortable enough?" Then, when Grant didn't answer, he turned his attention to negotiating the traffic making its way onto Atlantic Avenue. Once or twice he looked over at Grant, as if he were thinking about saying something but was hesitant. Finally he said, "I think maybe your uncle was being unreasonable." When, again, Grant didn't respond, he added, "It's not like you didn't get mixed up in the business back then, when that thing happened. I mean, there's lots of guys in this business never did what you did. You know what I'm saying?"

Grant said, "You're saying, you think he should let me work for him."

At that Albert didn't respond. He kept his eyes fixed on the traffic and was pointedly silent.

LINDSEY stretched out in the backseat. Through the open window over her head wind rushed into the car and tousled what remained of her hair. She had cut it short and, she thought, stylish—though not everyone agreed. Corinne, Kate's friend, thought it looked great. Others, though, clearly thought it was a dramatic response to Ronnie's death, which it was, but not like that, which made her furious, just that anyone would think it, that she'd make a display of her mourning by shearing off all her hair. She had been thinking about cutting it short for a long time. She had been looking at pictures online and checking out styles, and, okay, maybe she wouldn't have gone quite as radical if it weren't for her state of mind, but that was only part of it, and she liked the cut. Her hairline made a perfect semicircle high across her forehead from ear to ear, which accentuated the oval of her face. She could pull it off. Her auburn hair was thick and voluminous, so cut down to the scalp it looked like a shiny layer of fur on the sides and back of her head and along her forehead, only getting a little longer, a couple of inches, at the top of her head, styled so that it always had a roughed-up look, as if someone had just ruffled her hair affectionately. She liked the look. It was boyish and a little defiant.

She especially liked the look with sunglasses, which she wore throughout the funeral, through the words and the flags and the guns and the tears. The haircut gave her something else to think about, that was one thing—but it also gave others something to comment on other than *her loss*, which she thought at one point if she heard any-one else say to her—*I'm so sorry for your loss*—she might get violent. She could hardly stand it when they handed her the folded-up flag, and she had to just not hear it when someone thanked her for her brother's sacrifice or else she'd lose it and hell if she even knew what she'd do—start rolling on the floor and screaming. She didn't know what to say. She didn't have words.

And then the cut was also about not looking nice. Somehow she couldn't stand the idea of looking nice anymore, nice as in . . . what? Pretty hair, pretty clothes, pretty girl. She understood for the first time the attraction of piercings: those gold and silver rings through the lips, mutilating eyebrows and noses. They were antiadornment, and she understood how someone might want to brand herself or stick something through some fleshy part of her body and just leave it there. She was thinking about it. Maybe in New York, which was where they were going. They had a hotel in Manhattan, the Hudson, on West 58th, though Avery was in Brooklyn. It was a cab ride, no big deal. Avery'd been in Brooklyn for a month, and Kate was losing her mind. There'd be tattoo parlors and piercing places, and maybe not all patronized by twelve-year-olds and bikers. Hopefully. Hank didn't get it, the haircut or anything she tried to explain about not wanting to look pretty, but it didn't matter, he was there for her unconditionally, and she loved him for that, loved him more, though she knew she wasn't doing much of a job showing it.

He'd never been to New York. Forty and never been anywhere, really. Lindsey'd been to New York a dozen times. When she was a kid, her parents had taken her regularly. She lit a cigarette, took a drag, and then held it above her head by the window so the smoke would blow away. Hank sighed in the front seat, which Lindsey guessed was as vocal as he would get about the number of cigarettes she was smoking. She looked down at the cellophane-wrapped pack crumpled under her leg and then at the carton sticking out of a carry bag on the floor. She didn't know why she was taking such comfort in cigarettes. She had smoked rarely and on and off from the time she was fifteen, but she could count on one hand the number of times she had actually bought a pack, and she had never bought a carton until a week or so after the news. For the past three weeks, she had been smoking a carton a week, partly for the pleasure of the smoking and partly for the necessity of separating herself from others to go off and smoke.

Without looking at Hank, she said, "This is the last one I'll have for a while."

Hank said, "I didn't say anything."

Lindsey thought, *Yes, you did*.

Kate said to Lindsey, "So you're pretty sure it won't be too hard to get to Brooklyn from where we're staying?" Her hands were folded in her lap and she was sitting up straight, as if at attention.

Lindsey said, "Be like going to Roanoke from Salem, except you have to go over a bridge."

"Or through a tunnel," Hank said.

Lindsey said, "Is there a tunnel to Brooklyn?"

"Brooklyn-Battery Tunnel," Hank said, "according to my map."

Lindsey nodded to herself and took a long drag off her cigarette. It was some kind of thing in Hank's family, knowing maps and directions, or maybe it was just guys. First thing he did was buy maps and start studying them. Though her father wasn't that way: he could get lost going from the kitchen to the bathroom—and long before the Alzheimer's. But Hank's family, maps first thing. Once Kate had decided on going to Brooklyn and Hank had offered to take her, he'd gone out and gotten maps.

Kate twisted around in her seat and looked back at Lindsey. "Tell me again," she said, "that I'm doing the right thing."

Lindsey flicked her cigarette out the window. She sat up and re-attached her seatbelt. "Long as, like I said— We should make every effort to arrange a time to meet with her and not just show up like we're some kind of posse sent out to bring her in."

Hank said, "She's going to have to answer her phone, then."

"She was answering," Kate said.

Hank took his eyes off the road for an instant to quickly locate Lindsey in the backseat. "I may have to park myself outside the apartment building until I see her—if she won't answer the phone."

"Then what?" Kate said.

"Then tell her you're here and that you want to talk to her."

"And what if she just says no? Then what do I do?"

Lindsey said, "I should probably be the one to do that."

Kate said, "You two used to be so close." She looked as if she might cry before she spun around to face forward again and straightened her blouse. "I can't believe she didn't come back for the funeral. Ronnie was— I don't understand her."

"I'm seriously worried about this guy," Hank said. "Avery's with some guy only a couple years younger than me?"

Lindsey rested her head against the door and let wind rush over her face and through her hair. All of the family's speculation about Avery running off to New York eventually came around to this: the theory that the guy had conned her or bewitched her or in some way darkly influenced her. Lindsey doubted it. Avery had always been an intensely complicated girl, long before her father had died, or she'd gone off to college, or this guy from New York had showed up to whisk her away. It was part of why Lindsey had always liked her. Running off to New York— Avery, the way Lindsey understood it, had told Kate that she had gone to Brooklyn with this guy because she was tired of college and she'd gone to the city to find a life that fitted her better. That was pretty much how Kate had reported the phone conversation to Lindsey—but it didn't seem to be something Kate could comprehend or accept, nor could anyone else in the family. Once the analysis started, it inevitably came around to the guy, to some sort of power he must have over Avery. As if it were simply not possible that she could make this choice, as if she had to be tricked into it or in some way duped or manipulated.

"He's a gangster," Kate said, looking out at the road, not directing her remark to anyone. "This is a nightmare."

Hank said, "The guy didn't say he was actually a gangster himself."

"He said he works for gangsters," Kate said. "So what does that make him?"

Lindsey said, "Avery met him at the college, Kate. And that other guy, the professor there, he said he was a visiting artist."

"That's what *he* said." Kate spun around in her seat again. "But Kelly said he made his living working for gangsters."

Lindsey said, "I'm sure Kelly's a good detective, but the college wouldn't have brought this Grant guy in as a visiting artist if he didn't have some credentials. Plus Avery told you he was an artist, so—"

"So what about Kelly?" Kate said. "What reason would he have to make up something like that?"

"I'm not saying he made it up," Lindsey said. She heard a note of exasperation in her voice and tried hard to suppress it. "Most artists have to do something else to make money. Maybe he works for gangsters to make money."

"And again," Kate said, "what does that make him?"

Lindsey shrugged and looked out the window.

Kate was quiet for a long moment, then she said, "That haircut makes you look like a kid. Bet you ten bucks, next gas station we pull into, the attendant thinks Hank and I are your parents."

That made the three of them laugh.

Lindsey pulled a new pack of cigarettes out of the open carton at her feet but stopped herself from opening it. To Kate she said, "The detective, Kelly, he said it was the guy's uncle who was the gangster,

Kate. So picking up money, working for his uncle—it doesn't have to be that he's a gangster too."

Kate nodded and looked thoughtful but didn't say anything. She turned around in her seat again and stared out at the road, her thoughts obviously far away.

Hank behind the wheel, his blond hair catching the sunlight, his hands steady at ten and two.

Lindsey unclipped her belt and stretched out again. Beyond the window, trees flew by, then a field with a red barn, then cows, then trees. She was wearing faded jeans and old sneakers and a Smashing Pumpkins T-shirt that had been Ronnie's when he was a kid, a little kid, maybe thirteen, fourteen, because he'd never get a chance to be anything but a kid now. He'd left behind very little: music CDs, some clothes that were mostly jeans and T-shirts, a dirt bike was his biggest possession. He'd sold his car before he'd gone away, left his stuff scattered around with friends and family. Jake Jr.'s dad had come by with a couple of Ronnie's suitcases. He was a big man who used to play football in high school and still coached locally. He looked pleasant enough at the door, if serious, the suitcases on the ground, one on each side of him. When Lindsey let him in, he carried the suitcases into the living room and explained that they were Ronnie's, full of his clothes. He struggled to say how Ronnie had been like a part of their family, how Jake Jr. had loved him, how the boys had always been like brothers and Jake Jr. would never get over it, none of them would. He said, "That boy idolized you, but you must know that. *My sister Lindsey* this, *my sister Lindsey* that. Sun rose and set on you far as that boy knew."

Lindsey said, "Yes. Thank you," and when Hank joined them, she slipped away with the suitcases.

They were full of T-shirts and jeans, some memorabilia: his high school yearbook, a couple of journals with nothing much in them beyond *I did this* and *Willy and I did something* and a few entries about girls. Nothing much. He was like a cloud shadow that flew by. He left nothing behind but the few people who loved him and would have to live without him. Not much of a loss to the world, not like he would have done great things—not that any of that meant anything in the long run, in the real long run when everything eventually comes to nothing.

Lindsey found herself sitting on the edge of her bed in bright sunlight through an open window holding Ronnie's old Smashing Pumpkins T-shirt in her hand, and she took off the summery blouse she had on and pulled on the T-shirt and hugged herself and then she was crying again when she'd thought she was all cried out. Nothing to the world, his death meant nothing to the world. She hugged herself and cried. Then Hank came in and sat beside her and put his arm around her, and that was the only help. Keith was staying a few more days with his cousins. Holding Keith was a help, and being held by Hank. A help, but not Ronnie, not her brother—and that was the thing that infuriated her when people said they were *grateful* for his *sacrifice*. It was as if Ronnie were not real to them but an idea, or a kind of symbol they equated with something else—not real, not a real person whose death left a hole in other people, whose death led to more death in the people who loved him, every death a chain of deaths. It wasn't that they didn't genuinely feel for her, the sympathizers, the believers in war, only that they took some solace in the word *sacrifice* as if it somehow made Ronnie's death something other than the terrible thing it was. That was what infuriated her.

Kate twisted around and leaned into the backseat again. "Lindsey, honey," she said, "are you *sure* about this hotel?"

Hank said, his eyes still on the road, "She thinks you booked us into a riding academy."

"A what?" Kate made a face at Lindsey as if to say, *What is he talking about?*

Lindsey said, "That's Hank's colorful term for a hotel where prostitutes take their johns."

Kate pushed Hank's shoulder. "I do not," she said. "Just, I still can't believe a hundred and twenty-five a night in midtown Manhattan."

Lindsey said, "You can find decent cheap hotels in Manhattan, but this one is supposed to be nice. I mean, it's not a cheap hotel. I got it on Priceline."

"But you've never stayed there," Kate said.

"I checked it out online. Trust me."

"Really," Kate said, "you look, I swear, ten years younger with that haircut."

Lindsey smiled at Kate, touched by her attempt to raise her spirits—and amused. She did look a lot younger with the new cut, but she *was* only twenty-nine—which she thought sometimes both Kate and Hank forgot. Kate joked about being mistaken for her mother, but at sixteen years older, it was entirely possible. Hank was eleven years older, but the extra pounds in his gut made him look a little older than that, even though he was still handsome and Lindsey still found him attractive. She thought she always would. She loved his eyes, and they only got deeper and more attractive with age.

Kate nodded toward Lindsey's T-shirt. "Was that a popular band?" she asked. "Was Ronnie into them?"

Kate looked down at the black T, which pictured four long-haired youths under the band's name. "Guess," she said. "He had a couple of their Ts. One of them just said *Zero* in big white letters across a black shirt."

"Oh," Kate said, as if pained. "Really."

"Too much irony," Lindsey said, and then reached for the cigarette pack on the seat beside her and went about unwrapping the cellophane.

Hank said, "We'll be there in a couple of hours, maybe less."

Kate offered Lindsey a rueful smile, as if she were dreading what awaited them in the city, and then fell back into her seat, disappearing from Lindsey's view.

Lindsey fumbled with the crammed-together cigarettes, inhaling the aroma of tobacco from the newly opened pack. She managed to free one, lit it up, and then held the burning cigarette up to the open window.

From the front seat, Kate said, "I'm going to have to pee pretty soon."

Hank said, "Again?"

Kate said, "I think I'm nervous." Then she added, "I'm nervous. I felt like I had to pee soon as you said we were getting close."

Hank said, "Chances we'll see Avery today are pretty slim. Probably tomorrow." He took a moment and seemed to think about the timing of things. "Probably Thursday," he said. "In the afternoon, where she works." He paused again and then added, "Why don't you call her again?"

Kate said, "She hasn't answered her phone in a week."

Lindsey said, "Try her anyway, Kate. It can't hurt, and at least she'll know you've been trying."

Kate didn't answer, but Lindsey heard her rustling in her pocketbook and then the soft electronic beep of numbers being dialed.

Hank said, "Everything okay back there?

"Fine." Lindsey pressed the cigarette to her mouth between two outstretched fingers and pulled in smoke. She held the smoke in her lungs for a moment, savoring the feel of it, and then tilted her head back and exhaled slowly toward the open window, watching the trail of smoke move lazily through the air until caught in the rush of road wind, where it broke up like smashing into a wall before being pulled out of the car.

Kate said, "Oh, here's a surprise. I'm being transferred to voice mail." Then there was the click of the phone snapping shut and the sound of it being tossed back into her pocketbook. After a moment, she added, "I just pray there's nothing wrong."

Hank said, "We'll get it figured out. She's probably just—I don't know. That guy has her twisted around somehow."

Lindsey took another drag off her cigarette and then tossed it out the window. It wasn't that she didn't feel sorry for Kate. She did. Her girl, her daughter, in her senior year of college, had met a guy who, at first she was told, was an artist of some kind. Avery had met an artist of some kind and gone to live with him in New York. Kate must have repeated that sequence of events a few hundred times in the first week after she had found out, as if she might eventually comprehend it if she said it often enough. When Avery steadfastly refused to tell Kate where she was living, Kate hired a detective, and ever since she'd gotten the report—it had taken him all of maybe thirty-six hours to locate Avery and find out what both she and the guy, Grant, were doing—ever since the report had come in, she'd been beside herself. Avery was working as a waitress, Grant worked for mobsters, they were living in his apartment in Brooklyn. But aside from the gangster thing—and that was explainable, given the guy was his uncle—aside from the working for a gangster, the rest seemed downright romantic to Lindsey. Far from wanting to save Avery, Lindsey wanted to see how she was pulling it off. She wanted to meet Grant. If she could help Kate accept it and deal with it, that Avery had flown the coop, that would be a good thing. And then, of course, she was out of Salem. Keith was with his cousins. Her father had been going downhill so precipitously since the news of Ronnie's death that she doubted he would even realize she was gone. She might be of help to Kate, and she wanted to see Avery and meet Grant, and she was getting out of Salem. When she finally did see Avery, she'd have to thank her for running off when she did. *Timing,* she'd say, *your timing, for me at least, was perfect.*

AVERY and Zoo leaned over the raw concrete bridge outside the entrance to the Whitney, a fat art book between them open to Hopper's *A Woman in the Sun* while beneath them, visible through wide plate-glass windows looking into the museum store and café, Mei Mei gesticulated energetically, engaged in a discussion about something or other, a particular artist most likely. The man she was with was as impassive as she was animated. He was tall, six three, six four at least, skinny, dressed in a black suit and dark shirt with long gray hair that came down past his shoulders and onto his back. Next to him, in a purple tunic hanging off her bare shoulders and arms, Mei Mei looked like a little girl. While Avery watched, Mei Mei covered her eyes with both hands, as if she were so upset with whatever was being said that she had to hide. Avery said, "Who's she talking to?" and Zoo said, "Somebody important." They'd been waiting for Mei Mei nearly an hour. The plan had been to meet her at the Whitney at eight and go from there to a party someplace up in the 80s. It was a beautiful night, and they had agreed to walk the handful of blocks from the Whitney. Avery said, "Do you think Mei Mei's sexy?" and Zoo said, "If you like big breasts on small women, I suppose."

Avery was checking out Mei Mei's legs. She had on black panty hose, and the purple tunic only came down to midthigh. Avery said, "She dresses really oddly sometimes, don't you think?"

Zoo said, "Mei Mei?" and laughed. The way he said her name suggested that he knew her so well and there would be so much to explain that it would be crazy to even begin.

Zoo pointed to the yellow rectangle of sunlight where Hopper's naked woman stood, the shadows of her legs extending out behind her, dividing the rectangle of light into thirds. He'd bought the art book for Avery after she had seen *A Woman in the Sun* hanging in the Whitney and admired it. They had been killing time, wandering through the museum, waiting for Mei Mei to finish her business. She had been in the offices, negotiating with someone about a piece of hers that was to be in the next biennial. Zoo said, "The shadows of her legs seem unrealistically long, don't you think?"

Avery looked down at the print. It was dark, and she had to strain to see in the light coming from the museum and the street. A black town car, stuck behind a bus and a taxi on Madison, blared its horn until the taxi swerved around the bus, opening up a lane. "It's dawn," she said. "The sun's coming through the window in a straight line."

Zoo shook his head. "The shadows still seem too long." He flipped through the pages until he came to Bellow's painting of Dempsey getting knocked out of a boxing ring. Avery had studied the painting in an art history class. Bellows had made the boxer throwing the punch look like a god, while Dempsey flying out of the ring suggested Satan falling from heaven. "Everybody hated Jack Dempsey," Zoo said.

"Why?" Avery asked.

Zoo shrugged. "Dirty fighter, I think." He slapped the book closed and sighed loudly. "She's outrageous." He looked at his wrist-watch. "It's after nine."

Avery said, "We could just leave."

Zoo grasped his heart and looked horrified. "You don't know what you're saying."

"Why? What would happen if we left?"

"What would happen?" Zoo closed his eyes, as if it were too hor-rible to imagine. "We would never hear the end of it. Trust me. Ten years from now—and I have no doubt I'll still be hanging out with Mei Mei ten years from now—she'd be bringing it up. I mean—I'm absolutely serious, Av—she would never forget. It would become like Judas betraying Christ in the endless retellings—the night we abandoned her at the Whitney."

Avery looked down again at Mei Mei, who now had her hands on her hips and was spinning in small circles while the tall guy in black watched, unmoving. "Are you seeing this?"

"Probably something she's working on for the new thing."

"Zoo!" Avery said, exasperated. "What the hell *is* the new thing? Do you know? Because she's, like, talking about a film one minute, then it's sculpture, now it's dance—"

"Mei Mei's fearless," Zoo said. "She's a genius, really."

"You think so?"

"Why?" Zoo said, straightening up, looking a little surprised and a little defensive. "Don't you?"

"I don't know," Avery said. "She's a little too Matthew Barney, don't you think?"

"Don't ever—" Zoo said quietly, as if afraid of being heard. He took Avery's arm. "Don't mention Matthew Barney around Mei Mei."

"Why? Did something happen between them?"

"Just take my word for it," Zoo said, and he let go of her arm. "We don't speak that name."

"Oh, look—" In the café, the tall man leaned over and hugged Mei Mei, who hugged and kissed him in return.

"Thank God," Zoo said. "This party better be good. I haven't lain with another man in months."

Zoo had a way of making Avery laugh that she was grateful for. "Stop," she said. "I heard you with another guy a couple of weeks ago at most."

"That didn't count," Zoo said. "Trust me." Then he said, as if Avery's comment had just hit him, "What? Are you listening? Can you hear—"

"Oh, please," Avery said. "Actually, I've been dying to ask you," she said. "What do you guys do? It sounds like you're hanging Sheetrock or something, all that banging around."

"Bullshit," Zoo said. "You're lying."

"You know I'm not," Avery said. She picked up her book and hit him lightly with it.

"We don't mention Matthew Barney," he said, changing the

subject, "because Mei Mei is constantly compared with him—and she despises him."

"Why?"

"Why does she despise him?" Zoo said, and then he pointed to the café. "Oh, Christ . . ." Mei Mei had turned around on the stairs up to the lobby and was gesturing to the tall guy as if she had something more she wanted to say. While they watched, she yelled something and then turned and started back up the stairs. "She doesn't like him," he said, returning to the subject of Matthew Barney, "because he's, as she says, *a fucking male model*, and he's from Yale. She hates people from Yale. Especially guys from Yale. And she also, incidentally, doesn't like his work." Zoo dropped into his imitation of Mei Mei's high-pitched voice. "*A fucking male model climbing a pole naked and putting Vaseline on his dick? I'm supposed to care about that?* Mostly, though," he said, returning to his own voice, "she's jealous. But you can't ever tell her I said that."

"She's jealous of somebody whose work she hates?"

Zoo made a face. "Mei Mei doesn't like too many other artists," he said. "That's why she hangs out with me. I'm her entourage."

Avery hoisted herself up so that she was sitting on the rough surface of the bridge and took a moment to look over the bare concrete walls of the Whitney with their dizzying, slightly off-kilter lines. "This place is wonderful," she said. "Do you know the architect?"

Zoo said, "Le Corbusier, I think." He looked away, at nothing in particular, as if he were doubting himself. "I'm not sure about that," he said. "But the style is called Brutalism, which I remember because it's from the French for *raw concrete—béton brut—*but it's also, like," he gestured around him, "perfect, right?"

Avery nodded her agreement. *"Béton brut,"* she said, imitating Zoo's pronunciation. She glanced back to the glass doors of the entrance to be sure Mei Mei wasn't around. "You know," she said, "Grant has some issues with Mei Mei as an artist."

"Grant has issues with all of us."

"Not you," Avery said quickly.

"Not me," Zoo agreed. "I'm not successful enough." The topic of Grant seemed to change his mood, making him suddenly pensive. "What's he say about Mei Mei?"

"He questions her . . ." Avery had to think a moment about what exactly it was that Grant questioned, "craft," she said.

"Oh, bullshit." Zoo leaned back, as if putting distance between himself and the criticism. "Nobody works harder than Mei Mei. What's he want her to do, sculpt marble with a hammer and chisel to prove something? That's not what she does."

"It's not me," Avery said. "I'm not—"

"I know it's not," Zoo said. "I'm just saying. Grant, your boyfriend, hasn't made a good choice in about a million years. Except maybe," he added, "I'm hoping, you."

"Me?"

Zoo pointed to the glass doors, where Mei Mei was walking through the lobby with a middle-aged woman in a business suit. He took Avery's arm. "I'm not supposed to tell you this," he said, "but Mei Mei's thinking about hiring you as an assistant."

"Really?" Avery whispered. "To work on the new project?"

"I'm only telling you," he said, "so that you don't screw it up by comparing her to Matthew Barney or telling her that Grant doesn't adore her work. See where I'm going?"

"I should kiss her ass," Avery said.

Zoo laughed, as if something in what she'd said was funnier than she understood. "Mei Mei," he said, "if you haven't figured it out already, Mei Mei must be adored. If you're going to be her assistant, which would be a very good thing for you—"

"I get it," Avery said. A moment later, she added, "Who's going to be at this party tonight?"

Zoo said, "Everybody," and then Mei Mei came through the doors, leaving the woman in the business suit behind her in the lobby.

As Mei Mei approached Zoo and Avery, she mouthed, "They're all assholes," and waved for them to join her as she hurried away from the museum.

"This party had better be as good as advertised," Zoo said, falling in beside her.

"Wall-to-wall gorgeous art boys," she said. "Fresh out of some New England Ivy League college, I promise." She looked Zoo up and down. He was wearing a black paper-thin jacket over a plum-colored T. "You're especially handsome tonight," she said. She reached behind her and took Avery's hand, pulling her closer. "I think Avery brings something out in you, Zoo."

"You think so?" Zoo said. "And what would that be?"

"I think, perhaps, as you get older," Mei Mei said, observing Zoo as if he were a specimen, "you're getting more . . . avuncular."

Zoo looked away without responding, up at the trees lining East 75th, where they were walking against the flow of traffic toward Park Avenue.

A little wind came up, rustling through leaves and rippling the fabric of an apartment-house awning, and Avery felt a small electric trill of excitement walking hand in hand with Mei Mei, the blank concrete wall of the Whitney behind her, with its odd protruding windows. The night was beautiful, a quiet Wednesday evening, warm and breezy.

"I had a chance to look at your photographs," Mei Mei said, and she squeezed Avery's hand.

"Oh— Wonderful. Thanks." Avery had managed to download a series of her digital images off the server at Penn State. She had made prints and shown them to Mei Mei only a few days earlier. "What did you think?"

"Honestly?" Mei Mei said. "Never again look at another Cindy Sherman print, ever. Too, too much influence."

"I know," Avery said quickly. "I just thought—"

"And those dramatic self-portraits," she said, and she shook her head, "those nudes . . ."

Avery felt as though she were beginning to float a little as she walked. It was an odd sensation, as if she were suddenly falling into a strange suspended state as she listened for whatever Mei Mei might say next.

"Don't misunderstand—I loved the chance to see you naked, sweetheart. You're gorgeous, but . . ." She shook her head again and didn't go on.

Zoo looked across Mei Mei to Avery and said, "You're being complimented, Avery, though you could be forgiven for not knowing it."

"I am?" Avery tried to laugh as if she hadn't really just been crushed by Mei Mei's critique.

Zoo said, "Mei Mei never even looks at work young artists give her—"

"Push on me," Mei Mei said.

"Let alone comment on it," Zoo added. "She must think you have talent."

"*Talent*, Zoo, for God's sake." Mei Mei's smug tone disappeared. "The single most overused fucking word in the world." She twisted toward Zoo, though still holding fast to Avery's hand. "Who doesn't have talent, really? What's needed is will and desire. People with talent are waiting tables in every restaurant in the city."

Avery said, "I'm not sure what talent really means, beyond an aptitude—"

"Talent," Zoo said, "is the starting place for any artist. Without talent—without the *gift* of talent, which an artist is simply born with—all the will and desire in the blessed world won't do a damn thing for you."

"Yes," Mei Mei said, "but the point—"

"You should try doing a scene with a talentless actor," Zoo said, "who's only on the damn stage with you because he screwed every director in the city."

"Oh," Mei Mei said. "That's what we're talking about."

"What?" Avery said and peered over Mei Mei to Zoo.

Mei Mei said, "Where's Grant?" She let go of Avery's hand. "I hope he's not cheating on you already."

Zoo said, "Stop it, Mei Mei."

Avery said, "He sleeps all day. He's a vampire." She didn't want to tell Mei Mei that he had no interest in the party, that he'd said, actually, he'd rather eat nails than go.

Mei Mei said, "You know what he's doing, don't you?"

Zoo gave Mei Mei a look that seemed to take her aback for a moment.

"You mean transporting stolen goods across state lines?" Avery said. "He's never been shy about telling me what he does to make money."

They were crossing Park Avenue, stepping out of the street and up on the grassy median with its neatly kept arrangement of flowers and shrubs. Orange-and-white curb barricades lined the opposite side of the street under a long sign that screamed its building's address: *823 Park Avenue.*

Zoo said, "As I was saying earlier, Grant has been making bad choices for a very long time now."

"Jesus," Mei Mei said, as if she couldn't agree more.

"I've been hoping," Zoo said to Mei Mei, in a tone loud with subtext, "that Avery might finally be the thing to wake up the boy."

"Oh, for fuck sake," Mei Mei said. *"Saved by the love of a good woman."*

"Something like that," Zoo said. To Avery he said, "What happened to all his talk of change? Those first couple of nights back, he was all about changing his life?"

Avery said, "He's still like that. He just doesn't know what to do next."

"What about writing!" Mei Mei yelled. "I hate it that Grant turned into one of those writers that do every fucking thing in the world except actually fucking write something! Jesus Christ!"

Avery said, "He needs—"

"He needs to get off his ass and do something," Mei Mei interrupted.

"He needs some inspiration," Avery said.

At that Mei Mei and Zoo both looked at Avery as if she had just grown a third eye.

"Inspiration?" Mei Mei said. "Are you kidding me?"

Zoo said, "Grant's so lost he's not going to find himself again without a guide."

"And that's supposed to be Avery?" Mei Mei said, as if it were the most ridiculous idea in the world. To Avery she said, "How old did you say you were? Twenty-two?" She laughed and said to Zoo, "I can't believe what a romantic you are. Really."

Zoo said, "Let's change the subject." They were walking past Lenox Hill Hospital.

Avery said, gesturing toward the hospital, "Is that Brutalism?"

The hospital was built like a modern fortress, with long expanses of blank, windowless walls. "Looks like it," Zoo said, "but it has to be raw concrete to qualify." To Mei Mei he said, "How'd you get Terry to come to this party?" Then he added quickly, "She *is* coming?"

"I'm hooking her up with a Wall Street guy," Mei Mei said. "He's supposed to be good-looking."

Zoo said, "How'd this come about?"

Mei Mei shrugged as if the subject bored her. She pointed to a green apartment awning bracketed by a pair of potted shrubs. "Wait till you see this place." She took Avery's hand again and pulled her to her side. "Stay close to me," she said. "There are people I want you to meet."

At the door, Zoo pushed the buzzer, ran his fingers through his hair, and then glanced at Avery and Mei Mei with an air of disappointment.

"What?" Mei Mei said.

Zoo met Mei Mei's gaze and held it for a moment before turning away from her and watching the door as if he were seeing through it to the party.

"This is exciting," Avery said.

Mei Mei ignored her. She watched Zoo a moment longer, and then joined him in staring at the door.

HANK adjusted the pillow under his head and watched Lindsey in the bathroom. She had on a white terrycloth hotel robe, and she was bending over a white ceramic washbasin on a stainless-steel table. Given that their whole room was the size of a big walk-in closet, and the bathroom had about as much space as a pantry, he found it hard to think of the hotel as a bargain, New York or not—though on the whole, he'd have to admit, the place was something else. They'd parked in a lot and crossed West 58th, rolling their suitcases behind them over blacktop and concrete toward a set of modernish glass doors that opened onto two narrow escalators. The entry hadn't looked promising, but Lindsey had reassured them that she'd seen pictures on the web and that the place would be nice. Still, once they'd climbed the escalators they had all been surprised by the lavish expanses of polished wood and brick and the striking glass roof over crossbeams wrapped in hanging vines. Hank had laughed out loud, the way he did when he was both surprised and impressed.

Lindsey dabbed at her eyes with a blue washcloth and stepped back a few inches—which was all the space she had before she backed into the closed bathroom door—to look at herself in a mirror hanging over the basin. Hank was watching her from a double bed that filled the entire room save a foot or so on each side of it for bedside tables and a narrow gap at the foot where a sliver of a desk backed up against a glass wall that looked into the bathroom. Hank had showered when they'd first arrived. He was surprised, upon stepping into the bathtub, to find a glass wall between the shower and the bedroom. He couldn't see out to the bed, but he assumed from the lighting—and why else would you put a glass wall looking into a shower?—that Lindsey could see him clearly. He waved to her, heard her laugh, and then pulled a white plastic curtain closed for privacy. A moment later, once he had started showering, Lindsey came into the bathroom, reached across him, and pulled the curtain open. She said, "It's incredibly sexy," and then left him to shower feeling like he was on camera.

While he watched her in front of the washbasin, Lindsey ran the palms of her hands over her hair, smoothing it down. She leaned closer to the mirror and ran a finger along her forehead, tracing her hairline; then she stepped back, took off her robe, and got into the shower. If she was aware of Hank watching, it wasn't showing. She had left him asleep in bed, and he guessed she thought he was still sleeping as she crouched, ran the water and tested it on her outstretched hand, and then stood and tilted her head up, eyes closed, to the shower. The circular stream of water splashed off her face. She was right. Watching was incredibly sexy—though he was sure he was getting the better part of the deal. How many times had he seen Lindsey naked? Multitudes.

She was hardly shy. Still, watching her as she showered, as she tilted her face up and the water poured over her breasts and stomach and down her legs, the question pressed at Hank: When was the last time he had really seen her naked? When was the last time he had really noticed her? Suddenly it was as if he hadn't seen Lindsey, really seen her, in ages, and he watched her as if watching someone somehow different than the woman he had been living with for the past eight years. The haircut was part of it. She looked like a kid, like an artsy young kid, a little rebellious, a little wild. The word *sexy* repeated in his mind as he watched her soap her breasts and stomach, and there was a part of him, in his belly and his thighs, that came to attention, but another part was busy remembering the college girl he had met almost ten years earlier, remembering that she had been like that, like she looked now, again, a little rebellious, a little wild—and he felt slightly disoriented, as if he were looking back into the past and seeing the Lindsey he had first met at VCU, that girl in her paint-mottled jeans and band Ts.

In the shower, Lindsey shampooed her hair and rinsed it out in a matter of minutes, then went about lathering and shaving her legs, stretching out one leg against the back wall and shaving it quickly with smooth, long strokes, and then the other leg, and when she was done, she lathered her body in soap again, as if she were enjoying the shower too much to admit she was done and it was time to get out. Hank had been waiting patiently for her to come back to the bed, but when she lathered herself again, he tossed off the sheets and went to her. As he stepped into the shower, Lindsey looked down and said, "I told you it was sexy." She moved out from under the stream, offering it to him. She kissed his chest, and Hank touched her hair, running his hands along the silky mat of it behind her ears.

"I was watching you," he said, his voice a little loud over the running water, "and I was remembering back to Richmond. What was that T-shirt you used to wear, the one we'd always wind up arguing religion?"

Lindsey grinned but didn't respond right away. She soaped his chest and stomach with a bright green glob of body cleanser.

"The one," Hank pressed, "a guy's got a scissor and he's cut his puppet strings dangling from his arms and head, and then the marionette thing over his head, where he's cut the strings, is a crucifix."

Lindsey said, "Green Day." She wrapped her arms around his waist and pressed up against his lathered chest. "We'd argue about everything."

"I liked to get you going," Hank said. "We almost always wound up making love."

"Did we?" Lindsey pulled herself up, sliding against his body until he reached under her legs and lifted her onto him, and then the talk stopped as he leaned back against the shower wall and Lindsey moved over him with an energy that was both surprising and unnerving. She clutched his hair and pressed her tongue into his mouth as she wrapped her legs around him. "Lindsey," he said, wanting her to go slower, but she only answered with more hungry kissing that was as much licking as it was kissing, her tongue on his neck and chin and lips—and then she finished and she was still for only a moment before she started to shake, the whole of her body shaking from her feet to her head. Hank said her name again, gently, when he realized that she was crying. "Hank," she said, clinging to him as if she needed something from him, though she only held him tightly and cried.

KATE lay in bed clutching the cell phone to her chest. Her hotel room, around the corner from Hank and Lindsey's, felt like a coffin—a stylish coffin, with its polished wood floors and walls encasing elegantly designed furnishings, but a coffin nonetheless. She had already showered and was fully dressed after sleeping poorly through the night, starting at the sirens and squeals shooting up from the streets. She had gotten out of bed as soon as the dark started dissolving in the room's only window—if it was really possible to get out of bed in this room, which was mostly one big bed. She had to think that the room was designed for honeymooners who had only one purpose for being there. The glass wall in the shower made her laugh. From the bed, on her back, it looked like a giant plasma TV, and she couldn't imagine couples over a certain age wanting anything to do with it. She considered going over to Hank and Lindsey's room and knocking on their door and decided, yet again, that she would wait for them to call her or come get her, as was the plan.

She was surprised at how unpleasant it was to be traveling with the two of them. The active pretense got to her, not the lying—because it wasn't like subjects came up often that she had to lie about—but the acting, the pretending that there was nothing more than familial affection between her and Hank. It had been years since she'd spent any extended time with Lindsey. She saw her at every family gathering, so it felt as if she was always there, always around, but actually they hadn't gone anyplace together or done something together, something more than sharing a meal or banter, in years. Somewhere in Pennsylvania, Kate had looked into the backseat, meaning to say something to Lindsey just to break a long silence, and found Lindsey stretched out with her sunglasses on, looking blankly out the back window—and it had hit her then how young Lindsey really was. She looked like a kid, like a teenager sulking in the backseat. She reminded Kate of Avery more than anything. Avery sulking. Avery unhappy. And then it seemed impossibly strange to her that Hank was Lindsey's husband. There were fewer years between Avery and Lindsey than there were between Hank and Lindsey.

From someplace nearby, Kate heard the dull percussion of a helicopter, and she knelt on her bed and looked out the window in time to see a blue police copter swooping over the adjacent buildings. She found the city frightening. On the way in, on the radio, they'd listened to a story about a man who'd jumped on top of someone whom someone else had just thrown onto the tracks in front of an approaching subway train. Apparently the guy had covered the other person's body with his own, and they'd both survived, because apparently there's a deep enough space between the tracks for the train to pass over you. Lord. What kind of place? When Kate had asked Avery what she liked about the city, Avery had said, *The culture*. This was a phone conversation. *The art*, she had said. *The people.*

Kate knelt on the pillows and looked out her window at sunlight on rooftops and windows. She felt tears building. She felt a cry coming on—and she wasn't a big crier. Even in the hardest times after Tim's death, she hadn't cried much. She was so low at points that she felt as though nothing in the world could make getting out of bed worth the trouble—but the meds helped her get past that. She guessed she was depressed, but mostly she felt a terrible sadness, and why shouldn't she? Tim was dead. Avery was away. Then, when Hank came along, she let it happen. Tears started at the thought of Hank, and she wondered what was troubling her more, her baby Avery in the city with some gangster or Hank around the corner with Lindsey.

It was early still: a Thursday morning; people weren't even at work yet. Kate retrieved her cell phone from the bed and tried Avery again. When the phone rang, her stomach knotted the way it had been for weeks whenever she heard ringing on the far end of the line, out somewhere unknown. She waited, desperate for Avery to answer and fearing she wouldn't, as if every ring vibrated somewhere in her heart. And the disappointment, the frustration, there they were again, every time. The ringing would stop and the message start, *Your call has been forwarded to an automated voice messaging service*, and then the slight pause and Avery's voice, *Avery Walker*, and Kate would hang up as the robot went on, *is not available to take your call*. She only waited to hear Avery's voice come on the line, *Avery Walker*. She didn't bother leaving a message. She had left message after message with no response, so she had to assume Avery had stopped bothering even to listen to them. With every phone call, there were so many things that hurt, she didn't know why she kept calling. There was the not answering, and then the wondering where Avery was and what she was doing and how things had come to the point where Avery just clicked the button and disconnected her. And then there was the fear, the one she had to tamp down, that something was wrong, that there was some reason her daughter wasn't answering the phone. It was that fear that had brought her to New York. The detective, Kelly, had said Avery seemed fine, that she took the subway to work in the morning, spent time with friends in the evening, and had a late dinner at a Thai place on Manhattan Avenue with the guy, the guy she'd left college for, Grant Danko. "Grant Danko," she said his name aloud. Kelly said they seemed happy. They walked arm in arm from his apartment to the restaurant. They laughed over dinner. *Grant Danko*.

Kate stretched out on the bed, crossed her arms over her chest, and waited. All she needed, she thought, was a bouquet of flowers in her hand and she'd make a perfect corpse. Then she let herself, just for a moment, think about being dead. She scared herself a little when she did that, fantasized about being dead. Sometimes she could get elaborate in her fantasies, and there was a crazy mix of fear and comfort in thinking it through, thinking the whole thing through: how she'd do it, who'd find her, what Avery and Hank and the family would think. She wouldn't do it. She could never do such a thing to Avery, for one. She loved her too much to inflict that on her—and she loved herself too much, had too much hope left—and then there were her religious beliefs. So she knew she'd never do it, but still, she'd find herself, at night mostly, before falling asleep, thinking it through. Sometimes she'd think about jumping from a high place, someplace like Dragon's Tooth, a ridge of high jutting rocks with a steep drop to the valley. In those fantasies, it was the jumping that caught her imagination: standing on the rock ridge and doing a graceful swan dive into nothing. But she didn't like the thought of some rescue squad having to carry her body out, and chances were good she'd be such a mess that she couldn't have an open casket— and she wanted an open casket. Something about the idea of looking beautiful in her casket appealed to her. Sometimes she'd think through carbon monoxide in the garage, or cutting her wrists in the tub, and in those fantasies it was always Hank who found her. She imagined him crumpled in tears, kneeling by her body. Always she imagined that he'd keep their affair secret, that he'd never tell any- one, so it would be something between them for eternity, something he'd carry like a sweet wound.

Outside, another helicopter swooped by, this time so close that her window rattled. Kate closed her eyes. Her heart was beating hard, which didn't mean anything, her doctor had assured her, but it was annoying, hearing her heart thump in her chest. She'd feel better, she felt sure, once she saw Avery. She needed to see her. She needed to talk to her and touch her. Maybe Avery would help her understand. Maybe they could talk about her choices, and maybe there could be some way to understand—but really, more than anything, she needed to see her, she needed to hold her and touch her and see her. Then they could scream at each other and rail or whatever, but really, irrationally, she had a terrible need to see her, to see Avery, just to see her standing in front of her, real and solid and there.

Hank watched the ceiling, his arms folded under his head, as Lindsey curled up against him under the sheets, her leg thrown over his thigh and her head low on his chest. They had both been quiet for a long while. Lindsey had said that she didn't know why she had cried in the shower after sex, and that had left Hank thinking about the differences between men and women. He couldn't imagine a man doing that, breaking down into uncontrollable sobbing without something precipitating it. Hank had cried at the news of his brother's death. He had cried when he'd found out about Ronnie. It wasn't that he didn't understand crying, he just didn't understand it coming out of nowhere. After sex? At that moment? This was the second time it had happened to him, just like that, making love and then the climax, and then she was crying. The other time was Kate. The second or maybe the third time they had sex, but the first time she came—just the same as Lindsey, she started crying out of control, deep sobs, gasping for breath. It wasn't like Hank had a ton of sexual experience as a basis for comparing and analyzing sexual behavior. He'd always had long, committed relationships, so he'd only been with two other women before Lindsey—and nothing like that had happened with either of them.

"We should get going," Lindsey said. "Kate's probably been up for hours." She patted his thigh and then pushed the heel of her hand into the muscle, massaging him.

Hank said, "I don't know about this new plan." He unfolded his hands from under his head and sat up when Lindsey rolled off him and onto her back. They were both naked. Lindsey lay with her arms parallel to her sides, her palms flat against the bedsheet. She had kicked off the top sheet earlier. Hank ran his hands over her breasts and belly. He said, "You're beautiful."

Lindsey laughed, surprised by the compliment, and turned on her side to look at him, her chin propped in her hand. "I'm still not going with you," she said. "I don't think it's a good idea. We'll look like a posse sent out to bring her in."

"No," Hank said. "I understand. Do you know where you're going yet?"

Lindsey made a face that said she wasn't sure. "Thought maybe Times Square. I have good memories of going there with my family."

Lindsey said *family,* but Hank knew she meant Ronnie. As a kid, he was the one who'd loved Times Square. Hank had heard the stories. The flash and glitter of the place, as Lindsey's father told it, attracted Ronnie like it was a massive video game that he could walk around inside. Plus he liked the stores, and he knew his parents would wind up buying him something or other. *That* Hank had heard from Ronnie. "If Kate gets through to Av this morning," he said, "we might not have to go to the restaurant."

"I still think just showing up where she works is a bad idea."

"Maybe you can talk her out of it." Hank threw his legs over the side of the bed.

Lindsey said, "I'm worried about Kate. I've never seen her looking so stressed."

Hank fell back on the bed as if too tired to get up, "I think Kate's said almost exactly the same thing about you."

"I am stressed," Lindsey said. She stood and negotiated the narrow aisle toward the bathroom. "Why wouldn't I be?"

"Why wouldn't Kate be?" Hank said, talking to the ceiling. "Her only daughter dropped out of college. I'm worried. Aren't you worried?"

Lindsey said from inside the bathroom, "You know what?" She stepped out into the narrow corridor. "I'm really not worried about Avery. She's twenty-two, she's rebelling. I'm actually kind of excited about Avery."

Hank threw a forearm over his eyes. "For God's sake," he said. "Please do not repeat that to Kate."

When Lindsey didn't respond, he took his forearm away from his eyes and found her standing where she had been, unmoved, staring at him as if she wanted to say something more but was having trouble coming up with the words. A small part of him wanted to encourage her to say whatever it was she wanted to say, but a larger part of him was taken up with looking at her, at her mouth and nose and the brightness of her eyes, at her breasts, at her belly and thighs and legs, at the triangle of downy hair between her legs and the youthful sheen of her skin. Then she was saying something more about Avery, and Hank was listening and letting the words in, but mostly he was just watching.

SHE might as well be blind, given how little she could see of the glass and steel and concrete howling around her with people and cars, carriages with babies going by along with costumed joggers and pedestrians and police— Kate glanced over at Hank walking solemnly beside her, his hands in his pockets, his eyes straight ahead. At Columbus Circle, he stopped to gawk at the lines of cars and taxis and the hundreds of pedestrians swarming what looked to Kate like a gigantic roundabout. She knew it was Columbus Circle because of the street signs, and thus she assumed the marble statue atop the granite column was Christopher Columbus—but she really was having trouble taking things in. She had to stop and concentrate and tell herself to look, otherwise it was all a bluish blur of glass and motion. Hank appeared mildly awestruck. His mouth was open, as if he were about to comment on something. He gazed toward the circle and beyond it, into the towering walls of glass acting like mirrors reflecting the city back to itself, buildings reflecting buildings and people and traffic under a cloudless blue sky. Kate noticed two police buses parked on the circle in front of another monument, this one topped with glittering bronze figures. They were long white buses with *Police* in pale blue letters, and they looked as if the two of them could hold a small army. She tried harder to see, peering over the streets at the green-and-white umbrellas of the curbside food stands and past them to the startling green canopy of trees that had to be Central Park—but all she could see were people and cars and motion.

Beside her, Hank finally tore his eyes away from the circle. "It's this way," he said, and pointed down 8th Avenue.

"Are you sure?" She touched his back and then slid her arm through his and walked close to him. When he didn't respond, when he didn't squeeze her arm a little or say something to indicate he was happy to be walking arm in arm with her, she was quiet. After half a block, she pulled her arm free.

Hank said, "It should be on the next block." He took a slip of paper out of his pants pocket and checked the address. When they found themselves standing outside the restaurant, a green-and-white awning that read "Heriberto's" on the fringes announcing the place, Hank said, "This is it. Are you okay?"

"I'll be fine," Kate said. She gestured toward the restaurant's entrance. "It's obviously closed. You think I should just knock?"

"Knock," Hank said, "and if you don't get an answer, call." He handed her the scrap of paper from his pocket. The restaurant's phone number was scribbled under the address. "I'll be across the street." He pointed to what looked like another small restaurant, a few tables and chairs out on the sidewalk under a blue canopy. "Call me when you're ready." He walked away without so much as an encouraging touch. Kate's back went stiff and she almost called after him, but watched him walk away, his hands in his pockets, as if he were strolling leisurely along a grassy embankment somewhere. She watched him until he crossed the street, and then she knocked at a polished wood door. When her hardest knock clearly wasn't making much of a noise, she banged on the glass. A moment later the door opened, and Avery was standing there. For a couple of seconds, they looked at each other, wordless.

Kate said, "Avery, honey," and embraced her, crying already.

Avery said, "Mom," and hugged her. "What in the name of God are you doing here?"

Kate wiped the tears from her eyes. She was still standing on the street, the sound of traffic rumbling behind her. "I've been so worried about you," she said. "I didn't know—"

"Come in." Avery pulled Kate into the restaurant. Once she'd closed and locked the door behind them, the traffic roar was muted to a dull hum beneath the background sound of air conditioning. Across an expanse of variously shaped wooden tables and chairs— some round, some rectangular, some long, some short, a nicely arranged dizzying array—kitchen sounds clanked and clattered now and then. In the air was the slightest scent of flowers. "How did you get here?" Avery said. "Did you drive?" Then, as if the thought had just occurred to her and she found it worrisome, she asked, "How did you find me?"

Before Kate could answer any of her questions, a man came into the room through a swinging door that opened into a brightly lit kitchen, where Kate got a quick glimpse of a long grill before the door swung closed. The man was stocky and wore a black apron over a pale red shirt. As he entered the room, he called out Avery's name.

"Heriberto," Avery said, "this is my mother." She stepped beside Kate and put her arm around her waist with a smile, as if she were posing for a photo with her.

"Avery's mother!" Heriberto said, sounding wonderfully surprised and pleased. He swooped down on Kate and embraced her and kissed her cheek.

Kate said, "I'm pleased to meet you," and then stood there awkwardly, not knowing what to say next.

"Your daughter," Heriberto said, "is a wonder. We all love her. Where are you coming from? Salem, Virginia?" He said *Salem, Virginia*, as if it might be a small village in Africa somewhere.

"Yes," Kate said. "I got in last night."

"Where are you staying?" he asked, sounding, as far as Kate could tell, genuinely interested.

"The Hudson," she said.

"Oh!" he almost shouted. "Right here on 58th! Are you by yourself?"

"I came with my brother-in-law and his wife."

"Who?" Avery said and touched her arm.

"Uncle Hank and Aunt Lindsey."

Avery's smile faltered slightly. "The three of you?" She laughed, making a show of being amused.

"Well, you have to have dinner with us tonight," Heriberto said. "Avery," he went on, "if you can get your shiftless boyfriend to come, we'll make a party of it."

239

Avery said, "That's sweet of you, Heriberto, but my mom and I should probably talk first. Okay if I take a ten-minute break?"

"Is it okay if you take a ten-minute break," he repeated, and he looked at Kate. "Like I'm a slave driver." He pointed to a side door and said, "Use our little VIP den," and he looked at his wristwatch and added, "You have nine minutes left."

Avery kissed him on the cheek.

"I'll hope to see you again tonight," Heriberto said to Kate.

"Thank you," Kate said, and then Avery took her by the hand and led her into a small dining room with three round tables. They sat next to a large window that looked out onto a garden lush with grass and flowering plants, where there were more tables and chairs. When they were settled into their seats, Kate said, "This is a lovely place."

"Heriberto's a genius," Avery said. "You wouldn't believe the people that come in here. Steve Buscemi was in last night."

"Who's Steve Buscemi?"

"Actor," Avery said. "Really good. Robert Kennedy Jr.?" she said. "Lou Reed?" She shook her head. "Forget Lou Reed," she said. "I mean, I know you don't know who Lou Reed is."

Kate said, "It sounds exciting."

Avery nodded and then was silent. In her face, Kate thought she saw a hint of regret. It wasn't much, just something in her eyes. Otherwise she looked good. Any fears Kate had harbored of finding her wasted and in rags, living in a slum with degenerates and gangsters, disappeared at the first sight of her. She was wearing denim crops and a pullover with a neckline that swooped low over her breasts. She looked healthy. She had a short haircut that spilled onto her forehead in playfully uneven clumps and strands, as if she had just run her fingers through her hair and shaken it out. Kate wanted to tell her how much better the cut looked than the severe, straight line of bangs from the summer. "Avery," she said. "Honey . . . you could have been dead for all I knew. You haven't answered my calls in over a week. Do you have any idea how worried I've been?"

"I'm sorry, Mom, really—" She threw up her hands as if overwhelmed. "I've just been so busy," she said. "Really. It's been a whirlwind since I got here."

"Too much of a whirlwind to pick up the phone and say, *I'm alive, I'm okay?*"

Avery looked out the window as if taking a moment to measure her words. "You brought Uncle Hank and Aunt Lindsey?" she said. "You're not expecting me to go back home or anything like that, are you?"

"I was hoping," Kate said.

"Oh, Mom . . ." Avery slid her chair back a little, the look on her face a mixture of distress and pity.

"Avery," Kate said, "really. You haven't answered your phone in over a week. How did I know something terrible hadn't happened? What was I supposed to do? I could hardly breathe, I was so worried about you."

"I'm sorry, Mom. Truly." Avery leaned closer to Kate. "I wanted to call you. But— I don't want to hurt your feelings, really, but— Every time I've talked to you since I left college, you've been, *You're out of your mind. What are you doing?. You have to go back. Are you okay? Is he making you do this? Do you need me to come get you?* No matter

241

how many times I try to tell you that I'm good, I'm happy, you just don't seem to hear it. You're the same exact thing every time: I'm crazy to leave school in my senior year, how could I move in with Grant, and wouldn't it be better to wait until I graduate. Over and over again, Mom. I'm working my butt off to get myself established so I can stay here, and you keep telling me I have to go back to school."

"You have one year of college left," Kate said. "Then, if you still want to, you can come to New York. You'll have your degree, and you can establish yourself on your own terms. You can find your own place. I'd be happy to help you with that. Now you're just here with some guy—"

"He's not *some guy*."

"He's not?" Kate straightened up as if surprised. "Did you know him for more than a weekend before you left college and moved in with him?"

"First," Avery said, her whole body suddenly looking tight, "I can't just, over the phone, somehow explain my relationship with Grant to you. It's complicated, even for me."

"Try," Kate said. "Really. I'd like to understand."

"You don't get what I mean," Avery said. She looked down at her hands, saw that she was tapping her fingers on the table, and stopped. "I mean, I don't fully understand the connection to Grant. All I can tell you is, it's very intense, and I want to be with him."

"You're right," Kate said. "I don't understand."

Avery said, "Mom. I'm twenty-two. I'm sorry, but I get to choose my own way of life."

"Your way of life?" Kate said. "You've been on your own for approximately four weeks, Avery. It's a little early to be talking about your way of life, isn't it?"

When Avery didn't answer, Kate found herself staring across the table at her in silence. For a moment, all the words and arguments went out of her head, and she felt as if she were suspended in time, frozen across from her daughter, watching her through a thick pane of glass. She felt as though if she tried to touch Avery, her hand would bounce off glass, as if she would have to shout to be heard—and she didn't have the energy to shout. She watched Avery quietly as Avery watched her in return. What felt like minutes passed.

"Mom," Avery said gently, "I'm sorry to be causing you more grief. I swear. I'm so sorry."

"But not sorry enough to do anything about it."

"What can I do?"

"Pick up your phone, talk to me, for one."

Avery said, "We just went through that, but I promise, I will. I can't always answer the phone, but I promise I won't let so much time go by without calling."

"And recognize," Kate said, "that you have some responsibilities to me and to your family."

"I do," Avery said, "but right now my responsibilities to myself take precedence."

Kate closed her eyes and let herself float away from the table, just for a second. Then she asked gently, "What do you see as your responsibilities to yourself, Avery?"

"To figure out my own life—what I need, where I should be."

"And you don't think you should be back in college, finishing up your degree?"

Avery said, obviously exasperated, "No. I don't."

"Okay, " Kate said, equally exasperated, "You're twenty-two, as you say. I can't make you do anything."

"At this point in my life, Mom," Avery said, "I should be making my own choices, don't you think?"

"Fine," Kate said. "But if you're going to be independent, Avery, then you can't expect me to continue taking financial responsibility for you."

"I don't."

"What about the college? They notified me that they sent you a partial tuition refund."

"I think they should have sent me a full refund," Avery said. "I'd only been to a couple of classes before I dropped out."

"But I paid your tuition," Kate said. "How do you figure that money belongs to you?"

"Because I paid some of it. I paid some of it with my summer money."

Kate saw Avery's confidence crack a little and the troubled, anxious girl Kate knew emerged around the corners of her lips and in her eyes. "Okay," Kate said, "you can keep the money you earned over the summer, while you were living with me rent free and with no expenses, so that most of that money is really a subsidy from me anyway—but fine, keep that. That ought to last you a couple of weeks here. The rest, though, you need to send back to me."

"Okay, if that's what you want," Avery said. "Soon as I can."

"When will that be?"

"Soon as I can," she repeated.

"And what are you going to do about your portion of the rent in State College? I paid September for you."

"Oh, Mom," Avery said. "Please. Melanie can rent out my room in a heartbeat."

"With all your stuff in it? What do you want her to do? Toss your things out on the street?"

Avery looked out the window at the garden. "You could help me out with that," she said. "Get a couple of the boys to drive up with a truck and bring my stuff back to Salem. It's not that much."

Kate looked amazed. "You expect your cousins to just— State College is a six-hour drive, Avery. You can't—"

"All right, Mom. You're right. I haven't been taking care of my business. You're right. I'm sorry. I promise. I'll get it taken care of."

"How?"

"I'll figure it out," she said. "Really. I just need some time to get it together." Avery rubbed her eyes, and Kate noticed a flash of deep green ink on her shoulder. She reached across the table, hooked a finger through the neckline of her blouse, and pulled it down to Avery's biceps, revealing a tattoo. Avery had flinched at Kate's touch, but once the tattoo was exposed, she rested an elbow on the table and angled her body toward Kate so that she could get a good look. The tattoo was predominantly an intricate maze of lines and patterns in green and teal covering two red ovals, which, when looked at closely, turned out to be the eyes of some kind of cat-like creature. The overall effect suggested the night eyes of a animal peering out from behind a forest of interwoven lines. Avery said, "What do you think?

Kate said, "Oh, Avery . . ."

"I love it," Avery said. "I think it's wonderful."

"Good," Kate said, "because you're going to have to live with it the rest of your life."

"I know," Avery said. "I love it," she repeated. Out in the garden, the sun was shining brightly on a green lawn. She looked at the closed door to the dining room. "I need to be getting back to work," she said. "I'm sorry. I'll call you after I get off," she said, "or maybe later tonight. Grant's taking me to dinner."

Kate said, "When can we get together again? Hank and Lindsey want to see you too."

"I don't know. Sometime tomorrow. I'm not working Friday."

"When tomorrow," Kate said. "In the morning?"

"Morning will work," Avery said. "We can spend the day together."

"Okay," Kate said. Then she added, her tone, she hoped, conciliatory, "We can talk some more about all this."

Avery said, "I have to ask you, Mom: How did you find me?"

"What does that matter?"

"It matters," Avery said. "I didn't want to tell you where I was or what I was doing because I wasn't ready to see you yet. I explained all that more than a couple of times."

"Avery . . ." Kate said, "how do you think I found you?"

"I think you hired a detective. Grant said he thought he saw some guy following us last week."

"And?" Kate said. "What was I supposed to do, go to bed every night wondering if you were dead or alive? Yes. I hired a detective to locate you. Is that— Am I supposed to think I'm terrible now?"

"Not terrible," Avery said, and she got up from the table. "Just . . ." She shook her head as if she didn't know what to say and thought it was better to dismiss the subject. "I really have to get back to work." She straightened out her clothes. "Tell Uncle Hank and Aunt Lindsey I said hi." She gave Kate a hug and kissed her on the cheek.

Kate resisted the urge to bring up Ronnie's funeral. Instead she returned Avery's kiss.

Avery saw her to the door, and when it closed behind her, Kate found herself out on the street, the noise of traffic everywhere around her. She stood quietly for a long moment, her mind strangely absent of thought, and then she looked back at the door to the restaurant one last time before going to find Hank.

On 8th Avenue, the traffic was suddenly thin; a few yellow taxis rolled past, followed by a Fed Ex truck. Kate considered crossing in the middle of the block but thought better of it when she saw the light change at the corner and a line of cars stream across the inter-section. It was a mild, summery day, the sky blue and cloudless. She felt the pull of the weather and blue sky and mild temperatures in a bustling city, as if she might do something exciting, as if she *should* do something exciting—but all around those feelings was a background buzz of worry. She felt fragile, as if it might be possible to fall and shatter. At the corner, she waited for the light beside two men hold-ing hands. Both were dressed in suits, and one was significantly younger than the other.

When the light changed, she followed the couple across the street, then turned and headed for the restaurant where Hank was waiting.

In front of her, a thin black woman walked purposefully, as if heading somewhere important. She wore a neat skirt suit and carried a thin attaché case.

At the restaurant, she couldn't find Hank. She looked inside and then came back out to the street, where she stood amid a row of tables under a green awning. In a dark window, she saw her reflection and was startled. Her hair had gotten tousled somehow, and a big clump of it was sticking up on the back of her head. Once she saw it, she practically leaped to smooth it down, but still the reflection showed a skinny, small-breasted woman in black polyester slacks and a white button-up blouse. She looked nervous and schoolmarmish, her features pinched and tight, her skin pale. She looked like someone on the verge of fainting. A big truck blew its horn, and the deep loud blast of it made her jump. She couldn't imagine where Hank had gotten to. She thought maybe the restroom, and she'd wait a little longer—and then a waiter came out and approached her. He was black, with the broad face and muscular arms and chest of an athlete, and his voice was a perfect match for his body: deep and resonant. "Excuse me," he said, "are you Kate?"

Kate nodded.

"Hank had to leave," the waiter said. "He asked you to meet him at the hotel, and he said he'd explain when he saw you."

"Oh," Kate said. "Thank you."

When she didn't move, the waiter asked, "May I help you with anything?"

Kate looked around at the tables, which were empty except for a young couple chatting over coffee. "Can I sit out here?" she asked. "Can I get something to eat?"

"Certainly," the waiter said. "I'll get you a menu," and he disappeared into the restaurant.

Kate took a seat and looked across the avenue to where Avery was working, where Avery was busy doing something behind that plate glass and dark wood. Avery. Her Avery. Something must have happened with Lindsey, she thought. She'd gotten lost, probably. What else could have called Hank away? For a moment, it occurred to Kate that Hank was trying to get her at the hotel alone while Lindsey was off somewhere on the subway—she'd said she was going to take the subway—but then Kate ruled that out as nonsensical. If he'd wanted to go back to the hotel alone with her, he'd have just waited and they'd have gone back together. Unless he was planning something for her, which was so entirely unlike Hank that she dropped that thought in an instant. Most likely Lindsey. Most likely Lindsey was lost or something like that. Hank had told her, told Kate, that Lindsey thought Avery might just be breaking away, rebelling—as if dropping out of college in your senior year to run away with some guy on the back of his motorcycle was a little thing, only *rebelling*. It was a mistake. It was a dangerous mistake.

Kate looked across the avenue again. Knowing that Avery was so close and that she couldn't see her stung. She felt it physically, a pain in her heart. She touched herself there, over her heart. What had just happened? Between her and Avery, what had just happened? It was as if Avery and her arguments with Avery had gone out of her head as soon as she'd left the restaurant, and now it was coming back to her as she looked across the avenue. What had happened? Kate had tried to explain, tried to reason. That was all. That was what she was

EDWARD FALCO

there to do, and Avery— Why should a mother have to go through something like this?

Kate closed her eyes and tilted her face to the sun. Her daughter's name was in her head, echoing. *Avery, Avery. Avery, Avery.* It echoed with her heartbeat as all other thought disappeared, *Avery, Avery. Avery, Avery.* Then even Avery's name faded away, and all that was left was her heartbeat thumping and the traffic noise and, when she opened her eyes, all the people on the street walking past who seemed not to see her, and among whom she felt small and tired.

IN the midst of a dozen people on the curb before a white crosswalk laid out like a wide ladder over Broadway, Lindsey thought, *Bustling, the city is bustling.* The thought got stuck in her head and repeated, something about the word *bustling* exactly right for the speeding stream of yellow cabs and the red double-decker bus with tourists sightseeing on the open top and the half-ton panel trucks and a bright green dump truck and passenger cars and city buses and bicycles following tractor-trailers. The only kind of vehicle she hadn't seen—not a single one so far—was a pickup truck, which you couldn't be on the road five minutes in Salem without seeing ten of them. When the light changed, the stern red hand giving way to the bright walking figure, she followed the crowd into the street, where it thinned and elongated as some hurried while others strolled past six lanes of yellow cabs waiting as if at the starting line of a race.

Ahead of Lindsey, Broadway merged into 7th Avenue as Times Square opened up before her with its billboards and glitter. The sidewalk, she noticed, was lined with yellow police barricades, and then she saw two costumed figures strolling along the street with the exaggerated movements of clowns. One of the figures wore a Burger King crown and carried a globe under his arm, and he was being trailed by a second figure walking in a matched pantomime of arrogant strolling. As she got closer, she realized the figures were meant to be Bush and Cheney and that there was some kind of war protest going on. The street was partly blocked to traffic, and as she stopped to take in the scene, Lindsey saw a guy with a bullhorn. When he raised it to his lips, she heard fuzzy, blurred words of protest: *Iraq, oil, Bush, murder . . .* The people around her seemed oblivious to the protesters, who she saw now were spread throughout Times Square trying to hand people what she assumed were antiwar pamphlets and literature.

She crossed the street to get closer to the protesters, and when she reached Bush and Cheney, they were being interviewed by a man with a huge video camera balanced on his shoulder. The president and vice-president were dressed conservatively in dark suits with red ties, and Bush had the globe in one hand and a black container of oil in the other. The number *666* was painted in red on the front of Bush's crown, and in the same red paint a sign pinned on his back declared him *The Lying King*, which it took Lindsey a second to realize was meant to be a pun on Disney's Broadway hit *The Lion King*. Behind Bush, Cheney held a crossed control bar with strings attached to Bush's shoulders and legs. A rubber chicken dangled from a rope around Cheney's waist, which Lindsey guessed was meant to allude to his quail-hunting accident. The protesters figured, quail, chicken, people would get the point. The interviewer asked Bush, "What do the leaders of our country have to say?" and in response, Cheney manipulated the crossbar and Bush exaggeratedly drank from the container of oil and wiped his lips viciously. When the interviewer saw that Bush wasn't going to speak, he moved to Cheney and said, "Is it true you told Senator Leahy to go fuck himself on the floor of the Senate?" to which Cheney replied by manipulating Bush's strings, making him do a little laughing dance while he drank more oil. When the interviewer realized the people under the Bush and Cheney masks were going to remain mute, he said "Keep protecting our country, guys," and moved on.

Lindsey followed along beside Bush and Cheney on the sidewalk, watching them with an intensity of interest that surprised her. Their point was cartoonishly simplistic, and she found her interest modulating into anger as she watched the grotesque caricatures. She wanted to shout at them that it wasn't that simple, and then she found herself wanting to tell them about Ronnie. She wasn't going to do it—she knew that as she was considering it—but she wanted to stop them and explain, *My brother died in Iraq. This is not a joke to me.* She knew, of course, that what they were doing was theater, and that these people, people who were actually getting up off their asses and making their voices heard, were the last people on earth she should be angry with—but the anger kept growing nonetheless. *It's not a joke*, she kept thinking. *It's not a fucking joke.* And then she heard herself shout at Cheney as she stepped out into the street, "Do you think that this is a joke, this war? Do you think it's funny?" The words were hardly out of her mouth before a police officer stepped in front of her, and then two more appeared, one on each side of her, taking her by the arms and moving her back onto the sidewalk.

"All right," she said, and when the police tightened their grips on her arms, she shouted, "All right, Jesus Christ!" and pulled herself loose. For a moment the three officers stood around her in a semicircle, looking as if they weren't sure what to expect next. One of them said, "Please calm down, ma'am," and Lindsey closed her eyes and took a deep breath, as if following orders. She straightened her clothes, not looking at the cops. A few people had gathered on the street to watch the scene, and two of the cops turned around to disperse them. To the one who stayed with her, standing in front of her with his hands on his belt, she said, "They're making a joke out it. Like it's a fucking comedy." Lindsey surprised herself with the cursing. She hardly ever cursed. She looked up at the police officer and saw that he was a young man, her age, maybe even younger. She heard herself say, "My brother just died in Iraq. He died over there." She was ashamed of herself as soon as she said it, and when she glanced up and saw the look of commiseration on the young cop's face, something very much like fury raged in her—and she had no idea why. She wanted to hit him. Instead she turned abruptly and walked away. When she looked back, she saw the three cops watching her, two of them with their hands on their hips while the third talked into what looked like an old-fashioned walkie-talkie.

Lindsey walked for a block with nothing in her head but a red buzz of anger. She couldn't have said what exactly she was angry about, but her arms and legs tingled with it. When she was able to think again, her thoughts went back to the protesters and the circuslike atmosphere of the theatrics, and she couldn't help being furious. When the police were a few blocks behind her, she stopped to look up at the billboards and the lights and the moving images beaming down at her. Atop a building, a black billboard pictured the Phantom of the Opera's white mask under the words *Remember Your First Time* . . . Under that billboard was another with the black-hatted, green-faced witch of *Wicked*. Lindsey looked around her at the chaos of words and images and tried to shake the anger. What she needed, what Lindsey needed, was . . . What? That was the question, wasn't it? That thought played so loudly in her mind that she almost heard the words as if she had spoken them. *That was the question, wasn't it?* What did Lindsey want? What did Lindsey need? Now, with her mother long gone and her father fading to gone and Ronnie gone, now, what did Lindsey want? How had everything changed with Ronnie—and it had, it had changed—and how did that change what Lindsey wanted? "What?" she said aloud, with lines of people streaming past her. "What?" she repeated—and no one even gave her a second look, this young woman standing on the street looking up and saying aloud, "What? What?"

The buoyant mood with which Lindsey had started the day was gone. It had been transformed momentarily into anger, but then the anger disappeared too as she stared up into the green face of the witch and the white mask of the phantom, and a kind of recognition settled over her. The blast that had killed Ronnie had exploded her life too. She found her cell phone in her purse and started to dial Hank's number, thinking she had to tell him right at that moment, while the recognition was fresh and clear: she could no longer go on with her life as it was. It had to change. She wanted . . . And then, there it was again. What? What did she want?

She put the phone back in her purse, crossed the street, and wandered back in the direction of the protesters. She got caught up with a line of people, and she walked along as if she were going somewhere, but she was all in her own head. She was jealous of Avery. That was why she had come to New York with Kate and Hank in the first place. Avery had broken out of the picture. She had left Salem. It wasn't Penn State she had left, that was just college, an in-between where you met your husband and brought him back to Salem or he brought you back to his Salem—but Avery had shucked it, shrugged it off. She was in New York. She had a job and was surviving in New York and was living with an artist. Was she taking pictures in New York? Lindsey imagined Avery in a gallery office, showing a curator her photographs, and she thought it didn't even matter whether Avery managed any success. It was the doing it that mattered, that felt like a life to Lindsey. The people met, the wanting and the trying—that, in her imagination, felt like a life. At VCU, Lindsey would spend weeks in her studio covered in oils, so wrapped up in color and canvas, in textures and tones, that it was like sometimes she might forget to breathe, she was so inside the thing she was doing, and hadn't every professor she had ever worked with said she had talent? Yes. What happened? She met Hank. She had Keith. She moved back to Salem. For a while she had painted in the garage and taken the kids, Avery and Ronnie, to the museums and what galleries there were in Roanoke and Floyd and Blacksburg, but then that part of her life had withered away until at some point it was just gone, and she had packed up the paints and canvases and stored them in the attic, where she hadn't even looked at them now for years.

She was twenty-nine years old, and she felt like she was in her forties. Her husband was forty. The family members with whom she spent her time were all in their forties and beyond. But she was twenty-nine, and there were still other possibilities than a life in Salem, and . . . that was what she wanted. Other possibilities. Now her parents were gone, now Ronnie was gone, who was she? Other possibilities. She didn't know anymore. The her that she was in the mind of her father through which she saw and knew herself was gone. Last time she'd seen her father he hadn't recognized her. The her that she was in the eyes of her little brother— That was gone. No longer in the world, that her. Dead in Iraq with Ronnie. The she she was in her mother's eyes long gone. What was left was who she was to Hank and Keith, and the problem was that that her wasn't her, not really. Or, it was only a part of her, a good part of her, yes, but it was as if the anchoring self, the self out of which she could give, love, sacrifice, that self had gotten lost, and without that self, the rest wasn't loving or giving—it was draining and exhausting. She had to have that self back, the one she'd been born with and shaped and defined in childhood through the eyes of her family and through the selfishness of childhood and adolescence and that was lost now and that she had to regain. Other possibilities. Her own eyes on her own self. That was where time had taken her, to this place of need for remaking. That was what she needed. That was the what.

Somewhere in front of her, Lindsey heard a shrill voice calling out to the crowds of people hurrying along the street. She moved to her right, stepping out of the line of pedestrians, and saw a small crowd of young men and women clustered on a corner beside a green newspaper kiosk. At the center of the group were two young women, the girl whose shrill voice had pulled Lindsey out of her thoughts and a second woman standing next to her with an armful of pamphlets she was handing out to passersby. The girl with the shrill voice was reading from a prepared speech. She was short and thin and pretty. She had obviously practiced the speech and had some of it memorized. Her eyes moved back and forth from the paper in her hands to the passing crowd.

The speech was about the Iraq War and what she repeatedly referred to as "the Bush regime." Lindsey crossed the street and took up a spot directly across from the girl, separated from her by the constant stream of people moving in both directions. The speech was passionate if not eloquent as she argued that the Bush regime was destroying America and wrecking the planet, and—her principal point—people all over the world must take action. If they didn't, horrible things would happen. "Silence and paralysis," she yelled, "are not acceptable! That which you will not resist, you will learn or be forced to accept!" If people did take action, it would be hard, but they could stand up to the Bush regime. History, she argued, was full of examples of powerful regimes that had been overthrown by ordinary people joined together in resistance, just as it was full of examples of "people passively hoping to wait it out, only to be swallowed up by a horror beyond what they ever imagined." Then, with her voice growing ragged near the end of the speech, which she signaled by intensifying her rhetoric and raising her voice, she dropped the paper and opened her arms to the crowd. "The Bush regime must be stopped," she shouted, "and we must take the responsibility to do it! We in our millions must and can take the responsibility to change the course of history!" She stepped out into the pedestrian stream, the girl beside her offering pamphlets, and yelled out the final, climatic lines of her speech, repeating them over and over again: "The future is unwritten! Which one we get is up to us!"

Lindsey, who had been standing with her back against a storefront window, laughed and then slid down to the pavement, winding up with her butt on the ground, her knees pressed to her chin, and her arms wrapped around her calves. No one noticed her. She listened to the girl shout her slogan again and again, and she thought, *Okay, I get it*, half talking to herself and half talking to God. Though she thought she was mostly amused by the speech, her eyes were full of tears. She rested her forehead on her knees and disappeared into herself for a minute—in Times Square, surrounded by pedestrians and protesters and traffic. She felt so tired she thought she might actually be able to shut out all the sound swirling over her and fall asleep.

Sometimes everything was too much, and it was better to remember a blue pool of water where she'd gone swimming as a kid, with her mom and dad, before there even was a little brother. *Honey, how would you like to have a little brother?* She remembered that. How old would she have been? Five? Not even. But she remembered her mom holding her in her arms. *Honey, how would you like to have a little brother?* Or a ride on the Blue Ridge Parkway in the fall, which used to be an annual tradition. Why had she ever let that go? Her parents in the front, Ronnie with her in the backseat, Ronnie always sticking his head through the space between the seats to talk to Mom and Dad, which was fine with Lindsey, left her the whole backseat to herself, where sometimes she'd kneel and look out the back window at the mountains aflame in red and orange and gold and yellow. Even then, as a young girl, she'd thought she wanted to paint them, and that thought, that as a girl she'd wanted to paint the Blue Ridge in autumn, that thought in Times Square skipped her forward to VCU and an art professor, a young guy, she couldn't even remember his name anymore, who'd laughed at her. For him it wasn't about the Blue Ridge or memories of driving the Blue Ridge in autumn with her family, it was *landscape*. *Landscape?* he'd said, incredulous, and laughed at her—and that was that. She'd never even attempted it.

"Ma'am?"

Lindsey opened her eyes to find a cop kneeling in front of her. Blue uniform, black shoes, wide black belt with holstered gun. She looked into his eyes and saw that it was the same cop from before, the one she'd told about Ronnie. He touched her arm. "Why don't you get up from there?" he said. "Are you hungry? Would you like to get something to eat?"

Lindsey shook her head. Her eyes were wet, and she blotted them on her knees.

"Come on," he said. He offered her a hand.

Lindsey saw the protesters, the speech-making girl, the pamphleteer, others, watching. Between her and the protesters, the same unending stream of people strolling, hurrying, chatting with each other, most not taking much notice, though some watching the cop and the girl on the street, wondering, she guessed, what was going on.

Lindsey took his hand and pulled herself to her feet. "Am I under arrest?"

He touched her forearm, directing her to follow him as he started toward the corner and the street. "You're visiting New York?" he asked. "Where are you from?" He sounded like a New Yorker, the way he dropped the *g* on *visiting*.

"Salem," Lindsey said.

"Massachusetts?"

"Virginia."

"Really?" he said. "I didn't know there was a Salem, Virginia."

Lindsey wondered where he was taking her. She thought about asking and then let it go. "Well," she said, "there is."

※

Hank could have walked to Times Square in considerably less time than it took him to get there by taxi. He called Lindsey twice from the back of the cab, stuck in traffic, while the driver yawned and swigged water from a plastic gallon jug. She reassured him both times, explaining that there was no emergency. When she'd first called, he had resisted abandoning Kate until Lindsey had told him she was at a police station. "Actually," she had said, "it's more like a police kiosk." When the cab finally dropped him off, he saw what she meant. The glass-and-chrome structure, situated on an island in the center of Times Square, was the size of a big bus kiosk. Bright neon lights blared *New York Police Dept.* atop its overhanging roof, the first letter of each word—*N, Y, P, D*—larger and glittering gold, the remaining letters smaller and solid blue.

Hank paid the cab driver and stepped onto the island, where twenty or more people appeared to be milling around, some taking in the sights and sounds of Times Square, some waiting for a light to change so they could cross the street. He made his way through the people toward the front door of the station. Above the door was a yellow sign that pictured an American flag on one side and an NYPD police shield on

261

the other, and between them the words *THANK YOU* in giant letters. Hank was looking up at the sign as he approached the door, and when he looked down and to his right, he saw Lindsey on the other side of a glass wall, seated at a table across from a casually dressed good-looking guy, older, maybe in his forties, smiling at her as he held a coffee cup in both hands. He looked more like a movie star than a cop. Hank stopped a moment and then backed away from the door and into a group of people who were talking animatedly about the Iraq War. In the window, he saw his own reflection superimposed over the room behind it, so that he looked as if he might be standing beside Lindsey.

Lindsey's hands were under the table, folded in her lap. Hank couldn't quite read her expression. She seemed at ease but listening intently as the guy across from her picked up his coffee cup and held it out to her, as if in a toast.

In his own reflection, Hank saw that dumb ox of a flat face looking back at him. He looked dumb, always had, it was the broad features of his face, along with his size, big and bulky—football-player dumb. All his life, he had worked against it. He saw his reflection shift its weight from leg to leg as if nervous about something. Why someone as beautiful as Lindsey had ever taken an interest in him had always been a mystery and a source of pride—but he seemed to have forgotten that until this moment when he was watching her seated at a table with another man, a good-looking man, and he felt something like heat tingling in his arms and in his fingers. He sucked his stomach in and—as if he had suddenly had enough of looking at himself—started abruptly for the glass door.

He went directly to Lindsey's room, and she stood up at the sight of him. "Hank," she said. She looked to the guy at the table. "This is my husband." To Hank she said, "This is Detective Styne."

"Rubin," the detective said. He offered his hand to Hank. "I was just telling your wife: you need anything at all while you're here visiting, give me a call."

Hank shook his hand. "Thank you," he said, "but why would we need anything? Is there a problem?" He looked at Lindsey and shrugged as if to ask what was going on. On the phone, she had explained nothing.

The detective touched Hank's arm, friendly, as he slid past him. "I'll let you and your wife talk," he said, and then he pointed at Lindsey. "You have my card."

Lindsey smiled at him. "Yes, thank you," she said. When he was gone, she came around the table, gave Hank a look, and said, "That was rude. He was trying to be nice."

Hank threw up his hands and walked out of the room and then out of the kiosk with Lindsey following. On the street, he turned around and waited for her to catch up with him. "If it's not too much," he said, "would you mind telling me what's going on?"

Lindsey looked around her at the half-dozen people within earshot, looked back at Hank, and was silent. When the light changed, they stepped out into the street together and walked quietly side by side along Broadway, heading back toward the hotel. They were out of Times Square before there was enough distance between them and the scores of other pedestrians to talk with some degree of privacy.

"What happened?" Hank felt calmer after walking a couple of blocks. "How did you wind up at the police station?"

"Hardly a police station," Lindsey said. "I lost it a little, and they just— They made me a cup of tea. We talked—"

"What do you mean, *lost it?*" Hank stopped and pulled Lindsey aside, toward a storefront and out of the flow of foot traffic.

Lindsey hugged him around the waist and pressed her face into his chest, and Hank, surprising himself, hugged her tightly in return.

"Let's walk," she said. "I feel better walking."

"What happened?" Hank asked yet again. He took her hand, and they started along Broadway.

"The protesters," she said, "they must have—"

"What protesters?"

"You didn't notice them? They were all over the place."

Hank looked back toward Times Square.

"Trust me," Lindsey said, and then she took some time to explain about the Bush and Cheney actors, and the young cop, and the girl giving the speech. "That girl—" she said. "It was like, I don't know— God said, *Send her a message!*"

"Send who a message? You?"

"Yes, Hank," Lindsey said, as if it should have been obvious. "Send me a message."

"About the war? Why? You've been against the war—"

"Not the war," she said.

"Then what?"

"Everything."

"Honey—" Hank grasped his forehead with the palm of his hand. "How did you wind up at the police station? What happened?"

Lindsey thought about the question for a moment. Finally she said, as if the answer she was settling on was inadequate, "I sat down on the street to listen, and then I was just, I don't know, crying. That same young cop, the one I told about Ronnie, he brought me back to the station."

"Who was the other guy? The guy you were sitting with?"

"The detective?" They had reached the corner of 45th, and they waited with a small group of people at the light. "His family is all military except him. He's lost two nephews, one in Iraq, one in Afghanistan. He understood about Ronnie."

"That's what giving you his card was about?"

"Anything we need," Lindsey said. "He was serious."

"Honey—" Hank started to ask her what the hell was going on with her, and stopped. On the street, a double-decker sightseeing bus rolled by, followed by another exactly like it. Scores of tourists looked out over railings and down to the street. "I'm worried about Kate," he said, and he found his cell phone in his pocket and flipped it open.

Lindsey reached up and closed the phone before he could dial Kate's number. "Can we talk about us for a moment, please?" she said. "Kate will be okay."

Hank put the phone back in his pocket. "She's never been to New York before," he said. "I just abandoned her to come get you."

"Kate's all grown-up. She'll figure it out."

"I know Kate's grown-up—"

"Then forget about Kate for a minute, okay?" She looked up at Hank angrily. "This whole thing with Kate and Avery— Avery's fine. Kate's the one with the problem."

Hank folded his hands on top of his head for a moment, as if surrendering. "Her daughter drops out of college," he said, "she's here with some guy nobody knows—and it's not a problem? What are we doing here, then? Why'd we make the trip?"

"You made the trip," Lindsey said, "because Kate asked you. Ever since Tim died, you've been looking out for her. Which, honestly, Hank, at this point, really—" She stopped and put her arms on her hips as she faced him. "Enough is enough," she said. "It's been four years."

Hank's breath went out of him for a moment. A pair of men in shorts and T-shirts walked around him, looking worriedly at Lindsey as they passed. He said, "You've never said a word about having a problem with Kate."

"I don't have a problem with Kate. I'm just saying—enough. We have a problem, you and me. And you're worried about Kate."

"What problem?" Hank said. "What problem do we have?" Lindsey didn't answer for a moment. Then her face blanched, and she looked vulnerable in a way that made Hank want to hold her. "What?" he asked again, as gently as he could manage. "What problem?"

Lindsey said, "I'm not going back to Salem." The way she said it, it was if it were something she herself had just realized, and she was as surprised by it as she knew Hank would be. Then she looked at him as if he were someone she didn't know very well, and she walked away, up the street.

For a minute, Hank remained motionless, a statue bolted to the sidewalk. He watched Lindsey walk off as a clump of pedestrians approached and then split and made their way around him, and then his view of Lindsey was blocked, and still he didn't move. For a moment, he had thought Lindsey knew about Kate. For an instant, it had seemed possible that she had known about Kate all along. Now it felt like a crazy thought, but back there, in that moment, he had half expected her to say, *The affair has got to end*, and he had been ready to grovel and beg her to forgive him. That was the thing caught up in his thoughts as he stood like a lost boy in the center of the street, surrounded by the loud grumble of buses and the engine hum of traffic and the hundreds of overlapping sounds that made up any moment in a city like this: without a second thought, he would have begged Lindsey to forgive him.

There were times, in Salem, when he had entertained the possibility of leaving Lindsey. There were times when he'd thought he couldn't put up with one more of her sarcastic comments or one more complaint, and times when he'd thought he was just plain tired of her, and that he'd jump at a way out of the marriage if only something would present itself. These were always, he understood, background thoughts—the kind, he imagined, everyone who was married entertained more frequently than they would admit. Still, he was surprised at how genuinely insubstantial all those thoughts really were when the moment came that it seemed possible he might really have to make a choice—because there was no choice. There was only Lindsey, who was his wife, and whom he couldn't, in that moment, imagine not being his wife. What he felt in that instant was shame. It was as if he had been going along thinking somehow that it was completely impossible that Lindsey would ever find out about Kate, and the possibility that she knew was like getting hit with a two-by-four—and shame rose up in him and knocked the breath out of him before he realized that she didn't know. But still . . . He felt like he had come much too close to something that would have been more terrible than he had understood.

But she didn't know, and he wasn't moving because he needed a few moments to regain his balance and remind himself of that. She didn't know. He could put that issue, for the moment, aside. Then all he was left with was Lindsey saying she wasn't going back to Salem—which didn't make any sense. Hank took a few quick steps up the block and then broke into a jog. Lindsey was fifty people in front of him. When he caught up with her, she was walking briskly, as if in a hurry. He settled in beside her and matched her pace.

"We could come up with two hundred and fifty to three hundred thousand dollars," Lindsey said without waiting for Hank to speak. "If we liquidate everything and sell the house, we should come out with that much, at least."

Hank said, "That would be every cent we have."

"Exactly. That's what I just said."

"Why would we want to do that?"

"So we could start again." Lindsey stopped and took his hand and looked up at him. "I'm serious," she said, and then she started walking again and pulled him along.

Hank pulled his hand loose. "You want to pack up Keith and move to New York? You expect me to go along with that? Or am I even a part of this fantasy?"

"You're included," Lindsey said. She added, "It's not a fantasy. I mean it. I can't go back to Salem."

"Lindsey, please," Hank said. "Your son is in Salem."

"I could stay here while you make the arrangements. Keith is fine with his cousins. I could get us started here, and you could come back with Keith."

"And your father?"

Lindsey shook her head, as if the thought of her father was just too sad. "He doesn't know what's going on anymore," she said. "Eventually we could find a place for him here." She shuffled closer to Hank, bumping up against him. "We have enough to rent a place and put Keith in school, and still have plenty of time to find good jobs." When Hank remained silent, she said, "Do you understand I'm serious?"

Hank said, "You're stressed."

"Don't do that." Lindsey squinted the way she did when she was mad. "My mother used to do that."

"Do what?"

"Not take me seriously whenever I proposed anything she didn't want to hear."

"How can I take this seriously? You want to, just like that, move to Manhattan? I'm supposed to take that seriously?"

"Hank—" Lindsey stopped and put one hand on each of his shoulders, lining him up so that he was looking directly at her. "Try to listen to me," she said. "I'm not going back to Salem."

Hank looked at Lindsey and was silent. He was hoping she wouldn't press him for a response and was grateful when she dropped her arms and took his hand in hers and started walking again.

"I know this is going to be hard, and it sounds crazy, but will you just listen a minute?"

"Okay," Hank said. "I'm listening."

"We can do this," she said. "I know you're thinking this is crazy. But Hank, really, consider a minute." She squeezed his hand and twisted around to meet his eyes. "You never wanted to be a land-scaper, and I never wanted to be a housekeeper with a bullshit job sitting at a desk in an empty museum I couldn't even pretend meant anything. My mother died, and then we just wound up doing those things."

"It's not that simple," Hank said.

"Yes, it is," Lindsey said. "We're not in control of our lives."

Hank said, "Are you saying you married me because your mother had just died?"

"Oh, please," Lindsey said. "We've had this discussion before. All I'm saying is my mother dying had a lot to do with us going back to Salem and doing the whole ceremony and then having Keith right away."

"Okay," Hank said. "But—"

"I know this will be huge and scary," Lindsey said, "this move. But it's a chance to get our lives back. Please . . . think."

Hank pretended to be considering Lindsey's arguments. There was street work going on, and the explosion-loud report of a jack-hammer pummeled both of them for a moment, and they turned to follow the sound. When it stopped, Lindsey went back to her argu-ments and Hank walked quietly beside her. She was going into de-tails, explaining how it could be done, where she'd stay while he took Kate back to Salem, what to do with Keith, how to explain it to him. She was talking about finances and selling their home and moving companies and packers and New York real estate, and he nodded and half heard what she was saying but made no effort to really take any of it in. They weren't moving to New York. She'd figure that out for herself soon enough. Three hundred thousand might sound like a lot of money, but you couldn't buy a shack in New York for that figure—and it was a generous guess at every cent they had. It wasn't reasonable, no matter what kind of sense it might make or might not make.

Hank made an effort to listen, but he found himself thinking about how they might change their lives at home to make Lindsey happier. He might be able to convert the garage into a studio so she could start painting again. They didn't need the income from her job. She could quit that if she wanted and look for something better. He could take her out to dinner more often. They could make regular trips to New York, if that was important to her. He had no problem with the Hudson Hotel. They could spend long weekends there a few times a year. All that was doable. All that was possible.

Beside him, Lindsey reached into her bag and pulled out a pack of cigarettes. "Are you listening to me?" she said, and she tapped a cigarette out of the pack and lit it.

"Of course I'm listening," Hank said. "You want me to repeat it back to you?"

Lindsey gave him a look, as if she were considering taking him up on his offer. Then she started in again on her plans, saying she might be able to find a job in a gallery, she had the experience and the education, and he might be able to find a job in management, he had the degree and he could embellish what he'd been doing the last eight years in the construction business. Hank listened and tried to look like he was considering everything she said, weighing it all seriously.

What he was thinking about, though, was how he could keep her happy until this all passed. He was shuffling around the bits and pieces of his life, trying to figure out what could be moved and what could be changed to keep it all from flying apart. He meant to keep it all together, and thoughts were bouncing around in his head like a popcorn machine while he leaned close to Lindsey and every once in a while made a sound like he was responding to something she'd said.

Lindsey talked for block after block, until they were coming up on Columbus Circle and she said, "Why aren't you saying anything? You better be listening to me, Hank."

Hank said, "I'm listening. I promise."

Lindsey stopped and nodded toward Columbus Circle, to the city reflected in the walls of glass. "It's beautiful," she said, "isn't it?"

"Yes," Hank said, and he put his arm around her shoulder.

Lindsey leaned into him. "I love you," she said. "I hope you understand all this, Hank. I hope you understand what I'm saying."

"I understand," Hank said, and he squeezed her shoulder and kissed her on the top of the head.

"Good," she said, and she started in again, talking about New York and Manhattan as if it were already their new home.

GRANT snapped his cell phone closed and tossed it to the foot of the bed. The apartment was sweltering, and he was naked except for a thin strip of white sheet over his thighs, as if for modesty. He turned off the air conditioning at night, and Avery had forgotten to turn it on when she'd left for work. In the living room, strips of sunlight slithered around the sides and bottoms of the shades and lay in slivers on the floor and over the cluttered coffee table and on the leaves of a hanging plant that was Avery's one addition to the place. He guessed it was after eleven, and when he sat up and retrieved the phone, he saw it was nearly noon. Albert had laughed when he'd heard the sleep in Grant's voice, but the laugh was friendly, as if he were only amused at finding Grant sleeping late into the day. He had called to tell Grant to get dressed and ready, he'd be over in an hour to take him to Belmont. He wanted to talk about a few things. In that moment on the phone, in a corner of his mind, Grant had considered running, thinking Albert meant to kill him—when had he, or anyone in Billy's crew, ever wanted to talk to him about anything?—but by the time he'd snapped the phone closed, he'd put that fear out of his mind. Billy wasn't going to have his nephew killed over nothing, and Albert wouldn't take him to a racetrack to do it. If they wanted to kill him, they'd just call him into work and do it in the middle of the night, in a warehouse someplace in North Carolina.

Still, when he considered running, the first place that came to mind was Leigh's, and he wondered about that, sitting up in bed, his body slick with sweat. Why not Jesh at Penn State? Why Leigh? He wiped the sweat from his forehead and climbed out of bed to turn on the air conditioning, before collapsing onto the couch. In front of him, a half-crumpled pack of Viceroys leaned against an overflowing ashtray on the coffee table. He tapped out a cigarette and lit up. Albert had given no clue what he wanted to talk about, but one guess Grant entertained was that Uncle Billy might have changed his mind, and Albert might be bringing him an offer of some kind. It hardly seemed likely, given the way the previous day's conversation had gone. But it was possible. If anyone had asked Grant before yesterday, he'd have said that his uncle liked him. Grant had expected the conversation to go differently. He had expected Billy to be pleased. In the living room, with the air conditioner yet to make a dent in the heat, Grant exhaled smoke into a line of sunlight and watched it billow and swirl—and his thoughts moved from Albert and his uncle and Belmont Raceway to Avery.

She had come back from the party in a taxi, giddy and high, her eyes red from smoking. She came through the living room door grinning mischievously, leaned against it with her arms dangling behind her, and gave him a look that wasn't hard to interpret. He was on the couch reading when she came in, and he laughed and said, "Let me get high too." He went into the bedroom and retrieved a spliff from a small wooden box. By the time he got back to the living room, she was in her bra and panties, stretched out on the couch. He sat facing her with his legs crossed, and she put her feet in his lap. While he smoked, she chatted about the party and tried to unbutton his shirt with her toes.

Grant said, "That must have been good weed." He smoked and offered her the spliff while he was holding his breath.

Avery shook her head. "The place was unbelievable," she said. "It was like somebody dropped one of those old Victorian houses inside an apartment building by mistake."

"Money," Grant said, his voice high and squeaky, letting as little smoke out as possible.

"And celebs," Avery said. She laughed as if there were something funny about celebrities. "John . . . Turturro. And . . . that new novelist, the one in the news—"

"Stop," Grant said. He crawled over her and put his head on her belly while he reached to drop the spliff in the ashtray. "No celeb sightings, not permitted here."

Avery wrapped her hands around his back. "Something about being around all those . . . glitterati," she said, "it's got me hot and bothered."

"Uh-huh," Grant said, amused at the word *glitterati*, which he was pretty sure he had never heard anyone actually say before. "Money is sexy," he said, and he looked up along her belly to a strapless black bra that pushed up against her breasts. He pulled it away and she slid down under him, and two seconds later he was standing on the couch and she was against the wall and then they were in the middle of the living room, and against the door, and then, finally, in bed, where he finished before she did, and fell off her and onto his side, and said, "Sorry. You're too much."

She cuddled against his back and kissed his cheek. "You're spectacular," she said.

"You okay?" he asked. He wasn't sure she understood what he was asking.

She stroked his thighs and wrapped her arms around him and pressed her body into his. After a minute, after Grant had forgotten that he'd even asked the question, she said, "I'm delicious. I've never felt this good in my life."

"Really?" Grant said. He was looking at the wall, at a blank space below the bookshelves. "Even though . . ."

"I feel like . . ." She paused a long time, as if looking for the right words.

"Like what?"

"Like I was never happy a day in my life until I met you."

Now, on the couch, in the living room, with the air conditioning finally beginning to have an effect on the heat, Grant put out his cigarette and carried the ashtray into the kitchen. Avery had pulled up the blinds to let in morning light, so he found himself looking out through tall kitchen windows across their overgrown yard to the back of the Chinese restaurant on Manhattan Avenue, where a small man in a white apron held a long knife in one hand and a duck dripping blood in the other. He shook the duck as if trying to hurry the blood. Grant closed the curtains and got into the shower, where he ran the water as hot as he could bear it. He hadn't responded to Avery when she'd said she hadn't been happy until she'd met him. He had lain quietly a long while and when he had turned to look at her, she'd been sleeping. She had folded her hands under her head like a little girl, and he had pulled the sheets up and put a pillow under her head, and then he had surprised himself by kissing her on the temple—and that was the moment he was thinking about in the shower, when he'd kissed her like that. She'd been living with him for more than a month, which was a record for Grant. He hadn't expected her to stay for more than a week or two at most, and here it was double that and no sign of her getting ready to leave, no sign of her wanting to go back, only *I was never happy a day in my life until I met you*, which should have been the kind of sentimentalism that made him blush, only he had replayed the words a hundred times already trying to get a handle on how they made him feel, which seemed to be a mix of surprise and disbelief and gratitude. He had no idea why he should feel that way, which worried him. He tried to think back to Terry, who, in his private narrative, was the only woman he thought of himself as having loved—but it was so long ago, and so much had happened in between, and all those old feelings about Terry were colored by the way they'd changed as the relationship had changed, colored by current feelings and feelings from the recent past as she'd gone on to a good career and he'd done nothing but blind himself with drugs and a parade of women until the whole of life between then and now was a kind of speed blur, an afterimage, an ecstasy trail. His life hurtling away from him.

In the morning, they had made love again. There was a wildness in Avery that seemed to have little to do with him. He'd seen it in her from the start, through the drunkenness out on that balcony,

whenever she was quiet, when she wasn't speaking and lost in whoever she thought she was—then there was that electricity about her.
Zoo saw it in her too, they all did, and there was something about the
balance that was attractive, the chaos and order, as if they were both
extreme in her, and it made him wonder what it must be like inside
her head, and then it came to him, like a fact, that it was only a matter
of time before Avery, like Mei Mei, like Jesh, like all his friends,
found what she wanted to do and succeeded at it. He seemed to be
drawn to such people, and whatever it was that they had, she had it
in excess—and he didn't. Or he didn't anymore. He had either never
had it, or it had been snuffed out in him or he had snuffed it out, or
it was there but buried and lost. He didn't know what was what or if
he was even thinking straight when it came to that, to who he was
and what he was supposed to be doing—but the thought of Avery
joining Terry and Jesh and Mei Mei while he still eked out a living at
bullshit made his muscles go tense until it felt like he was cramping
all over. He threw his head back and stretched up toward the hot
water and made his mind go blank while the water eased him again
and he willed himself loose and calm.

By the time he was showered and dressed, it was after one o'clock,
and he locked the apartment and went out to wait on the front steps.
Another gorgeous day, summery, though October was around the
corner. At the entrance to McCarren Park, a panhandler in a wheelchair was hitting up a girl in a bright yellow dress for change. He had
his cupped hands out as the girl rummaged through her purse, came
up with a clump of coins, spilled them into his open palms, and disappeared into the park. While Grant was watching the drunk count

his money, Albert pulled up in front of the fire hydrant and tapped his horn.

"Hey," Grant said, settling himself into the car, "look at you." Albert was wearing khakis and a plaid, short-sleeved shirt. "I haven't seen you in anything but a suit since forever."

Albert said, "I don't wear a suit to the track," and he pulled out into the street. "BQE's jammed, but what the fuck—" He glanced over at Grant. "We're in no hurry, right?"

"You got a horse?" Grant asked.

"Filly called Benny's Future's been funding my retirement. She's in the seventh. You like the track?" he asked. "You go?"

"Handful of times," Grant said. "I know how to handicap a race, that's what you mean."

"No kidding. You can show me, then." He turned the air conditioning down and gestured out the window toward a girl walking along the street in denim shorts and a skimpy tank top. "Look at that," he said. "How come they got all the beautiful girls this part of Brooklyn?"

Grant followed the girl, turning so he could see her face. "I know her," he said. "You're out of luck. She's taken."

"You think that makes me out of luck?" Albert said.

When Grant didn't answer, a comfortable silence replaced the banter. Albert and Grant had spent enough time traveling together over the years that they knew how to be silent in each other's company. Even with traffic, Grant figured, they'd be at Belmont soon enough. He considered asking Albert what this trip was all about. If Albert had talked Billy into giving him a job, the question was, what job? He decided not to push, to let it play out. He was curious, though, and as he sat back in the passenger seat, trying to relax and enjoy the ride, he realized he was also at least a little excited.

"So," Albert said, "you don't mind my asking—" They were merging onto the BQE, and the traffic, as Albert had warned, was bad. "Look at this," he said, "son of a bitch."

"Asking what?" Grant stretched as if barely interested, his palms flat against the roof of the car.

"Anything in particular precipitate your wanting to meet with Billy yesterday? You got something going on in your life?"

"Not really," Grant said. "I've got a girl living with me. That's new."

"Something serious?" Without waiting for an answer, he added, "How old are you, Grant?"

"Thirty-seven."

Albert's eyes were on the traffic, but his thoughts were obviously elsewhere. He looked as though he were working out an elaborate calculation.

"What's up, Albert? You want to talk to me about something?"

Without looking away from the traffic, Albert said, "Obviously I want to talk to you about something, Grant. I said as much when I called, didn't I?"

"So? Go ahead." Grant twisted to face the driver's seat. "You have something you want to say to me in confidence?"

"I've been watching you a long time," Albert said. "Many years."

"And?"

Albert hesitated again. He edged the car into the far left lane as the traffic started to move a bit. "And," he said, "the nature of this business you're exploring an interest in—" He paused again, as if looking for the right words. "The nature of this business is ruthless. You need to understand that."

Grant said, "I know what you guys do for a living. That was you sitting beside me that night, wasn't it?"

"That was self-defense," Albert said. "That was a no-brainer. Somebody's about to shoot you, you shoot first. That's easy, my friend."

"Really?" Grant said. "Didn't feel easy."

"Trust me," Albert said. "What I'm talking about now— This particular business, it's ruthless. Everyone gets into it knows that. I know it. Billy knows it. You need to know it. It's an understanding."

"I get it," Grant said. "It's a ruthless business."

"You get it on one level," Albert said, and then he stopped and his thoughts seemed to change track. "Listen," he went on, "I'm not ashamed of the choices I've made. At the heart of everything, Grant—" Albert took his eyes off the traffic to glance at Grant, as if to emphasize the importance of what was coming. "At the heart of even very good things, like the church, for instance, there's ruthlessness, there's doing the thing that has to be done to keep everything running the way it needs to. There's no pity, there's no ideals, there's nothing but what has to be done."

Grant watched the lines of cars and trucks slogging through traffic. Much as he tried to ignore it, he found himself annoyed at Albert's patronizing tone. "Even the church?" he said. "What seminary'd you go to, Albert?"

Albert ignored him. He swerved into the right lane, and the car behind them braked and hit its horn. "As I said," he went on, "I've been watching you for a long time, waiting for you to figure out who you are."

Grant said, "I wish you'd get around to whatever it is you're trying to say."

They had just turned onto the LIE. Traffic eased up, and Albert dropped one hand off the steering wheel. "Billy's getting old. He's running his business into the ground." He looked meaningfully at Grant as if to ask if he understood what he was being told. "He should retire to Florida someplace, but he's not going to. He's never going to. Anybody he thinks might present a threat to him, he keeps where he can watch them. You think Billy never brought you into the business because you were too good for it or something? You think he's keeping you out of it now because you're too old or whatever bullshit he told you?"

"What are you trying to say, Albert?" Grant was surprised by the degree of annoyance in his voice. "You think Billy sees me as a threat? Is that what you're saying?"

"You've been a concern of Billy's since the first day he laid eyes on you. He's kept you where he could watch you."

"That's crazy." Grant was quiet a moment, and then he laughed as if, on second thought, the notion were even more preposterous. He didn't know if Albert was trying to con him or if he was just out of his mind.

"I'm offering you fifty grand," Albert said, "and a share of the business. I already have my reputation. I'm a known quantity. You? You do this, people will fear you. There's certain parties lost respect for Billy. They're not afraid of him. Instead of doing what needs to be done, we've been running like chickenshit assholes. Why do you think the pickup and dropoff is different every other trip? You? After this? They'll respect—and fear."

Grant thought he understood what Albert was saying, but he found it so unlikely that it was as if he really didn't quite comprehend it.

"I'd be the one running things." Albert's tone had gone business-like, as if he had thought everything through and now was taking the time to explain. "Are you following me, Grant?"

"Is this all you?" Grant said. "Is this all your idea?"

"No." Albert seemed both surprised and pleased by the question. "I've got the people lined up that I need. This is something that's in process, but I've had my reservations. You're the last piece in the puzzle. Actually," Albert said, "it feels like fate. After you talked to Billy yesterday, I was, *Okay, now*—"

Grant said, "I'm not sure I know what you're talking about."

"You know what I'm proposing, though, right?"

Grant nodded.

"I'll be blunt as I can," Albert said. "No one's ever called me a genius, but I'm smart enough to know my limitations. Billy's going. That's happening—and he brought it on himself." He gripped the steering wheel hard, with both hands, as if to emphasize his resolve. "If it wasn't me, it'd be somebody else. Question is, how to do it. It doesn't do me any good, I take over and I don't handle all the situations we've got going on. That's been my hesitation. With you, supposedly somebody I'm bringing along but actually helping me run the whole show from the start. Like that, listen—" Albert's hands flew off the steering wheel for an instant, as if frustrated at not being able to adequately explain himself. "Listen," he said again, settling down. "I'm thinking, once you see how things work, you'd come up with some good ideas. My experience, your ideas . . . See what I'm saying?" He looked at Grant. "You still there?"

"I'm here," Grant said.

"You hearing me?"

"Yes," Grant said. "I'm hearing you."

"Good." Albert patted the seat beside him, as if patting Grant on the head. "Right now, you come in, you can expect, as is, you can expect to be making a lot of money very soon. But we figure things right, could be even more, a lot more, for both of us. There's no limit, really. Your uncle, if he doesn't have a couple million stashed in offshore accounts, I'll kiss your ass."

"A couple million?"

"At least."

"And I have to be the one to do this, why?" Grant started to massage his temples and then stopped quickly when he realized what he was doing. "You want to do this," he said, "but you don't want to do it alone? You want a partner?"

Albert shook his head. He looked worried again. "As I already said, this is something that's going to happen. I want you because—"

"All right," Grant said. "I get all that. But why would I have to be the one to actually do it? This is my uncle we're talking about."

"That's the point," Albert said. "You have to be the one—for it to go the way that's best all around. You didn't do it, there's no way you could have anything to do with anything. Be some people, even, think you should go away."

"Because he's my uncle," Grant said. "People'd think— But if I did it—"

"That'd be your reputation," Albert said, "and reputation, in this business— It's a big deal. That, and you're a Danko. Your uncle's reputation accrues to you. It don't make sense, but that's the way it is. People'll talk about you and your uncle like you're the same person. Watch."

"Christ," Grant said. In his head, he was telling himself to remain composed—but words seemed to be slipping out of his mouth with a will of their own. "And if—" he said, and then he managed to stop himself. He had started to ask what would happen if he said no. Anything Albert said in response to that question, though, would be meaningless. What could he say: *Then I'm going to have to kill you to keep you from going back to your uncle?* What could Grant say: *I promise I won't tell my uncle?* Now that the proposition had been made, Grant wasn't at all sure what his options were.

"And if you say no?" Albert said, finishing the question for him. "Then that's sticky," he said, "but it's not like I haven't thought it through." They were coming up on the Cross Island, and Albert slowed down as they approached the exit. "My thinking is," he said, "that after yesterday's words with your uncle, you'd be taking a serious risk, you went back to him with this. I mean, I don't want that to happen, and I don't think it's going to. A lot of this business is instinct, and I wouldn't be making this proposal if I wasn't pretty sure what your answer would be. But if I'm wrong?" he said. "I think I'll come out okay."

"And me?" Grant asked.

Albert didn't answer. He made a show of putting on the turn signal and checking traffic as he changed lanes. After a while, once they were on the Cross Island and close to Belmont, he said, "One more thing: you can't be doing any more of that Saint John bullshit. That's behind you."

"That's been behind me a long time," Grant said. He turned on the radio and started fiddling with the channels.

Albert touched his wrist and then turned the radio off. "I need an answer."

"I don't get to think about it?"

"Think," Albert said. "But I need an answer before we leave the track."

Grant leaned back in his seat and looked up at the ceiling of the car, as if he were wrestling with his thoughts for one last moment. He said, "I don't really need time to think. I've had all I can take of living on bullshit, and Billy made himself pretty clear yesterday about letting me in the business."

"That's exactly right," Albert said. "Long as he's running things, you'll never do anything more for us than drive a truck."

Grant sighed, as if relieved at having made a decision. "So?" he said. "What's next?"

Albert looked proud of himself. Grant tried to look as if he too were pleased at his choice when, in truth, he had no idea yet about what to do, or what he should do, or even what he could do. He was acting for Albert's benefit. Belmont was a huge racetrack with extensive grounds, and it seemed entirely possible to Grant that, should he say no, or should Albert even think he was considering saying no, he'd wind up under a pile of hay and manure somewhere.

"You should have been in this business a long time ago," Albert said. He gestured to the glove compartment. "Open it."

Inside the glove compartment, Grant found a gun on top of a stack of bills.

Albert said, "Check it out."

Grant closed the glove compartment. "I'll check it out later," he said. "When are we thinking of doing this?"

"Tomorrow. Billy and I are going fishing in the morning, out of Canarsie. It's something we do a few times a year. You'll be waiting on the boat. I'll pick you up at five A.M., drop you on the boat. Then I'll go get Billy and bring him. We'll do it once we're out on the water."

"Tomorrow," Grant said.

"Tomorrow," Albert repeated. He opened the glove compartment, pulled out the cash, and tossed it to Grant.

Grant flipped through the bills. "This isn't fifty thousand,"

"It's money to play the horses."

Grant flipped through the bills again. They were all new hundreds.

"Five grand," Albert said. "A bonus to play around with. I'm telling you," he added, as if suddenly excited, "Benny's Future in the seventh. Make the bet, you can triple that five grand. Add the fifty grand you'll earn tomorrow— That's a good start, no?"

Grant didn't answer. He looked out the window at traffic.

At the entrance to Belmont, Albert handed the booth attendant a five and sped through to the parking lots, which were largely empty. "No one comes to the track anymore," he said. "It's all OTB and television—and now, with computers, bookies are dying."

Grant nodded and tried to look interested, though his thoughts were clumped around Albert's proposition and his response. On the way to the clubhouse, they drove past a chain-link fence separating the concrete and blacktop of the parking lots from the dirt of the track area, and they passed two grooms walking a pair of racehorses. The horses, their coats glistening, manes braided, tails combed out, looked to be in much better shape than the grooms, both of whom appeared scrubby and in need of a bath. Grant had folded the stack of bills and slid it into his pants pocket, and he laid a hand over the bump it made as if to remind himself that it was real, the situation he now found himself in, riding beside Albert on his way to a day at the track.

For years after he'd shot and killed that hijacker out in the middle of Nowhere, North Carolina, for years after that night he'd had dreams—still did, though rarely now—in which he'd murdered someone in the past, and somehow, in the dreams, he was always discovering it for the first time, as if he might have done it and forgotten it, or as if he weren't really sure that he'd done it, that he'd murdered someone, and then, in all these dreams, there'd be the moment when he realized it was true, he'd actually done it, really, he'd murdered someone, and often he'd wake up from the dream feeling sick and frightened, in the middle of the night, not knowing, still stuck in the dream's reality, whether or not he'd actually done it, actually murdered someone—and often it would take several minutes before he found his way back to the daily world, the waking world, the world in which he knew what had happened that night, had worked out what had happened, the killing an act of self-defense, a matter in which he had no choice, something he'd done with only an instant to think, if you could even call it thinking, grabbing the gun off the seat, thrusting it toward the figure coming into the window, seeing that figure leveling a gun at him, firing, the explosion like a cherry bomb going off next to his ear, the figure flying back and away into the speeding dark as he hit the gas and then the crumpling metal as the truck plowed through the car and off into this life he was leading now, on the way to the racetrack, trying to shrug off the dreamlike feeling of it all, of the whole situation, which was like one of those dreamscapes, one of those dream stories, as if he might wake up and find himself in his bed, in the middle of the night, alone.

"You all right?" Albert said. They were pulling up to the valet's stand in front of the clubhouse. "We're here. We're at the party. You ready to make some money?"

"I'm ready," Grant said. He pushed the door open as soon as the car came to a stop, happy to get out into the sunshine and air.

AT the Hudson, Lindsey stripped out of her clothes, threw on an old T-shirt, and collapsed into bed for a nap while Hank went to the bathroom to splash water on his face and take two Advil. He had started to develop a headache on the walk back from Times Square, and by the time he was on the narrow escalator, on his way up to the lobby, the back of his head was throbbing and the ceaseless noise of the city was threatening to unhinge him. The elevator was a sanctuary. He would have been happy to stop it between floors, stretch out on its carpeted floor, and luxuriate in the silence. Lindsey too had seemed worn out. She had slumped against the wall and looked vacantly at the elevator doors.

In the bathroom, he sat on the john and massaged his temples. The room was blessedly quiet, the sounds of the city muted and distant and dimmed by the white noise of the air conditioning. He took the cell phone from his pocket, worried that Kate hadn't called him yet, and grimaced to see that she had, several times, but that his ringer had been turned off. He didn't bother retrieving her messages; rather, he pulled himself to his feet and went to Lindsey, meaning to tell her he was going over to Kate's room. When he found her asleep, he kissed her on the back of the head and closed the door behind him quietly as he went out into the hall.

On the way to Kate's, he stopped in the narrow hallway and hung his head, taking a moment for himself in the quiet corridor. He felt a sharp annoyance toward Kate that was troubling, given that she hadn't done anything to deserve it. He hardly ever argued with her, yet he felt as though he were storming to her room, ready to scream at her. First her husband died suddenly, and now her daughter had run off and refused to even answer phone calls—and instead of feeling sympathy for Kate, instead of being there for her and trying to help, he felt as though he wanted to scream at her. He touched the back of his neck and rolled his head—and something popped so loudly he half expected a nearby door to open.

In Salem, when he visited Kate, it was usually in the evening. Early in the affair, he would sneak away from work and bring some takeout with him, Chinese or Italian or something from Mac and Bob's. The last year or more, though, he'd usually call and she'd make something for him, so it was a lot like going home—going to his real home with Lindsey and Keith. He'd come through the door at Kate's, and she'd greet him with a kiss, just as Lindsey usually did. Only at Kate's he made sure the door was closed and they were out of sight. And at Kate's he ate lightly so that he could eat again when he got home. And at Kate's, after dinner, they went directly to her bedroom, where their sex had quickly fallen into a routine. He'd go into the bathroom and wash up, and when he came out she'd be waiting for him in bed, the covers pulled up to her neck. She was shy about being seen—which was exactly the opposite of Lindsey, who would walk around naked all the time if it weren't for Keith.

At Kate's room, he paused another moment and then knocked.

Kate opened the door instantly and looked down the hall, as if checking for Lindsey. He stepped around her into the room.

Kate said, "Where did you disappear to?"

"Where's the thermostat?" Hank answered, hugging himself. "It's below zero in here." He scanned the walls.

"By the window. I was sweating from the walk back." Kate watched him as he leaned into the window frame. "What happened?" she said. "Why did you leave me there?"

Hank turned the thermostat up to 70 and sat on the bed, his back against the wall. "I was waiting for you," he said calmly, though his head felt like it might crack open, "and Lindsey called me from a police station."

"A police station?" Kate put her hands on her hips and waited for more.

"There were war protesters in Times Square. She sat down on the sidewalk and— She was crying, and a cop brought her to the station."

Kate took a few steps toward Hank and then collapsed onto the foot of the bed. She held her head in her hands.

Hank watched her silently. Her hair was a mess. It was pushed back, as if she had been running her hands though it. Her blouse had sweat stains under the arms, and her pants were unbuttoned at the waist and unzipped a little. He moved beside her and touched her back.

She exhaled loudly with a sound between a sigh and a moan. "God," she said, "everything's a disaster."

Hank moved closer and kneaded her shoulders. "It's not a disaster," he said. "It's not that bad," and he pressed his thumbs hard into the back of her neck, the way he knew she liked.

Kate let her head and arms go loose while Hank massaged her. "She loved Ronnie, and now the kid's dead at, what? twenty-four?" She tensed up again and made a sorrowful sound, a quick, guttural groan. "Tell me that's not a disaster."

Hank kissed her on the back of the head, which was a way of comforting her and saying he'd be happy if they dropped the subject of Ronnie and Lindsey. "How was Avery?" he asked. "How did it go?"

"She's lost weight, at least six or seven pounds."

"Is she too thin?"

"No. She looks good. She was like— She was pretty reasonable. We had a decent talk."

"Why hasn't she been answering her phone?"

Kate shrugged. "She said she was sorry."

"And?" Hank said. "Is she coming home?"

"She'll call tomorrow," Kate said. "We can all spend the day together. Then . . . I don't know. We'll see." Kate didn't sound overly upset, but her eyes were wet with tears.

Hank said, "It doesn't sound like you had a bad talk."

"I love her," Kate said, "and this is what I get." She covered her face with her hands. "For God's sake," she said, as if angry with herself. She dried her eyes with the back of her arm.

Hank said, in as calm a voice as possible, "You said she looks good. She looks like she's okay."

"She looks great. She looks confident and self-possessed."

Hank squeezed her shoulders as if to say, *See, she's okay*, and then he lay back on the bed with his feet on the floor. "I have a splitting headache," he said, and a moment later he added, "You're not going to believe this."

"What?" Kate seemed to be dragging herself up out of deep thought as she turned slowly to face him.

"Lindsey says she's not going back to Salem. She wants us to start a new life here, in New York, immediately."

"Are you serious?"

"Be a strange thing to kid about."

"And Keith? How could she—"

"I'm supposed to go get Keith, sell all our possessions, and come back here with the kid and the money, where we start fresh, start all over again."

Kate looked like she couldn't quite grasp what Hank was telling her.

"It's temporary insanity," Hank said, "but I have to figure out how to deal with it."

"I don't understand, *deal with it*?" Kate said. "You can't just move to New York. That's pretty simple."

"It's not that simple."

"Why not?" she said. "You'd consider pulling Keith away from everything he knows to bring him someplace where he has no family, no anything? Isn't Lindsey thinking about any of that?"

"She's not thinking clearly," Hank said. "This is all about

Ronnie." He rubbed the back of his head, meaning to remind Kate that he had a headache and could use a little tenderness.

"I'm sorry," Kate said, "but I think it is simple. You can't consider uprooting Keith like that, out of nowhere."

"She's my wife," Hank said. "I can't just dictate to her. I have a responsibility to listen. I have a responsibility to hear her out."

"You have responsibilities to your son."

"And not my wife?"

"Not when she's behaving like this, no."

Hank covered his eyes with his forearm and sank back into the darkness. He hoped Kate would be quiet for a moment. His headache, remarkably, seemed to be subsiding, the Advil finally, he guessed, kicking in. Out in the darkness somewhere, Kate said, "Let her move if she wants to move. Tell her you won't go with her and you're keeping Keith. You'd win a custody fight with Keith's whole family in Salem."

Hank opened his eyes to find Kate unmoved at the edge of the mattress. "There's not going to be any custody battle," he said.

"Are you sure?" she asked. "My experience with Lindsey, she doesn't fool around about things."

Hank sat up straight and touched his forehead as if he were checking for a temperature. "She needs some time," he said. "She'll figure out that this is all ridiculous. I don't believe she actually wants to pick up and move to New York."

Kate watched Hank quietly. She looked as if she were working through something puzzling. Then she said, as if amazed, "You're going along with her, aren't you? Did you tell her you'd do it, that you'd move here with her?"

"I didn't tell her we were moving to New York, no."

"But you didn't tell her you weren't," Kate said. "You didn't tell her it was out of the question."

"No." Hank turned his back to Kate as he slid to the opposite side of the mattress and propped up a couple of pillows under his back. "I didn't tell her it was out of the question, no."

"So she's down the hall," Kate said, "planning this move to New York. She's down there working out the details."

"She's sleeping," Hank said, and he didn't try to hide his annoyance with Kate.

"You know what?" Kate said. She put her hands on her hips. "I'm sorry, but I think you're behaving like a coward."

"Kate," Hank said.

"You're behaving like a coward, and Lindsey is behaving like a fool. I'm sorry, but someone needs to tell you."

"Kate," Hank said again, "you're way over the top. Keep in mind you're stressed too."

"I'm stressed, but that doesn't mean I'm wrong. I'm sorry for talking to you like this," she said, "but it's crazy, Hank. To really consider picking up and moving to New York is crazy."

Hank didn't say anything for a while. He watched Kate where she sat hunched forward, her hands over her eyes. She looked worn out. Finally he said, as gently as he could manage, "This isn't about Keith and Lindsey, this conversation we're having. It's about us."

"What *us?*" Kate said without taking her hands away from her face. "When has there ever been an *us?* There's me and you and what we're doing, what we do with each other. There's no *us.*"

Hank nodded, and then he sat up and pulled Kate's hands away from her eyes. "I'm sorry about all of it," he said. He hesitated a moment and then said, "It was a mistake, and I want it to be over."

"Really?" Kate backed away so she could see him better. "Everything, just like that, over?"

Hank walked around Kate toward the door. He tried to think of what to say next but came up with nothing. He felt like a fist was closing around his heart.

"Don't worry," Kate said, "I won't tell her." She paused, watching him. She said, "You're a bastard, Hank."

Hank said lamely, "I'm not a bastard."

Kate nodded, meaning yes, he was. "You do whatever the hell you want, don't you?"

"You know that's not true." Hank touched her on the arm, and she jerked away from him. "Kate," he said.

Kate turned her back to him. "Just get out of here," she said. "Really. Just go away, please."

For a moment, Hank considered changing his mind, apologizing. Saying he didn't know what had gotten into him, he was angry. She looked wounded. Her body hunched over.

Kate said, "Really, Hank. Will you get out of here, please?" Her body seemed to stiffen a little more with each word.

Hank spent another long moment struggling to come up with something to say before giving up and quietly leaving, going out the door like a kid being punished and sent to his room. Once in the hallway, though, with the door closed behind him, what he felt more than sorrow or compassion was relief. He was done with it, with the whole thing. He'd have the awkwardness of the long drive home, but they'd get through it and then they'd move on. It felt exhilarating in a way that surprised him. It felt as though he had just found his way out of a maze, and he hadn't even known he'd been in one. When the door to Kate's room clicked shut, he felt like the bastard she had told him he was, but by the time he rounded a corner on the way back to his room, he was feeling lighter and more energetic, as if he had been dragging something heavy for a long time and he'd just managed to cut himself loose.

IN Brooklyn, on the bench in front of Enid's, Avery crossed her legs demurely as she considered a whitewashed door on the other side of the street. The door looked battered and had a small window at eye level, and under the window were the words *Bright Red Door*. She didn't know what to make of it. The doorway was covered by an ornate wooden arch that looked misplaced jutting out of the bare brick wall surrounding it, as if the brick had once been covered by a facade that had been stripped away and someone had thought the elaborate arch too beautiful to remove. She made a mental note to photograph the door once her camera arrived. She had just called Chack, and he had offered to empty her room, put her stuff in storage, and mail her camera and other photography gear to Brooklyn. She told him he was a lifesaver and smooched the phone—and when she heard his laugh booming through the handset, she felt nostalgic for Penn State, as if she were a middle-aged woman thinking back to her college days. The ambiguity of the door was what interested her.

In this neighborhood, painting *Bright Red Door* on a white door was very likely intentional, a statement of some kind about the relationship between reality and language. On the other hand, the door appeared to actually have been bright red at one point, before it was whitewashed, and it seemed possible that the sign was meant to identify it for someone, *this is the door that used to be the bright red door*. Either way, it was interesting, and she'd photograph it, though documentary photography of doors, even interesting doors, wasn't going to get her anyplace in the art world.

At the party, the talk had been all about art, but it was clear that, among Mei Mei's friends anyway, all the traditional distinctions were passé. *Photography, painting, sculpture*—no one talked that way. Their notion of art was dynamic and fluid, as if it encompassed everything. There was some talk of an artist who had rented an amusement-park whirligig, filled the seats with paint, surrounded the ride with wall-sized canvases, and then let the thing fly. There was a gallery in Chelsea, apparently, showing her work. As the evening progressed, Avery saw clearly that she was going to have to start from scratch in her thinking about herself as an artist. When she walked into the party, she would have identified herself, had anyone asked, as a photographer; by the end of the evening, she wouldn't have known what to say. Not that anyone asked, or even had much of a chance to ask. Mei Mei kept her close, often on her arm, and directed the conversation to herself and a handful of other artists about whom she wanted to gossip. Not long into the party, someone in their circle pulled a spliff out of her handbag and started passing it around. After that and a few more identical episodes, Avery found herself relaxed and having a good time among the swirling chatter of beautiful bodies, several of which belonged to people she had previously seen only on screens or in newspapers and magazines.

Behind her, on the other side of the plate-glass window, a young couple with identically dyed platinum-blond hair broke into loud laughter, and Avery turned around in time to see them lean over their table, kiss, and then break into laughter again. She looked away as a waiter approached them carrying a tray of food. She checked the time on her cell phone and saw that Grant was late again, which was something she was coming to expect. She was wearing a new red dress, with black flats, and she was looking forward to his reaction when he saw her. It would be the first time, she was pretty sure, that he had seen her in a dress—and she loved the dress. Zoo had picked it out for her. They had been downtown together, on Broadway, and she had seen it in a boutique window and oohed and ahed over it; that night, he had shown up with it wrapped in a gift box. If he weren't Grant's closest friend and she hadn't known that he was wealthy with family money, she wouldn't have accepted it. She had, though, and she had been waiting for the right time to surprise Grant. When Grant called and told her he wanted to take her to dinner at Enid's, she decided it was the right time—and now she was sitting alone on a bench waiting for him.

Late at the Park Avenue affair, after most of the partygoers had left, Avery had found herself alone with Mei Mei on a balcony that looked out over a field of rooftops. They were both high and Avery was giggling like a little girl as Mei Mei riffed on the relationship between sex and success in the New York art world, spinning out story after story about who had had what kind of sex and with whom, as if artists documented it all and sent out a newsletter, with pictures, the next morning. Then there was a moment—they were leaning over the balcony railing—when Avery glanced at Mei Mei and saw that her breasts were mostly exposed. It was the way she was leaning on the balcony: her breasts rested on the railing, pushed up, and the tunic fell forward. Avery's eyes fastened on the sight, and when Mei Mei noticed what Avery was looking at, she pulled her down to her with one hand behind her head, casually, and kissed her on the lips, a deep tongue-in-mouth kiss, and then let her go and looked at her a moment, her eyes playful and wicked, before they both broke into laughter. Others joined them on the balcony, and the moment passed as if there were nothing particularly significant about it, as if it were a comic moment between them—but the thrill of the kiss was real, and Avery had thought about it on and off ever since.

Across the street, the white door that read *Bright Red Door* looked back at her as if it represented a secret message she couldn't quite interpret, God talking to her in puzzles and parables; then Grant pulled up in a yellow cab, startling her, since he rarely took cabs. He got out of the backseat, busy slipping his wallet into his pocket; at the bench, he leaned down to kiss her and then stood back a moment to look her over. "You're gorgeous," he said. "Where'd the dress come from?"

Avery said, "You're late. Dinner and arriving in a cab? Have we come into money?"

Grant took her hand and pulled her up. "We have," he said, "as a matter of fact. A work bonus."

Inside Enid's, they stood quietly side by side near the entrance and waited to be seated. Across the room, a girl in a miniskirt crossed her legs in an ancient photo booth, the curtain pushed aside, an *Out of Order* sign taped next to her head. Avery looked up at the tin ceiling, at a shelf dangling from the rafters, holding a junked receiver, its wires connected to nothing; at a big curving-arrow liquor sign that had obviously once hung outdoors and now added to the flea-market atmosphere of the decor, as did the gold-sequined camel hanging on a wall with peeling paint. Grant said, "I'm hungry," and then, as if his wish had conjured her up, a pretty girl in a granny dress appeared, led them to an open table, and dropped two menus in front of them. Grant watched the girl walk away. "I'm getting the meat loaf," he said. "It's good here."

Avery took a minute to look over the menu. "How about the sweet-potato quesadilla?"

Grant shrugged as if he'd never heard of such a thing. "Doesn't sound especially appealing."

Avery held the menu to her breast, her hand over her heart as if pledging allegiance. She said, "Guess who paid me a visit at work today?"

"Who?" Grant looked up from the menu.

"My mother," Avery said, her face a mix of shock and wonder.

"Your mother?" Grant said. "How did she find you? I thought—"

"Remember when you said you thought someone was following us? At the Thai place?"

"Really? She hired a detective?"

"Unbelievable," Avery said, and she opened her hands in a gesture of resignation.

"So, what?" Grant said. "What happened?"

"Nothing." Avery's tone suggested that she didn't want to dwell on the subject. "We talked. I'm going to spend the day with her to-morrow."

"Doing what?" Grant seemed amused.

"She drove up with my aunt and uncle," Avery said. "I don't know. . . ." She threw her hands up, meaning she didn't want to talk about her family anymore. When Grant looked down at his menu again, she slid back a little from the table. "Zoo got me this dress," she said. "Are you jealous?"

Grant smiled broadly and then laughed, as if the thought of Zoo made him happy. "And you imagined it was a present for you?" he said.

Avery had to think about that for a minute. "Oh," she said. "Okay. Well? Do you like your present?"

Grant folded his hands on the table and looked Avery over care-fully, as if he were examining her, attempting a diagnosis—and as he observed her, his expression grew more serious. "Do you know," he said finally, "you've practically transformed since you got here?"

"Transformed? That's a little over the top, don't you think?"

"I don't think so," he said. "I mean, literally."

"Please." Avery leaned closer to him. "What was I, a pumpkin?"

Grant looked away, toward the bar. "It's partly the hair and the weight," he said, and then he turned to meet Avery's eyes again. "You lost weight and cut your hair, and you're dressing differently, but—"

"What?" Avery said. "Something else?"

"Something else."

"And what do you think it is?"

"Us, maybe," he said, as if trying to sound cavalier as a cover for being serious.

"Us?" Avery made a face that said, *Tell me more.*

"Did you mean it last night when you said you'd never been happy a day in your life until we met?"

Avery pulled her chair closer to the table. She said, "Are you getting serious on me, Grant? I feel like you're about to tell me you love me."

Grant didn't smile or laugh, as Avery had expected. He only watched her, his hands folded in front of him.

"That would be amazing progress," Avery said, "for a relationship that began with a rape."

Grant looked confused. "The lake? You were an animal that night," he said. "We were both animals."

"I'm not arguing that," Avery said. "I'm just saying you never asked."

Grant studied her face. He said, "I can get myself excited just thinking about that night. What do you feel when you think about it?"

Whenever Avery thought about that night on Raystown Lake, she found herself in the moment when he first entered her. Her back is against the tree and she feels him inside her and then she's at the moment again where she can resist what's happening or throw herself into it, and she remembers the sound that comes out of her throat as she pushes down on him and feels him up in her belly while she wrestles him, hugging him violently, moving brutally, and she remembers that in that moment, in the moment when she chooses to attack rather than resist, it's Grant who's off balance, Grant who has to struggle to keep from falling. In Enid's, thinking back to that night to answer his question—*What do you feel when you think about that night?*—she came to the same place she always came to, a place of confusion where there were no real answers to reasonable questions because reason was someplace else in that moment, and what was left in its place didn't answer questions. "*Excited* is a good enough way to describe it," she said. "I feel excited when I think back to it."

"Then let's forget the rape stuff," Grant said, and he reached across the table to take her hand.

Avery nodded as if to agree with him, though the agreement meant nothing because the whole issue was an ongoing confusion.

Grant said, "We do something to each other. We make each other different somehow."

Avery squeezed Grant's hands and then pulled hers away. She cocked her head. "You're behaving oddly," she said. She squinted at him. "What's going on?"

"I'm trying to be serious," he answered. "Is it that strange?"

"Yes," she said and laughed. "It's making me nervous."

Grant settled back in his seat. "Okay," he said. He picked up the menu and looked it over.

"All right," Avery said. "How do we make each other different?"

Grant didn't answer. A moment later, the waitress came back, and they ordered. At the bar, a couple broke into laughter and the noise level in the restaurant seemed to go up a notch.

Avery said, "We've already determined that you make me crazy and happy. What do I do for you?"

Grant thought a moment before he said, "You make me want to do something with my life."

"Like what?"

"Like something more than drive a truck."

"You think it's me," Avery said, "making you unhappy with your life?"

"In part," he said. "There's something about you that—" He stopped, at a loss for words.

"What's going on with you tonight?" Avery asked. "I feel like something's wrong."

Grant didn't answer immediately. He seemed frozen in place, sitting upright in his chair, staring at her. Then he said, "I'm thinking of becoming a murderer."

"Oh. Really? Any particular reason?"

"To get ahead. There's excellent money in it."

"And you think you're qualified for the job?"

"Sure. I've done it already, actually."

"You've murdered someone?"

"Yes," Grant said, "but in self-defense, a long time ago."

Avery said, "You're making me a little nervous, Grant. We are kidding around, aren't we?"

Grant closed his eyes and his body seemed to go soft, as if he were taking a quick nap at the table.

"Grant," Avery said, "tell me you're kidding. Quickly."

When Grant opened his eyes, he was wearing his familiar smirk. "I'm speaking metaphorically," he said. "I'm thinking about taking a straight job. Something where I could make a good living."

"Oh," Avery said. "Thank God." She looked around the restaurant and saw their waitress at the bar, flirting with the bartender. "I'm getting hungry," she said, and when she looked back, Grant's smirk had morphed into a sneer. He seemed suddenly angry. "You mean," she said, "you're thinking of giving up on a career as an artist? Is that what—"

"Are you mocking me?" he said. "What career as an artist? You see anything in my life that looks like art?"

Avery said, "You're friends with artists," and then hurried to come up with something else to say when she saw the look of fury that came over him, as if he thought she really was mocking him. "What about Saint John?" she said. "You got serious attention for that. I mean, you were written up—"

"That was always more Jeshua than it was me," Grant said, and then their waitress appeared at the table and slid plates in front of them. Neither Grant nor Avery looked at her. When she was gone, Grant said, "Have you ever read Revelations?" When Avery shook her head, he said, "Violence?" He forked a bite of his meat loaf, lifted it to his mouth, and then put it down again, as if he'd lost his appetite. "Armies of locusts with men's faces, with shields and swords, and when they sting you with their tails, you suffer for five months before you die."

"Lovely," Avery said. She held up a bite of the quesadilla. "This is delicious."

Grant played with his meat loaf, jabbing it with his fork and moving it around on his plate. "My Saint John," he said, still looking at his food, "he could be angry. He'd mock the boomers, the ex-hippies—"

"I've got an uncle who was a hippie," Avery said. "I've got a picture of him with hair down to the middle of his back."

"My mother got caught up in all that too," Grant said. He stopped playing with his food. "That whole generation, they tore everything down, but they didn't give us anything in its place." He put his fork down gently, though he looked like he wanted to throw it at someone. "Sex is fine," he said, meaning that was what the boomer generation had taught its children. "Drugs are not really a problem." He asked Avery, "How old were you when you started having sex?"

"I was in college."

"You're the exception, then. I was fourteen; the girl was fifteen."

"Did you like it?" Avery asked. "Was it good? Or am I supposed to think that's too young; that's bad? Because the way I remember it, at fourteen and fifteen, all anybody can think about is sex."

"That's not the point," Grant said. "The point is a system of belief that you can live by. Without it, we're clueless."

"Grant," Avery said, "you're scaring me. This is your Saint John character talking, right? This isn't you."

Grant smiled enigmatically.

"Who are you?" Avery asked. "Really?"

"Me?" Grant said. "I'm the anti-Christ."

"Really," she said. "You. Grant. What do you believe?"

"Nothing," Grant said.

Avery leaned over the table and held her head in her hands.

"Relax." He touched her hand. "You're beautiful, and I'm fucked up. It's that simple."

"Oh," Avery said, going back to her food. "You're complicated, and I'm simple. Is that it?"

"You're not simple," he said. "You're anything but simple."

"Thank you."

"You're welcome. Want to go over to Galapagos when we're done here? One of my artist friends," he said, "is performing tonight."

Avery said, "I'm sorry I said that. I didn't mean—"

"Not a problem. You want to go?"

"Sure," Avery said, and she took the last bite of her quesadilla. Grant watched her a moment and then, finally, went at his meat loaf, which he had only picked at before. Avery considered asking him again what he really believed, about values, about behavior, but decided against it. Instead she said, "Something's bothering you tonight." She waited, then added, "We don't have to talk about it. That's fine. I just want you to know I can see it."

Grant looked up to smile at her and then went on eating.

HE used her and went home to the woman he really loved. That was the truth of it. Home to the woman he really loved, and anything else was a lie she deluded herself with—about time she faced that. If it took this to make her face that, good. About time. He showed up after work, had sex with her—which he hardly seemed to even like— and then went home to the woman he loved, if he was even capable of love, which was an open question. There was that truth about men, about all men, about Hank, about Tim: they were driven to sex, a woman could see it in their eyes, the way they looked hungry. It wasn't need, it was beyond need, it was a drive. That was all it had ever been for him, for Hank, an animal drive—the rest of it, the stories, the words, all pretext, all a game. That was all it was. That might be, in the end, all everything was. Romance, philosophy, love, all of it. He loved Lindsey because she was young and beautiful, but she'd be old soon enough, and he'd look elsewhere. That was the blessed truth. Can you call that love? If you want a woman when she's sexually attractive and then lose interest when she's not? How can you call that love? It was more about propagation, about making babies. Which was why it was an open question, if he was even capable of love, if men ever were really, any of them, capable of love.

Kate was standing in the narrow corridor looking at the closed door through which Hank had just left. The room was quiet, only the soft hum of the air conditioning and the occasional sounds of traffic. She seemed unable to move as she stood and looked at nothing, a steady flow of thoughts transfixing her, keeping her standing quietly, her arms heavy at her side. Something was ticking somewhere. It sounded like a pipe steadily contracting or whatever it was pipes did when they clicked like that. Out in the hall, someone walked by chatting with someone else. Their voices swelled and diminished and then were gone, and the room was quiet again.

Tim had cheated on her. Twice that she knew of. It was odd, but, though it seemed like the end of the world the first time it happened, and she almost divorced him the second time, now . . . she seemed now to have forgotten it. Or if not forgotten, then put it aside. At the time it was a terrible secret: night after night she cried, fearing someone else would find out, the family might come to know, almost as if that bothered her as much as the betrayal, if not more, that others would know. She had told no one. Not even Corinne. But Salem was a small town and she knew there were people who knew and she feared it would get out and she hated that, others knowing, almost though if no one knew it was not as bad, it could be more easily survived. Why was that? Because she needed the story they made: Kate and Tim and Avery. It was about that. She needed it: Kate loved Tim, Tim loved Kate, Avery was their beautiful girl. Why did she want that story so desperately? If Tim cheated, he ruined it, but only if others knew. If no one knew, then the story remained unchanged, and it was the story that was so important because it was the story that they lived in their public lives, in their lives involving others. But why was that more important? Avery had never known about the affairs. The family still didn't know. But Kate knew, and truth was that while Tim was alive the knowledge was like something sharp lodged inside her and while he was alive she could feel it all the time and now that he was dead she didn't feel it anymore. It was like that. She forgot it was inside her, though it was still there, and now she remembered what men were like, all of them. *Dogs*, other women said. *Men are all dogs*.

Kate leaned against the wall and watched the closed door as if she might bolt out of the room. She'd had a dream weeks ago where she was on an elevator and something went wrong and it descended into a basement beneath a basement, a sub-basement that no one knew about. She was trying to get somewhere and she had to walk through an abandoned building and in order to get to the street she had to take this elevator. In the dream she found herself in a gutted room looking into the elevator and she knew taking it would be risky, she worried about it but she needed to get out to the street so she got on the elevator and pressed the down button and then it rattled and shook and went down one floor and then lurched and dropped deeper and the lights were out and she knew she was stuck in this sub-basement no one knew about and that the doors weren't ever going to open and no one would hear her if she called out. She woke from the dream gasping and clawing at the air as if trying to dig her way up. And now, in her hotel room, the dream came back to her as if with a will of its own. She felt like she was floating. Things didn't feel quite real.

She talked to herself. She told herself, *Okay, there's a lot going on.* She was away from her home, in a city that frightened her. *Avery. Avery, my only child . . . Avery is living with— Avery is living with this person in this city.* And then Hank. *It was a mistake.* Just like that. *It was a mistake, and I want it to be over.* Kate sat on the edge of the bed, more dropped than sat, and leaned forward, rested her head on her knees. She imagined Avery living in New York with this guy or some other guy and Hank and Lindsey here. Maybe they'd be friends. Maybe Avery would stop by for dinner. Hank and Lindsey and Avery and whoever, while Kate was back in Salem living in her house like a mausoleum. It felt like a mausoleum sometimes.

She was tired. She lay down on the bed and kicked off her shoes. Then her clothes felt constricting and she took them off, stripped naked and got under the top cover. She pulled the blanket to her neck. She needed a nap. She needed to pull herself together. This was what it all came to. Tim dead. Avery gone. Hank used her and tossed her away. And to whom exactly was she going to complain? In the eyes of others, Hank was doing the right thing, going back to his wife. Who was she to think she had a right to wreck his family? And what was she even thinking anyway? She'd always known it was an affair and it would end, but here she was again and now it was like somehow she was back in the day Tim had died, waking up that morning . . . She hadn't thought about that morning . . . a weekend, a Saturday morning. They'd made love the night before. He was already cold to the touch. Not rigid but stiff. He didn't feel right. She had awakened to their beautiful room with light coming in through the skylight, bathing them, the dark mahogany of their sleigh bed soaking up the light, the lightweight down comforter peeled off their shoulders. They were both naked. They had made love the night before, and that was something at least. The doctors said there was probably no connection, he'd been carrying this weak spot in a blood vessel in his brain from the day he was born like a clock ticking down to that night, but it probably happened soon after they made love and he may well have been dead already when she said good-night and kissed his sleeping cheek and then rolled over. He always fell asleep after sex. She always kissed his cheek and said good-night. They were both naked in the morning light. She rolled onto her side and started to cuddle with him, pressing herself against him, and she felt it right away, not that he was dead but that something was wrong. He was cold like sick cold, like cold and sweating when someone has the flu, but no sweat. She felt it right away. When she tugged on his arm it didn't feel right, the way it bent. It moved stiffly, not loose, the arm falling down and the hands open, but a stiff movement and cold that frightened her. She sat up and called his name loudly to wake him as she pushed his shoulder, turning him onto his back. His eyes were closed. He looked like he was sleeping. She put her head to his chest and there was nothing, no heartbeat, and that was the moment she knew. She didn't scream. She didn't even cry. She got out of bed and pulled up a chair and sat beside him for a long time. She told herself there was no rush, and there wasn't. Kate in the morning light sitting white and naked in a dark chair watching Tim's body, not Tim, Tim wasn't there. Then the long blur of days and weeks . . .

Kate touched her neck and felt the wrinkles in her throat that would in a few more years be like her mother's neck that she thought was disgusting when she was a girl and her mother bent to kiss her. Why do some memories stay lodged in the mind for a lifetime? Her mother bending down to kiss her and her repulsion at the sight of her neck. Why? Under the covers, Kate touched her small breasts and ran her hand down her chest to the pouch of her belly. A pouch of belly, exactly not what the young girls showed off between low-cut tight jeans and halter tops: tight smooth skin. A belly pouch, a sagging body. Hank didn't look at her when he touched her. He closed his eyes, sucked her breast, and worked at her like a task to be accomplished: touch the right places till she shivers. And most of the time she shivered just to be done with it. She always knew when it wasn't going to happen, which was most of the time, and then it was an act from the beginning, her eyes closed too, acting out all the stages. Sometimes she wondered if he didn't know, or did he think any woman could come every time? In the end, it didn't matter. It was a kind of game. All she really wanted was him in bed beside her. What she wanted was a man in bed beside her to hold and be close to, and what they wanted was the penetration and release so they could at last sleep.

She was so angry.

It was a mistake and it's over, just like that.

She was tired and sleep was nowhere near. Sleep was on another planet somewhere.

Kate got up and paced the room and then lay down again. Her heart was beating hard. Aloud, she said, "Go back to what?" and she hadn't even been aware of thinking along those lines, of wondering what she had to go back to in Salem. The words just came out, as if there were a whole other level of thinking going on in her somewhere beneath consciousness and the sentence just slipped through. *Go back to what?* Her house frightened her. Her job bored her. She'd never meet anyone interesting there, and if she did, who would be interested in her anymore, pouch of a belly, sagging body, and it wasn't as if she'd ever been especially interesting. Lindsey was interesting, which was why Avery had gravitated toward her in her teens, all those years always Aunt Lindsey, Aunt Lindsey. She had passions and pretensions: she loved art, she wanted to be an artist. Plus, she was young and beautiful, which helped. Kate didn't have anything like that. She wasn't an interesting person. Might as well face that. Tim got bored with her, affair one and affair two. That she knew of. Avery traded her for Lindsey as a teen and then ran off first chance she got, on the back of some guy's motorcycle. Leaving Kate exactly what? She was very tired and sleep was nowhere near. What would her life be with no one in it but her? Her own family was so far away, and she hardly knew them anymore. What was she supposed to do, go back home? What home? Tim in the ground moldering to dust. Avery couldn't get far enough away fast enough.

She got up and paced again, lay down again, and then she was in the bathroom looking for her Klonopin and it was like the hand of God touched her, such relief, such a rush of release. She poured a glass of water and dumped all the Klonopin in. She started to leave the bathroom, the glass in her hand, then turned around and went back for her handbag. Whatever thinking was going on was going on someplace else. She wasn't making any choices. *Turn around. Go back for those Tylenols and those Percocets, drop them in too. Swirl the water around. Go back to bed. Drink it all down. All of it. Wipe your mouth. Wait quietly. Sleep.*

GRANT had dressed neatly for his dinner with Avery at Enid's, and he liked the picture they made together as they approached a cluster of people gathered at the entrance to Galapagos. The night was warm and blustery, a little bit of summer in the heat still rising from the concrete sidewalks and a little bit of fall in the breezes gusting along the corridors of streets and up toward the rooftops. Avery had to hold her dress, her right hand grasping her thigh as if without thought, as if it were something a woman knew to do instinctively. In the plate-glass shop windows, he admired her. The girl he had met in State College was still there in her speech and manners, but physically she was gone, as if the Avery of Penn State had been a cocoon and inside it had been another Avery, the one who wore this red dress like she'd been born to model it.

Ever since he'd left the track with Albert, he'd been considering telling her. Why, he had no idea. Why would he tell someone, anyone, that he was thinking about murdering his uncle? What could he expect her to say but *You're a madman and I'm out of here?* And he had no way to even explain why he was thinking about doing it except that he was, he was thinking about it—and maybe he wanted to tell her so she could talk him out of it, and maybe he hadn't told her yet because she might talk him out it. She looked good walking beside him in her red dress, and he looked good himself in dark slacks and a white linen shirt, untucked and loose and flapping about him in the breezes. It didn't hurt that he had money in his pocket and more at home. He had come out of college with a disdain for money, for the preoccupation with money that narrowed people's lives, turning everyone and everything into commodities. They all railed against the culture of money, Jeshua, Mei Mei, Zoo, all of them. It was understood, they were artists. They were different. Then somehow, mysteriously, they all started making money. First Terry, writing for TV. Then Heriberto next with the restaurant. Then Mei Mei all of a sudden traveling around the world getting fantastic commissions. Zoo, who had been rich all along, kept his second-floor apartment in Brooklyn and nothing too fancy going on—but it was different with Zoo because whatever money he needed was always there, just a matter of transferring funds.

Grant didn't have funds to transfer. He lived week to week on a few hundred dollars, and for a long time that was fine because money didn't matter, but now it did. It did matter. He was tired of being without it. Avery beside him in her red dress. He'd either be there when Albert showed up at five in the morning or he'd go to his uncle and look for a way out. Either way, someone would wind up dead. If he didn't kill his uncle directly by pulling the trigger, he'd be killing Albert indirectly—or getting himself killed. But he didn't think so.

He thought he could still talk to his uncle, maybe get Leigh to inter-cede, or his mother, though either choice would require that he get on it pretty soon, within the next couple of hours: call Leigh, call his mother, meet with his uncle. Or go home and go to sleep and wait for Albert, the gun and nearly fifteen thousand under the bed, Benny's Future having come in, just as Albert had promised.

They had walked from Enid's to Galapagos, Grant and Avery, sharing only a few words. Someone observing would have seen two young people walking comfortably side by side, lost in their own worlds. Grant wondered if she were thinking about him. He wanted her to be, but he doubted it: he was right there, and she was far away. In State College it had been all him, all Grant, and Avery doing the wanting. Now he hoped she was thinking about him and felt a pull, a need, to impress her. He was tempted to tell her that he had started writing, which would be a ridiculous lie, and even the momentary temptation embarrassed him, his cheeks turning red for a moment. She unbalanced him, the ground tipped and lurched while he walked beside her, and this all out of nowhere, coming on slowly, a little more each day, till it was as if some part of himself slipped away around her and he was even more off balance than before, which was just great, which was all he needed. He wanted to tell her. It made no sense, but he wanted to while knowing absolutely that he couldn't. She was beautiful in that dress. The way she walked was self-assured but not haughty or self-aware. He wondered if she knew. "Did I tell you you're gorgeous?" he said, and he touched the small of her back as they came up to the entrance to Galapagos.

"You did," she said and gave him a look that said she was flattered but didn't need to hear it again. "Where's your friend performing? Front or back?"

"Back room," Grant said. "I think there might be some nudity involved."

"Long as he doesn't make us get naked."

"Might," Grant said.

"Might what?"

"Might suggest that some of the audience members take off their clothes."

Avery stopped at the entrance and looked at Grant as if she were trying to determine whether or not he was serious. Grant opened the door for her, and then they were standing in a long red-brick foyer that featured a reflecting pool in front of a bare wall sliced by a bright streak of blue light. *NO SMOKING* in large dark letters on the wall: it looked like both a warning and a piece of art, surrounded as it was by so much space and the reflecting pool and the blue light.

Avery hesitated inside the door. "Is he going to ask me to take off my clothes? Really?"

Grant grinned and said, "I'm pretty sure you'll get asked."

"Well," she said, and put her hands on her hips, "I'm not going to."

"Nobody's forced."

"That's nice." Avery took a few steps toward the inner entrance to the bar before she stopped and turned to face Grant, who was following her. She leaned against a pipe railing that separated a walkway from the reflecting pool. "I'm not sure I want to do this," she said. "I have enough trouble with the burlesque things they do here; I don't want to be sitting around surrounded by a bunch of naked guys."

Grant leaned against the railing beside her as a half-dozen people came through the front entrance chatting and laughing. Avery and Grant flattened themselves against the pipes to let them pass. Grant said, "When did you start having trouble with nudity?"

"I don't have any trouble with nudity," she said. "I'm just not interested in being leered at."

"That's funny," he said. "You didn't have any problem giving Mei Mei nude pictures of yourself. You didn't think she'd be leering at them?"

Avery seemed too surprised to answer. "My prints?" she said finally. "You're comparing sharing my prints with another artist to stripping naked in a smoky bar surrounded by horny guys?"

"Sure I am," Grant said. He pushed off the railing and backed into the brick wall so that he was directly in front of her. "You think, what, because it's art it's not about sex? You don't think Mei Mei got off on seeing you naked? You don't think you were aware of that, that Mei Mei would be turned on by the pictures? You don't think you were using your youth and your body to attract her interest?"

Avery went from looking surprised to looking stunned. She stared at Grant as if he had just morphed into an alien; then she turned her back on him and went into the bar alone.

Grant waited, leaning against the brick wall, for a sudden flush of anger to subside. He felt the urge to hit her, and he told himself he was out of control. Out of nowhere he was jumping all over her for sharing her prints with Mei Mei. He hadn't even thought anything like it before: then he was just saying it, as if there were some other level of thought and feeling going on in him that he didn't ordinarily have access to, and it could take over under the right circumstances—

which made him feel as if he never really had any control over what he did or said, as if this other part of himself might rise up at any moment, and that was frightening, the thought of it, so he talked to himself leaning against the brick wall looking down into the reflecting pool and told himself to get it together, to get control of himself.

It was all the stuff going on in the back of his mind. The stuff with Billy and Albert. He wasn't thinking about it consciously, but it was either do nothing and find Albert at his door in the morning or do something soon, while he could still call Leigh, who could still call Billy. Doing nothing was the same as doing something. It had clear consequences. Once, when he was maybe seven or eight, his father smacked him in the face so hard that he flew across the room and bounced off the refrigerator. Why did he remember that particular blow so clearly? There were so many beatings. But it was as if that particular blow was down there with all the other stuff that percolated endlessly and it for some reason rose up now and then, as it had now when he should be inside with Avery making amends if he could. He watched the blue light on the reflecting pool. He was going to have to do something soon; there was no choice. After he bounced off the refrigerator, his eye swelled up instantly. He couldn't see out of it. He remembered how much it hurt and how he couldn't see and was afraid, and then his mother was there holding him in her arms, holding an ice pack over his eye, cursing at his father, and he remembered the look of concern and fear in his father's face as his father watched it all: Grant crying, his mother holding the ice pack to his eye while she cursed her husband. *He was not my father,* Grant reminded himself—but it was hopeless. In his mind his grandfather would always be his father, his grandmother his mother, and his mother his sister. It would never change.

Grant took a breath and leaned over the railing and looked down at his reflection looking up at him. He thought he looked good. He was still young and he looked good and that was something. He could leave with another girl tonight if he worked the bar, he was pretty sure of it. It wasn't hard. He'd look around until he found a girl who was looking, and there were always a few girls looking at a place like this. As often as not someone would approach him, the way Melanie had when he'd met Avery. If he had to do the approaching, then one subject was good as another to open the conversation because the real conversation was only *I'm looking for someone, and I see you're looking for someone, are we good? Am I somebody you want, are you someone I want?* His work was to give her the information she needed as unobtrusively as possible. The physical stuff was right there, up front, so what she wanted was background: *Who are you, what kind of work do you do, what kind of person are you?* He talked softly—*I'm a good guy*—and he talked about his friends—*I have successful friends*—and he talked about art, about some of his work, mentioning reviews—*I'm someone important*—and who said what about him and where, worked into the conversation as subtly as possible, but it didn't have to be that subtle because that was the information she was after, after all. She, whoever, knew he looked good, and when she, whoever, found out he had some accomplishments and the hope of more, usually he'd wind up at her place or she at his, and where it went from there had to do only with her, and almost always he'd wind up sleeping with her, if not that night then soon after. When he hated himself, he thought it was the only thing he was really good at. He couldn't count the number of women he'd slept with. Through his twenties and his early thirties it might have averaged a couple a week. Those days were all drugs and women, and he'd thought he was doing fine.

His father's pet name for him was *Idiot. Hey, Idiot, come here. Idiot, get me a beer.* Grant could entertain endlessly with these stories. It was like a comedy routine he had at his disposal whenever he wanted to make someone laugh. *My father's pet name for me was* Idiot. *No, really. He'd be like, "Idiot, what time is it? Idiot, tell your mother to get me dinner."* But it was gospel, that was his father: a slur and an insult for everyone. He'd call his wife a cunt, his daughter a whore, as vile a mouth as Grant had ever encountered. At the dinner table once, talking about one of his employees whom he had just fired—and no one ever lasted more than a few months in his employ—at the dinner table he'd said of this employee, *May he die with a prick in his heart!* At the dinner table. Grant spit into the reflecting pool and then quickly looked around to see if anyone had seen him do it. The place was full already but not packed, people talking and laughing at tables, the bar mostly full, a few stools open. He didn't see Avery.

He went through the second entrance and into the long red-brick cave that included the bar and stage, and there he found Avery leaning against a column, her eyes focused on an array of lights behind the bar, over shelves stocked with liquor bottles. She seemed lost in thought. A young guy with a mop of blond hair and a scraggly beard waited a few feet behind her, a minute or two away, Grant figured, from hitting on her. He was half tempted to wait for the guy to make his move and then interrupt. Instead he maneuvered through clusters of people and touched Avery's shoulder. She turned a hard look on him. He was about to tell her he was sorry, that he didn't know why he was being the way he was, but she didn't give him a chance. She said, "Has Zoo been talking to you?"

"About what?"

"About my working as one of Mei Mei's assistants."

Grant had no idea what she was talking about. "You want to work as an assistant for Mei Mei?"

"Of course I want to work for her. First of all, she actually pays her assistants a real salary, with health insurance and benefits. Second, do you realize the kind of connections I'd make?"

Grant's face went a little red. "That's fine," he said. "You asked her?"

"No one's asked anyone yet," she said. "You didn't know about this?"

"Know about what?" Grant extended a hand alongside her head and leaned against her column.

"Know that Mei Mei was thinking about offering me a job as her assistant."

"She's thinking about it?" On stage, a series of colored lights flashed and then a group of musicians appeared carrying instruments. A girl with a shaved head and face full of piercings approached a standing mike and cupped it in her hand as if it were the back of a lover's head. Grant said, "It's going to get loud in here in a minute."

Avery said, "We can go outside."

"What do you mean, she's thinking about it?" he asked. "She told you she's *thinking about* hiring you?"

"Zoo told me," Avery said. "In confidence."

"Oh." Grant looked away, to the stage. There was some kind of problem with the sound. The musicians were talking among themselves and pointing into the wings. "Long as you know she wants to fuck you," he said. He leaned close and kissed her neck. "She'll be relentless, and she'll either get you in bed or she'll fire you. Did Zoo explain that?"

Avery put her hand to her neck, over the spot where Grant had just kissed her. "What's wrong with you tonight?" she said. "Did I do something? Did something happen?"

Grant shrugged and made a face as if he couldn't imagine what she was talking about. "Way it is with Mei Mei, is all. I mean, you know that, right? You know her assistants are, like, concubines."

Avery looked like she was someplace between being angry and wanting more information. She said, "I don't know what you're talking about."

"Oh, please . . ." Grant was still leaning over her. "All of Mei Mei's assistants sleep with her, the men and the women. They're on call. Her assistants are her sex life so she doesn't have to bother with any of the romantic bullshit. She hires her lovers. Sleeping with her is part of the job."

Avery said, "I don't believe that," and glanced at the lines of liquor bottles over the bar.

"Yes, you do," he said. "You know it's the truth. Tell me she hasn't been flirting with you." Gently he touched Avery's chin and made her look at him. "Tell me," he said.

She pushed his hand away. "So what? Yes, she's been flirty. What's that mean?"

"It means she thinks you'll sleep with her. Otherwise she wouldn't be offering you the job. It's part of the deal."

"Grant," she said with a pleading tone, as if she wanted him to be lying to her.

"Come on," he said, and he could feel the anger that he had been successfully resisting shift around inside him and float up into his face and eyes. "Please. You know what's going on."

"No, I don't," she said. "Yes, I know she's flirty. Yes, I know she's slept with some of her assistants. I'd heard that. Like, Jesus, there's something odd about that, like that's not the most common thing in the world. But that's a long way from saying it's part of the job. Nobody's suggested anything like that to me."

"I just did."

"I don't believe you," she said. "Zoo is your best friend, and he's my friend now too. He'd have told me something like that." Avery folded her hands over her chest. She seemed to have convinced herself with the point about Zoo. "You're exaggerating," she said, "because you're jealous of Mei Mei."

Grant took a step back and turned around so that he was looking out at the reflecting pool, toward the street. For a moment it was as if he were someplace else. Someplace outside or above the racket and the crowd. When he turned around again, he found Avery watching him. He said, "I'm sorry, but you can't work for Mei Mei. Or you can," he said, "but then we can't be together."

"You're kidding," she said, and a second later added, "Are you serious?"

Others around them were watching now. A few were looking at each other or looking away, but they were listening, and others were watching as if it were theater. Grant leaned close to Avery and whispered in her ear, "I'm not kidding. You can't be sleeping with Mei Mei and living with me."

Avery said, "I'm not sleeping with Mei Mei."

Grant said, no longer whispering, "You will be if you take the job, and even if you're not, everyone will assume you are—and I'm not dealing with it."

Avery threw up her hands and then, apparently at a loss for words, pushed past him and started for the exit.

Grant grabbed her shoulder and turned her around. "Why don't you spend the night at Terry's?" He took his cell phone out of his pocket and held it up to her. "I'll give her a call and tell her you're spending the night there."

Avery seemed off balance. She shook her head as if trying to shake off dizziness. She said, "Why don't I just give Mei Mei a call?"

"Go ahead," he said, "but then don't come back except to pick up your stuff."

Avery gave him a look that said she was sorry for him, as if he were pathetic. Then she turned and walked away.

Grant started for the bar, bumping the kid with the blond hair on the way, knocking him back. The kid pretended nothing had happened. From the stage, music started up, sudden and loud. The girl with the shaved head screamed into the mike, and waves of sharp sound bounced off the surrounding red brick while a gruff bass thumped along the floor. Grant found a space at the bar, and when he looked back to where Avery had been standing, she was gone. He caught a glimpse of her red dress by the reflecting pool just as she disappeared behind two guys coming in and then another glimpse of the dress as she went out the door. At the bar, she left his thoughts, as if nothing had happened, as if he had just quietly walked into Galapagos for a drink. The music a staticky blanket draped over the crowd. He waited to catch the bartender's eye. High on the wall to his right, a blue neon light announced *BACK ROOM* above a red neon arrow, and Grant recalled that he had come to see a friend perform. He looked at the time on his cell phone. It was after nine. His friend was already performing, and Grant stretched over the bar and called out to the bartender, who didn't look his way when he shouted but then came over after he served someone a beer. Grant said, "Makers on the rocks. Double," and put a twenty down on the bar. The bartender was a young guy, maybe in his midtwenties, with long wavy brown hair. He put a tumbler with ice in front of Grant, poured two shots of Makers, snatched the twenty, went to the cash register, and came back in a second with change. Grant took the drink, pushed two singles toward the kid, and left the bar.

In the back room, his friend was on stage naked, his blue jeans and orange T-shirt in a heap beside him. There were a handful of people at a half-dozen tables, and a few of them were naked too, their clothes in piles on the tables. Everyone was laughing. Grant finished his drink and put the empty glass down on a ledge behind the door. The room was dark, bathed in eerie blue-and-violet light. Leigh went to bed early, and it might already be too late to call her, to put that in motion. Grant felt as though he were on the cusp of something, teetering on the brink. As if, if he closed his eyes, by the time he opened them again he'd have made a choice. In the cab of that truck something inside him had said *yes* even if he couldn't hear it; even if he was unaware of it, there was something inside him, whatever it was, that said *yes*. First the gun was on the seat beside him. They were being hijacked, he'd figured that out. There was always a swirl of something going on under the surface, stuff not even conscious just churning swirling constantly, and what anyone does or doesn't do has everything to do with what's churning what's swirling and whatever it was something inside him said *yes*. They're being hijacked and a kid comes through Albert's door and Albert says, *Son of a bitch*. Before that happened that wasn't part of the swirl and now it was, Albert saying, *Son of a bitch*, and then, *Just do what they say*. Guy in the seat next to Albert, guy on the sideboard with a gun to Grant's head. There's that moment. *Pull it over*, the guy says. All this is like the moment before. The stuff that leads up to the moment that begins when Grant sees the gun on the seat. First the gun on the seat beside him, but before that the guy on the sideboard tries to point to where he wants the truck pulled over and he loses his balance and falls off into the darkness and the kid beside Albert breaks up laughing a high childish giggle and Albert knocks the gun out of his hand. That's when the moment starts. The gun is on the seat. Something inside Grant says, *Pick it up*. Why? He could let it sit there; he could let Albert pick it up, but something inside him says, *Pick it up*, and he picks it up just as the guy who fell off the running board leaps back up onto it and sticks his gun into the window at Grant's head and Grant shoots him and the guy flies out into the darkness again. There's nothing like what could be called thought happening between the first moment when Grant picks up the gun and the moment he fires it. It's a slide, a sequence, a moment stretched out: gun on seat, gun in hand, gun fired. But nothing happens without thought.

On the stage Grant's friend was calling his name and waving for him to come into the room. Grant smiled in recognition but didn't move. There was an undressed girl with bright red hair and heavy breasts on a slim body grinning at him. She yelled something. The music was loud behind him and they wanted him to close the door. Nothing happens without thought. The mind tells the body what to do. He picked up the gun and at the moment the barrel hit the guy's forehead something inside him whatever it was said *yes*, said, *Do it*, said, *Pull the trigger*—and the body flew off into the dark. Something inside him whatever it was out of the churning something said *yes*. Grant smiled and backed out of the room and closed the door, his friend still shouting his name.

People were crowding into the bar, the night just beginning. A throng packed in front of the stage, the band rocking, all the musicians save the drummer jumping up and down in rhythm. Grant started for the door, making his way through the press of bodies. He might have taken off his clothes and gone into the back room and sat next to the girl with red hair and riffed with his friend but that would have been a decision and he wasn't ready to make one yet. There was still time, though it was running out fast.

He put his hand in his pocket and slid it over his cell phone. Jeshua wore a jacket to class and lectured on theater and art. Jeshua who had once stabbed himself in the chest in front of the Metropolitan Museum of Art as a comment on the tyranny of institutions. Grant laughed out loud and a girl pressed up against him looked a little nervous, as if she might be pressed up against a maniac. He slid past her and pushed toward the door. Jeshua was gone: he had transformed into another Jeshua. He was with a girl named Lee Ann, a graduate student in her twenties, and they planned on getting married in the summer. Grant hadn't told anyone. He hadn't even thought about it much. It was as if he didn't really believe it and couldn't take it seriously and so dismissed it. Jeshua, though, had been clear. He was getting married in the summer, her family was planning a church ceremony and a reception, and Grant and the whole crew could expect invitations in a few months. Jeshua had explained that he had been pressured to ask Lee Ann's brother to be his best man, and he hoped Grant would understand. This was Jeshua. Jeshua who had stabbed himself in front of the Met, who had tattooed the anarchist *A* inside a circle on his ass, who had spent half his life in the city drunk or drugged. He was getting married and explaining to Grant why he couldn't ask him to be his best man. He went on and on about his anxiety over going up for tenure. Mostly he talked about Lee Ann, whom he said he loved. He said love changed everything. He said they wanted to have kids. Doors might open for others, but Grant didn't see any doors opening for him. He was embarrassed for Jeshua, which was why he hadn't talked about him much since coming back from Penn State. He was embarrassed for him not because he'd morphed into someone else but because the someone else he'd morphed into was embarrassing. Time was so fucking weird, the way it went slow and fast simultaneously.

At the entrance, on the way out to the reflecting pool and the street, Grant saw Zoo leaning against the door frame and scanning the room. A moment later, Zoo saw him and gestured toward the street. It never failed that Grant was glad to see Zoo, something like a small space inside him relaxing and opening at the sight of him. The sidewalk and street outside the bar were crowded with twenty-somethings, kids dressed in black, some with crazy hair, some with piercings, all tattooed, and most of them, Grant knew, products of Ivy League schools and parents with money to pay for their apartments in Williamsburg or Manhattan. You couldn't move sideways here without bumping into an artist. Grant pushed his way through the crowd on the sidewalk and crossed the street to where Zoo was waiting for him, framed by a store entrance. He was wearing leather sandals and dark slacks and a loose white silk shirt, his broad face framed by the way his hair fell behind his ears.

Grant said, "What are you doing here?" Zoo didn't do the bar scene. He spent his life rehearsing or acting, or thinking about rehearsing or acting, or taking care of his friends.

Zoo made a face that said there was a story to tell. He touched Grant's arm and directed him toward the river. For a while they walked without speaking, and then, when they were away from the crowd, nearing Kent Street, where the surroundings grew quiet and empty, Zoo said, "Avery's mother attempted suicide."

Grant stopped but didn't say anything. He watched Zoo and waited for more.

Zoo touched his arm as if to say, *Come on, let's walk while I explain*, and they started walking again. "Her uncle came by looking for Avery—"

"To my place?"

"He rang my buzzer when you didn't answer."

"Where's Avery? Does she—"

"Yes," Zoo said. "I drove him over here, and we saw her walking. He saw her, actually. I was coming up on Wythe, and he made me stop."

"This is so fucking weird," Grant said. There was no traffic on

Kent, a street of potholes and broken cobblestones surrounded by warehouses and abandoned industrial buildings. The East River hidden behind walls and gates and fences, the lights of Manhattan on the other side of the river. They were walking toward 3rd and a sliver of undeveloped land that reached down to the shore, where they could sit on boulders by the water and look out at the bridges and the skyline. "How was she?" he said. "She must have—"

"She got shaky and teared up," Zoo said, "but given what was going on—"

"So, what? Her uncle just—"

"He said the mother's okay, but she attempted suicide in her hotel room."

"Where is she?" Grant asked. "The mother."

"Roosevelt."

"She'll be all right?"

"They pumped her stomach. They're keeping her overnight."

"Fuck," Grant said. "How did Avery look?"

Zoo shrugged. "I made the uncle tell me what was going on before I'd tell him where you were. He seems all right."

"She say anything to you? Avery."

Zoo was quiet a moment, his eyes on the cobblestones at his feet. "I loaned her my car," he said, "and she's, *I can't have it back to you till tomorrow morning.* I'm, *I don't get that,* and the uncle tells her there's no need to spend the night unless she really wants to. Then she gives me this look which I took to mean she wasn't coming back to your place tonight regardless. Did I get that right?"

"Got that right," Grant said.

"What happened?"

335

"Argument. Bullshit." Grant clasped his hands behind his neck and looked away, toward two tall thick sheets of aluminum that were part of a fence and looked like they might at one point have served as gates but were stitched together now with what appeared to be giant staples. The left sheet was riddled with a score of bullet holes, as was the top of the right sheet. It looked like someone had opened fire with an automatic weapon.

"Bad?" Zoo asked. "Fixable? What?"

"I don't know," Grant said curtly, meaning he didn't want to talk about it. He said, "How come you still hang out with me, Zoo? Other than Terry, I haven't had a relationship that lasted more than four months since what's-her-name in my midtwenties."

"Rochelle," Zoo said and laughed at Grant forgetting her name. "And that was maybe six months."

They were coming up on North 3rd. A couple holding hands strolled toward the water, followed by a girl in a leather miniskirt and a pale yellow blouse. Her hair was thick and long and fell in waves over her shoulders. Grant guessed she had walked out on a party and come here to be alone, which was why people came down to the water at night in Brooklyn. Except this spot was rarely empty. Somebody was always by the water trying to be alone, or some couple making out up against the fence, under the razor wire that protected a warehouse yard. "Seriously," he said. "Why are you living in a rail-road flat upstairs from me? You could be living anyplace you want with your money."

"Please. How could you get by without me? It's a burden I carry."

"That's your answer?"

Zoo said, "What were you expecting?" and there was a touch of something unpleasant in his voice.

Grant said, "I feel like I've been asleep the past twenty years."

Zoo sighed, meaning he found the subject tiresome.

Grant stopped. "Really," he said. "How is it possible that I'm thirty-seven and driving a truck? What happened to all that time?"

"And what am I supposed to say to that?" Zoo took a step back from Grant. "If there's one thing you can be depended upon for, Grant, it's to make the wrong choice. Like, for instance, right now. What's this about with Avery? I thought, God help me for being an idiot— I thought she might actually turn you around."

"Why?" Grant said. "Why would Avery turn things around?"

Zoo looked away as if to say, *If you don't know, I can't tell you.* "She's staying someplace else tonight?" he said. "What happened?"

They were at North 3rd, and the street opened onto a dirt lot that reached down to a line of boulders along the shore. The couple Grant had seen a moment earlier was sitting on rocks up against a tall chain-link fence topped with loops and curls of razor wire. The guy had his hand on the girl's knee and together they looked through the fence toward the Empire State Building and the skyline of Manhattan. The girl in the miniskirt was sitting atop the biggest boulder, looking toward the Williamsburg Bridge and beyond, to the Manhattan and Brooklyn Bridges. In the moonlight, the East River glittered. Grant stood face to face with Zoo and said, "Mei Mei wants to hire Avery as an assistant?"

Zoo said, "Oh," as if Grant's question explained everything.

Grant went ahead of Zoo down to the shore and found a boulder near the water where he couldn't see anyone else. It was quiet, and with only a little imagination it was possible to believe he was alone. He had come to this spot—with Zoo, with Terry, all of them—scores of times since they'd first discovered it, when they were teenagers and in school at NYU. He had made love to Terry here, up against the chain-link fence, where the couple was sitting at the moment. He had been drunk here and drugged here and sober here, between Brooklyn and Manhattan, looking out along the river toward the line of bridges and the city lights. Killing was part of the rhythm. What did a code of ethics do except paint a gloss over it or provide a screen to hide it? People killed when they needed to or they thought they needed to, endlessly. This morning the streets of Iraq were littered with corpses, while the couple by the fence hand in hand looked out at the long array of lights. A part of every dollar earned apportioned for killing. If he killed his uncle, someone else, whom his uncle would have killed, would live. If he didn't kill his uncle, he'd be killing Albert, and whomever Albert would have killed would live. Maybe. Who could do that kind of math? Something deeper than ethics was needed, something beyond belief, some kind of guidance. Terry and Mei Mei and Heriberto, it wasn't just the money, it was their power to shape themselves and the way others saw them so that they were there, identifiable and located, while Grant every day seemed to dissolve a little more, disappearing. Already they were forgetting him and it was only a matter of time before Terry moved away and Zoo finally got the break that everyone knew was coming and Heriberto opened a restaurant in Malaysia or somewhere while Jesh settled down with wife and kids and Mei Mei bought a place in Barcelona and Grant became someone from back then, from a long time ago,

What's he doing now? Has anyone heard anything? No, because what would there be to hear? It was getting late. Soon Leigh would be in bed, and if he called he'd have to wake her.

After Leigh left the house, she never really came back. She got a job with an insurance company and an apartment in the city but Grant only knew that she was gone. He remembered her moving out. She had a big red suitcase and a white cardboard box and there were two girlfriends with her to help her move. They were all working in the city and sharing an apartment. He must have heard that later. He must have heard a lot of what he knew later and gotten it mixed up with what he actually remembered, which was Leigh and the red suitcase and the white box and her girlfriends and how he cried and clung to her leg because he didn't want her to leave. And then she never came back. He saw her rarely from that day on, but her moving out was not the issue and had never been the issue. She made a choice he could understand. It was reasonable. But not telling him? Never telling him? Never at any point sitting down and saying, *This is it, this is what happened?* That was what he couldn't forgive.

Zoo settled onto a boulder beside Grant and slipped off his sandals. "Mei Mei can do a lot of good things for Avery," he said. "You know that."

For a long time after the killing, it was as if a curtain had been yanked away and suddenly everything was different: what he saw, what he thought, what he felt. Or the angle of perception skewed. Something. But nothing remained unchanged. Even the simplest things. Scissors looked different. Supermarkets scared him. The streets were full of dead birds, he saw dead birds everywhere. He couldn't sleep. He couldn't eat without effort. The way the world turned into a projected image sometimes, as if he were watching a movie. All that and more, that intense for a few months only, but the aftermath stretching out over years.

"Grant?" Zoo said. "Are you going to talk to me?"

"About what?"

"Mei Mei's going to be Mei Mei," Zoo said. "I'm not saying she won't try to sleep with Avery—but that doesn't mean Avery's got to go along."

"She might, though."

"Why? What makes you say that?"

Grant listened as a train rattled over the Williamsburg Bridge, its lights glimmering like the glimmer of light over the river. "Mei Mei's got a lot to offer her, and she's hungry. She doesn't even know how hungry she is."

"For what? For fame?" Zoo said. "For success?"

"For everything."

Zoo scratched the back of his head and looked straight up as if suddenly interested in the stars. "We can't know what Avery will do."

Grant pulled a crushed pack of Marlboros out of his pants pocket.

Zoo groaned. "Another wise choice," he said as Grant lit up.

Grant inhaled deeply and then blew a line of smoke up toward the clouds. "I don't smoke much," he said. "It should be the worst choice I make."

"So what will you do?" Zoo rolled up his pants legs and put his feet in the water. "Don't you think you should at least call Avery?"

"Why? Tell her I'm sorry her mother tried to off herself?"

"Tell her she can come back here tonight," Zoo said. "This isn't the time to send her off somewhere else." Then, as if the thought just occurred to him, he said, "Who do you think she'd ask?"

"Terry'd let her stay there," Grant said. "You'd let her stay with you."

"Bad idea," Zoo said. "Not given what just happened with her mother. Really—" He shoved Grant to get his attention. "You need to call her."

Grant shook his head. "I've got to be at work early tomorrow. I've already promised."

Zoo said, "What's that got to do with anything?" and he watched Grant, waiting for an answer. When Grant only took another long drag off his cigarette before leaning back and stretching out on the boulder, Zoo started to repeat the question and then stopped abruptly and let it go. He stretched out also, his feet dangling in the water beside Grant, and looked up blankly at the handful of visible stars.

A blue-and-white police car inched along West 59th while the cop at
the wheel was turned entirely around talking to someone stretched
out in the backseat. On the rear door, the bright red letters *C-P-R*
were aligned vertically; spelled out horizontally in pale blue beside
them were the words *Courtesy, Professionalism, Respect.* While Hank
watched, standing in front of a long wall of plate glass under the
squat red-and-white cross of the emergency-room sign, the cop
leaned into the backseat, grabbed a disheveled young man wearing a
suit and tie by the collar, and sat him up straight, then turned around
and sped off toward the intersection. Behind Hank, separated from
him by sliding glass doors, Lindsey and Avery were deep in conversation. Avery had on a bright red dress and black shoes. She looked
glamorous, as if she had just walked out of a posh party somewhere.
Lindsey, who had thrown on crumpled slacks, slipped into tennis
shoes, and left the hotel in the same olive-green T shirt she had been
sleeping in, looked like the art student she used to be. She hadn't

taken time to put on a bra, and Hank noticed Avery's eyes falling to Lindsey's chest, as if she were a little disturbed to be able to make out her aunt's breasts so readily.

Hank, watching his wife and his niece through glass, shifted his focus to his own image reflected in the window and saw a guy looking back at him with worry in his eyes. At the hotel, after his scene with Kate, he had gone back to his room and fallen asleep beside Lindsey before the raspy electric sound of voices clicking on and off through walkie-talkies woke him. Out in the hall, he saw an EMT in a blue tunic talking to a wiry police woman. The gun she wore looked impossibly big, her belt heavy with stuff clipped and fastened to it. Hank closed the door behind him as if it were important—though he didn't know why—to hide from Lindsey whatever it was that was going on out in the hallway. When he asked the cop nervously, "Is there something wrong? Is there a problem?" she didn't answer at first. He didn't know what he was thinking, terrorism maybe, a fire. She wrote something on a clipboard for the EMT and then looked Hank over as if he might be potentially dangerous. She said, "We have a situation down the hall." Hank said, "What kind of situation?" and when the cop said, as if annoyed, "It's nothing to worry about, sir," Hank said, "I have family staying down the hall." She asked what room, and when Hank told her, she asked for a name. Hank's knees got watery. He resisted saying Kate's name.

"Name?" the cop repeated. She seemed suddenly angry.

"Kate," Hank said. "Kate Walker. I'm her brother-in-law, Henry Walker."

By the time they reached Kate's room, the EMTs were wheeling her out on a stretcher, and Hank leaned against the wall to steady himself. He thought she was dead when he saw her, her face was so white. Then Lindsey was there saying, "What? What the hell?" and more cops appeared, and there was a lot of talk and noise that for a while Hank couldn't make out because everything went fuzzy and strange as if he were seeing it through glass that distorted shapes and altered sound, and the next thing he knew he was sitting on the floor with his head buried in his knees trying not to throw up while a sweet-faced EMT held his shoulder and talked to him, asking him questions, and Lindsey knelt beside him, her hand stroking his hair. "I'm okay," he heard himself say, and then he pulled himself together and said it firmly, "I'm okay." He took a deep breath, and when he exhaled, it came out as a sigh that was so full of despair it sounded like an animal groaning. Everyone looked at him.

"Where are they taking her?" he asked the cop, and then it was all Q&A for a long time before finally Hank and Lindsey went back to their room and grabbed what they needed and then went out to the street and found a cab—and all that time, everything that happened, answering the questions, going back to their room, taking the elevator and then the escalator to the street, getting into a cab in front of the hotel, everything happened with an air of unreality. When he had been asked if he knew of any reason why Kate might try to take her own life, he hadn't answered. The truth stuck in his throat. Lindsey interrupted to save him, saying, "Avery," saying, "She was distressed about her daughter, Avery," and Hank let it go at that. *Avery.* She was distressed about Avery. It was all unreal anyway. It was playing out like a movie, like someone had written a script and somehow he had learned his lines and was reciting them.

By the time they got to the hospital, it was clear Kate would be okay. They had pumped her stomach and done all the things they do when people try to kill themselves with pills, and they had moved on to deciding what to do with her next. Kate was sleepy and groggy and would be for a good while, but awake enough and lucid enough to say she didn't want to see anyone, especially not her daughter, whom she specified by name: "Don't let my daughter, Avery, in here. Don't let her see me."

Lindsey, nonetheless, sent Hank off to find her. "She needs to be here," she said, and now Avery and Lindsey were talking like confidantes in the lobby behind a wall of glass while Hank looked at his own reflection and then started off to pace the street again, as he had done a dozen times already, walking past the ambulance bays and the entrance doors and then turning around and walking back to the ER. He still couldn't quite grasp what Kate had done. He knew, of course: she had taken all the pills she had with her and tried to kill herself. Housekeeping—a young woman, a girl in her twenties—had gone into the room after knocking and not getting an answer. She saw a glass broken beside the bed, water pooled on the hardwood floor, and a thin white arm dangling loosely over the mattress. She called down to the desk and took Kate's pulse and so could tell them that Kate was alive when they arrived, the hotel attendants, who had seen this kind of thing before. All this had been explained to Hank, and as he paced the city street he imagined it, he imagined the scene—but he still couldn't really grasp it.

"She tried to kill herself," he said aloud, the words emerging with a will of their own, always followed by a curse—*son of a bitch, goddamn it*—the curse an expression of disbelief, of stunned disbelief that such a thing was possible, not only possible but had actually happened. Avery had been relatively composed around Hank, though he could see the pain in her eyes clearly enough that he felt sorry for her. He had told her friend, the Asian guy, what had happened. He hadn't wanted to tell him, but it was clear the guy wasn't going to take him to Avery otherwise—and then he turned out to be decent, lending them his car, obviously concerned. On the drive to the hospital, Avery cried silently, the tears welling in her eyes and then falling down her cheeks. Without being asked, she said, "There's no way I could have known she'd do this."

Hank said, "Of course not, Avery. Nobody's blaming you."

Avery shot back, "Why not?" bitterly.

Hank almost told her. He kept playing with the wording in his head. *I'm sorry to have to tell you this, Avery, but . . . I was having an affair with your mother. . . . Your mother and I had an affair. . . . Kate and I have been involved with each other. . . . After your father died, Kate and I spent a lot of time together, and, then, though neither of us planned for it to happen . . .* But he never got the words out.

Beside him in the car, Avery looked as though she were carrying the weight of the world. Her red dress glared in contrast to her slumped shoulders and the look in her eyes and about her face. He wanted to tell her. He wanted to explain that it wasn't all about her. But the words never came out, and then they were on the block with the hospital and he was pulling into a parking garage across the street from the ER, and Avery was out of the car the second it stopped, and then it was too late.

On 59th, a midnight-blue Lincoln sped along the street before coming to a sudden stop in front of the ER. While Hank watched, a child in a black miniskirt—she looked like she couldn't be more than thirteen—slid out of the backseat, pulling at the arm of a boy who stumbled out after her, followed by another girl. Once they were all out of the car, it sped away and the girls helped the boy into the ER. The boy was skinny and appeared to be drunk or drugged, and at the sight of him Hank thought of Keith, and suddenly he wanted to talk to his son. He took his cell phone from his pocket and saw that it was already too late to call, and then Lindsey came up to him. Behind her, he saw Avery standing inside the emergency-room doors.

Lindsey said, "Who are you calling?"

Hank slipped the phone back into his pocket. "Keith."

"He's in bed," Lindsey said, surprised. "Did you call Liz's?"

"No," Hank said, and then added, "Did you see those kids?" meaning the teenaged girls and the boy. "They looked like they were just barely teens."

Lindsey took Hank by the arm and directed him back toward Avery and the ER. "Keith's seven," she said, "and I've talked to him twice this evening. He's fine."

"A city like this has got to be tough to raise a kid in," he said, and he looked meaningfully at Lindsey.

Lindsey ignored the comment and the look. "I talked Avery into trying to see Kate again."

"Why?" Hank stopped. "Kate doesn't want to see her. What good's it—"

"Of course Kate wants to see her," Lindsey said as if Hank were an idiot not to realize it. "This whole thing is all about wanting to see her."

"It's about what?" Hank stepped in front of Lindsey, turning his back to Avery. "You think Kate did this as a ploy to get Avery back?" He spoke in a loud whisper.

"I think it's possible there's a degree of manipulation in what she did, yes."

Hank's face went red with a wave of fury that almost made him dizzy. "Did you tell Avery that?" he said, nearly choking on his forced calm.

"What are you so mad about?"

"Did you tell Avery that?" he repeated.

"No, I didn't," Lindsey said, "though I was tempted." She leaned close to Hank, the way she did when they argued. "Truth is, after this," she said, whispering too, "I think it's best all around if Avery comes back to Salem and looks after Kate, at least for a while, because that's not something I want to do, and it's not something I want you to do, and frankly, I think Avery's stuck with it. But honestly, yes, I'm partly really pissed off at Kate for doing this. It does seem like a giant manipulation. Avery tries to break free and she does *this* to hold on to her? For Christ's sake, Hank. Really."

"You're unbelievable." Hank took a step back from Lindsey as if she repulsed him. "The woman tries to kill herself, and you're pissed off at her."

"Sorry," Lindsey said, "call me heartless, but I think it was a selfish, stupid, manipulative thing to do. And I think she knew there weren't enough Klonopin to kill her."

Hank looked at Lindsey as if he were seeing her for the first time. "You do sound heartless," he said, "and honestly, I'm—" He couldn't find the right word, so he only shook his head and remained where he was, blocking her path.

Lindsey covered her eyes with her hands and stood stiffly a moment longer before her body suddenly loosened, as if some inner buttress gave way, and her shoulders collapsed first before her whole torso lurched forward. "I'm sorry," she said, and then she was sobbing, and when Hank wrapped his arms around her, she fell into him, her head pressed against his chest.

"There might have been things going on with Kate that we don't know about," Hank said very softly, almost inaudibly. He felt a hand on his back, and then Avery was there beside them.

"I'm so sorry," Avery said, and her voice sounded as if it were coming up out of a well. "I didn't mean—" she said.

Lindsey wiped her tears away. She said, "This is not about you, Avery."

"Oh, of course it is." Avery's hands flew up as if she were suddenly angry. "Let's not pretend," she said. "I'm all she's got and I left and then this." She rubbed at a spot on the ground with her foot as if she were trying to erase something. "I'm sorry I'm causing her all this pain, but Jesus— She never—"

"Avery . . ." Hank moved closer to her, wanting to put his arms around her but not at all sure he should. "Av," he said, "you can't assume she did this because of you. I know she's your mother and you think you know—"

"Look—" Avery raised her voice. "I'm so—" she said and then suddenly turned her back on Hank and Lindsey, as if she couldn't bear to have them see her.

Lindsey moved beside Avery and put her arm around her and rubbed her back a little. "We're not saying it has nothing to do with you, Avery. Only, you're not responsible. It's not about you like that."

Avery hesitated a moment and then nodded. She said, "I don't know what I'm supposed to do."

"Let's see if we can get her to talk to us," Lindsey said. With her arm still around Avery's back, she directed her toward the ER doors.

Hank followed. Inside the emergency room, on the way to a corridor that would lead them to the room where Kate was resting, he noticed the two teenaged girls sitting side by side, holding hands. Their eyes were red, and one of them had mascara stains down her cheeks. They were watching Avery as if she were a celebrity walking past.

In the corridor, Lindsey said to Avery, "Listen, it may be too soon to bring this up, but I'm hoping you'll consider coming back to Salem for a while to be with Kate, just until she's feeling a little better."

When Avery didn't answer, Hank said, "You don't have to deal with it this instant. Let's see how things go."

Avery nodded and looked grateful for the reprieve.

Hank fell in behind the women as a pair of nurses rolled a gurney along the corridor. They were chatting casually back and forth over an older woman stretched out rigidly with her hands folded on her chest. The woman was heavily made-up and wearing a black evening dress, the top of which was visible above a white sheet. She watched the nurses with wide, frightened eyes. As she passed, the smell of perfume momentarily overwhelmed the mild antiseptic smell of the corridor. At the door to Kate's room, which was actually several rooms divided by curtain partitions, with multiple entrances, Avery stopped and took a step backward and away from the door with her eyes closed. Lindsey put a hand on Avery's shoulder. From the doorway, a gap in the curtains surrounding Kate left her exposed in her hospital bed, an IV taped to her arm, her head propped up on pillows. Her hair was disheveled and her face still looked unnaturally pale. She looked like a corpse. The wrinkles around her eyes and mouth cut into her skin like scars.

"Wait out here," Lindsey said; first she put both hands on Avery's shoulders as if she were only going to touch her encouragingly, then she changed her mind and wrapped her arms around her in a tight hug.

"Okay," Avery said. "I'll wait in the corridor."

To Hank, Lindsey said, "Let me go in and talk to her alone a minute."

Hank said, "We'll wait out here," and he put his arm around Avery's shoulder but took it away quickly when she stiffened at his touch.

"My God," Avery said as soon as Lindsey was out of sight. She whispered, "She looks terrible," and wiped tears away from her eyes.

Hank said, "She'll be okay," and before he could say anything else, he was interrupted by Kate's voice, at first only loud and firm, saying, "Get out! I don't want to see anyone!" and then yelling, "Get out!"

Hank started for the entrance as the same pair of nurses who had passed with the gurney a moment earlier scrambled into the corridor, followed by a young woman in a blue smock who Hank assumed was a doctor. In the doorway, he met Lindsey, who pushed him backward, making room for the hospital staff to get in the room. Hank turned around, looking for Avery, and saw her crouched against the corridor wall, her face buried in her knees, her arms around the back of her neck.

Lindsey knelt on one side of her and Hank on the other. Lindsey rubbed her back with a small, circular, massaging motion.

Hank said, "Avery. I'm sure she's just not ready—"

"Sure," Avery said. "I understand. She's probably—" She stopped abruptly. Hank wasn't sure whether or not she intended to continue and so was quiet.

Lindsey said, "Maybe it's better if you just go home for now."

Avery nodded.

Hank said, "You can see her in the morning."

Avery said, "They're definitely keeping her overnight?"

"Definitely," Lindsey said. "We have to see the doctors in the morning about getting her released."

Avery nodded again and then pushed herself to her feet and rubbed tears from her eyes. To Lindsey she said, "You can call me in the morning? Let me know what's going on?"

"Soon as we know when they're releasing her," she said. "I've got your cell."

"All right," Avery said, then added quickly, "And they're sure she's going to be okay?"

"Absolutely," Hank said. "The doctor told me. She's just going to feel lousy for a while."

"No permanent effects?"

"None." Hank touched Avery's arm. "I'm really sorry," he said. "Avery, I'm really terribly sorry."

Avery said, "I'm the one who should be sorry," and then her eyes filled up with tears and she tried to shake them off, as if she were angry with herself for being emotional.

Hank said, "Let me walk you out to the garage," and waited while Avery and Lindsey exchanged hugs.

On the street, as they approached the parking lot, Hank said, "You can't assume this is all about you, Avery. You can't take all this on your own shoulders."

Avery said, "Do you know something I don't?" She wiped tears from her eyes with her arm. "Is there something going on in her life I don't know about?"

"That's not the point," Hank said. "I don't know what's going on in your mother's life."

"Well, I do," Avery said. "Nothing's going on in my mother's life but me. I'm all that's going on in her life, and now I've—" Again she stopped abruptly, seemingly in the middle of a thought.

Hank walked beside her and waited. When he realized she wasn't going to continue, he said, "Nobody's life has *nothing* going on in it, and I don't believe Kate would do something like this just because you moved away. That doesn't make sense."

Inside the garage, Avery slid her ticket under the cashier's window and pulled out her purse.

Hank pushed the purse away and slid his credit card under the window. A moment later, the attendant was on his way to get her car.

"Really," Hank said, picking up where he'd left off, "it doesn't make sense that your mother would do something like this because you're not doing exactly what she wants you to be doing. It's got to be more complicated than that."

"I'm sure it is," Avery said. "Mom's life was always about Dad, and then about me. Now Dad's dead and I left and it must be like, I don't know? What's she got to live for?"

Hank said, "That may be part of it."

"Part of it . . ." Avery said dismissively, as if it obviously was the whole of it.

Hank said coolly, "You ought to consider that you may still be looking at your mother from the perspective of a daughter, someone who thinks her mother's life is only all about her."

Avery didn't answer.

"Look," Hank said, trying to be conciliatory, "you'll see her again in the morning. You'll be able to talk to her."

"I hope," Avery said. "She's probably going to feel humiliated."

Hank pulled a couple of singles out of his wallet and handed them to the attendant, who had driven the Mini around and was holding the door open for Avery. To Avery, he said, "She's going to need to talk to you." The attendant walked away quickly. He looked South American, and given he hadn't said a word, Hank guessed he didn't speak English. He seemed nonetheless to understand that he should leave these people alone.

Avery got into the car. Looking up through the window, she said, "We could probably all use a good night's sleep. Maybe I'll figure out what the hell to say to her by the morning."

Hank touched her arm and said lamely, "It's going to be all right."

Avery leaned toward him out the window, and Hank gave her a kiss on the cheek. "I'll see you tomorrow," he said and watched her a moment longer before walking away, back toward the hospital entrance. Crossing the street, waiting for a truck to pass, he turned to look back at the parking garage and saw that Avery was on the phone and talking to someone while she watched him watching her. Once the truck went by, he crossed the street hurriedly. Behind him, he heard the Mini Cooper pull out of the garage and then rush up 59th. By the time he turned to follow the car's progress, he saw it approach a red light on 10th, pause, and then run the light.

A crowd of women passed Lindsey and Hank as they were walking back to their hotel from the hospital. The doctor looking after Kate had recommended they leave and check back in a couple of hours. The women were all very young, and they were laughing and shouting back and forth excitedly. There were a score of them, a little parade of happy young women, and when they were finally past, Hank said, "We're not moving here, Lindsey. It's not happening. Not with me. And not with Keith."

"Hank," Lindsey said, as if she had disregarded his words as soon as she'd heard them, "we both need a drink. We're upset and tired, and we need to take a minute and talk reasonably about what we're going to do."

"That's fine," Hank said. They were on the corner of 58th, and he gestured down the block to the hotel. "They have a bar in the lobby. But I'm serious," he said.

Lindsey moved closer to him and pressed her cheek against his shoulder. "You're upset," she repeated. "Someone you love just tried to take her own life." She stopped and put her arms around him, holding him in a tight hug.

At first Hank went cold at Lindsey's touch, wanting, out of anger, to resist, but then his body sank into her and he laid his head on her shoulder. Her hand came up and touched the back of his neck. She held him tightly and said something, something soft that he couldn't make out over the wind and didn't need to—he knew the sense of it if he couldn't make out the exact words. She was saying it would be okay. He was being comforted by his wife because the woman he'd betrayed her with had just attempted suicide. Somehow he was on a street corner in Manhattan while an autumn wind tossed trash and dirt at his feet and a helicopter passed overhead and his wife held him, comforting him, and all this was happening, was just happening, and for that moment he gave up on figuring it out, on figuring out what to do or what he should do, and he let himself be held by Lindsey while everything went out of his head so that despite all the noise and motion around him, the city felt still and quiet and small, everything shrunk down to that particular moment and space.

SHE could still change her mind. Avery was already in Mei Mei's building, and Mei Mei had already sent the elevator down, but she could still change her mind. The lobby was clean and nicely decorated, with a huge oil taking up most of one wall, a Cy Twombly–ish abstraction that looked like holy scribbling in colors from wine red to mauve to ocher. Waiting for the elevator, she kept her gaze steady on the painting and ignored the stare of a doorman—an older guy with gray hair and deep-set eyes who sat behind a desk in a corner of the lobby facing the door and the elevators. A girl in a red dress by the elevator doors. She needed to talk. On the phone she'd said Grant had thrown her out and her mother had tried to kill herself and she needed a place to stay for the night—but even as she was saying it she wondered what she was really saying, what she was really doing. Grant had hardly thrown her out. He'd said, "Why don't you spend the night at Terry's?" meaning he didn't want her at the apartment— but that was hardly thrown out, *Grant threw me out.* She heard herself saying it on the phone and wondered why she was putting it that way. For sympathy? Or because she wanted to suggest that she was now available? Was she available? Was she interested in Mei Mei in that way? What was she doing? Her mother was in the hospital. She'd had a fight with Grant. She'd take a minute and explain: he hadn't thrown her out, he'd only said. But he did mean that he didn't want her to stay with him, that he wanted her to stay someplace else, and he'd been arrogant and controlling: *You can't work for Mei Mei.*

Avery thought, *Hell I can't.* She thought, *Here I am. We'll see what I can and what I can't.*

How many other women, she wondered, had the doorman watched come to Mei Mei's elevator at this hour of the night? She wondered what he was thinking, if he was imagining, looking at her, the two of them together, Mei Mei and the girl at the elevator, imagining them entangled, if he'd get off on that when he went back to whatever bed he slept in wherever, if he'd imagine them together. Avery had been with a girl once before. Briefly, a couple of weeks, when she was sixteen. It was all the rage then to be bi, all the talk: You should love someone for who they are, and if you love them then sex is cool is an expression of that, so what did it matter which sex? Sue-Ellen wore a 42G sports bra, a white Lycra minijacket that zipped up the front and was the only thing she felt comfortable wearing that kept her breasts hidden enough so the boys didn't all hoot and giggle. Sue-Ellen had been raised to be a cheerleader, but boys had been teasing her about her breasts from the time she was ten years old, so she'd fallen in with the skaters and the druggies, the *On the Road* crowd, and for a few weeks they were a couple, she and Avery. They had sex in Avery's bedroom while Kate was still working. Etched in Avery's memory, the first time she unzipped that sports bra, the way her own stomach felt and the flush of heat all through her. Mei Mei knew she could have stayed with Zoo. Everyone would know that.

What exactly was she supposed to do? Her heart felt like a block of steel when her thoughts came around again to her mother. What? Apologize? Enroll in school again? Kate's face was a wooden mask, wrinkles carved into her eyes and mouth. Fluids dripping into her, her head propped up, her hair disheveled. It felt like an assault. That idea and that word, *assault*, floating around in Avery's thoughts. She felt assaulted, though she couldn't pin it down, she couldn't say how or why. She didn't want to think anymore, and she was angry with Grant. *You can't work for Mei Mei.* As if he employed her. As if he somehow had the right or the power. Avery didn't think so, and she called Mei Mei from the parking garage and Mei Mei said, *Come right over, honey.*

And what did that mean, *honey?* Were there people who knew exactly what they were doing before they did it? Or was everyone like Avery, who never seemed to know what she was going to do next? Here she was on her way to see Mei Mei because Grant had been the way he'd been and she wanted some comfort, and she thought she'd get it from Mei Mei, but Avery knew there was more going on. That kiss at the party. She still felt it. It wasn't like it was with Grant, it was a different thing, but it was real and she felt herself drawn to what it was. Maybe it touched her in a way she needed to be touched. Maybe a million things. Maybe the job. Maybe it was that simple and low. She didn't know. She didn't know how anyone ever did.

The elevator doors opened and she got on.

Grant wouldn't know for sure. She could say she needed a place to stay; she couldn't let him dictate where she stayed; she stayed with Mei Mei to make him angry; nothing happened. Maybe nothing would. She was mad at Grant, but she wasn't sure just how angry, and she didn't know what would happen with Mei Mei. In the mirrored back of the elevator Avery quickly fixed up her eyes, grabbing a tissue and mascara out of her purse. Nothing in her head anymore, waiting for the elevator to ascend. Someplace underneath, some level of churning thought expressed itself in the tingly sensation of her skin and the slight roiling in her stomach—but nothing in her head. She leaned close to the mirror and fixed her eyes, and by the time the elevator slowed and the doors whooshed open she was composed and empty-headed, and she walked the carpeted hallway purposefully on her way to Mei Mei's apartment, the door open a crack.

Inside, a pair of black cats perched side by side directly in front of her, as if guarding the place. Avery closed the door and called out for Mei Mei tentatively. The apartment was huge, a converted loft with no interior walls; instead of rooms there were spaces defined by furnishings—living room space, office space, kitchen in the far corner. City light came through a long wall of uncurtained windows and provided enough illumination to see, if not clearly: a dimly lit, quiet space. Avery took a step toward the cats and neither of them moved. She dropped to one knee and extended a hand cautiously. First one cat rose and brushed against her arm, and then the second one rubbed up against her calf and purred. Avery called out, louder, for Mei Mei, and Mei Mei's voice came back to her from a far corner of the loft. "I'm up here," she said. "Come on up." She followed the sound of Mei Mei's voice through the loft, which was cluttered with what would look like junk to someone who didn't know she was an artist—rolls of fabric, sheets of metal and plastic, bits and pieces of various objects: parts of pinball machines painted with garish scenes, a stack of old LPs, bowling pins piled on the seat of a recliner.

"Where are you?" Avery called out before she saw a spiral staircase nestled in a corner and a circle of dim light at the top of it.

Halfway up the spiraling flight of steps, Avery smelled the unmistakable, tangy odor of marijuana. She ascended the stairs, rising out of the floor into an attic-like space with rough brick walls and no windows, light coming down instead through a long wide skylight that looked up into a black sky interrupted by only a couple of tall buildings and their array of lights. Mei Mei was sitting on a white couch in a white silk robe, with three remotes in her lap and another in her hand. Several feet in front of her, a plasma TV hung on the brick wall like a blank painting or a window into nowhere. On shelves under the TV, electronic devices were lit up, one of them blinking rapidly, as if warning of some problem. Mei Mei said, "Oh, fuck it," and hit a button that made the blinking stop. "I paid a fortune for this shit," she said, "and if I hit one wrong button, that's it. I've got to call the tech guy to get it working again." She lifted a giant spliff from an amber ashtray on the coffee table beside her. "It sounded to me like you could use some of this." She dangled the spliff over the back of the couch toward Avery.

Avery laughed and said, "It looks like a little ice-cream cone." She took the spliff from Mei Mei and brought it her lips as she went around the couch and sat at Mei Mei's feet. She took a long drag, rested her head on the back of the couch, and looked out the skylight at a handful of dim stars.

"I got a head start on you," Mei Mei said, and she tucked her legs under her. She scooted up against Avery and turned her around slightly so she could massage her shoulders. "I'm sorry about your mother," she said. "Will she be okay?"

Avery said, "She'll be all right. But— Jesus—" She took in another lungful of smoke and held it.

"Go easy," Mei Mei said. "It's intense."

Avery exhaled a stream of smoke toward the stars. "It's what?"

"Potent," Mei Mei said and dug her fingers into the cords of muscle at the base of Avery's neck.

"Jesus." Avery let her head flop forward. "That feels good."

As if encouraged by Avery's response, Mei Mei lifted herself onto her knees and squeezed behind her so that she could reach around her shoulders. "I spent the evening with Terry," she said as her fingers worked up into Avery's hair and scalp. "Talk about sad," she said. "She's drinking a bottle of wine a night plus who knows what pills. It's pathetic sad, really. She's in between boyfriends, and it's like— I don't know . . . the end of the world."

Avery brought the spliff to her lips again and took another hit. Already she could feel the odd, disorienting feeling she got from weed.

"Our whole crew," Mei Mei said, "our whole gang . . ." She sounded for a moment as if she had more to say, but she only shrugged and waved it away.

Avery said, "My mother—" She shook her head. "God . . ."

Mei Mei massaged her shoulders harder and then kissed her on the back of the neck. "No one knows anybody else's heart," she said.

Avery nodded. "But you wouldn't have seen this coming in a billion years."

"That's usually the way it is. People are always so shocked, but really, how common is that? No one sees it coming?"

Avery said, "I had a high school teacher who shot herself. It was like, she was doing a bake sale the day before. Everyone was, *This is just not possible.*"

Mei Mei said, "Tell me what happened with Grant."

Avery scooted forward a little on the couch, giving Mei Mei room to come around behind her and hold Avery between her thighs as she massaged the base of her neck. "I can't talk," Avery said. "This feels too good."

One of the black cats from the doorway appeared suddenly, leaping up onto the coffee table, and a moment later the second cat leaped onto the couch.

"Have you met my babies?"

"Downstairs," Avery said. "What kind are they? They're beautiful."

"Burmese. Sables. Aren't they gorgeous?" She stopped working on Avery briefly so she could pet one of the cats; then, when the second cat leaped onto the arm of the couch, trying to get closer to Mei Mei, she scooted them both away. "There are things you should understand about Grant," she said. She unclipped the back of Avery's dress and pulled it open so she could massage lower down her back.

Avery made a soft, throaty sound. She could tell Mei Mei was naked under her robe. She could feel the heat of her body.

"Grant is largely about his own darkness," Mei Mei said. "I mean, at least this is my opinion of him—and I've known him since we were both kids." She kissed Avery gently on her shoulder, as if to say, *I'm telling you this out of friendship.* "Others, the people who come into his life—they're all only a part of his story. He can't perceive others, not really."

Avery said, "What do you mean by that, *He can't perceive others?*"

"I mean," she said, "others don't really exist to him except as characters in his own story. Do you get what I'm saying?"

"Not really," Avery said. She could feel the weed kicking in. The couch seemed to be floating, traversing a slow circle.

"You," Mei Mei said, and then paused as if taking a moment to follow her own thoughts. "It's like the real you, *Avery*—you're not even there. Who's there, for Grant, is this girl who's an interchangeable element in the story he's trying to tell about himself." She paused again, then added, "It's like there's a slot, a place where a character is needed—the beautiful young girl who loves him—and at the moment he's working to make you fit there."

"I don't know," Avery said. She closed her eyes and leaned back.

Mei Mei kissed her on the temple and then peeled the front of her dress down to her waist and ran her hands up along Avery's stomach and under her bra, pulling the bra up and off her breasts. Avery twisted around in her arms so they could kiss. She leaned back and closed her eyes, letting herself be touched as, blindly, she touched Mei Mei, her hair, her face, her breasts. When she opened her eyes, Mei Mei was shaking off her robe. Her body was youthful and lean, her breasts disproportionately large for her thin frame. For a moment they were both quiet, looking at each other, taking each other in; then Mei Mei slid along the couch and pulled off the rest of Avery's clothes. When she leaned down to Avery again, Avery again closed her eyes and let herself fall into a space where there was no thought at all, only feeling.

SEWAGE bubbles over the white porcelain lip of a john, a brown sludge spilling out of the commode and onto the tiled floor. Grant barefoot pushes back at it with a squeegee of some kind, but it's useless. It keeps coming. It pools and puddles, clumps of it sliding toward his feet. It's hopeless so he stops and rolls up his pants legs. Grant's sleeping. He's fallen asleep for a moment after lying in bed for hours looking at the dim shapes around him in his dark bedroom. The last time he checked the clock beside his bed it was three-thirty A.M. and then when he awakened from his dream it was three-forty-five and he figures ten minutes about, that's about how much sleep he'll get this night and he wishes it were otherwise because he may need to be sharp and he won't be, not without any sleep. He thinks about getting up and showering and getting dressed and ready and then he thinks he can still get an hour's sleep before Albert shows up at five, so he closes his eyes again and tries to push the remnants of the dream out of his thoughts.

Often, in his sleep, Grant is chased, he runs, he's in a dark room and someone he can't see is in the room with him, he's lost. Lost maybe the most common—he's in a neighborhood he knows one second and in the next second surroundings turn strange and he can't get home.

A car rolls past his living room window and shadows float right to left in procession. A car on the street its lights music that makes the shadows float right to left, a kind of dance.

He stirs and checks the time again.

Out on the street a girl's voice shouting. It sounds like it's coming from the park. He's made his choice but it's almost as if he doesn't know it. He hasn't said *I'm going to kill my uncle*. He hasn't said it but here he is sleepless in bed waiting for Albert and he knows where he's going and what he's agreed to do. The gun is under the bed with the money. Grant leans over the mattress and comes up with the gun. He lays it on his chest and looks out at the shadows. She's yelling something about keys, about the keys in her purse.

He was an altar boy for a couple of years, and Father Sardonica made him learn Saint Francis's prayer. *Lord, let me be the instrument of thy peace.* That was his name, Father Sardonica. *Thy peace* which is bodies floating up out of the East River every spring thaw. They have a boat, that's it's job, to gaff the bodies that float up out of the river. They have no idea, most assumed suicides, but not all. Worldwide one million suicides each year. He could tell Avery that if he thought it would help. He'd read it only recently. Worldwide, an attempt every three seconds. Now. . . . And now. . . . Now. . . . And now. . . . If he thought it would help. The priest said *Dominus vobiscum*. He said *Et cum spiritu tuo*. Grant never knew what it meant until Saint

John. *Lord be with you. And with your spirit. Gloria in excelsis Deo.* Picture of a pickup truck, the back filled with dead children: Iraq right after Shock and Awe. Peace on earth to men of good will—*not* peace on earth and good will to men. Grant takes the gun by its grip and points it at his own head and then lays it back down on his chest.

He can't pray. He wants to but he hasn't and he can't anymore. It's been too many years. It's in him, though—a boy raised by a mother who dragged him to church every Sunday and at least one weekday morning before school when she'd make him sit and watch while she knelt before the stations of the cross. Nights like this he wants to, but he can't. He's almost forgotten the stations of the cross. St. Mary's. On Grand Street? No. A cavernous church in the old style, marble and gold, tall ceilings, holy echo. He'd sit in the back pew and watch her, the old woman who was his mother. Up one aisle kneeling at each plaster relief and whispering a prayer, one hand touching the frame of a sculpted scene: Christ carrying the cross, Christ scourged. Christ's blood on the tongue. Body and blood. Christ's face on the cross agonized, a crown of thorns. Grant was born into this, but he couldn't do it anymore. He used to talk to God all the time. When making love, he'd thank God because he felt close to a great power. When he finished, he wasn't in his body, he was lifted up. He used to pray, but then, after, he couldn't.

A dozen years, more, thinking it through, over and over, and never figuring out a thing. Time buries it doesn't heal, and some things won't stay buried.

Grant puts the gun back under the bed and sits on the edge of the mattress a moment, looking out at the pair of windows that face the street. His stomach is upset. He's naked and lays a hand over his belly: his fingers play over the contour of muscle under skin. He's nauseated and thinks for a moment that he might throw up. A car goes by on the street, rolling slowly past his windows, pushing the shadows. He guesses it's a police car. There's a station down the block. A smell like something burning comes in from the street. He gets up and sniffs the air. He looks out the window, peeking through blinds, and sees that the street is empty. In the kitchen, he opens the fridge and stands a moment in its light. His skin tingles from the cool air flowing out into the warm air of the kitchen. He finds an orange in the vegetable bin, slices it into quarters with a kitchen knife, and sucks the juice out of the slices one by one. He tosses the remains into the garbage. It's a quarter after four. He stretches out on the love seat behind the kitchen table, neck propped up on one end, feet on the other. It's hardly worth trying to sleep at this point though he thinks even a half hour would be something. He goes into the bathroom and pees, and then shaves and brushes his teeth before pulling on jeans and a T. He finds his sneakers in the closet and puts them on and then makes his bed and stretches out on top of the quilt to wait for Albert. He props up his head with pillows. He folds his arms under his head and crosses one leg over the other.

He hadn't thought about Father Sardonica in many years. Sunday mornings in the rectory, he was good-natured and funny. Grant a quiet kid who hung his head like a beaten dog and Father Sardonica would joke with him, muss his hair, and make him laugh. Childhood was a long bad memory with bright moments, Sunday mornings in the rectory among the brightest. Grant liked the processions when he got to swing the censer while the priests sang in Latin. *Thurible.* The word rose up out of the pits of memory, and Grant spoke it with pleasure. *Thurible.* He liked the smoke wafting out of the thurible, the thick sweet smell of incense that filled the church. He'd fucked Zoo once, more like raped him, and they'd never spoken of it again. The night after the shooting, Zoo knew something was wrong. He hovered the way he did when he wanted Grant to talk to him. He hovered and waited. He sat next to Grant on the couch, same old, but then he put his hand on Grant's leg and Grant looked at him like he knew what he was doing and why was he doing it? Zoo's look went from frightened to defiant. Grant was high on some mix of hashish and pills, so was Zoo. Zoo pulled down Grant's jeans and Grant let him and then yanked him up by his hair and slammed him down on the couch, on his belly, and when he was done he went to bed and left him there. Neither of them had said a word about it since, a dozen-plus years. Censer smoke, thurible, purple robes. Sometimes he's so angry it's a fire burning him up, only it isn't really anger alone, it's a chaos of too many feelings to name that come out as anger. Sometimes there are moments when usually a touch or something in the eyes moments of peace. Sometimes there are friends and sometimes there are lovers, but sometimes it all works in its own way and time.

Grant's running again. He's running full out along a dark street and someone's there, someone's behind him, someone he can't see. Again. Then something, what? Again, more, then continuous and he's awake and someone's banging on his door.

"Hold up!" Grant felt like he'd just been beat up. "I'm coming," he said, and he dragged himself off the bed and opened the door, where Albert was waiting in the hall, a big grin on his face. Grant said, "I must have fallen asleep." He ran the palms of his hands over his head, massaging his scalp.

Albert said, "You ready?" He stayed in the hall. He was in a suit, and he held the jacket slung over one shoulder, hooked with one finger.

Grant stretched, reaching up to grab the top of the door frame, and then he was fully awake. He looked over Albert. "Going fishing in a tailored suit?"

Albert's grin disappeared. "I've got a change of clothes in the car."

Holding the door frame, Grant leaned out into the hall, stretching. "You look like Frank Sinatra in Vegas," he said, then laughed and walked to the bathroom, leaving Albert standing in the hall.

In front of the bathroom sink, splashing water on his face, he heard Albert come into the apartment and pull up a chair at the kitchen table. Grant peed again, his face still dripping water, then washed his hands and turned one last time to look at himself in the mirror over the sink. He stared at his own reflection, looking as if he might punch himself in the face, then left the bathroom, walking past Albert as if he weren't sitting at the kitchen table watching him. He went into the bedroom, where he retrieved the gun from under the bed, checked to see that the safety was on, and stuck it down the back of his pants, under his T-shirt.

"For Christ's sake." Albert was in the kitchen doorway. He went to Grant's closet, found a denim jacket, and tossed it on the bed. "Put the gun in the pocket," he said, "and fold the jacket over your arm."

Grant did as he was told, then started laughing. "Who wears a suit to go fishing?"

Albert told him to shut the fuck up and handed him a couple of pills. "Take these," he said. "They're Dramamine." He watched Grant pop the pills into his mouth, then went out the door.

On the street, Grant got in the passenger seat and Albert hung up his jacket in the back. While Grant waited, a big dog loped down Lorimer. It was bulky and gray-black, with a white mask over its eyes and snout, and it stopped a moment at the car and looked at Grant, their eyes meeting, before it continued loping toward Bedford.

"What the hell was that?" Albert got into the driver's seat and buckled up. "Fucking thing was huge."

Grant closed his eyes and slumped against the door, making it obvious, he hoped, that he didn't feel like chatting. Albert didn't have any problem with that. He started the car and turned the radio to an all-news channel before he pulled out onto the street.

Grant settled into the seat, his head mostly full of what he was hearing on the news: more bombings in Iraq, mosques blown up. His heart was beating hard, though, and his arms and hands were a little shaky. He told himself he was nervous and that it was natural, given what was going on. He didn't feel it, though, the nervousness, and that was odd. He was aware of it—because his heart was pounding like a sledgehammer and he was twitchy, his arms and hands doing little spasm things—but he felt so peaceful that he thought he might fall asleep if the radio weren't going.

"So," Albert said, "you'll be okay?"

They'd been driving about fifteen minutes at that point. Grant considered feigning sleep, but then he heard himself say, "I guess I'm a little nervous. My heart's pounding."

Albert turned the radio off. "Think about the money," he said. "You're going from crumbs to a feast. You hear what I'm saying?" He paused a moment, as if waiting for Grant to answer. "Your uncle's a prick," he said. "You don't want to know the people he's put in the ground. What goes around comes around, you know what I mean, Grant? Are you hearing me?"

"I hear you," Grant said. He didn't move or open his eyes. "Billy's a prick. He's got it coming."

"Exactly," Albert said. "This all gets easy once you've done it a few times."

"Time number two," Grant said.

Albert laughed, and when Grant opened his eyes to see what he was laughing at, he saw that Albert was looking at him. "What?"

"I was just remembering," Albert said. "Sit up, will you? We're almost there."

Grant sat up. They were in Canarsie, by the water. Through the alleys between houses he could see boats docked on a sliver of a waterway in moonlight. "What are you laughing at?"

"I was just remembering," Albert said again. "Last time we took a guy out for a boat ride—" He stopped, looked like he was trying to remember something. "Long time ago. Billy made me cut the guy's chest open. I mean, we already blew most of his head off—but you got to cut up the lungs, guys'll pop up even if you got chains. So Billy's wearing a suit and I'm, you know, I'm dressed like you. He's standing on the other side of the boat, I swear. He's like ten feet away from the body. I stick a butcher knife in the guy's chest, and blood—I swear to God, it's like a fire hose, I don't know what the fuck I hit, his heart, maybe—blood shoots clear across the boat, all over Billy's suit. Fuck! Pissed off? I thought he'd kill me next." Albert pulled the car into a sandy lot, up against a chain-link fence, cut the engine, and then reached behind him into the backseat for a canvas gym bag. He dropped the bag next to Grant's thigh and rifled through a pile of neatly folded clothes. "All right," he said. He zipped up the bag and slung its carry strap over his shoulder. "Time to go."

Grant stepped out of the car into a breeze coming off the water. He put on his jacket against the chill, swinging it around his back, and the gun flew out of the pocket. At the sound of the gun skittering over the ground, Albert turned and then looked from the gun to Grant before he picked it up, cleaned it off with a handkerchief, and handed it back without saying anything. From the water, a man's voice said something about tackle, and Grant and Albert both turned toward the sound. Albert seemed to think about something for a moment, then he continued walking across the sandy lot and onto a dirt path that led down to a line of boats docked behind houses.

Grant followed in the dark. There was enough moonlight for him to see his way and to make out the scene, which was strangely rustic. Small Brooklyn row houses with gated backyards, but beyond the yards, water and docks and boats. The smell of fish in the air, clinking bell-like sound of metal tackle and knock of boats against docks in a little breeze. Then an engine starting and the watery sound of churning water, and a boat backing out of its slip. Albert stopped at a locked gate and watched the boat maneuver slowly onto the waterway, the hum and churn of the engine accelerating slightly as it started out toward Jamaica Bay. He found a key in his canvas bag, unlocked the gate, and held it open for Grant. "It's that one right there," he said, and he pointed to a long sleek boat. "Bayliner," he said, keeping his voice down, as if not wanting to wake anyone. "Beautiful galley. It's like a living room down there—television, everything."

Grant said, "Billy's?"

Albert said, "We use it when we want."

On the dock behind the boat, Albert said "Be light in about a half hour," and he hopped onto a kind of lip only a few inches off the water and then through a spring-latch doorway onto the deck. Grant followed and watched as Albert unlocked the galley door, turned on a light, and stepped down into what looked like a compact living room, with a plasma television, a bar and counter, a cooking area, and cushioned seating. "It's nice in here," Albert said and closed the door behind Grant as he gestured for him to take a seat. "Look around," he said. "Try to familiarize yourself. You can wait in here, but I have to turn the lights off." He said, "This is the john," and he opened a door to a small bathroom, all white and contoured plastic, with an eye-shaped porthole window over a sink. He held the door open long enough for Grant to get a good look and then went to the other side of the galley. "When you hear me on the dock—I'll make some noise—you go in here." He pulled aside a red curtain that revealed a small closet with a couple of rainjackets dangling from hangers. "You okay?" he asked.

"Sure." Grant heard a little bit of shake in his voice and was annoyed by it.

Albert hitched up his pants legs and took a seat next to the counter. He leaned toward Grant. "Listen," he said, "this won't be diffi-cult. We're going out on the ocean for blues. Your uncle knows how to handle the boat, so he'll mostly be out there doing his thing. It takes about an hour to get where we're going. We'll be down here on and off, but mostly we'll both be up on deck. I put a pillow in the closet. There's enough room for you to sit comfortably. When we get to where we're going fishing, we'll both come down here before we get started. You're uncle will probably go in the bathroom to take a leak. That's when you come out of the closet, and you do it when he's in the bathroom. We don't want blood all over the carpeting."

"What happens if he doesn't go to the bathroom?"

"Then I'll come over to the closet and get you. You come out with the gun in your hand, and you tell him to get in the bathroom." He paused as if thinking. "He won't do it," he said. "He'll know why you want him in there. He'll start talking some bullshit to you, trying to save his ass. You ignore it. Don't even fucking hear it. I'll get be-hind him and throw him into the fucking bathroom. When he's in there, you do your part." Albert raised a finger for emphasis. "If," he said, "I can't get him into the bathroom, or he tries to fight, shoot him wherever the fuck he is. We'll deal with the mess. You understand?"

"Sure," Grant said, "but you'll want to be careful not to be too close to him. I haven't fired a gun since the last time, in the truck."

Albert said, "I'll be out of the way," and looked at his wristwatch. "One more thing," he said. "Don't come out of that closet and get nervous and shoot him in the back or anything like that. He's got to see you."

"Why's that?" Grant said. Quickly he added, "I mean, it's not a problem. But what's that about, him having to see me?"

"We don't shoot people in the back. We do this, we're looking the son of a bitch in the eye." Albert got up, went to the galley door, and turned off the lights. For several seconds he stood silently by the door, as if memorizing the layout of the galley with the lights out. Then he went out onto the deck and locked the door behind him.

Grant stretched out on the carpeting and waited for his eyes to adjust to the dark. He knew he was going to do this. He was going to do this, and in return he was going to make a lot of money immediately and a lot more down the road. It wasn't complicated. It was a choice and he'd made it and now he was lying in a dark galley, the breeze a low whistle out on the deck, the just barely perceptible sensation of the boat rocking. After the first shooting, when he'd stayed with Beppo and his family on Lake Maggiore, he'd go out on the water in a wooden rowboat. He'd row. Sometimes all day. Sometimes at night. A red boat, the paint chipped and peeling, a rusty set of oarlocks, a splintered set of oars. He'd go out first thing in the morning, in the dark, and he'd get in the boat and row. He didn't go anywhere, and the trick was to find his way back, out on the water in a little red boat before the sun came up, and he'd stop and watch the sunrise. Several nights he slept in the boat, on the water, tied to a snagged tree. He'd bring a sleeping bag and slither down under the thwarts. He was twenty-four. The stars were huge. He'd never seen stars like that. Grant couldn't remember the last time he'd thought about those weeks on Lake Maggiore. Maybe he'd never thought about them since, it felt like that. Lying in his sleeping bag in the dark, he couldn't sleep through the night then or for months after. Lying in the sleeping bag in the dark, he could feel the water moving under the skin of the boat, and the stars were so huge they were like a performance. One night there was a shooting star so long and bright it scared him. Nothing like the little pinpoint streaks of light he'd seen before, this was a phosphorescent white-blue blaze across black sky, a slight arc, like a filmstrip comet. It lasted seconds. He was frightened when he saw it, he'd never seen anything like it, and then when it was done, it was magnificent, a magnificent thing he'd witnessed—but frightened when he first saw it, he remembered the fear. Blue streak of light over a red boat on black water, Grant wrapped in a sleeping bag under thwarts, nowhere. Nowhere he'd ever been before. He remembered wishing that Kellen were with him. He left without a word and then when he got back he never contacted her again. She was like another life, the life before.

In Iraq, they were blowing up mosques. Grant had seen footage of men blown into small pieces by a turret gun mounted on a Humvee. They flew apart in the eerie light of night-vision cameras, the bodies black shadows in green-blue light crossing a road and there was some staticky talk from the Humvee, the men inside the Humvee, and then the explosive *rat-a-tat-tat* of the gun and the bodies came apart. They were kids who pulled the trigger. They made a choice. Maybe they believed what they were doing and maybe they were right, but the bodies still flew apart in that eerie light and in the morning vultures picked at them or their children found them or their wives or family. Grant had no illusions regarding the thing he was about to do. He was doing it for the money. Billy had millions in offshore accounts. His heart was beating loudly. Who was innocent? Who escaped?

Avery wouldn't have to know. He could come up with something, a story for her and Zoo, for everyone else. He could say nothing had changed but his uncle had died and left him money, a role in his legit businesses. He could come up with a story. He'd work in the background, behind Albert, and in time he could walk away from it, maybe with Avery, maybe Europe again, this time with resources. Grant didn't know what he would do in the long run, but he knew that with money there were possibilities and that without money there was nothing. They'd all move on, all with their successes or what was given to them, and he'd still be driving a truck. What could he expect, he didn't even know what to dream? Not as if the world wasn't endless carnage, mosque bombings to random massacres.

Grant got up and felt his way through the galley to an eye-shaped window where he could kneel and look out over water. Almost sunrise, that faint lightening of sky. A pair of seagulls, low and squawking. His stomach growled and he worried that it would make a noise while he was hiding. He didn't know what he felt about Billy, but the urge to strangle him had been real. He ruled out anger. This wasn't about anger. He felt his way to the counter and a small refrigerator. When he opened it, light streamed out into the galley and Grant stopped and listened. When he didn't hear anything, he found a few pieces of bread and stuffed them into his mouth. He washed them down with a swig of bottled water. He closed the refrigerator door, crouched in the darkness, and a few minutes later, outside, first the gate opened and then Billy said something and Albert answered, something about blues. Albert said they were already gassed up. Billy said something else, and Albert laughed. Grant went to his hiding place and settled into a comfortable position, his back against the closet wall, pillow under his shoulders, the gun held to his chest. His thumb played over the safety. On the dock, near, Albert went into a coughing fit. Billy asked if he was okay. Yes, fine, something in his throat.

When Grant broke up with Terry, he walked out of her apartment and went to a bar, where he picked up a girl and took her home with him. She was short. She was maybe five two, five three. She was pretty and her body was nice, perfectly proportioned. She was like a doll, he remembered thinking that. Also, she was amused. She acted amused through the whole routine: the come-on, the pickup, the ride to his place, sex, talk after, good-bye. As if she found it all, including the sex, amusing. Grant wondered if she ever thought of him again the way the memory of her drifted up, if he ever drifted up into her thoughts. What was it about him that amused her? What did she see? He should have asked her, did she see something in him? Was he a fool? Did she see that and did she go home with him only for the sex, and did that amuse her too? Was he a clown? Did she see that?

The boat rumbled, and the faint smell of gasoline. Grant was angry suddenly. He didn't know why, anger seemed to come out of nowhere. He settled back into the pillow and when the galley door opened his heart rocketed so hard he thought it might actually be audible. Then footsteps into the galley and to the closet and Grant lifted the gun beside his head, with his thumb slid the safety off, lowered it to the curtain. Albert took a step back when he pulled the curtain aside and saw the gun pointed at him. "Relax," he whispered. "But be careful not to fall asleep."

"Not likely," Grant said. The sun had risen, daylight through the streak of galley windows. Albert snapped the curtain closed. The door clicked behind him as he went up on the deck.

Once the boat was moving, Grant settled into the rhythm of it, the maneuvering out of the slip, the slow push through the channel, the bouncing over water as they picked up speed. The movement was comforting. For a moment, he saw himself crouched in a small dark space, clutching a gun, waiting, and it was as if he were looking at himself in a dream. He had daydreams of violence now and then, he thought most men did, maybe women. Once he'd been stuck in traffic on the Thruway, trying to get back into the city, and the traffic was stopped, all the way up near Harrison, a long way to go. He decided to get off at the next exit and try to find 9W, some alternative route. He pulled out of the line of traffic, meaning to drive on the shoulder to the next exit, which he knew was close because he could see a sign for it ahead, and the car in front of him swerved to block him from using the shoulder. He wanted to smash the guy's head in. He wanted to beat him with a crowbar. Every time Grant tried to swerve around the car, the guy blocked him. Then the car behind him tried to move up, to keep him stuck on the shoulder. Grant was a kid driving a beat-up Chevy. The car blocking him was a white Lincoln. The car behind him, a late-model BMW. For weeks after that night, Grant would have occasional fantasies of getting out of his car with a gun and shooting up the Lincoln. Sometimes he'd shoot out the window, shoot the driver, pull him out of the car through the shattered window, and leave him bleeding on the road—and then he'd shoot the driver in the car behind him. Then he'd get in his car and drive off on the shoulder. It was one of several fantasies in which he did violence to others—but the moment of seeing himself in the closet wasn't like that, wasn't like he was seeing himself about to step into a violent fantasy. It was the opposite. In his sleeping dreams, he was always running, always being pursued. In the moment of seeing himself crouched in the closet with the gun, it was like a sleeping-dream image, but he himself was the guy he was running from, or he himself was the other guy in the dark room, the guy the dream-Grant knew was there but couldn't see.

Someone came down into the galley and used the bathroom, then stopped to open the fridge, then went back up on deck. From the sound of the footsteps, Grant guessed it was Billy. He was in a dream, Billy, and he didn't know it. There was someone else in the room with him. There was something in the closet.

Avery was probably with Terry. Grant had left his cell phone on the kitchen table. He had expected to hear her walking up the stairs to Zoo's. He half thought she would come back to the apartment anyway, even though he had told her not to. Part of him had lain there all night hoping for it, waiting to hear her at the door and see her framed by the hall light. She would have gotten into bed with him, and he wasn't sure what he would have done after that, probably nothing different. Probably told her Albert would be picking him up early, not to bother getting out of bed. Probably. Or he might have told her. It didn't seem impossible. He might have slept. He had almost told her at Enid's. He had wanted to tell her, he could feel words wanting to rip their way out of him. If he started telling her, he might have told her everything. He might have gone all the way back. All the way. The first story he published, the central character was a child, a boy of seven. The boy loves his mom and he's afraid of his father. He has a sister, whom he also loves. Boy, mom, sister, they're a circle of love. The father is the conflict. The father is fighting with his daughter, the boy's sister. Father doesn't like daughter's friends.

Daughter plans to run away. She confides in her little brother, tells him her plan. The boy tells the father. He doesn't want his sister to go, he doesn't want her to leave. The father catches the daughter as she tries to sneak out at night, to run away. The father beats her, and the boy watches. That's the climactic moment of the story: the boy watches—and is glad. He's glad to see the sister he loves being beaten. That's why the story worked. Because the boy is glad.

All the way back.

Avery, her head on his chest, his arm around her back.

The boat engine rumbled loudly, and the boat seemed to heave up, as if climbing a wave. The engine cut out, and a sudden deep quiet emerged as the boat came to a stop. They were out on the ocean. Grant had been on the ocean before, he recognized the slow up and down of the swells, the quiet sway and rock. Seagulls followed the boat. They squawked and squealed, the only sound for a minute before the galley door opened and Albert and Billy came down. Albert, "I'll cut up the bait." Billy, "Let me take a piss." Grant waited for the sound of the bathroom door opening. The gun was clutched to his chest and he flipped the safety off. The bathroom door opened. Grant stood up in the closet. He pushed the curtain aside with the gun and stepped out into the galley.

Albert was in front of the refrigerator. He looked at Grant and then looked at the bathroom door. Grant crossed the galley to the bathroom. The swells were deep and long. He lost his balance for an instant, and from inside the bathroom, Billy laughed and shouted, "I missed the john!"

Albert whispered, "Go ahead. Make sure he sees you."

Grant's head was empty. He wasn't thinking a thing, just moving—yet he felt taken up so entirely with unseen and unheard calculations that he moved slowly. His blood like sludge. It took forever to get to the bathroom door, Albert behind him watching. Grant, the gun in his right hand. With his left hand, he opened the door an inch and then, with his foot, opened it full and held it open. Billy turned around holding his dick, daintily, between two finger. White contoured plastic, an eye of light over the sink. When he saw Grant, a look came over Billy's face, at first mystified. Grant must have seemed to him to have appeared out of nowhere. He looked from Grant's eyes to the gun. Then he gathered himself together. He seemed different in sneakers and jeans and a ratty white I-heart-NY sweatshirt. His hair the same neat gray, carefully combed. His eyes lucid, smart. He looked at Albert and zipped up his pants.

"I don't get it," he said to Grant. "What the hell is this?" To Albert, he said, "This a joke?"

Albert leaned against the refrigerator. His eyes were fixed on Billy. "Do it," he said. His voice bitter, eyes on Billy, speaking to Grant.

Grant said, "He's paying me fifty thousand." He was trying to buy time because his arm was shaking, and the way he was holding the gun, with his elbow bent, controlled the shaking some, but he knew if he tensed to fire, his hand would wave around like a flag. "He's giving me a piece of the business," he added, breathing, and the breathing stopped the shaking a little.

Billy laughed. "He offered you a piece of the business?" He took a casual step forward and sat down on the lip of the bathroom door.

Grant backed up. Albert moved away from the refrigerator.

Billy looked at Grant and said, "Asshole. You'll never get off this boat, let alone see fifty thousand dollars." To Albert, he said, "You fucking idiot." He sounded amazed, as if he finally understood what was happening and found it unbelievable.

Albert said, "Take a deep breath and do it, Grant." To Billy he said, "Your own nephew. Your own blood."

Billy said, "Albert despises you, Grant. He'd have killed you years ago just for doing that Saint John shit, had I let him."

Albert said, "What are you doing, Grant?" A touch of anger coming into his voice. "I told you he'd try to save his ass. Get this over with." He looked at Billy. "Put this arrogant son of a bitch out of his misery."

Billy said to Grant, "He's going to bring you into the business?" He opened his hands. "You can't be that stupid. He's going to share the business with you? Why? Why the fuck would he do that? You bring nothing. You know nothing. You have absolutely zilch to offer. Why?"

The shaking in Grant's arms stopped. His composure came back to him. He turned to Albert.

Billy said, "You're here so he can watch while my nephew kills me and then he gets the pleasure of killing you—who he's hated from day one." He slapped his hands together, washing them. "No more Dankos," he said. "And he thinks he winds up with the business."

Albert said to Grant, "Get this over with before he cries."

Billy said to Albert, "I should have known as soon as you started showing up in suits." He laughed.

Albert said to Grant, "Are you going to do this or what?"

Billy said, "You're too fucking stupid to run the business, Albert. You think studying vocabulary books—" He turned to Grant. "You know he studies vocabulary books? He took a fucking course." He laughed again, as if suddenly he was having a good time. He turned back to Albert. "Even if you pull this off, you won't last a month." He corrected himself. "Forget that," he said. "You won't last two weeks."

Albert said, "You think so?" He reached for a gun, holstered under his jacket.

Grant pointed his gun at Albert. He shouted something. He was surprised at how loudly he shouted.

Albert froze for a moment, his gun out of the holster, pointing at no one. Then he started to move, fast. There was no question about what was happening. Albert's body was moving fast to the left as the gun came around toward Grant. Grant saw it all the instant it started. To stop Albert from shooting him, he'd have to shoot Albert. He had maybe a second to do it, and the whole thing was in that way like the moment in the truck all those years ago, when he lifted the gun from the seat of the cab at about the moment when the figure of a man was coming into sight through the driver's window and the figure had a gun and pointed it at him, just as Albert was pointing it at him in that instant, and something inside Grant raised up the gun and fired. But this time, this moment was different. This time Albert was pointing the gun at him and Billy was moving fast, a blur moving toward Albert, and Grant had time to pull the trigger but this time something inside him said *no*.

Billy flew at Albert, Albert pointed the gun at Grant, Grant pointed the gun at Albert, and then a voice as real as if someone were standing beside him and whispering in his ear. The voice said *no*.

MEI Mei stirred, turned over onto her back, pulled a heavy white quilt to her chin, and then pushed it down again, low on her breasts. Her mouth opened and then closed and her eyelids quivered as her eyes moved side to side rapidly and then were still. Avery lay beside her in bed, fully awake, her arms folded under her head. It was early, she guessed around six, six-thirty. The streets were quiet, the traffic light: now and then the building rumbled when a big truck went by. Mei Mei's skin dark against the white quilt, a deep tan, youthful. Avery gently placed her hand on Mei Mei's shoulder. Her skin was so light it seemed to flare where it touched Mei Mei's skin. The night had gone by in a blur and then they were in Mei Mei's bed and Avery felt sweaty and weak, suddenly knocked out. She fell asleep with Mei Mei cuddled against her and her thoughts skittering back and forth between Grant and her mother, Mei Mei making soft falling-asleep sounds as Avery tried to think about what she was doing and couldn't—and then her mind blanked out all inquiry with sleep.

From where Avery lay, she could see a bank of clouds through the skylight. The day would be somber and dark. Mei Mei flung her arm up suddenly and then turned on her side, her back to Avery. She nuzzled into a fat, watery blue pillow that matched the sheets crumpled around her. Avery considered getting up and driving to the hospital; a second later, she considered going to Brooklyn, to Grant's. There were practical concerns that had to be thought through. What if, really, Grant wanted her out of his life? Where would she live? If Mei Mei offered her a job as her assistant, she'd have enough money to get her own place—but not immediately. Immediately, she was living off money she had just promised to return to Kate—not that that was really possible. She didn't have enough to live even in a cheap New York hotel for more than a couple of weeks. Under other circumstances, Zoo would let her stay with him—but not under these circumstances. He was Grant's friend first. Heriberto wouldn't do it either. She wouldn't ask. She wouldn't come between Grant and his friends. Mei Mei had to offer her the job. She didn't make enough at Heriberto's to live in Manhattan. She'd have to find a place out in the boroughs, and she'd have to borrow money from Kate even for that, and after yesterday— It was possible that Mei Mei might let her stay with her. And it was possible that Grant would believe her when she told him nothing had happened between her and Mei Mei, that she had just stayed with Mei Mei to make him angry. In any case, if Mei Mei offered her the job, she could find a place to stay until she got her own apartment. She'd have a place to stay and a future. She'd meet the people she needed to meet. She'd travel. Mei Mei had shows coming up in London and Berlin. Avery had never been out of the States. Where was

Grant at this moment, what was he doing? And Kate? What was Kate thinking?

Avery turned onto her side and touched Mei Mei's hair. It was silky and straight, not a bit of curl. She pulled the quilt down slightly so that she could kiss her shoulder. Mei Mei stirred and then turned over, rubbing the sleep out of her eyes. Avery smiled and said, "Good morning," and Mei Mei slid away from her, as if trying to get distance so she could see more clearly. Avery saw that Mei Mei didn't recognize her. There was a second, maybe two, of an utterly mystified look in Mei Mei's eyes, as if she couldn't imagine who this girl was in bed with her; then the look shifted as her memory must have come back, and she dropped her head into the pillow, closed her eyes, and sighed sleepily.

"Hey," she muttered into the pillow, "darling. Would you mind getting me a glass of orange juice? It's in the fridge downstairs. My throat's dry."

Avery didn't reply for a moment. Then she said, "Sure. No problem," and went from the bed to the couch, where she gathered up her clothes and held them bunched to her chest as she navigated the spiral staircase, stopping at the bottom step to sit a moment, staring out across the expanse of the loft, before starting to get dressed and then stopping and laying her clothes on a step while she padded around naked looking for the bathroom. When she spotted a door on the other side of the loft, between the living room and kitchen areas, behind the chair with the bowling pins, she gathered up her clothes, and as she was walking past the line of windows on her way to the bathroom, she saw an older woman in an apartment across the street, watching her. The woman was sitting at a table in another loft, behind another line of windows. She had short gray hair and a weathered face that looked wrong for the youthfulness of her clothes, blue jeans and a neat white blouse. She had a book open on the table, a coffee pot beside the book, and a black mug poised in front of her as if she were about to sip her coffee—but she was looking across the avenue, obviously watching Avery. When their eyes met, Avery put her clothes down on the chair, dropped her arms to her side, and stared until the woman laughed, toasted her with her coffee cup, and went back to her book. Avery didn't know what to make of the toast.

In the bathroom, she sat on the john a long time and tried to get her thoughts together. Grant, her mother, practical concerns. She couldn't focus. She still couldn't quite believe that Mei Mei hadn't recognized her right away. It was probably just waking from a deep sleep, but Avery couldn't shake a sense of indignation—as if she were one of so many young women in Mei Mei's life that she couldn't recall which one she'd slept with the night before.

She washed up and got dressed. In the refrigerator, she found a bottle of orange juice and poured two glasses. When she returned the bottle to the fridge, she noticed a variety of out-of-season fruits in a clear bin, and she arranged a bowl nicely with blueberries, strawberries, and grapes—all plump and fat as if it were midsummer. She carried the orange juice and fruit up the spiral staircase and found Mei Mei in her robe, sitting on the couch, both cats in her lap, poring over a thick stack of notes and photographs and sketches. She put the bowl on the table, sat next to Mei Mei, and kissed her on the cheek. Mei Mei said, "Sweetie," distractedly, without looking away from the notes. Avery folded her feet under her on the couch and took a sip of her orange juice. After a minute, Mei Mei said, "Give me a another second, honey," and she scooted the cats out of her lap, took a fountain pen from the coffee table, and began jotting something in the margins of a sketch. When she was done, she tossed the pen and paper onto the table and turned to Avery with a sweet smile. "So," she said, "how are you this morning?"

Avery said, "I'm fine, thank you."

"Found the kitchen with no problem?"

"Except for your neighbor." Avery looked behind her to the wall, in the direction of the neighbor's loft. The cats leaped up onto the arms of the couch, almost simultaneously, and perched there like bookends.

Mei Mei said, "I don't know a blessed thing about her. I've been in this place five years."

"I didn't put my clothes on until I got to the kitchen bathroom— and she was watching me like I was R-rated entertainment."

Mei Mei said, "You get used to her. She sits and reads and watches me, like, 24-7. I can't imagine how boring her life would be without me."

"That doesn't bother you?"

"Not really." Mei Mei picked up the cat beside her and put it in her lap. The cat next to Avery protested with a yowl but didn't move. "I make my life public in everything I do," she said, and she stroked the cat. "My whole life's like someone sitting in a window watching me." She nuzzled her cat and then leaned back and looked Avery over, obviously looking at her critically, as if she were judging a work of art. "You're attractive," she said, "but you'd look even better with shorter hair and a good cut." She put the cat back on the arm of the couch. "I'll send you to my girl," she said. "She's terrific." She added as an afterthought, "She can give you a wax too."

Avery said, "A wax?" and as soon as she said it, she realized what Mei Mei meant. "Oh," she said, and laughed.

"You'll like her," Mei Mei said. "She's, like, a fortune—but I'll take care of it." She smiled then, meaningfully, and said, "So. I'd like you to work for me as one of my assistants. Are you interested?"

Avery answered without hesitating, but it was as if she had suddenly been possessed and someone else was speaking. "I don't think so," she said. "But I'm flattered that you'd make the offer."

"You don't think so? Why on earth not?" she said. "What else are you going to do?"

"I don't know," Avery said, "but it's not something I want right now." The cat beside her leaped into Avery's lap. She stroked it once and put it down on the floor.

Mei Mei looked confused. Some of her imperial air melted away. "Do you—" She sounded like she wanted to explain something but then changed her mind. "Fine," she said. "Whatever." She looked at her notes. "Call me whenever you like. We'll get together again."

Avery said, "Don't be angry."

"Why would I be angry?" Mei Mei picked up a sketchbook and rested it on her knees. "I assume Grant's not going to know about any of this. I just gave you a couch on a night when you were distressed. That sound about right?"

Avery nodded.

"Good." She looked at Avery as if waiting for her to leave.

Avery said, "I just think—"

"I don't need an explanation," Mei Mei said. "It's your life. I'm sure you understand what you're doing." She shrugged, as if she were mystified but it wasn't her business.

Avery hesitated another second, then found her purse on the coffee table, smiled awkwardly at Mei Mei, and left with both cats following her. In the living room, she saw the neighbor sitting at her table again, gazing across the avenue. This time when their eyes met, she went quickly back to reading. Avery left the apartment, the cats perched like palace guards watching her as she closed the door behind her, and only when she was in the elevator and on her way down to the lobby did she ask herself why she had just turned down the job she had been so excited about the possibility of getting. She didn't have a good answer. She was now, she thought, officially screwed. She had little money, and if things didn't work out with Grant, she'd have no place to stay. She looked in the elevator mirror and saw a worried-looking young woman looking back at her. She wanted to find Grant and tell him she had slept with Mei Mei. When she asked herself why she would want to do that, she had no answer. She thought it might not be the best idea to go back to Brooklyn, given that she seemed to be out of control, given that she didn't seem to have any idea what she would do next. But she knew she was going to Brooklyn. She was getting into Zoo's car, returning to Brooklyn, and seeing Grant. After that, she'd think about Kate. Why that order, she didn't know. Aunt Lindsey would call when Kate was ready to see her.

In the lobby, the elevator doors opened on a middle-aged Asian man carrying a load of parcels to the counter. He was bright and friendly and said, "Good morning!" as if he were genuinely glad to see her. Avery nodded and whispered, "Good morning" as she made her way out onto the sidewalk, where the day was bleak, with a misty rain that dampened her skin and hair. She crossed the street to the parking lot and fifteen minutes later was stuck in traffic on Canal Street, on her way to the Williamsburg Bridge. She dropped the visor and then flipped it back up and pulled a compact out of her purse. She grabbed a brush out of her purse and touched up her makeup. The traffic moved suddenly, and she tossed everything onto the passenger seat so she could shift gears and move up a few car lengths, and when the traffic stopped again she picked up the compact and the brush and tossed them back into her purse. "Son of a bitch," she said and slapped the steering wheel. She wasn't thinking about what had just happened with Mei Mei or what might be about to happen with Grant. She was thinking about Kate. "Damn," she said, and tears welled up thick and fat in her eyes and spilled heavily down her cheeks. She was thinking about Kate but not clearly, not focused, only that her mother had tried to kill herself. The phrase kept floating to the surface of her thoughts: *She tried to kill herself.* She wished the traffic would start up again. She felt trapped with her thoughts.

By the time Avery reached the bridge and the traffic started moving easily, the tears had quit and left her with a dull headache. She dug her phone out of her purse and tapped out Lindsey's number, her head jerking quickly back and forth from the roadway to the phone. Alongside her, Manhattan in a gray mist. A train rumbling over the bridge. The call went directly to voice mail.

"Aunt Lindsey," Avery said, "could you or Uncle Hank pick me up in Brooklyn and take me to the hospital? Or let me know when you want me to meet you there, and I'll take a cab. Call me, okay?" She paused and added, "Tell Mom I love her," and then clicked the phone shut, brushed tears out of her eyes, and said, "Shit," and then "Shit shit shit shit shit shit," and slumped back in the driver's seat. On Bedford, she parked illegally at a bus stop, hurried to a nearby coffee place, and ordered a cappuccino. The mist had turned into a light drizzle, and people on the streets were wearing raingear or carrying umbrellas. She supposed she looked ridiculous in her red dress, her hair wet and dripping down her neck, her eyes puffy from crying. She checked her wristwatch. It was almost eight. Grant would still be sleeping, and with that thought she ordered a second cappuccino and then carried them both to the car in the rain, secured them in the cup holders, and drove the rest of the way down Bedford, where she found a parking space near Grant's apartment on Lorimer.

At the door, coffee cups in hand and purse hanging from her shoulder, she paused and considered whether to ring the bell or use her key. She decided on the bell, and only when Grant didn't answer did she find her keys and then push through the series of doors, with the coffee cups in hand, as if bearing presents. She expected to find Grant in bed. She unlocked the door and then shouldered it open and headed straight for the bed, which she found empty and neatly made. She put the cups down on the kitchen table and checked the bathroom. She couldn't tell whether or not he had spent the night in the apartment. At the sight of the bed, her first thought was that he hadn't come home, that he had spent the night with someone else. He never made the bed in the morning. She checked the kitchen and the fridge. The same three eggs were in the carton that had been there the day before. There were no dishes in the sink, and the same dishes in the drainer that she had put there yesterday. She checked the cabinet and saw that the new box of cereal was still unopened. She knew he hadn't spent the night there—he was never up and out this early—but she kept looking around the apartment, looking for evidence that he had in fact spent the night and somehow, for some reason, was out early. But she didn't find any such evidence and there was no reason to think she should have. He had picked up someone and spent the night with her. That was pretty obvious. What else? Avery sat on the edge of the mattress, then grabbed a pillow and propped it under her head as she lay back and stared at the ceiling. She imagined Grant in bed at that moment with another woman, having athletic sex with her—and she had no problem at all with the imagining. There wasn't any part of her that thought for a moment he wouldn't do it. Why should she think that, given where she had spent the night? Grant would come back and lie to her if he felt like it, or not lie if he didn't feel like it. There weren't any rules between them. Why should she expect rules?

Avery lay a long while on the bed in silence. The street was surprisingly quiet, people walking by now and then, snatches of conversation coming through the windows. Cars. Shouts from the park, a mother calling children. Morning sounds. Avery didn't know what she felt. Or she knew what she felt but didn't understand why. She felt injured. As if she had been wounded or hurt in some way, physically—and she was stretched out on the bed unable to move. She lay there listening to the clock tick for the better part of an hour before she finally got up—some part of her not directly under her control making her move—and stripped out of the red dress. She laid it out on her side of the bed, the straps on her pillow. She showered and

395

washed her hair, taking her time with it all. She supposed she was partly waiting for Grant to come back and partly waiting to hear from Lindsey, and partly she didn't know what she was doing.

When she finished showering, she put on an old pair of jeans, a comfortable blouse, and her painting sneakers, the ones splotched with colorful stains. She sat on the couch a moment looking blankly at the window, as if she were on a bench at a subway stop, waiting for the train to arrive. She checked her phone to be sure the ringer was turned on and that she hadn't missed a message. When she confirmed that Grant hadn't called at all, not last night or this morning, she started packing. She found her duffel bag in the closet and stuffed it full of her clothes. She went down to the basement and grabbed a few boxes for various accumulated stuff. She rested the duffel bag against the refrigerator and stacked the boxes beside it—where Grant would see it all as soon as he opened the door. She went upstairs and knocked on Zoo's door, just to be certain he wasn't in, though she knew he wasn't, she hadn't heard a sound, and when, as she expected, he didn't answer, she made a cup of tea and went out to sit under the awning on the front steps with mug in hand. She supposed she was waiting for Grant or Zoo, but when a car pulled up to the curb and her aunt got out, it occurred to Avery that she might not really have been waiting for Grant or Zoo at all. She was glad to see Lindsey. She put her mug down and met her on the sidewalk with a hug.

"You know," Avery said, "you look about ten years younger than you did last time I saw you in Salem."

Lindsey ran a hand over her hair. "It's the cut," she said. She stepped back to look over Avery. "You're stunning. You look even better in daylight."

Avery said, "I lost a lot of weight when I first got here. Nervous mostly." She paused and sighed and threw up her hands. "How's Mom doing?" Before Lindsey could answer, she added, "I know I behaved terribly. I don't know why—"

Lindsey stepped into Avery and put her arms around her. She held her tightly and kissed her on the cheek.

Avery said, "I'm so sorry about Ronnie," and pulled back from her aunt's embrace so she could look at her. "I know I should have come home for the funeral."

"Why?" Lindsay said and brushed the tears away from Avery's eyes. She took her hand and pulled her down to sit next to her on the stoop. "I wouldn't have noticed if you were at the funeral or not, Avery. And about Kate, nobody's blaming you," she said. "It's not like that."

Avery said, "I'm just— I'm so—" She shook her head, unable to come up with a coherent sentence.

Lindsey put her hand on Avery's knee. "Avery, like I said, nobody's blaming you."

"It hasn't been," Avery said, "because I don't care, or—" Again she was unable to complete her thought. "I've mostly been happy here," she said.

Lindsey said, "You look like it's been good for you," and there was something in her tone that suggested she meant to wrap up that line of conversation and move on to something more important.

Avery was quiet. She waited, trying to signal that she was willing to listen.

"Honey," Lindsey said, "I have to ask you again. I wish you would consider coming back to Salem with us, if only for a few days.

I was, myself," Lindsey said, and then she seemed to reconsider. "I don't want to go into all this right now," she said, "but I was planning on staying here, in the city, myself—"

"Here?" Avery said. "Manhattan?"

Lindsey reached for Avery's hand and held it tightly. "I can explain it all to you later, but yes, here. I wanted to stay and look for a place while Hank took Kate back to Salem, but then— Your mom is not talking to anybody. Not me, not Hank, no one. They almost didn't let her go home. Hank finally convinced them she'd be better in Salem. The doctor thought there was too much risk that—"

"What?" Avery said. "She'd try again?"

"Apparently."

Avery said, a little anger creeping into her voice, "This is crazy." Then she was quiet a while. She looked down at her feet, not really seeing anything or thinking anything either, though she could almost feel a maze of silent gears and cogs turning somewhere within her. "When are you going?" she said. "When are you leaving?"

"Right now. We're packed up and Hank's with Kate as we speak."

"Right now," Avery said.

"It would be a huge help for you to come with us," Lindsey said. "Once we're back in Virginia— She has her own doctors there. People who know her."

Avery looked past Lindsey toward the park, where a girl was walking hand in hand with a blond-haired little boy. "All right," she said. "Give me a minute. I'm already packed."

Lindsey looked surprised but didn't ask questions.

Avery got up and unlocked the door and held it open for her. "Come on in," she said. "I just have to make a few calls."

LIKE bobbing, up and down, sea swells, his own breathing. Muted noises, sharp sounds. This goes on and on. Moment of light, moment of shadow. Then he rises up into excruciating pain, as if someone were slowly pulling a hacksaw through the cords of his neck. He's in a kid's bedroom: there are bright posters of red cars with twinkling blue windshield eyes and smiling white grill mouths. He calls out and his mouth is full of blood. He's spitting blood and choking. Figures appear. He falls into darkness. This goes on and on until slowly he emerges into a pattern of rising up to a bedroom with pale blue walls and kids'-movie posters and descending into dreams.

The dreams are palpable. They happen to him.

There are people in the blue room. They attach IVs, they take needles in and out of his arm, they roll the IV pole. He figures out that he's alive. He figures out what's happening. There are no city sounds from outside. There are hardly any sounds from outside at all except big jets flying over now and then, loud enough to rattle windows. He comes to recognize a short older man with a boxer's battered nose. He opens his eyes and he's alone in a room dark except for the various lights of monitors and machines. He moves his legs and arms. His neck hurts and he touches it, the left side of the neck, low, near the collar bone. It's bandaged. A blanket of bandages.

When he wakes it's daylight and Billy is there, gray suit, dark blue tie. He's standing beside the man with the battered nose, who Grant now understands is his doctor. The thought of speaking moves slowly in Grant's head. He wants to say, *Where am I?* but nothing happens. Billy goes away. Grant falls back into dreamy thought. In his mind he says, *Thank you*, and he's talking to God. He's thanking God because he's alive. He's been shot in the neck, his mouth has been full of blood, blood gurgled choking in his throat— and still he's alive. He can move his arms and legs. He says, *Thank you* to God as if God is standing there in the dark beside him. When he opens his eyes, his mother is there, in a wheelchair. Her body has grown old and frail, but her eyes are piercing. She watches him intently. Billy is behind her, an arm on her shoulder. From the other side of the bed, someone says his name, and it's Leigh in a chair beside him. When he manages a smile for Leigh, she lays her head on his belly and cries. Her arms wrap around him. He touches her, his hand on her shoulder. In the dark again, he asks for God's help. There's another voice in his head and it says, *Who are you talking to, Grant?* and Grant says, *God*, defiantly. He knows he doesn't know what that means. He knows he's not thinking it through. Still he answers, *God*.

He's alive and broken. The surrounding darkness swells and coalesces and waits as if in anticipation, as if whatever it is inside the darkness has all along been waiting. Words rise up. He's sorry, he's sorry, he wants, he wants. Petty, whining. He's ashamed and he tries again. It's dark. He's breathing. The pulse of the world tick ticks while he searches for words.

Off the Island

HE had 179 friends. In his picture he's wearing gray fatigues and holding a green beer bottle up to the camera. His name is above the picture: *Ronnie Wills*. Beside his photo, the exclamation "Booyah!" and under that "Male. 25 years old. Salem, Virginia. United States." But Ronnie would never be twenty-five years old. When Lindsey first clicked on his MySpace page, blaring music came through her computer's speakers. She learned how to turn it off quickly. The music was a Smashing Pumpkins song called "Zero," which she knew was one of Ronnie's favorites. Why it was one of his favorites, she had no idea. The sound was raw and repetitive, and she could understand it in that way, in the way a driving rhythm overwhelms all the senses but the sense of sound and its suggestion of movement. It was like both being buried in sound and picked up and carried along by sound. She could understand the desire and the need for that, but the lyrics—which she had to look up on the Internet to fully make out—

were angry and maudlin in a way she never in a million years would have associated with Ronnie.

She was in the kitchen with her laptop open in front of her, a cup of coffee in hand. Outside, snow covered the slopes of Roanoke Mountain and turned her lawn and the surrounding fields into a pristine white expanse under a hazy morning sun. It was only a little after dawn. Keith had been up and down all night with a cold and a fever, and she and Hank had taken turns looking after him. He was sleeping peacefully now, but she could hear Hank breathing hard and making occasional dull, grunting sounds, the way he did when he was dreaming. The kitchen was cold, and Lindsey was wrapped up in a fat red terrycloth robe over crumpled flannel pajamas. She had looked at Ronnie's MySpace pages scores of times since Willie, home on leave, had first showed them to her. Willie had given her Ronnie's password, and she had logged on to his pages and read his blogs and his blurbs and his messages. It was all largely superficial and silly. One- and two-sentence blogs: *Hey! Nasiriyahs the shits, Bro. What up with you?* Same thing with the messages: *Jake's got nothing going on. Quiet here too. Bor! ing!* The pictures were what you would expect: him and his buddies in military gear, standing around Humvees on dusty roads, drinking beer together in a tent somewhere.

In most of the pictures, he looked like her skinny little brother, same scrawny body and dopey cute face, only sometimes carrying an elaborate-looking weapon and mostly dressed in fatigues or uniform. There was one picture that was different, and she found herself coming back to it often. It was open on the screen in front of her as she sipped her coffee. She looked back and forth from the drifting snow outside her kitchen window to the picture on her laptop, which showed Ronnie in profile, a close-up of his face against a black background. His skin was scraped and bruised, as if he had just been in an accident. His hair was messed up, his forehead was cut and smeared with blood. A scrape close to the corner of his eye, a layer of skin rubbed away, a blood-red smear. His earlobe was red and raw and a bruise discolored his cheek, high near the eye and temple. He appeared to have hit the ground hard with the side of his head. The look in his eye, though, his expression—that troubled Lindsey more than the scrapes and bruises. He didn't seem angry as much as intensely focused or deadly serious. Maybe solemn, but more blank, a blank intensity . . . Lindsey couldn't find the right words, but in that picture, Ronnie looked like someone she didn't know, or almost didn't know. He looked like some other Ronnie, a bloodied and fierce version of himself, and she kept coming back to it as if there were a hint in it, a hint of a mystery. If she could solve the mystery, it might help her understand what had happened. Why Ronnie had gone to Iraq and why he had died there. When she looked at that picture she thought what had drawn him to war might have been something other than innocence and foolishness and a simplistic willingness to believe in lies and slogans, as she had always assumed. It frightened her a little, the picture—but it also fascinated her. It was almost as if, in that picture, she had a second brother, one she had known and not known—because that was the sense she got from the photograph, that she somehow knew this Ronnie even though she had never seen him before.

Lindsey snapped the laptop closed and took her coffee to the sliding glass doors of the living room, where she watched the snow fall for a while before she made her way through the quiet of her house to Keith's bedroom. She found him sleeping under a pale yellow blanket, his head pressed into a pillow that pictured Harry Potter waving his magic wand. She touched the back of her hand to his forehead. He was still a little feverish, but he was sleeping soundly. She took off her robe, laid it on the floor beside the bed, and got under the covers with him. She ran her fingers through his hair and then curled up behind him, wrapping an arm around his chest and pulling him close to her. He stirred a little and then opened his eyes and turned his head, and when he saw Lindsey, he snuggled into her and dropped right back to sleep. Lindsey kissed the top of his head and then watched snow collecting on the leaves of the chestnut tree outside his window. She closed her eyes, thinking she might catch some more sleep before he woke again, but her thoughts kept drifting back to Ronnie and the war. She felt both like she had to do something and like there was nothing she or anyone else could do that would ever change a thing. There would always be fighting. There would always be little brothers dying. When it was clear that she wouldn't be able to sleep, she rested her chin on top of Keith's head, the way she liked to do, and held him close while she watched snow falling on the tree beyond his window. The scene was peaceful as a pleasant dream, and it soothed her.

AVERY almost turned back midway on the drive from Virginia. Snow had been falling lightly when she had left her mother's house in Salem. She'd thrown her duffel bag into the back of the Jeep, looked up at a mist of snowflakes already accumulating on the front lawn, and gone back into the house to check the Weather Channel on the Internet one more time. When, once again, it predicted light snow, she jotted a good-bye note to Kate, who was off on another weekend junket to D.C. with Corinne, and then drove the half mile to I-81, where she settled in for the long ride to New York. Four hours later, someplace in Pennsylvania where she could barely see the road for the snowfall, she almost lost courage and turned around. The sky was dark and snow was falling the whole trip. She decided to push on for another hour rather than turn around, and if the snow got worse to stop and get a room for the night—but in another hour, the snow had tapered off, and by the time she reached the tollbooths of the New York State Thruway, the snow had stopped entirely and the clouds had blown away, leaving a bright blue sky and sunlight glittering off fresh snow on the roadside. At the moment, a few miles, according to signs, from the exit for Rifton, New York, the sun was fading as dusk came on, snow and ice on either side of the road like bright brackets around a dull line of highway.

Grant was in Rifton. He'd been there since shortly after Avery had left New York for Salem. For a time, Avery had thought the whole thing with Grant was going to end as suddenly as it had begun. When she first got back to Salem, she tried calling him repeatedly and was repeatedly transferred to voice mail, where she left messages that went unanswered. When she called Zoo, he was mysterious. He sounded pained, but he avoided her questions and told her nothing. Eventually she gave up. With no place to go back to in New York, she took a job working for her grandfather, where she was overpaid to do clerical work. She settled into a routine of spending her days working and her evenings with Kate—when Kate wasn't busy doing something or other with Corinne, or Corinne and her friends. Then, before the holidays and a few days after Avery's twenty-third birthday, Zoo called and arranged to visit for a weekend. He arrived on a Friday evening, and Avery had to pry him loose from Corinne and Kate before she could take him out to dinner, where he told her Grant's story. They were at Billy's Ritz in Roanoke, seated by a window that looked out at the market. There was a point in the evening when Avery felt so light-headed she thought she might faint. Zoo touched her arm and handed her a glass of water, which she sipped slowly.

Zoo said, "Grant couldn't tell you all this over the phone, and he couldn't make the trip down here either. He wants to see you. He was hoping, if I explained—"

"Why couldn't he?" Avery said. "Why couldn't he tell me?"

Zoo brushed his hair back off his forehead and looked down at the tablecloth as if he were searching for the right explanation. He said, "Grant's not doing so well." For a moment, he seemed to want to say more, but then he let it drop and went back to picking at his meal.

Avery wanted to be assured that Grant was finished with his uncle—and Zoo assured her. "From what I understand," Zoo said, "neither of them wants anything more to do with the other."

"Are you sure about that?"

Zoo said, "I'm sure. The place where he's staying upstate is his sister's."

"The sister in Pennsylvania?"

Zoo nodded. "Leigh," he said. "She's the one's been looking after him mostly."

"What's he been doing for money?"

"Leigh, I'm guessing. They seem to have reconnected."

The next day, Zoo spent the morning charming Kate before he and Avery went for a drive and a hike. They talked mostly about Grant, but Zoo also talked about himself. Being away from the city seemed to open him up. It turned out that he had met someone on the same night that Grant had disappeared, and that he'd been with him ever since. "This time it feels right," Zoo said about his new boyfriend. "It's the first time, really, in a very long while."

Avery parked her Jeep in a lot at the bottom of the Cascades, a popular short hike to a waterfall. The climb was steep at times, and

Zoo and Avery were mostly quiet as they concentrated on walking the rocky path. To the right of them, the fast water of a stream rushed over and around rocks and boulders. All around them, trees and greenery climbed up hillsides. The day was unseasonably warm, and they shed their jackets and tied them around their waists. At one point on the walk, in the middle of climbing a flight of rock stairs, Avery turned around and asked Zoo what had happened to the guy who'd shot Grant. She had been trying to imagine Grant being shot in the neck, what that must have been like, and the question had suddenly occurred to her.

Zoo said, "I asked Grant the same thing."

"And?" Avery said. "What did he say?"

"He said, 'Nothing good, I assume.'"

"That's all?"

Zoo said. "I don't think it's too hard to guess what happened to him."

"This is all—" When Avery couldn't finish her sentence, she turned and kept climbing.

At the falls, they sat together quietly on a boulder and watched a torrent of foaming water spill into a blue-green pool. Zoo asked Avery how she was getting on in Salem, and Avery explained that she felt like she was in between things and waiting. He asked about Kate. He said Kate looked good to him. She looked like she was doing well. Avery agreed and then hesitated, not sure whether or not she should tell Zoo the whole story. Zoo read her hesitation and pressed her.

"What?" he said. "Tell me."

Kate had told Avery about her affair with Hank shortly after returning from New York. She hadn't wanted Avery to feel responsible for what had happened in New York, so she told her every-thing. She said she didn't know why she had done it. She could still hardly believe it had really happened.

Zoo seemed neither especially surprised nor shocked once Avery finished telling him what she knew about the affair. He asked, "Does Hank's wife know?"

"Lindsey?" Avery said. "No. Her brother just died in Iraq. Her father's completely gone with Alzheimer's. Mom made me swear not to tell her."

"Don't you want to, though?" Zoo asked. "Don't you think he should pay a price?"

"He's paying," Avery said. "They're moving to Chicago. They've already sold the house. Lindsey got into the Art Institute, and Hank has work lined up."

"That's his price? Moving to Chicago?"

"You'd have to know Uncle Hank and his family," Avery said. "I'm sure he's going because of the thing with Mom."

Zoo said, "I'd still tell her."

"And make her suffer for what he did? For what he and my mother did?" She shoved him. "No, you wouldn't."

Zoo thought about it for a moment and said, "You're right. I wouldn't." He added, "One more thing I've wanted to ask you," then hesitated.

"Yes?" Avery said. "What?"

Zoo said, "I think I know the answer already, but— Why did you turn down Mei Mei? She was— She couldn't believe it."

"I have no idea," Avery said. "I wanted it, I wanted it, I wanted it— Then she offered, and I said no."

"I don't believe that," Zoo said. "That you have no idea." He rubbed Avery's back and put his arm around her shoulders. "I think you know exactly why you said no."

Avery said, "Thanks for coming to see me, Zoo."

Zoo said, "I'm just Grant's messenger boy."

"No, you're not."

"No, I'm not," Zoo said. "You're right again."

Avery said, "Why do you think I said no to Mei Mei?"

"Integrity issues."

"Integrity?" Avery said. "Me?"

Zoo went about taking off his shoes and socks so he could dip his feet into the water. "What about photography?" he asked. "Are you still doing it?"

"Not since I've been home. But I will," she said. "I'm waiting."

"For what?"

"When it feels right," she said, and she looked up into the cascades, where water rushed over the cliff as if powered by an impossible force. A white mist drifted over the blue pool at the base of the falls.

Zoo left the next morning. That evening, Avery called Grant. Since then, she had been in touch with him, at first irregularly but lately almost nightly in long phone conversations. Now, in late February, months after Zoo's visit, she was approaching the tollbooths for the New Paltz exit off the New York State Thruway, where small hills of snow on the side of the road were covered with a fresh coat of white powder. Daylight was fading quickly, and she could already see a fat full moon, pale and ghostly, low on the horizon. She checked the MapQuest directions spread out on the seat beside her. Rifton was less than ten miles from the exit. At the thought of seeing Grant again in a matter of minutes, a rush of nervousness came over her. She hadn't expected to be nervous, given how much they had talked on the phone in the past month. Grant talked about being full of sorrow—but when she asked if he were depressed, he insisted he wasn't. *It's not the same thing*, he said. He'd been spending his time reading and walking along the river and a close-by lake. He was reading a little bit of everything. Once a week, he'd get up at dawn, put on his backpack, and hike eight miles into New Paltz, where there was a college and a library. He'd return the previous week's books, check out a new stack, then spend the day reading in the town's coffee shops before making the hike back. When Grant told her this, her first response was that she couldn't imagine him wearing a backpack.

By the time she had passed through the town of New Paltz and was approaching Rifton, it had grown dark. She left the main two-lane highway and found herself on a narrow road that ran alongside a river; and then, a few minutes later, she was there. She pulled up in the dark in front of a two-story blue-gray clapboard house with a peaked roof. The house backed up onto a thick stand of trees, beyond which, once she opened the car door, she could hear the river. The quiet was otherwise striking. The only sounds in the dark were the ticking of the Jeep's engine cooling down and the whisper of flowing water. She could see the house clearly in the moonlight, but there were no interior lights on—and she stood for a moment outside her car, wondering if she might be in the wrong place. She looked up and the sky was bright with stars, and then she heard Grant say her name and she followed the sound of his voice to a covered porch. When he said her name again, she saw him sitting in a tall rocking chair in the shadows. "Grant," she said, and then, "Oh, my God," when she got close and could see him more clearly. He had let his hair grow. It was thick and full, and it fell in dark waves toward his shoulders. He was wearing boots and jeans and a blue corduroy shirt under a brown winter jacket. Avery said, "If you hadn't said my name, I wouldn't have recognized you in a million years."

"The hair," Grant said, and he brushed it back off his forehead.

"It's cold," she said and wrapped her arms around her chest. She pointed at the Jeep. "I left my coat . . ." She jogged back to the Jeep and retrieved a white quilted coat from the backseat.

Grant followed her, and once she had pulled on her coat, he embraced her, holding her tightly, pressing his cheek against hers. "I'm glad you're here," he said. "I'm glad you came."

Avery said, "Me too," and then they stood there awkwardly, looking at each other until she nodded toward the house. "Are you going to invite me in?"

"I thought we'd take a walk first," Grant said. "You must be cramped from the drive."

"I am," Avery said. "Good idea." She found gloves in one coat pocket and pulled them on, and a red wool hat in the other pocket. The hat had earflaps and a cord that tied under her chin.

"Cute," Grant said, and then he zipped up his jacket and led her behind the house to a path through the woods. The path was so dark that Avery reached out and took hold of Grant's sleeve for balance. When the trail opened up, they were on a rocky riverbank, where a second snow-covered trail followed alongside the water. Grant said, "It's gorgeous out here, isn't it?" He gestured toward the dark blue line of the river. "It opens up in a little bit into Sturgeon's Pool."

"Sturgeon's Pool?"

"A lake," Grant said, and he reached back for her hand.

The trail was only wide enough for one at a time, and for a long while they walked single file, with Grant talking over his shoulder and Avery speaking loudly to be heard. When the path opened onto a semicircular clearing covered in snow, Grant said, "Here we are." Beyond the clearing, the river widened into a tree-lined lake.

Two chairs were positioned at the shoreline, looking out over the water. Grant pulled a hat out of his coat pocket and used it to brush snow off the chair closest to Avery. When he was done, he gestured for her to sit while he went about clearing snow off the second chair.

Avery said, "This must be pretty in the summer."

"You don't think it's pretty now?"

The lake water was still, and it reflected stars and the moon and a handful of drifting clouds. "It's lovely now," she said. "It's beautiful."

Grant dropped into the chair beside her and reached for her hand. "I took Zoo out here last time he visited," he said. "He thought I was crazy."

"He didn't think it was beautiful?"

"It was below zero and snowing. Did he tell you he bought our house?"

"Your house?"

"The building on Lorimer. He bought the whole thing."

"Really?" Avery said.

"He's giving the downstairs to Brian, the new love of his life."

Avery said, "Good for him," and then they were both quiet again for a while. Stretched out in front of her, the night blue of the lake surrounded by white-capped trees darkened as a wisp of cloud floated past the moon. She watched a blaze of stars shimmering in the water and found herself thinking uncomfortably about Mei Mei. She had already talked to Grant about that night. She'd told him everything.

Grant said, "What are you thinking?"

"I'm thinking—" Avery said, and she took off one of her gloves and reached under her. "I'm thinking that my pants are soaked through and my butt is freezing."

"I know," Grant said. "Me too."

"Time to go?"

"Time to go."

Before they made it all the way back to the house, Avery really was freezing. From her thighs to the middle of her back, she felt a tingling numbness. "I think I have hypothermia," she said. They were coming out of the woods, walking around the house toward the front porch. She said, "I need to get my things out of the Jeep."

From the back of the Jeep, she pulled out a big cardboard box full of her stuff, including her camera gear, and handed it to Grant.

Grant said, "How long can you stay?"

Avery pulled her duffel bag out of the car and slung it over her shoulder. "I told my family I'd be gone a week," she said. She leaned close to Grant and kissed him on the cheek. "We'll see how things go."

Grant held the box in his hands and watched her as if he were trying to read her mind.

"Grant," Avery said, "I'm truly freezing."

Inside the house, it wasn't much warmer in the living room than it had been out on the street. Grant turned on the lights and then turned them off again when he found a candle, lit it, and put it in a holder on the brick mantel of a fireplace. In the brief time that the lights were on, Avery saw that the house was largely empty. A few boxes were scattered around on a bare hardwood floor, along with a pair of braided oval rugs. The rugs were situated in front of the boxes, and on one of the boxes was an open notebook and a pair of yellow pencils. It looked like Grant had been sitting on the rugs and using the boxes as desktops. Grant had disappeared out the front door once he'd lit the candle, and when he came back in, he was carrying a half-dozen fireplace logs in his arms.

Avery said, "I'm going to freeze to death before you get a fire going."

"Upstairs," Grant said, and he nodded toward an arched passageway off the living room.

In the dark, Avery followed Grant up a flight of stairs. The moon through a window at the top of the stairway provided the only light. She asked, "What's the story with the dark? Is there a problem?"

Grant said, "I'm not ready for bright lights yet." He hurried ahead of her, taking two steps at a time. In a moment, he was out of sight.

Avery stopped at the window and looked out at a view of snow-covered woods, and beyond the woods, the river. She heard a crash above her and assumed Grant had dropped the logs somewhere, and then he appeared again in the light of a fat white candle on a yellow coffee plate, which he held out in front of him. "Up here," he said, and Avery followed him, climbing the second flight of stairs to a short hallway that led to a bedroom that was nearly empty except for a couple of stacks of books by a bare window and, again, a pair of boxes that appeared to serve as desks. On the side of the room near the door, a queen-sized mattress lay on the floor, covered with a down comforter, fat and white and big enough to swallow up the mattress in its airy quilts. Avery sat on the corner of the mattress and in a minute was out of her wet clothes and huddled under the quilt, curled up between sheets and a second blanket that was under the comforter. "Oh, my God," she said.

"The sheets are cold, I know. They'll warm up." Grant was kneeling in front of the fireplace, arranging logs over a pile of crumpled newspapers.

"This is your sister's house?" Avery said, shivering. "Doesn't she believe in furniture?"

"It was on the market." Grant lit a match and held it to the newspaper. In an instant, the fireplace was glowing and he came back to sit beside her on the mattress. "She was trying to sell it, and then—" He pulled off his boots and pants and flung his jacket across the room. "She's letting me live here for now." He climbed under the comforter and lay beside Avery with his head propped up on a pair of pillows. Avery was curled up in a fetal position, her forehead against Grant's waist. She turned on her back slightly and then reached one hand cautiously out from under the comforter to touch Grant's hair where it spilled down onto his shoulders. "You look so different," she said. She noticed then, for the first time, a small, jagged circle of raised skin low on his neck, just above the collar bone. She ran her fingers over it.

"That's where the bullet went in." He took her hand and pulled it around to the back of his neck, where she felt an apple-sized patch of raised skin that was smooth to the touch but crisscrossed with a maze of bumps and ridges. "That's where it exited."

Avery already knew the story of the wound. He had almost died. He should have been in a real hospital but got good care where he was taken, to the home of a doctor. She knew that for a while he had been in a lot of pain. She asked, "Does it still hurt?"

Grant said no and then slid down under the comforter and kissed Avery on her shoulder, the one with the tattoo. "Animal eyes," he said. "I missed them."

Avery said, "I hardly notice it anymore."

Grant kissed her shoulder again and then wrapped her up in his arms. "You're warm already."

"You're not," she said. "Your legs are all icy." She threw her legs over his and held him tightly. When she kissed him on the lips, she felt his body stiffen slightly under her, and then he looked away. She let him loose and he rolled onto his back and pulled the blankets to his chin. She asked him what was wrong and he turned his head to the side, as if he were listening for something. The fire crackled and cast a flickering light on the walls. She said again, "What's wrong?" and ran her fingers through his hair, petting him.

Grant turned away from her. "I find myself thinking a lot about that night at Penn State, at the lake," he said. "The first time. The way things started between us."

"We've talked about that," she said. She pulled at Grant's shoulder until he was facing her again. "I thought we agreed to forget about that."

"I lied," he said, "when we talked about it." His face was only inches from Avery's. The fire snapped and popped, and the smell of wood smoke filled the room. "I said I didn't know what you were talking about when you said it felt like rape. But I did. I knew what you meant. I knew you weren't ready. When it happened, I mean. I knew you weren't—" He closed his eyes.

"Okay," Avery said. "Still. It's history. You shouldn't have. You know you shouldn't have."

"I know," Grant said.

Avery touched his temple with her fingertips, and with her thumb she pulled an eyelid up. Grant took her hand in his and kissed the back of it. "I was angry," he said. "It's one of the things I've been thinking about."

"Why do you think you were angry? Your father?" Avery was remembering things Grant had only recently told her, in their phone conversations, about his father.

"I don't know my father," Grant said.

Avery waited for an explanation.

"My sister Leigh," he said, "was raped when she was fourteen. She let her parents raise me. She's my mother."

Avery touched his shoulder, massaging it. She played through the implications of what he had just told her. She asked, "How long have you known that?"

"Long time," he said. "I've known for a long time that she was my mother, but we only just now started talking about it." He paused a moment and seemed to collapse a little deeper into his pillows. "I didn't know she was raped," he said. "I mean, it had occurred to me as a possibility, but I never— I never really thought it. I thought she— I thought she had gotten pregnant too young and just . . ."

Avery said, "She should have told you."

"She didn't want me to know," Grant said quickly, as if defending Leigh. "He was a stranger. He attacked her at knifepoint in her bedroom." Grant looked up at Avery out of the dark. "Would you want to tell your kid that he was fathered by a rapist?" Without waiting for an answer, he said, "I can't believe she even had me. I can't believe she carried—" He stopped talking, as if he were suddenly done with the subject, and curled up with his head under Avery's breasts. He said, "I'm sorry," and then he was quiet.

Avery knew he meant he was sorry about the lake. "Grant," she said, calculating the connections he must have been making between what he'd done and what the man who'd raped his mother had done. "Grant," she repeated, "that's not you."

"I don't want it to be," he said, and then he took a deep breath and tightened up, his body stiff against her. Avery pulled the comforter over his shoulders. She didn't know what to say, so she lay quietly in the dark and watched flames shooting into the chimney, red at their outer edges, blue and white where they growled and consumed the firewood. A moment later, Grant's body went slack, and she realized, from the way he had collapsed into sleep, that he was exhausted. She brushed his hair out of his eyes and looked down at his face in the firelight. He didn't look peaceful, even in sleep. His lips were pressed together, and she ran her fingers over them lightly, as if she might relax them with her touch. An urge to hold him close came over her. She wanted to kiss him but didn't want to disturb his sleep. On the ceiling, the fire threw moving patterns of light and dark, and she noticed a thin haze of smoke, a little puff of it, drifting through the room toward the open door to the hallway. When she closed her eyes, she could still see patterns of light through her eyelids. She settled toward sleep, listening to wood sighing and groaning in the fire, with Grant curled up against her in the quiet.

Acknowledgments

An excerpt from this novel was published in *Gargoyle 54*.

Thanks

To the National Endowment for the Arts and the Virginia Commission for the Arts, for their support.

To the Corporation of Yaddo and the Virginia Center for the Creative Arts for the gift of a peaceful place to write, surrounded by a supportive community of writers.

To the people at Unbridled Books, particularly Fred Ramey and Caitlin Hamilton Summie, and especially Greg Michalson. Greg has been doing great work with writers since his days as an editor at the *Missouri Review*. I am indebted to him for all his help.

To Steve and Clorinda Gibson, lifetime friends and literary companions; Steve Yarbrough, who is, as Greg calls him, "one of the good guys"; my brother Frank, who discovered a love of art in his youth and shared it with his family; and Neil Olson, my agent, who, bless him, is still interested in fiction.

And finally, I'd like to thank Judy, whose presence in my life is both a gift and a wonderful surprise.